D1020603

BOOKS BY ANNA TODD

After
After We Collided
After We Fell
After Ever Happy
Before
Nothing More
Nothing Less

SHORT STORIES IN *IMAGINES*

"Medium"
"An Unlikely Friend"

the spring girls

anna todd

GALLERY BOOKS

New York   London   Toronto   Sydney   New Delhi

G

Gallery Books
An Imprint of Simon & Schuster, Inc.
1230 Avenue of the Americas
New York, NY 10020

The author is represented by Wattpad.

First Gallery Books trade paperback edition January 2018

GALLERY BOOKS and colophon are registered trademarks
of Simon & Schuster, Inc.

For information about special discounts for bulk purchases,
please contact Simon & Schuster Special Sales at 1-866-506-1949
or business@simonandschuster.com.

The Simon & Schuster Speakers Bureau can bring authors
to your live event. For more information or to book an event,
contact the Simon & Schuster Speakers Bureau at 1-866-248-3049
or visit our website at www.simonspeakers.com.

Interior design by Bryden Spevak

Manufactured in the United States of America

10 9 8 7 6 5 4 3 2 1

Library of Congress Cataloging-in-Publication Data is available.

ISBN 978-1-5011-3071-7
ISBN 978-1-5011-3072-4 (ebook)

To all of the "little women" out there
who are trying to figure out
just what it means to be a woman;
I'm here for you, and so are your many sisters.

the
spring
girls

1

meredith

"Christmas won't be Christmas without any presents," Jo declared from her spot on the rug.

She sat at the feet of her oldest sister, Meg. Jo's long brown hair was unruly, as it always was. She was my strong girl. She was the only one of my girls who didn't hog the bathroom. Her delicate fingers, the black polish on their nails chipped, picked at the frayed edges of the Afghan rug under her folded legs. The hand-woven black-and-red textile had once been bright and beautiful, and I remembered when my husband had sent it to our house back in Texas from his former post in Kandahar, Afghanistan.

In my head, my husband's company's FRG leader's scratchy voice reminds me to use proper military lingo: my husband's *FOB* in Kandahar. The biggest forward operating base in Afghanistan, she would also necessarily add. Denise was always on my case. Come to think of it, she even had comments about the rug when I got it. She said he could have sent it to the base and paid no fee.

None of that mattered to my girls. From the moment it arrived, they loved that rug as much as I did. When I ripped open the package from their dad, who had been living across the world for the past eight months, the girls—particularly Jo—were excited to own such a beautiful, culture-filled treasure from a place so far away. Meg loved that we now had a lavish handcrafted object in our simple home. She was my most materialistic daughter, but I always knew that if I tried to teach her right, she would use her love of shiny things to do something magical *and* worthwhile with her life. Amy was too young to really care about the rug, and of course Beth knew it was coming because her daddy knew that she was the only Spring Girl who could be trusted to keep the secret. Plus, on a more practical level, since Beth was basically homeschooled, Frank knew she could watch out for it. Later, he explained to me that he wanted to mail the package straight home so that we could be treated with the rug as a surprise on our doorstep, rather than as a pickup chore on the base. I'm not sure if I told Denise that, she would understand.

Of late, our beautiful rug wasn't as beautiful anymore. Dirty shoes and heavy bodies had worn it down, and the colors blended into a mud brown that I tried my best to clean, but the color just wouldn't come back.

We loved it not one bit less.

"We're supposed to get snow in New Orleans. That feels like Christmas to me," Meg said, brushing her fingers through her brown hair. It was grown to her shoulders now, and she talked Jo through instructions about how to ombre her hair so it looked like she had blond ends and dark roots. It was so cold that year that the roads iced over, and it felt like every day there was a wreck clogging the only major highway in this town. The sign outside our Army post keeping track of the number of days without a road-related fatality went back down to zero nearly every day instead of weekly. The highest number of days without a death that the sign at Fort Hood ever got to was sixty-two.

That morning didn't feel as cold as Channel 45 said it would be. I wondered if my sister would make it to our house or if she would somehow use the weather as an excuse. She always had excuses. Her husband was deployed with mine, and their dirty laundry had been fully aired, left around in pieces, from his making jokes about her weight to a group of privates, to his sleeping with a female medic last month.

"Did Aunt Hannah call yet?" I asked my girls.

The only one who looked at me was Beth, who replied, "No."

Since moving to Fort Cyprus the summer prior, Hannah had been engaged twice, married once, and is soon to be divorced. I loved my younger sister, but I couldn't say I was upset when she moved closer to the city a few months back. She got herself a weekend bartending gig on Bourbon Street at a little bar called Spirits, where they serve mixed drinks in light-up skulls and make a tasty po' boy. She had a good personality for a bartender.

"Is she coming?" Jo asked from the floor.

I looked at Jo, into her milk-chocolate eyes. "I'm not sure. I'll call her in a little while."

Amy made a small *hmp* in her throat, and I stared at the blank TV.

I didn't want to talk to my daughters about adult things. I wanted them to stay as young as possible, but to also be very aware. I told them of things happening around them. I discussed current events with them, the war going on around us. I tried to explain the dangers and blisses of being a woman, but as they grew older, it got harder and harder. I had to explain to them that sometimes things would come easier to the boys and men around them, often for no good reason. I had to teach them to defend themselves if one of those boys or men tried to harm them. Having four daughters ages twelve to nineteen was not only the hardest job I'd ever worked, but it would be the most important thing I would ever do. My legacy wasn't going to be that I was an Army wife; it was that I'd raised four reliable, responsible, and capable little women to unleash out into the world.

I felt a heavy sense of duty; if nothing else in my life, I wanted them to carry their strength proudly and their kindness openly.

Meg was the princess of the family. She was our miracle baby, coming to us only after two painful and soul-wrenching failures and finally making her entrance into the world on Valentine's Day evening. But it's not like when it happened, Frank and I were out on some romantic date sipping ten-dollar glasses of Yellow Tail merlot. Rather, Frank was sitting behind a desk at his company building, trying hard to stay awake. Every hour he had to do a walk around the barracks behind the building. He always seemed to be assigned to charge of quarters. (CQ, as Denise would note.)

He hated when he had to do it, and so did the girls, but the Army required it once a month. That night, I had to call the company phone four times before someone finally answered and corralled my husband. Just as my contractions became unbearable, he made it home and we rushed into his car. We thought she was going to be born right there in our 1990 Chevy Lumina. Staring at the fuzzy dice hanging from the rearview mirror, I counted as they swayed back and forth, back and forth, and tried to keep at bay the faint smell of the Marlboros that Frank used to smoke in the car before we found out we were expecting. Frank held my hand and told me jokes and made me laugh so hard that I was crying and trying to keep myself from peeing on the fuzzy black seat covers. We were so cool back then.

By the time we got to the hospital, I was too far into labor to get an epidural, and so while Meg came out screaming into the small hospital room, it was all I could do not to scream myself. Still, that was just one night, just a moment. Becoming a mother changed something deep within me; I felt the scattered pieces of my life lock into place, and I knew that I had a new role.

Jo was next, and her birth took a toll on my body. She was breech and refused to turn her stubborn little body the right way, so a C-section was scheduled by my doctor.

Beth was easy, only thirty minutes of pushing. Her birth was calm like her, and she took to my breast easier than the rest of my girls.

Lastly, our unplanned little Amy surprised us on a Taco Tuesday when I realized my stomach no longer liked tacos, even though the rest of me did. After Amy, I asked my doctor to ensure we didn't have any more surprises.

Amy was just as fiery as the spicy food I craved when she was growing inside of me, and I looked at her now, then to the rest of my girls. For a few minutes, no one spoke, and I pretended, just for a few heartbeats, that Frank was here, sitting in this old recliner he's had since our first apartment. In my mind, he was singing along to the radio. He loved to sing and dance, even if he was awful at both.

"I saw online that White Rock cut the music program again," Beth said, yanking me back to reality.

"Yikes, really?" asked Meg.

"Yeah. It sucks for the students. It barely existed before, and now it's practically gone, no new instruments, no field trips. Nothing."

Amy looked over at her older sisters, trying to keep up with their conversation.

"Are you *kidding* me?" Jo spat. "I'm going right down to Mrs. Witt's office. That's bullshit that they—"

"Josephine, watch that mouth," I said, still eyeing Amy. Jo always cursed, no matter how hard she claimed to try not to. Given that she was almost seventeen, I didn't know what to do about it.

"Sorry, Meredith."

She also had begun using my adult name, for some reason.

Across the room, the phone rang from its cradle on the charger, and Amy jumped up to answer it.

"What does the caller ID say?" I asked.

Amy bent down and squinted her eyes. ". . . Something bank. Fort Cyprus National Bank."

My chest tightened. On Christmas Eve? Really? That bank was already corrupt enough with their high interest rates and less-than-noble marketing. They were known for standing pretty women in the entries of the PXs and Walmarts to lure soldiers to open an account with a smile and the phantom promises of early direct deposits from the Army.

"Just let it ring," I instructed.

Amy nodded and silenced the ringer. She watched the little red light on the port until it stopped blinking before asking, "Who's calling from the bank?"

I turned the television on.

"What movie are we going to watch?" Meg interrupted. "I think . . ." Her printed nails skimmed over the rack of DVDs at her feet, and she tapped one. "How about *The Ring*?"

I was grateful to Meg for changing the subject. Meg was always good at reading a room and constructing and polishing true-ish stories to distract, charm, or disarm someone.

"I hate *The Ring*," Amy whined, and looked at me imploringly.

It wasn't funny when Meg dressed Jo up as the girl from the movie who climbs up the well. I didn't laugh at all. Okay, maybe a little, but I was still upset at my oldest girls for tormenting their little sister.

"Really?" Jo's voice had a spooky tone, like she was trying to scare her sister. Jo reached out to tickle Amy's sides, and Amy jerked away.

"Please, Mom, tell Meg we aren't watching *The Ring*!" Amy pulled at my sweatpants.

"What about *The Skeleton Key*?" Beth suggested. That was her favorite movie. Beth loved anything with Kate Hudson, and living just outside New Orleans made the movie especially terrifying.

"Jo, what do you want to watch?" I asked.

Jo moved over to the DVD stand, making Amy yelp when Jo's knee landed on Amy's toes as she passed.

"*Cabin Fever* or . . ." She picked up *Interview with the Vampire*.

It made me feel like a cool mom when my girls liked movies that I loved growing up. *Interview with the Vampire* was my favorite movie for a good twenty years. To this day, Anne Rice is the only author whose entire works I've read.

Meg said in a quiet voice, "That movie reminds me of River . . ."

Even hearing that boy's name made my insides feel like a Ferris wheel on fire, but fortunately my girls' penchant for drama distracted me. Amy moved to her feet and grabbed the movie straight from Jo's hands and tossed it under the Christmas tree. Jo yelled an indignant "Hey!" and Meg blew a kiss to Amy.

"John's calling!" Meg yelled, and disappeared from the room before her phone even rang.

"*Cabin Fever* it is," Jo said, and took the remote from the table.

While Jo fiddled with the DVD player, Amy ran to the bathroom and Beth disappeared into the kitchen. The house was quiet except for the beeping of the microwave, then the soft hum as it spun around whatever Beth was making. My house wasn't usually quiet like this. When Frank was home, there was always music playing or the sound of him laughing, singing . . . something.

The silence wasn't going to last long, and I wasn't sure that I wanted it to, but I was going to enjoy it while it lasted. I closed my eyes, and shortly I started to hear kernels popping and smell a decadent butter odor.

Jo was sitting cross-legged next to the TV, staring down at her candy-cane-striped socks. To a stranger Jo may have looked sad, with her pouty lips and her downcast eyes, but I knew she was calm. She looked like she was thinking about something important, and I wished I could read her thoughts, to help take a little of the weight off her shoulders. I no longer wanted silence.

"How's the piece coming along?" I asked her. I didn't get much time alone with Jo now that she had a job—a job that she seemed to love, since she spent so much time there.

Jo shrugged. "It's good. I think." She ran her hands up and down her cheeks and looked at me. "I think it's good. I think it's really good." A shy but blinding smile split her face, and she covered her mouth. "I'm almost done. Should I use my actual name?"

"If you want to. You could also use my maiden name. When can I read it?" Her smile dissipated even faster than it had arrived. "Or not." I added a smile to show I wasn't upset. I understood why she wouldn't want me to read her work yet. Of course it hurt my feelings a little bit, but I knew she had her reasons, and I never wanted to add any pressure on her.

"You could send it to your dad," I suggested.

She thought about it for a second. "You think he has time? I don't want to distract him."

Sometimes she sounded too adult for me.

The bathroom door opened in the hallway, and Amy came walking back into the living room, her bedroom blanket in tow. My parents had given it to me at her baby shower, but it was really worn now, the colored patches that made up the little quilt a bit duller.

Amy, with her lip-gloss obsession and blond hair, was trying to grow up too fast. She wanted to be like her older sisters more than anything, but that was the typical youngest-sibling thing. My sister was the same, always following me around and trying to be my equal. Amy was now in seventh grade, which debatably was the hardest grade to push through. I couldn't remember much of my own seventh grade, so it couldn't have been so bad for me. Ninth grade—now, *that* I remember.

Jo always teased Amy, warning her sister that she should start preparing for high school now. But Amy was at that pivotal age in her life when she thought she knew everything. She was at the awkward stage in her appearance, too, where she hadn't quite grown into her features. The bratty little girls in her class liked to make fun of her bony frame and her lack of a period. Just last week, Amy came in asking when she was allowed to shave her legs. My rule had always been that my daughters could shave when they started their period, but when I told Amy that, she had a twelve-year-old's meltdown in the bathroom. Honestly, I didn't even know where I got that rule, probably my own mother, and given what Amy was going through, I helped my girl shave her legs that day.

Meg was not only the oldest, but she was also the second-in-charge of our government-owned home. Sometimes it was easy to pretend that it was our home, until something happened like getting a ticket for my grass being too long. I had looked out the window to find a man standing in my front yard, bent down and measuring my grass. When I went outside, he cowered back to his truck, but not before handing me a ticket. Apparently the housing office didn't have anything better to do than measure people's grass.

I hoped that one day we would be able to buy a home of our own, maybe after Frank retired from the Army. I didn't know what state we would settle in when he was finally done, but something like the middle of nowhere in New England sounded nice. But Frank often talked about moving to a sleepy beach town where you could wear flip-flops every day. Of course, it would depend on where our daughters ended up, too. Amy wouldn't be out of the house for another six years, and Beth . . . well, I wasn't sure if Beth would ever want to leave, and that was okay, too.

Beth brought in two bowls of popcorn, and everyone got comfortable in the small room. I stayed in Frank's chair, Amy sat next to Beth as Meg walked in and plopped down on the opposide side of the couch, and Jo stayed on the floor near the TV.

"Is everyone ready?" Jo asked, and hit play without waiting for a reply.

As the movie started, I went back to thinking about how fast my daughters had grown. This could be the last year that we would all be together for Christmas. Next year, Meg would more than likely be with John Brooke's family in Florida, or wherever their vacation home was. I couldn't keep track sometimes. It wasn't that Meg dated a ton, but she'd had a few boyfriends. Unlike my mom, I kept a close eye on my daughters and the guys they brought around, although so far that really just meant watching Meg. Frank minded more than me, but I knew firsthand that being too protective of our daughters could be worse than making sure they were educated about dating and relationships.

When Meg was sixteen, I took her to get on birth control, earning me an awkward lecture from my own mom.

She wasn't one to give anyone advice: she had had two kids before she was twenty-one.

The house phone rang again, and Jo leaned over and shut it off.

Meg's phone rang next, a pop song that Amy immediately started singing along to.

"Technology, man," Jo commented from the floor.

"It's Mrs. King." Meg sighed, getting to her feet.

Jo grabbed the remote and paused the movie. Meg disappeared into the kitchen.

Amy lay down where Meg had been sitting, even though she would just have to get back up when her sister got back. "I'm too young to work, but when I'm old enough, I'll work at a better place than a coffee shop or a makeup store."

"You're being obnoxious," Jo said.

"You're being obnoxious," Amy mocked in a voice that sounded a lot like Jo's.

Being the youngest, Amy liked to point out the flaws of her sisters any chance she could. I had a feeling that it took a heavy toll on Amy's confidence to exist under her three sisters, who in her own way she looked up to. Sisterly love was tricky because she loved her sisters more than anything, but at the same time, she was jealous of nearly everything about each of them. Meg's wide hips, Jo's confidence, Beth's ability to cook anything and everything . . .

When Meg returned to the living room, Jo started the movie again.

"Did she pay you yet?" Beth asked, mirroring my own thoughts.

I didn't mind Meg working for Mrs. King, even if the woman intimidated me with her huge house and tiny purebred dogs. I had never met Mr. King, but I had met their three children on a few separate occasions. Meg had had a real thing for the boy, Shia, and I could see why. He was nice, with a big heart and a freight train of passion. I thought if there was a man who could keep up with Meg, it would be Shia King. I didn't know much about what had happened between them, but I figured if Meg wanted me to know, I would.

Meg shrugged. "She just hasn't yet. I don't know why."

Jo rolled her eyes and threw her hands into the air. Meg's brown eyes bulged out of her head in response.

"Well, haven't you asked her?" I said.

"Yes. She's been so busy, though."

"Doing what? Throwing parties?"

Meg sighed. "No." She shook her head at me. "It's the holidays—she's busy."

"I'm surprised you're okay with this. I thought you were tougher than that," Jo said.

"I *am*."

"Yes, she is. You're not tough as Jo, though—Jo's as tough as a boy!" Amy laughed.

Jo shot up to her feet. "What did you say?"

I sighed from the chair. "Amy." I said her name harshly enough for her eyes to snap to me. "What did I tell you about that?" I wasn't having that in my house. My girls could dress however they wanted.

"I said you *act* like a boy." Amy sat up on the couch, dodging Meg's attempt to hold her on her lap. I knew if it got too heated, I would have to interfere, but I wanted to let the girls at least attempt to work things out on their own. Just like Meg with Mrs. King, though the nerve of the woman for not paying for honest work did grate at me.

"And what exactly does that mean, Amy? Because there's no such thing as boys being stronger than girls!" Jo's voice was loud and her fingers were bent into air quotations. "Being tough has nothing to do with being a boy. If anything—"

"Not true! Can you lift the same as a boy?" Amy challenged.

"You *aren't* serious." Jo's mouth was a hard line.

Meg put her hands on Amy's slim shoulders and pressed her flowery fingernails into her sister's sky-blue nightie. Amy let out a stubborn huff of breath, but she lay down and let Meg play with her hair.

Jo waited, her hands on her hips.

The movie played in the background.

"Let's enjoy our winter break. This is better than sitting in math class, right?" Beth asked. My sweet Beth was always trying to fix things. She was the most like Frank in that way.

Jo had his political and social passion, but Beth was a natural caregiver.

Beth and Jo stared at each other for a few moments before Jo gave in and sat down quietly on the floor.

However, before long Amy began in again on her favorite topic of the last couple days. "Ugh, it's not that much better than math. It's not fair. You don't understand that all the girls at my school are going to come back with all new clothes, a new phone, new shoes." She counted the list on her fingers and lifted her cell phone in the air. "And here we are with no gifts under our tree at all."

My heart ached and my head swam with guilt.

This time Beth spoke first. "We make more money than half the girls at your school. Look at our house and look at theirs. Our car, too. You need to look around and remember how it used to be before Dad was an officer." Beth's words were sharper than usual; they seemed to settle into Amy, because she frowned and her eyes darted around the living room from the beige walls to the fifty-inch flatscreen we'd bought from the PX, tax-free of course.

Amy looked at the Christmas tree. "*Exactly* my point. We could have—"

But, as had often been happening during the break, Jo forcefully interrupted Amy to remind everyone that the family only had extra money when Frank was dodging bullets and IEDs in Iraq, and so we had to respect that and not seem like we were being opportunistic on the back of his risk.

I hated when they talked in specifics like that; it was a little too much. I wondered if I still had that Baileys in the fridge. I thought I did.

"Plus," Jo went on, all worked up into a lather, "all the girls in your grade *steal* most of that stuff anyway. You really think

Tiara Davis's family can afford to buy her Chanel sunglasses? Only officers can, and you don't have any officer's kids in your grade beside that one kid who moved from Germany, what's his name?"

Amy nearly growled his name. "Joffrey Martin. He's a jerk."

Jo nodded. "Yeah, him. So, don't be jealous. No one else has any money around here unless it's the first or the fifteenth."

"Except the Kings," Meg said under her breath.

Her words expressed more than annoyance at not being paid. Everyone in the room could easily detect the longing in her voice for the finer things in life, and the King's had all the finer things. There were even rumors that they had gold toilets in their expansive mansion, though Meg said she hadn't seen any.

I knew how much Meg loved working for Mrs. King as an assistant. I hadn't been quite sure how my princess Meg would do following orders all day, but since Mrs. King had plucked Meg from her job at Sephora and asked her to work for her, she hadn't fired her yet. So far her job description remains unknown, aside from doing Mrs. King's makeup and walking her yappy little dogs. Last week Meg loaded the dishwasher, but she told me that Mrs. King told her to never touch a dirty dish again. I wasn't sure that I liked that message, but Meg was nineteen and I had to let her decide what kind of woman she wanted to be.

"No one likes the Kings anyway," Amy said.

"Yes, they do!" Meg defended.

"Okay, so you like them. That isn't saying much. That's like saying people like Amy," Jo teased, but Amy wasn't having it.

Amy shot up like a firecracker to yell at her sister. "Jo always—"

Meg put her hand on Amy's chest and laid her back down on her lap. "Amy, it was a *compliment* . . . Anyway, John Brooke is going to be an officer, too. When he graduates from West Point in a few weeks."

I felt like a teenager when I rolled my eyes at Meg at this. "Don't throw around rank like that. You sound like a snob."

What Meg didn't say was that she didn't so much mind being a snob if it meant she got Chanel sunglasses or a pool in her backyard, like Mrs. King. I'd heard her say those exact words to Amy last week.

"Yeah, Meg," Amy added.

"Shut up, Amy."

"Meredith, do you know how rich they are?" Meg asked.

I shook my head. I only knew that Mr. King helped big corporations get out of lawsuits. I wasn't fascinated by the Kings the way my daughters seemed to be. I was the opposite of my oldest daughter; I absolutely hated when people thought they were better than others, which happened too often in the Army community. Before Frank got his latest promotion, I felt like I fit right in with the enlisted wives. Everyone was equally lonely, equally broke, equally stressed over the war and taking care of their households. Some of the enlisted wives even worked, and I loved that. I had a small group of friends, one young wife who had just had her first baby and a woman my age who had just been stationed at Fort Cyprus from Fort Bragg.

After Frank became an officer, I was no longer accepted by my lower-ranking group, but I didn't fit in with the officers' wives circle, either. Being an officer's wife came with more social responsibility that I simply didn't want. I already had four daughters to raise and a husband to support while he was away.

Denise Hunchberg, the leader of our old Family Readiness Group, was pleasant once upon a time, but she'd become increasingly catty and crazed with the little bit of power she had. It drove me insane to sit back and watch her use her so-called authority to bully the younger wives. Every time she scolded me or mocked another wife behind her back, I would mentally lick my fingers and wipe the awful woman's penciled eyebrows off her smug face.

Sometimes when I was feeling especially petty, I thought about telling Denise—a woman who acted as if her status in the FRG was the same as leading the free world—that her husband slept with the female medic, twice, during the battalion's last deployment. When Denise's little finger was waving in my face for forgetting to bring hot dog buns to the last fund-raiser that I actually went to, I almost told her off. But I knew better. I was too smart to do something stupid like that. It would be an awful thing to destroy someone's family, and on top of that, a husband would get the heat for his wife's mouth, so her behavior had to stay mature, almost regal.

Officers' wives were held to a different standard than enlisted wives, and I couldn't do that to Frank. Sometimes I felt that Fort Cyprus was like being a fish stuck in those fish tanks in Walmart. Too many fish, too little food, and nowhere to go but the other side of the dirty tank.

Our daughters needed to keep a good reputation, too. Well, as good as four teenage girls could. Word traveled faster than light at an Army post, and the Spring Girls had been sprinkling seeds for gossip all around town.

Something had turned in the conversation while I pondered Denise, because I was brought back by Amy saying, "And Dad has a safer job than everyone else. He doesn't even have to carry a gun."

No one told her she was wrong.

I had told her that little lie once to make her feel better. I mean, what the hell was I supposed to tell my seven-year-old when she asked if her dad was going to die?

For her part, Jo always tried to ignore the huge gun strapped across her dad's chest in every single picture he posted on Facebook. Jo hated the idea of guns and said so often. She would be content never to hold a weapon in her life. I was the same.

"I wouldn't call being on a base in the middle of Mosul *safe*," Jo said, not bothering to hide the darkness of her tone. She had long ago given up on pretenses.

Never-minding Amy's lack of details, my daughters knew where their dad was and how dangerous it was in Iraq. They knew that men died there, from both countries. Men like Helena Rice's father. He left two days before her last year of high school and was dead before Christmas. Helena and her mom were now moving back to wherever they came from before the Army told them where to live. They were only given ninety days to evacuate their home on post.

It was awful. Just plain awful.

"It's the safest post," Amy said.

Another lie I told her.

"No—" Jo began, but I interrupted by saying her name.

I felt tired all of a sudden. Sometimes I had moments like that, when I wished Frank were here to help explain such heavy things to his girls.

"*Meredith,*" Jo snapped back at me, though her demeanor softened a little when she felt Beth's eyes on her.

"Jo, come on. Let's just watch the movie."

I was so tired; I'd been very tired lately. I wanted to get up and check the fridge.

"Sorry, Beth, that my concern about our father's life is disrupting your movie," Jo snapped, crossing her arms around her chest.

If Jo would have said that to Amy or to Meg, or even me, she would have gotten an earful, a lecture, or even a slap from Amy. But Beth didn't say a word. A few seconds passed, and Jo turned up the volume on the television. I felt the tension seep out of Jo's shoulders, along with mine.

We just missed Frank, that was all.

The Spring Girls went through phases of missing their father. Meg missed her dad the most when her boyfriend showed the other boys at her school pictures that were supposed to be for his eyes only. Jo missed her dad the most when she was chosen to be the youngest editor her school newspaper had ever seen; then she missed him, even more, when she got her title taken away. Beth missed her dad the most when she was playing music and couldn't find the right note. Amy missed her dad the most when she wanted to hear him sing her favorite Disney songs. And lastly, their mother missed her husband when life got just a little too heavy for her shoulders to bear.

The five of us missed our lieutenant for all different reasons, and we couldn't wait for him to return next month. It felt like he had been gone so much longer than one year, and two weeks of R&R wouldn't be nearly enough.

During those two weeks, he would always try to spend a year's worth of time with his girls. Last year, we drove from Louisiana to Florida and spent a week at Disney World. I could feel Frank's anxiety growing with each burst of fireworks in the sky above us. He left during the show, and I would forever remember the way he looked as he walked back to the hotel, his shoulders shaking as each blooming flower of fire lit up the dark sky. The explosions were beautiful to Jo with her wide eyes, and to Amy with her big smile. The booms made my blood pump, worrying about my husband, who couldn't handle the chaotic blasts of color.

When Frank disappeared into the noisy crowd, I ran after him, and apparently Meg left Jo in charge and ran after a boy she'd met in the line to walk through Cinderella's castle.

Jo smiled and leaned down to her sister's ear. I couldn't hear what she said, but I was sure I didn't want to know.

In the kitchen, the oven beeped and Beth jumped up. If the other girls heard the sound, they didn't show it. Beth spent a lot of time in the kitchen. Lately, I had felt less and less like cooking, and Beth was the only one of my daughters who noticed when the laundry was piled up.

"Are we watching a movie, or what? Everyone quit moving around and talking!" Amy exclaimed, to which Jo rolled her eyes.

Every year, I made my four girls watch horror movies on Christmas Eve. It's been a tradition since my and Frank's first Christmas alone. We were stationed in Las Vegas, and I was feeling homesick. Halloween was always the best part of my years growing up. My mom went all out, and I had adopted her love for the holiday, so when I sought out comforting things from home, I happened upon an all-night monster marathon that Christmas Eve. Ever since, I've kept the habit up and brought my girls into it.

All of my girls got into Halloween and spooky things, but since we'd moved to New Orleans, Beth and Amy had become more and more entertained by the voodoo tales and urban legends surrounding the Big Easy. I prided myself on having the scariest house on the block, no matter where we lived. I reminisced about my childhood and told ghost stories about haunted places in my hometown in the Midwest. When I was young, my friends and I spent our weekends touring "haunted" places near our small town, which comprised the few good memories I had of that place. So it was lucky that on that Christmas Eve I hit upon a TV horror marathon, instead of one about, say, depressed rural areas and alcoholism.

Jo pointed to the screen. "I love this part."

She picked the same type of movies from the same time frame every year, always virus- or zombie-themed horrors. Last year it was *28 Days Later*. Meg always chose movies off the lead actor. Last year her celebrity crush was Tom Hardy, and I had to agree with her on that . . . which was a weirder occurrence than ketchup on tacos.

"Me, too," Amy said.

I caught Jo smiling at Amy and my heart warmed.

The house fell to a steady quiet, aside from the screams on the television.

2

jo

As usual, I was the first one up on Christmas morning. Typically, I would wake up before the sun rose and go downstairs to peek at the unwrapped gifts from "Santa." Afterward, I would wake up Beth, then Meg. Amy always woke up the moment that Beth did since they shared a room.

That year was different, though. I had no urge to rush quietly to the living room and check for gifts. At least our stockings were still hung up that year. The stockings were always my favorite of all things Christmas because my parents would just cram as much little shit, mostly candy, as they could inside the giant sock. I would dump the whole thing on the floor, and I would have to keep my sisters from touching my stuff, even though they had their own. Amy was the worst at that; she was known to trade out her stuff with ours on the sly if she liked ours more.

We each had our own itchy thick stocking with our name threaded across the top. My mom's mom made one for each of us when we were born. Mine was the ugliest, with a Santa on the front who looked a little deranged and a lot drunk. His belly was lopsided, and his beard was a dark gray, like his teeth. His smile was just slightly sinister, and with the whole thing fraying over the years, it was like Bad Santa had rotted the fabric itself. It made me smile each year we unpacked it for use.

Meg always complained that Target had cuter designs on their stockings. Instead of an exquisite piece of jewelry from a distant royal relative, the Spring Girls got old stockings from our grandma—who Meredith hadn't spoken to in nearly two years. Even so, I had to pick a side, and only one of those women put food in my stomach. As much as I liked my grandma, I wanted to support Meredith.

So this year, Meredith went through the trouble of hanging up the stockings (the day after Thanksgiving, for God's sake). I cared less about the absence of Christmas gifts in the house than my sisters did. Even Beth, who didn't care about clothes like Meg did, or books like me, or herself like Amy, got excited about presents. If Christmas were a person, it would be Beth. Beth was fresh-baked cookies, soft laughter, and giving.

I would be Halloween, I thought, as I pulled open the top drawer of my dresser and gathered the little books I'd bought for my sisters. I'd spent half of my paycheck on them. I'd been making enough working as a barista in a book/coffee shop and I loved having my own money. I knew Beth would likely be the only one to read the book of poetry—and she'd be proud of me for using my money to give everyone gifts—but I hoped Amy and Meg would at least open theirs. If not, at least the author would make a few bucks from my purchase.

I dreamed of the day I could write words that people would actually read. I would even be okay with only selling four copies. I would even be fine if one lonely person bought anything I wrote and felt somewhat connected with it—heck, if they just *finished* the thing I'd be thrilled. Beth always told me I was too hard on myself, too eager for the future and too quick to be offended, but I didn't exactly agree with her. If the past and present both kind of sucked, and no one seemed to learn from their mistakes, why wouldn't I be looking to the future? The future was sort of all I had to look forward to.

Beth was the only one who actually read every single article I managed to get into the school paper, and she always told me how talented I was. She praised my silly stories about school dances and debate-club meets, but I couldn't wait to write about the world outside the walls of White Rock High School. I didn't want to write about Shelly Hunchberg winning some sparkling, shallow crown made of cheap plastic and fake diamonds that reflected the light of what could only be described as soon-to-be-failed dreams.

I wanted to write about the madness happening in my nation, across the world. I wanted to use my voice for something more than stroking Mateo Hender's ego with a page full of pictures of him on the football field in his uniform, thick pads puffing out his already-overbeefed body. I was tired of posting the ROTC stats, and since White Rock High was made up of 90 percent military brats, no way was that going to stop. I could deal with that—ROTC was pretty cool to watch—but I needed more freedom.

I wanted to write about the things that would matter in two years, when Shelly is pregnant with Mateo's baby and he's enlisted or working at the local drive-thru. I should have been able to write about the number of troops who came home to their families last week—or the ones who didn't. The twenty-car streak of paying it forward Meg and I saw at Starbucks would never make the White Rock High newspaper. It could easily have; it was a simple, cute story. Mr. Geckle was a fool.

"Our readers are too young to read this," Mr. Geckle told me while waving his wrinkly finger at my article about the blooming protesting across the country.

"No, Mr. Geckle, they aren't. They are teenagers, my age." I waved frantically at my own body as if Mr. Geckle had any idea what it was like to be a teenager in the two thousands.

"Too biased, too controversial," he mumbled, dismissing me with a feeble wave of his hand.

I wasn't having that, and I was sure he was fully expecting my reaction to be less than dismissible. He had known me for two years at that point.

"It's true, it's all true." I picked up the page and followed him around his desk.

The fake wood of his expansive desk was marked all over with pen and students' initials. The school just gave up on replacing the tables after the second round. It was sort of a thing at my high school, to write initials on teachers' desks. I always said that it was immature, pointless even, until now.

It wasn't until I was standing in front of him getting my best piece of writing shot down because he didn't want to give enough credit to the mental capability of his student body that I saw the carvings as something different. A rebellion. I loved it. I wanted to reach across the graffiti-marked desk and grab Mr. Geckle's monogrammed pen out of the pocket of his shirt and carve my name into the fake wood. I promised myself I would force the courage to come back later and carve my name right into his desk so he would never forget me—or how wrong he'd been about my ideas.

But Mr. Geckle would just keep telling me no, over and over. He cemented my worry that real stories would never make it to the eyes of my peers. Not here in this tiny high school at the bottom of Louisiana. Lucky for them there's the internet, so they aren't completely unaware of the happenings of the world outside the Army post. I wasn't going to give up completely, but I had to accept that my stories were never going to be cover stories. The Mateos and Shellys of the world make cover stories.

My phone buzzed in my sweatpants, and I shoved the four black books into the front pocket of my hooded sweatshirt to shut off the alarm I had set.

I needed to call my work and tell them that I could pick up any empty shifts they had during my winter break from school. I didn't want the time off like the rest of my coworkers. I loved the holidays at Pages. It was the stuff of a writer's dreams. A postmodern coffee shop with black metal and wood tables, big murals of local art hanging on the walls, and pop-culture-reference tip jars. The day I had my interview, the choices on the two tip jars were VOLDEMORT or DUMBLEDORE. I tossed a dollar into VOLDEMORT, just because it was empty and I felt particularly rebellious that day. I smiled and thanked the hyper girl behind the bar. She must have taken a shot or two of espresso that morning.

Between hyper Hayton and my boss, who encouraged my creative hand and always asked to read my writing, I mostly loved my job.

I sent a quick text to my boss, then immediately remembered it was really early, and a holiday. Whatever, he's done it to me before. I scooped up the books and quietly walked over to Meg's twin bed on the other side of the room. She was asleep, softly snoring (though she swore she didn't) with her legs curled up to her chest. Her arms moved a little as she slept, and her shirt slid over, exposing one of her breasts. Meg seemed to get all the best genes of the family. She got Meredith's boobs and hips, our dad's smile. I remembered when I was in junior high and would stare at myself in the mirror, feeling so undeveloped compared to the outrageous curves of my sister's body. Now, I don't wish I had bigger boobs so much, but big breasts weren't all Meg had. She also had lacy panties in her top drawer and she had sex with River Barkley, and then a few more boys.

On top of that she had a red Prius. I couldn't wait to drive. I had just gotten my permit, and I knew Meg was counting down the days until I could help her chauffeur everyone around. I knew she hated when she had to take Aunt Hannah back to the French Quarter or Amy to Girl Scouts. Meg, for some reason, felt that her hours were more valuable than mine. Maybe that was true. She was a year out of high school, closer to being a full-on woman than me.

She moved again, and I wondered if she was having a nightmare. Maybe Sephora had run out of eye-shadow palettes or Shia King had blocked her on Twitter. She'd had a meltdown when all of her old friends from Texas had blocked her, though she refused to tell us exactly what happened with her circle there and why her friends all took River's side. Or why she couldn't stand Shia King anymore.

Meg loved to stalk his whereabouts online. She followed him from Cambodia to Mexico, staring at (but not liking) all of his pictures. She would try to tell me how horrible he was, but that was hard to believe when I saw him posting pictures in small villages around the world. One was of him reading to a small girl in Uganda, her arms wrapped around his lean shoulders. Their skin was nearly the same color. The little girl's skin was only slightly darker brown. She was so beautiful.

Meg couldn't stand Shia, but I was fascinated by him. A handsome, popular, rich kid who dropped out of college to travel the world and use the money from his trust fund to become an activist. I could see that Meg would be bothered by the idea of that, I suppose, but I thought it was a cool story and was impressed that he and both of his sisters moved away from here. I remember when Meg asked Meredith if anyone cared that Shia was black, and Meredith spent over an hour explaining to us that we could date anyone: boys or girls, black or Asian or interracial. Meg never asked again. Of course, Meg didn't seem to have a type—every boy she brought home looked different from the last.

My fingers carefully lifted the bottom corner of Meg's pillow, and I slid the poetry book underneath her sleeping head. She didn't stir, just snored and looked beautiful while doing it. I always thought she was gifted with her looks. Her soft hips and big chest used to make me a little jealous, but the older I got, the less I cared about boobs and things like that. Meg was proud of her body, even if she spent too much time complaining because she had to wear a heavy-duty bra and carry around extra weight strapped to her chest.

As Beth's own chest blossomed, Meg warned her about boys harassing her even more than they might me. Meredith said that wasn't true, that boys can harass any type of girl. I didn't know which was true, but hoped that I never had to find out.

Meg used her looks to her advantage for sure. She always tried to give Beth advice on how to handle boys, but Beth always just blushed and shook her head, not soaking any of Meg's words in. I figured Meg knew what she was talking about. Especially living in a town full of soldiers. Meg loved it. She always said that she loved a man in uniform. Like her boyfriend, John—

"What the hell?" Meg jerked up from her bed and let out a little scream, startling me. She looked around, clearly confused, her dark hair stuck to her mouth. "What the hell are you doing, Jo? You scared the shit out of me." Her hands swiped across her face and tucked her hair behind her ears.

I covered my mouth with the books and tried to stifle a laugh. "I was playing Santa."

Meg smiled at me and shoved her hand under her pillow. Her expression grew into excitement, and I remember thinking how young she looked when she pulled the book out. Her eyes scanned my gift, and even though it wasn't makeup, she beamed at me, even squealed a little when she pulled the book to her chest. "Thank you." I covered my mouth when I smiled, but Meg saw it. "It's no Naked palette, but I knew you would come through, Jo."

I liked the idea of that, that I would be expected to do something for my sisters. Beth was usually the one who would think of everyone before herself. Not this year; this year, it was me.

Maybe we would all get along that holiday, I thought.

"There, I did my good deed for the year."

Back to form, she rolled her eyes. "You could have just gotten your license so I wouldn't have to be the only one chauffeuring Amy and Beth around. That would have been a better present."

"Beth never goes anywhere."

"You know what I mean."

"Not really."

I stared at Meg's poster of an actor she liked. He was in nearly every movie that year. She followed him on Twitter and thought she was going to meet him when he came to a convention in New Orleans that past fall. When he got engaged the week before, Meg gave away her meet-and-greet tickets.

"Just remind Meredith to take you to get your license. You've had your permit for seven months, dude."

"Seriously, Meg, it's seven in the morning, chill. I've asked Meredith to take me three times this week. She's too busy."

Meg's eyes narrowed. "Doing what?"

I shrugged, stepping toward the door. I didn't have an answer, and I still had three books to deliver.

"Meredith's doing more than you, Princess," I reminded her.

Meg stuck her middle finger up at me.

"You should read the book, really, this time."

When I turned back around to look at her, she was opening the book at a random page. I was hoping the words would attach themselves to her the way they did me. Lately I had begun to feel like I wanted to get closer to Meg; I wanted to grow up. I wanted all three of my sisters to find themselves in the words of the artist. Especially Meg. She could relate to more of the poems than the rest of us, I was sure of it. Some of the poems made me crave to fall in love with someone; I even craved the heartbreak after.

Next, I went to Beth and Amy's room across the hall. It was dark inside and the door creaked when I pulled it open. Amy had taped a SPRING GIRLS ONLY sign on her door last night when she got in a fight with her friend Tory. Amy never kept friends long, but when you have three sisters who love you unconditionally, it doesn't matter as much. We had to put up with her bossiness, Tory didn't. Neither did Sara, or Penelope, or Yulia . . .

Amy's half of the room was a cluttered mess. It was worse than Meg's and my sides put together. Beth kept her side spotless, and Amy's sloppiness drove Beth half-crazy, and she cleaned it once a week. Amy always waited it out.

Amy's bed was empty. I glanced over to Beth's, expecting to see Beth snuggling our littlest sister in her slightly bigger bed, but, nope, Amy wasn't anywhere.

I slid my fingers across the soft black cover of the book, stopping on the illustration of a bee on the front. Even the cover of that book was perfect. I loved every single poem inside.

When I lifted Beth's pillow, she woke up. "What's wrong?"

I shook my head and pressed my finger to my mouth to silence her. "Nothing, go back to sleep. Sorry."

When I was done playing Santa, I made my way downstairs to the kitchen. I was happy to find the four stockings were stuffed with candy and surprised to see three gifts on the counter. They had been laid down in a straight line next to the empty fruit basket that my mom had bought for decoration but refused to put fake fruit in because somehow that would be ridiculous.

The three gifts were left unwrapped, so they were meant to be from Santa. None of us believed in Santa anymore, though Meredith refused to acknowledge that. She wanted her girls to stay as young as possible for as long as possible, which was hard when our world was so full of hate and war and injustice. But, I had to admit that when I was staring at the line of unopened gifts, my heart leaped a little when my eyes landed on the last gift, a book.

The words *The Bell Jar* were clear on the front in purple. I had mentioned wanting this semi-autobiography written by one of my favorite writers, Sylvia Plath—one of the only things I hadn't read by her. Meredith didn't care for my dark obsession with the woman whose name carries such a black flag around, but I had been utterly fascinated by her ever since I stumbled upon a post about her on Tumblr, before my dad made me delete my account. I hugged the book to my chest. Meredith came through this year.

She was doing the best she could with my dad in the Middle East for the fourth time in eight years. She had a lot on her shoulders, to be two parents instead of one. It was hard enough for her to be one, given that she had four teenage daughters. I grabbed the book and gently touched the woman's silhouette on the cover. It was beautiful; my chest throbbed. Only books could make me feel this way. I wished I could write a great novel, even if I was more of a column writer. I wanted to work for *Vice*, or maybe even the *New York Times*.

Who knows? If I can get out of this Army town, I can do anything.

Meg's gift was a bag to hold more of her makeup, and Beth's was a cookbook, which was really a gift for our mom, too, because this meant Beth was another step closer to being everyone's servant. Beth literally did everything in our house and was hardly ever thanked for her servitude. Her quiet order just came and went so naturally around us—picking up Meg's makeup, tossing my socks into the hamper, then washing all of our clothes. On the bright side, this book promised thirty-minute meals, so Beth would have more time to do everyone's laundry.

The sound of the fridge opening startled me, and I dropped Beth's book on the counter. Amy stood there, searching the shelves in the fridge for breakfast. A glass jar of jelly fell to the floor, hitting my bare foot. It rolled past me and under the kitchen island.

"Shh, you're going to wake everyone up!" I scolded.

Amy's Christmas-themed pajamas draped over her small frame. They were covered in snowmen and pretzels. The pretzels didn't make much sense, but I remember loving them five years ago when my parents got them for me for Christmas. Sometimes I felt bad for Amy, the youngest of us all, because she always got stuck wearing all of our hand-me-downs. With each daughter born, my parents had to make their dollars stretch that much further. When we were younger, it was the reason Meredith could never work; a sergeant in the Army didn't make enough to feed six mouths, unless he's deployed, of course, so there was no way they could have paid for child care for four kids. Now that we're older, Meredith's lack of a degree meant she could get few jobs around Fort Cyprus anyway. Only a few of my friends' moms worked, so it wasn't anything out of the norm. A few moms I knew sold those scented-wax cubes or leggings, to make a little extra money for the house, but it still wasn't much.

In reality, most of the families I knew from our old housing neighborhood only had excess money during paydays, deployments, and tax season. The idea of that drove me nuts; that was the type of story I wanted to be writing. Now that Dad was an officer, we should have had more money and been better off, but somehow it seemed that we had less.

"Why are you up?" I asked Amy.

She shut the fridge door and sat bread, a cup of yogurt, and a carton of orange juice on the counter. She looked like she had been up for a while; her hair was even brushed, and that was not a normal thing at this time of day. I always woke up before the rest of my sisters. It was time I got with Meredith, uninterrupted by the voices arguing over what to watch before school.

"Because it's Christmas." She shrugged her shoulders, and the neckline of the pajama top slid down her shoulder.

She looked so slight in the oversized clothes, it was like I was looking at her for the first time in a long time. I was sure there was some sort of metaphor for my clothes being so big on her little body, but I still hadn't had coffee and my brain wasn't ready to be metaphorical just yet.

Amy opened the drawer in front of her and grabbed a butter knife. "Want some?"

I looked at the counter. Toast with yogurt spread on it?

"It's good. Trust me," she said, like she was much older than twelve.

I decided to go against my usual instincts and trust her. It was only toast.

She made us breakfast and I made coffee. After we ate the toast, which was surprisingly not awful, Amy picked up Beth's cookbook.

"What did you get?" I asked.

From the front pocket of my old pajamas, she pulled out her phone. It now had a sparkling gold phone case on it. It wasn't my style, but it was cute. Amy loved sparkles and shine, but I was more of a denim-and-cotton kind of girl.

"That's so cute," I told her, touching the gold glitter. It was rough to the touch and flaked a little under my thumb.

"It is, right?" She smiled. I was happy that she was happy about it. "Do you think this will be the only present we get?"

Amy's hair was so blond in our dark kitchen. I remembered when she was born and how white her hair and skin were. The rest of us were dark like our dad. We were all dark hair, dark eyes, except Meredith and Amy.

Amy and Meredith both looked like something out of a Disney movie. Amy was the more fair, but irony decided to make her insides the darkest of us all. I remember Meg's jealousy over Amy's blond hair when we were younger, but personally I liked my dark hair. Meg wanted to be Cinderella, but I was more than fine being more like Belle. Belle had a library and got to talk to candlesticks and clocks. With or without the prince, I would be fine.

"It might be, but that's okay. Christmas isn't supposed to be only about gifts, remember?" I tried to look into the living room, but couldn't see the tree.

Amy sighed and took a drink of her orange juice, pulled out her phone, and didn't speak until Meredith shouted our names from the living room.

3

"Girls!"

"Mom's up!" Amy exclaimed, as if I hadn't heard her. Amy shoved her sparkly gold iPhone into her pocket and rushed to the living room.

I grabbed my coffee mug from the counter and refilled it. I started a new pot for Meredith and plodded into the living room. When I entered, everyone was on the couch, save Amy, who sat on the floor at Meg's feet. Beth's soft voice was reading the password to Meredith's laptop for the tenth time this week.

"We got a letter," Meredith started to tell us. Her hands were wrapped around a coffee mug, and her face turned to mine. Her light eyes were swollen and tired. Another holiday without my dad. I thought it would get easier as the years went by, but Meredith seemed to be taking this one harder than the three before.

"An email? From Dad?" Amy bounced around before landing on Beth's lap.

"Yes. Your dad. Who else?" Meredith told us. She sat her mug down on the side table and I peeped inside of it, but it was empty. It wasn't stained with coffee, and it smelled a little sour. Weird.

I felt bad for not being surprised or excited to hear from my dad. It always seemed like the longer he was gone, the tighter I had to hold on to the memories I had of him, and if I read too many impersonal emails from the online version of him, I would forget the life of him.

My dad was always bright, his energy consuming. He lit up and took command of a room with his laughter and his witty commentary on all things. I loved to just listen to him talk; his views on the world were so passionate and fascinating, and I loved it. Meredith said I got my bleeding heart from him. And I was fine with that.

But his bleeding heart couldn't be felt through the coldness of the screen.

I tried to smile for my family's sake.

"Let us read it! Where is it?" Amy tugged impatiently on the sleeve of Meredith's shirt.

"It's an email, she has to open it. Be patient, Amy." Beth petted Amy's hair, and the little one instantly calmed down.

I tried to hide the void expression covering my face, but I was never good at hiding anything, especially from my family. Everyone around me always knew what I was thinking before I ever had the chance to say a word. It drove me insane. I couldn't lie; I couldn't hide my frustrations from my sisters or my parents, no matter how hard I tried. My dad always said I was as open as my favorite book. When I got dropped from the journalism program at my high school and demoted to ad manager of the yearbook, I came rushing through the door. I tried to keep my expression flat, not to draw attention to my failure. But the moment the door opened, every single face in my house turned to me, and my family started clucking around me like crazed chickens. All I said to my mom was "I'm fine," but in that mo-

ment I felt like my entire career had ended before it even began. I hated being a young senior in high school. I wasn't even
seventeen.

To make it worse, my senior year was to be spent in the
sticky-sweet Louisiana sun, where my skin burned while Meg's
tanned, and my hair turned to ash while Amy's bleachy blond
was kissed by the sun. I'd always hated the sunshine. Really. I
knew it was a stereotypical wannabe-edgy teen thing to say, but
I didn't care about being cool and dark. I just hated the way I
looked when my face was set in a constant squinty scowl and
my legs stayed pale year-round no matter how many summer
rays beamed down on them. I hated the way the constant sunshine made everyone float around and have an excuse to wear
too much suntan lotion and too-bright smiles. It was weird,
like walking around in a land of zombies. Sure, not the *Walking Dead* kind of flesh eaters; these were less brutal, just Army
wives and brats with big smiles and too many dangly bracelets
and sadness behind their eyes. I couldn't hate that part, though.
I was carrying the same sadness. Our post deployed more soldiers than any across the country, and a huge part of family was
gone, a dad or mom or husband or wife.

Christmas felt especially brutal this year without Dad. On
top of how the glue of my family was sitting in a tent across
the globe, we somehow had no money. I didn't get it. I thought
about how many times I had heard my parents' hushed, angry
voices talk about money. Everyone always said money was the
root of all evil, but Meg told me, "It's sure as hell easier to be
happy when you are rich," and that made more sense to me. I
thought that money must only be evil if you didn't have any.

I missed my friends in Texas almost as much as I missed
my dad. Well, one of my friends; I had finally made a best

friend right before we got orders to move to Louisiana. We had been in New Orleans for a year, and I hadn't tried to make any friends yet.

That's not true; I made eye contact with the old man next door. Twice. A week later I waved.

I stayed lost in my own jagged trail of thoughts throughout Beth's reading of my dad's email. I did smile once, when she read my name. He missed me, it said. I missed him, too. I figured that I would never miss him that much again, but I had no idea what was going to come into my life, or leave it.

My mom and sisters sighed and cried over the laptop, and Meredith said that she would try to schedule a Skype call with our dad that week. I thought about how his camp in Mosul was probably decorated a little, and it made me feel a bit better. When he was at Bagram or Kandahar, they decorated for almost every holiday. On the Christmas that he spent in Afghanistan he had lobster and steak for dinner. It was the least they could do for those troops who were away from their families for the holidays. This time he was at one of the most dangerous bases in Iraq, so I hoped they at least had a tree. We'd sent him a care package full of candy and cookies from Beth, Bugles from me, toiletries from Meg, and a painting from Amy.

"Don't forget we have the battalion Christmas party today. One of you better get in the shower," Meredith said, and sat back as Amy and Meg fought over who would shower first.

While my sisters showered and attended to their appearance, I lay on my bed and typed a few sentences into my notes. I had been working on the same essay for over a month, which was long for me. I looked at my new book, *The Bell Jar*, and opened it to the first page.

4

When Meg pushed out through the front door, we all followed. Meg had that thing about her that made everyone want to follow her. She would have made a good politician or actress. It was something in her brown eyes or the certainty evident in the set of her feminine shoulders.

I wasn't sure what it was, but people flocked to her like bees to honey. Meg made friends with boys easier than girls, which she told me was because girls were threatened by her. I didn't understand that; personally, I was intrigued by her sexuality and fascinated by the way experience danced around her and shone like a spotlight on her. She loved being the center of attention. I was the opposite, but could still appreciate the way she was.

"Let's go, girls!" Meg called to us as she sped up.

The toe of my boot got caught on the doorframe, and I stumbled forward. I would have fallen on my face if not for Beth's sturdy grip on my elbow, steadying me until I could catch my footing. I caught my bag on my shoulder before it fell, but the same couldn't be said for my new copy of *The Bell Jar* and my cell phone. My phone slid down the small hill that was our driveway, and I cursed after it.

"Watch your step," Amy said with a braggy sort of smile on her face and laughter in her voice. Sometimes she drove me crazy.

I reached out my hand to slap her arm, but she dodged out of the way and ran down the driveway. I ran after her and grabbed the long sleeve of her sweatshirt and jerked her to me. Just as she squealed, I looked up and saw a boy standing in the driveway next door. He looked my age, maybe Meg's. His blond hair was grown past his ears, and he was wearing a tan sweatshirt. The same color as Meg's. They would be matching if he weren't wearing black jeans instead of light denim. His most noticeable accessory was his smirk. He was trying not to laugh at me, and that would have pissed me off if I'd had time to process it.

"Jo!" Amy screamed as she jerked my hand, pulling me to the ground.

My knee hit the cement hard, and I heard Meg yell my name. I hadn't realized Amy had hit the ground already. But there I was, lying next to her with my arm across her chest. My knee throbbed under my torn jeans, and I could see red seeping through the tear in the black fabric.

Amy was laughing and Meg stood over me, reaching for my hand. Beth was already helping Amy to her feet. When I looked across the yard, the boy was still staring at us. He was covering his mouth, trying to hide his laughter.

I wanted to flip him off, so I did.

He laughed harder and didn't look away; he just waved at me. He waved with a big smile on his face as I climbed up to my feet and dusted off my jeans. He just kept that awkward shaking hand in the air until I waved back, with my finger still up. My hand was burning too from where the cement had torn the skin of my palm.

"Who's that?" Meg whispered, and pulled my jacket down to cover my back.

I looked to my sister. She had on this red lipstick and looked so put together. The exact opposite of me with my scraped-up skin and ripped jeans.

"I don't know."

"Ask him," Amy said.

He was walking down the driveway of Old Mr. Laurence's house.

"No," Meg and I both quickly said.

"Hey!" Amy yelled to the boy. She was like that.

I started moving my feet, ignoring the pain in my knee. My sisters followed me down the driveway and to the sidewalk.

"What's your name?" Amy yelled at the stranger.

We were passing him, and I couldn't get my feet to move fast enough.

"What's yours?" He tilted his chin like he was saying "Hey" or "'Sup."

"He just gave you the chin tilt," I said to my sisters. I was sure he heard me, but I didn't care.

"He's—" Meg said, probably checking his fingers for a wedding ring.

To me, he looked too young to be married. Older than me for sure, but too young to be someone's husband.

How different he was from anyone Meg had ever dated. His hair was long, so he wasn't a soldier, and Meg didn't date anyone who wasn't a soldier. She was like that.

The boy was walking fast, following us. I wanted to speed

up and put some distance between us, but I also didn't want to bust my ass again.

"I bet that's the grandson that Denise was telling Mom about," Beth told us. She always knew everything that was going on in the adult world around us.

"Probably," Amy agreed.

"Stop staring at him," I hissed at my sisters. They all looked like drooling puppies.

"He looks like the type of guy who makes out with his long-term girlfriend over torn sheets of poetry he wrote for her," Meg said, still gawking.

I knew she only said "makes out" for the sake of our twelve-year-old sister bobbing beside her. I knew what she meant, and I knew what boys that looked like him did with their girlfriends, plural.

"He does, doesn't he?" Meg asked us again. Beth and Amy both nodded.

My sisters burst into laughter, and Amy bounced in front of me and turned on the heel of her boots.

The boy was only a few feet away from us. When he reached us, he walked next to Amy like he knew her. He kept pace with us. "I live next door now."

"Good for you," I said to him.

He turned back to me and smiled at me with bright, straight teeth. A rich kid, no doubt. "Oh"—he cocked his head to the side, and his light hair touched the top of his shoulder—"it'll be good for *you*, too. We'll be friends, I'm sure."

His voice had a hint of an accent, but I couldn't tell you what kind.

His cocky smirk mixed with his black eyes reminded me of the villain in a Saturday-morning cartoon.

"Doubtful," Amy said. "Jo doesn't have any friends."

He laughed again. Amy turned and walked sideways, looking straight into his face. I pinched her arm and she swatted at me. I wanted to slap her.

"We'll see," he said, and separated from us.

The four of us turned toward him, walking backward. Our black boots were a line in the sand, an omen for this new neighbor boy.

"Don't hold your breath!" Amy yelled, and Meg told her to shush.

He was back in the driveway where he came from just as a town car pulled up in front of Old Mr. Laurence's house. He didn't say a word as he climbed into the shiny car. He did smile toward us, but something about the way his eyes clouded made me think he was a little afraid of us.

Good.

Sometimes I felt like we were a force of nature. In that moment we were a powerful blowing wind, coming together to destroy a town.

Okay, maybe a little dramatic. But we *were* a force of nature, the four of us Spring Girls.

5

The community center was packed with volunteers and children running around like chickens. Meg took off her jacket as soon as we walked through the door and hung it up on one of the hooks on the wall. The walls were covered in construction-paper crafts. Long banquet-style tables were lined up across the entire span of the room. Each table had something different on it—crafts for sale on one, crafts to make on another. An old man in a Santa suit was in the corner, and the scratchy, familiar voice of Denise Hunchberg came over the speaker, calling out the names of the winners of the raffle.

"Leslie Martin, Jennifer Beats, Shia King," her smoker's voice croaked. I walked with my sisters and looked for the food. If I was going to be here and be expected to smile, I needed food.

I walked behind Meg, but in front of the others, as we did a lap around the room. I found my spot: two long tables were covered with food, next to another with a face-painting station. Next to that sat a man drawing caricatures. The Christmas party felt like a fair, and I loved fairs. I watched the artist for a few seconds while he drew the Sullys' family portrait. In front of him sat two kids and a mother, but the artist added Mr. Sully, who was in Iraq with my dad, to the drawing, using a small picture of him.

The battalion's holiday party always brought out so many families. Last year, even though Dad was home, we came by and spent our day with the other families who had a mom or dad deployed. We had just moved to Fort Cyprus, and my parents wanted us to make friends with the neighborhood. To start over. Dad led the dance circle, and I spent the entire afternoon watching him teach little kids how to do the electric slide and the Macarena.

"Hey, girls, where's your mom?" Denise Hunchberg asked the moment she spotted the four of us hovering by the tables of food.

"She'll be here soon," I assured the nosy FRG leader. Her husband and youngest child were so nice, but she and her oldest daughter, Shelly, reminded me of weasels. Shelly was awful. She looked nice and innocent, but I'd witnessed too many bitchy popular-girl fits to believe she was anything but a wolf in sheep's clothing, and I did my best to stay away from her.

Denise nodded and told us she couldn't wait to see my mom. She wasn't a good liar.

Meg told me she was going over to the face-painting station to help, and Amy ran after her. Beth stayed with me, and we perused the table full of baked goods, aka my happy place, then started handing out blocks of sugar and cornstarch to already-hyper children.

Meredith showed up an hour later with two pans of sweets. Her famous peppermint bark and her gooey brownies were scooped out of her arms the moment she walked in the door.

Denise gave her a quick hello and a lengthy reminder of Meredith's tardiness before shoving a brownie down her throat.

"Jo Spring? Is that you?" I recognized the voice, but couldn't put my finger on who it was until I turned around.

Shia King. There, in front of me. He looked older somehow, much older than he did just four months ago, when I had seen him last.

The top of his hair was grown out more than it had ever been, and the sides were shaved close to his head. He was taller, too, and he looked like a man.

This new Shia seemed far from the mouthy teenager who I'd caught Meg kissing in the living room the day of her graduation party. Balloons had been everywhere, and confetti was in my hair and Meg's dress was so tight and mine was so long. I was gnawing on a piece of pretzel dipped in chocolate icing, running through the house, high on sugar and caffeine. Wearing a tiara on my head, I had been trying to find my oldest sister, and when I found her, she was spread across Shia's lap, her creamy thighs open, covering his dark skin, and her floral dress was bunched at her waist. His hands were in her thick brown hair, and I covered my mouth and watched them. I couldn't make out what he said when he stopped kissing Meg, but whatever it was, it made her jump off of his lap and push at his chest. When he grabbed her by the waist and whispered something else, she kissed him again. Seconds later, he said something else and she shoved at him again. This time, she climbed off him and moved toward me in the hallway. I ran away before she could see me, and as far as I knew, Meg hadn't spoken to him since that day. She still watched him through social media, but they weren't on speaking terms, she swore.

"It's me," I mumbled, struggling to erase the image in my mind of Meg's mouth touching his.

Shia King smiled and his arms flew around me. "How are you?" he asked, squeezing my rib cage. He lifted me off my feet.

No one except my dad had ever hugged me like that before.

I kind of liked it, even if it took me by surprise. He felt warm, and I wondered if he thought I was Meg. We didn't look much alike, though some said we did. My hair was all one color and long and my eyes were lighter than hers. She had more cushion to her and more confidence.

"Good," I huffed out. My rib cage was burning from his strength. Ten more seconds and it would collapse. I was sure of it. "Are you back in town?"

I didn't remember him knowing me enough to be giving me so generous a hug, but I also couldn't remember the last time anyone had hugged me even half of this.

"Yep, I'm back for a week." He put me down on my feet. "For the holidays. Just enough time to dip my toes in the swamp and jump back out," he joked.

His eyes sparkled under the awful yellow lighting of the ballroom.

I studied his face and noted the changes in him. He was wearing a worn T-shirt that had the shape of the earth printed in colored ink. The land was covered with stacks and stacks of buildings, and one lone tree was in the center, somewhere near Colorado. He was wearing loose joggers and dirty sneakers with no laces. I bet it drove his mom crazy, that he would leave the house looking like the rest of us. Mrs. King was sure to want her offspring to dress their best.

While Shia asked about Meredith and Amy's art, I looked around the room at the chaotic party and searched for Meg's red shirt. She looked like an old Hollywood starlet that day. Her hair pinned back with thick dark-and-light curls, and her eyelashes long and fluttery, like the wings of a butterfly. The blush and highlighter on her cheeks were striking, one of the many perks of working at a makeup store. Her makeup was always flawless, and even if she was constantly teetering on the line between too little and too much, she managed to pull it off. I was decent with makeup, but nothing close to Meg.

"How's your family? How are you? Man, you look different," Shia said. His light eyes darted back and forth between my eyes, mouth, and forehead.

When I'd seen him for the first time, he was scrawny with eyes too big for his head. He was always cute, but too old for me to actually pay attention to.

"Thanks?" I murmured. I wasn't sure if he was being nice or not.

His eyes told me that he was, but Meg's constant complaining about him told me otherwise. I wasn't ready to trust him. Meg was my sister. He was a stranger who most people had something bad to say about. That had to say something about his character.

Or maybe it didn't? I was starting to think that was all a big conspiracy theory. Like when Shelly and Mateo broke up for the third time last summer over a new girl named Jessica. She had bigger boobs and a shorter skirt than Shelly, so when Mateo ditched Shelly in pursuit of the new girl, Shelly told everyone how awful Jessica was. Come to find out, Jessica was actually great, to the point it was hard to keep a straight face when she rejected Mateo.

His smile said he was more of a Jessica than a Shelly, though.

"How's your family?" he asked again.

I didn't know how much to tell him. I never really knew him, despite how he was acting now. I wasn't sure if I should tell him the shallow version, the typical "Oh, everyone is fine and dandy! Sunshine and happiness galore!"

I studied his face and his hands and the way he stood with his back straight but his shoulders slightly slumped.

When I paused too long in reply, he got more specific. Pressing his hand against the back of his neck, he asked, "How's Amy? She must be so grown now."

"She's in seventh grade."

"So basically grown." He smiled and his eyes were alive. "What about Beth? Is she still playing piano?"

How did he even know that Beth played music? I tried to think about him and how well I knew him, but could only remember a few brief interactions.

"Yeah, she plays some still." I felt my pulse quicken under my chest, and I swallowed, looking directly into his eyes. I didn't know if I was supposed to tell him anything, but the longer I stood with him, the more I thought Meg had to be hiding something. I couldn't find a single reason to hate him, from the statement T-shirt he was wearing to the way his hands moved when he talked. I didn't know exactly why Meg disliked him so much, but I knew it had something to do with love, or lack of. Standard grown-up problems.

I found myself wanting to ask him about his travels instead of telling him about the rest of my family. I looked at the tree on his shirt again, and when my eyes went back to his face, they caught his. So, I just told him about Beth. I told him how she spent her days and nights wishing she could make it as a musician. I told him that she had been composing her own music lately, instead of just covering the songs from pop radio.

"She was always so talented," he said, like he remembered something about Beth that I didn't know. "When I was in Peru, I met this woman who teaches music to deaf children—it's fascinating."

I had to think about where that was on the map longer than I wanted to admit.

I thought about Shia in Peru and I felt so young, and I realized that I was so inadequate to be out in the world in the way that I had planned to be by seventeen. I wanted to do things for people like I heard he did. I wanted to help in a bigger way than just fighting with internet trolls in Facebook comments.

"How was Peru? It looked beautiful," I said, remembering the pictures I saw of his trip on Facebook. Meg had made me sit there for two hours, clicking on pictures of his new life abroad. We followed him from California to Brazil to Peru. I thought about how full his passport book must be and then remembered that I didn't even have one.

Shia's eyes closed slightly and his head tilted in confusion. "Did it?"

I thought I was going to have to explain to him why I had been scrolling through his photos of Peru, of Mexico, and of the Philippines. I couldn't just say, "Oops, my sisters and I were cyberstalking you and know your entire life."

At least the one he portrayed on the internet.

Just then Meg walked up to us, her cheeks glowing and shimmering. Shia's back was to her, and as she got closer, I watched as her face twisted into an expression that immediately told me she didn't expect or want to see Shia King here at the party. Even though I knew this would be trouble, I was still glad that she saved me from the awkwardness of having to come up with some kind of reasoning for knowing what was happening in his life when I barely knew him.

Meg approached us and stood next to me, her game face in full effect. Grown-ups were good at game faces. When Shia saw her, her expression said she couldn't have been happier to see him.

"Meg!" Shia smiled at her, but it was faker than Meg's glue-on eyelashes, which fluttered and fell onto her cheeks when she closed her eyes. A girl at her work did them for her every week and she loved them. When everyone around me started getting them, I considered letting Meg's old boss at the makeup store do them for me, but then I watched a YouTube video and decided my eyesight was more important. I'm not willing to sacrifice that much for beauty . . .

Not yet, at least. I was still in high school. I hadn't even grown into my skin yet. Well, that's what the internet said, so I thought it had better be true. I was still staring at Meg's eyelashes when she finally responded to him.

"Shia." She paused, then upped the wattage on her smile. "Hi." Meg matched Shia's fake grin and doubled it, unleashing the biggest, brightest glowy-eyed smile I had ever seen across my sister's face. "How are you? How's life? Where are you living now? Canada?"

He laughed and licked his full top lip. His lips were the kind boys don't usually have; they were pouty and perfectly bowed. Meg always obsessed over her lips, complaining how thin they were. She used to tell us how she wanted Amy's blond hair and my big lips. I wondered if all pretty girls picked apart their looks like Meg did. It seemed like such a waste, to have it and still find things wrong. I grew up hating my lips, especially when I was young and the kids in my grade who hated themselves

would tease me, puckering their lips and calling me "fish face."
Oh, how much I hated middle school.

"No." He laughed. It wasn't real, I thought. "Actually, I'm going to DC for two weeks, then to stay with a friend outside of
Atlanta. How's life here in Fort Cyprus? The same"—he paused
and his eyes darkened—"I assume? Doesn't seem like much has
changed around here."

Meg's Barbie smile faltered for a split second, and Shia
leaned toward Meg and whispered something in her ear. Her
eyes, looking into mine, rolled into the back of her head, but
when Shia's eyes met hers, she composed herself and returned
to her smiling demeanor. She was good at being comfortable in
every situation—or at least appearing so.

She was so good at being a woman, I thought.

"Everything is great here. John's coming back from West
Point in a few weeks. He finished top in his class, isn't that
great?" Meg waved her hand around and didn't look at Shia's
face.

I watched his hard expression crumble like dead flower petals. I felt like I was missing something, but I wasn't exactly sure
I wanted to find out what. Boys and girls dancing around things
wasn't something I wanted to know about yet.

"I know. I talked to him a few weeks back," Shia said.

Meg's shoulder's stiffened. What kind of game were these
two playing? I didn't know, but it seemed exhausting. I hoped
when I started dating, I wouldn't fall into that.

"Is that so?"

"Yep" was all Shia said, and then he told us both how great
it was to catch up.

Meg turned away from him and didn't watch him walk away
like I did.

"He's such an asshole," Meg huffed. She grabbed a roll of wrapping paper and slapped it against the table. "He thinks he's so much better than everyone." Meg's hands were slightly shaky, but I pretended that I didn't notice. "I don't give a shit what he's doing. John will be home soon anyway."

"And John coming home will change things how?" I asked, wanting her to share her secrets with me, but also knowing that she would expect a secret back. That's how Meg was, and I sort of liked the give-and-take of it.

Meg just sighed, looped her arm through mine, and walked me away from my station at the holiday party. We pushed past Lydia Waller and her boyfriend, Joeb Waller (they weren't related, but sharing the same name was still weird), who were holding hands.

"When they get to the pole, who do you think will let go first?" Meg whispered into my ear.

"Neither." I laughed, and we watched them move around the support pole instead of separating their hands. Joeb looked like someone who would have sweaty hands, and Lydia looked like someone who liked it.

I turned back to my sister, and she squeezed my arm tighter. "I can't believe he's here out of all places to be. He's here."

"He's from here and his parents are still here," I muttered. It wasn't such a surprise to me.

Meg was frustrated and flustered, and it was an odd but slightly fascinating thing to watch my elegant sister, who never so much as has chipped nail polish, be so turned around by someone. I could feel the tension radiating off her; who knew Shia King had so much power?

"How am I supposed to work at the King house if he's there? It was bad enough to see pictures of him hanging on the walls of the house. None of them was recent, so it was kind of easy to pretend the light-eyed, beautiful brown-skinned boy wasn't Shia, but still I hoped he wasn't planning on staying long.

"Oh, Jo, how lucky you are," Meg's dramatic voice told me. She didn't elaborate on why I was lucky, and I didn't ask her to.

Then she shot me a defensive glare. "What? Why are you looking at me like that?"

Damn my face for being so transparent. I needed to work on that before pursuing my dream career as a journalist. I needed a game face.

I shrugged my shoulders at my sister, and a soulful, smooth voice singing "Hello" took over the radio. I thought I had heard this song more than any other song in my life, aside from that Black Eyed Peas song that played every other second of my entire seventh-grade year. I looked over to the makeshift DJ table in the corner and saw Beth standing behind it. She was always where the music was.

"I just don't get what's going on with Shia? I thought you guys couldn't stand to be in the same room as each other? Now you're standing here acting like you were his first wife or something?"

"Nice way to put it." Meg's eyes rolled back. She was the best at this.

"I'm just saying." I wanted to sound mature enough to get an actual answer.

"What do you know about boys, Josephine?"

"Not much."

I knew about boys from the internet, but not real-life boys. I wondered how different they could possibly be. Boys on the internet seemed better than the game masters Meg got mixed up with.

"You have so much to learn." Meg wrapped her arm tight

around me. I let her. "Remember when I was dating River and we always fought, then made up, fought, then made up? Like that time when he kissed Shelly Hunchberg?"

I nodded. I hated Meg's ex-boyfriend River Barkley. He was the worst. I remember when we were in Texas and Meg put an entire bottle of Tabasco into her ex–best friend's Starbucks cup, and everyone laughed when she threw up all over the gym floor.

"Well, Shia is like River, but much worse. He is the definition of a snake," Meg warned me. She even included a little *hisssss.*

I couldn't help but look around for him, and when I found him, he was hugging Meredith and his entire face was lit into a smile.

"Worse than River? Yikes." I looked away from Shia.

"So much worse than River," Meg groaned, and we kept walking. "Do you like anyone, Jo?"

I shrugged. "Not really. No."

It was weird to talk about boys with Meg. Sometimes she would get in a mood where she would talk about boys with me, but she didn't usually ask me anything. She talked and I listened.

"Anyone at all?" she gently prodded.

"No. Now tell me what happened between you and Shia? Did you guys sleep together or something?"

The words felt weird coming out of my mouth. Meg divulged things here and there, but I was ready for more. I was trying to land in the sweet space between little sister who she trusts and mature sister who she can share her relationship secrets with. It was a thrilling yet dangerous shift, and I felt it inside me as it was happening. I felt my doll's bows being traded in for a padded bra, and my crayons upgrading to tampons.

"Yes. But more than that. He made me think—" Meg cut off her own sentence, and I felt disappointment creeping in. I was almost seventeen and ready to hear whatever she was going to say.

I tried not to picture Shia and Meg having sex, but it was nearly impossible.

I followed Meg's eyes and saw Shia standing just a few feet away. A group of girls from my grade were huddled around him like little old ladies admiring a newborn.

Meg huffed. "Ugh, I need to find out how long he's going to be here."

"Don't let him get to you, Meg. John will be back soon."

I liked John Brooke. He was a short man with cropped red hair and a gentle smile. He was infatuated with Meg; she reminded us every day how much he missed her and how hard it was for him to be away from her.

Meg's eyes opened wide, and for a second I thought she had already forgotten that John existed.

But then she took a heavy breath and exhaled. "You're right, Jo. John will be back and Shia will go away. It's been so long since Shia and I were a thing anyway, why should I even care?"

I wasn't sure if she wanted me to answer. "You shouldn't care. If you pretend like you don't care, you win anyway. Isn't that how it works?"

Meg smiled at me. "Oh, Jo. You're so right. Who would have thought?"

I simply nodded, and she led me farther toward the back of the building. We passed Meredith as we walked, and she didn't notice us. She was too busy talking to Denise about something. It could have been anything from the struggles of deployments to the shade of Denise's new hardwood floors.

It depended on that woman's random moods. She was always like that.

Her daughter Shelly was like that, too. One minute she was nice, praising me for my two-page spread about the dirty drinking water in Flint, Michigan, and the next she was talking about me behind my back and calling me Joseph as an insult. A lot of people at my school couldn't seem to wrap their head around me and why I didn't see the point in waking up early and putting lipstick on before the sun was even up.

Since I had known Shelly's biological dad when I was younger, and I knew her stepdad, General Hunchberg, too, I thought she got her personality from her dad, Mr. Grisham, a teacher at our middle school in Texas. Rumor had it that Denise, an Army brat herself, married Mr. Grisham right after high school, and when he got medically retired from the Army ten years ago, Denise couldn't stand the civilian life. It drove her insane that she never got her American dream of being an FRG leader and getting to move into one of the big houses that was specifically built for generals and their families.

Denise had big plans, and being married to a health teacher wasn't a part of them. She wanted the attention; she wanted the respect and the recognition for the patriotic sacrifices she made being a general's wife. Denise Hunchberg needed the luncheons and bake sales. Here she was with Meredith, being the patriot that Denise is, stuffing peppermint bark down her throat and washing it down with a nice glass of boxed wine. I thought it was funny in an awful way that Denise and her family followed us to this post too.

"Where are we going?" I asked Meg when she pushed against the black bar on the heavy back door of the ballroom. The cold air rushed in with the loud squeak of the metal, and I looked

behind us to see if anyone saw us. No one seemed to notice the
two girls leaving through the back of the party. It felt liberating
in a way.

"Outside. Don't talk about Shia," Meg warned me, and before I got to ask her why, my eyes fell on three boys standing
in the grass.

I only recognized one of them, the young guy from Old
Mr. Laurence's driveway this morning. His hair seemed even
messier now, down past his ears. Was it that long earlier? I
couldn't remember for sure, but I didn't think so. His hair was
so thick, like a puddle of yellow paint, spreading down his neckline and onto the collar of his black jacket.

"What's up?" the tallest, biggest of the guys asked. He had
the body of a comic-book superhero. His arms were massive and
his chest expansive, making his uniform tight at the middle. I
wondered if they even made uniform tops big enough to fit him.
The name sewn over the chest was Reeder. I didn't know him.
I would have remembered if I did.

"Nothing in there," Meg said, looking back to the building.

She was still holding on to my arm as we walked down the
small set of stairs to get to the grass. I didn't notice that the
corner of the concrete porch was chipped until the toe of my
boot caught and my foot slipped. I quickly caught myself, using
Meg as a crutch, and she held me up. My heart pounded in my
chest. Really, again? That was the second time that day I had
tripped in front of him. I was quickly turning into that wannabe
quirky girl who always trips and makes a flat joke about her
awkwardness.

When I looked up, the long-haired boy was the only one
staring at me. The smirk on his face made me want to run back
inside the building or call him out—I wasn't sure which was

the better option. He looked like a boy who never got called out for anything. When I weighed the consequences for each, embarrassing Meg and having her not see me as mature seemed worse. I had already felt so much closer to her that day, I didn't want to ruin it.

I looked away from him and watched my sister start her engine of social cool. She said, "Hi," to all three, and the blond-haired boy we had met that morning stuck his hand out for her to shake. She took it, letting go of my familiar hand, and told him it was nice to meet him. Did she not recognize his face from earlier today? I wondered.

The guy standing between the long-haired boy and my sister was wearing a uniform, too. His said that his name was Breyer. I never wondered what soldiers' first names were anymore; they usually didn't want to be called by them anyway.

Breyer had stubble around his mouth that was so dark it looked almost like paint. The closer to his thin lips, the darker his beard was. He pulled a pack of cigarettes from the pants pocket of his uniform, and the big guy, Reeder, handed him a lighter. He pushed the stick through the line of his lips, and smoke clouded around his face. It was menacing, and my imagination was running wild. It only took the smallest of things to make me imagine so much more. When I was younger, I used to spend my time writing stories about vampires, and wizards, and magical lands inside closets like Narnia, but as I grew up, I found myself attracted to nonfiction and the journalism side of writing.

"How's the party?" Reeder asked.

"Lame for me, but cool for the kids." Meg held her hand out and took his cigarette from him. I never knew she smoked. What I *did* know then was that she trusted me, at least enough not to tell Meredith, or the other girls.

It had warmed up already since we left the house this morning. So much for snow on Christmas in southern Louisiana.

"Aren't you two supposed to be working?" she asked the two in uniform.

I watched their eyes and how they looked at her. They were admiring her with a zoned-out expression on their faces, like they would follow her to the other side of the Dothraki Sea if she wanted them to. Dragons or not. Comparing Meg to a khaleesi felt like comparing Joan of Arc to a politician's trophy wife.

Reeder laughed, and the sound was like an echo. "We are. We're on patrol."

Meg laughed, and the smoke rolled out of her mouth in perfect swirls of gray. "Looks like it."

Both guys laughed at her comment, and I figured they would laugh at just about anything she said if she wanted them to. The blond-haired one didn't seem to be paying attention; he was staring off into the empty field behind us.

"Laurie, how long you staying here?" the big one asked, looking directly at the boy from this morning.

Laurie? His name is Laurie Laurence?

What an awful choice his parents made.

"At the party, or this town?" Laurie asked. Drama seeped from his response, and I pictured him sitting over a cup of coffee and a half-finished manuscript. My imagination again.

"The party." Reeder blew smoke from his mouth and looked a little annoyed. He immediately took another drag, then glanced at his phone.

"Two more minutes," Laurie said.

I stepped closer to him, and my mouth opened before I gave it permission to. "And the town?" I asked.

Meg stared at me like I had just asked him if he wanted to have sex with me in front of his friends.

Laurie—his name was so strange—smiled at me. "Not long. My dad sent me here to bond with my grandpa while he's overseas. He will be home in a year, so I'll go back to Texas when he's back."

A year could be a very a long time, depending on what one did with it . . .

"Iraq or Afghanistan?" I asked.

"Neither. Korea."

"Oh." I had heard awful things about being stationed in South Korea. My dad told me that the local people didn't want them there, so most of the soldiers stayed on the base, hardly ever going outside the gate.

Laurie didn't say another word before dismissing himself. I watched his back as he strode through the grass field and disappeared between the thick clusters of trees at the beginning of the woods.

"So, are you two going to work at all, or can we go somewhere?" Meg asked the two who remained.

I didn't go with Meg that day. I didn't even wait to hear their reply. I went back into the party and helped hand out food to families who missed their soldiers on Christmas.

6

The next week went so fast. The time between Christmas and New Year's was always so weird. The decorations are still up from Christmas, and the entire post basically shuts down for two weeks. I remembered feeling ready for the new year that year—I was so ready.

I was going to be seventeen in just a few days, and I already felt so much older. Meg had been spending more time with me, too, while she played sick to Mrs. King. Meg had me call her employer every morning since she'd seen Shia at the battalion's Christmas party. Mrs. King was trying not to sound irritated over Meg's illness, but I could hear it in her voice. I was always good at knowing what people were feeling, even when they wouldn't say it. Especially then. Or so I thought I was.

"What time should I put the meatballs in the oven?" Meg asked Beth, who knew more about cooking than everyone else in the house combined.

"Around nine-thirty. So they are ready around ten when we will start the party."

The kitchen was a mess, a tray of meatballs and three Crock-

Pots covering the little counter space we had. On the small kitchen island were bags of chips, and one small bag of Bugles for me. They were my favorite food, and I could have lived off their salty goodness alone.

I grabbed the bag and popped it open. I ate a handful before I climbed onto the counter to get the bowls from the cabinet. Our family always did the same thing every year: we covered the kitchen with food and tried to stay awake until midnight. Amy usually didn't make it past ten, but this was her year, she claimed.

"Beth, can you make me a cup of coffee?" Meg asked. "Not with mom's coffee machine, with the pod thing. It's only six and I'm already tired."

Beth, of course, said she would, even though her hands were busy crushing crackers for her famous cheese ball. Since I was a vegetarian, Beth always made me my own small ball with no bacon and extra shaved almonds. I ate every bit of it.

"Look," Amy said as I dumped a bag of chips into a big red bowl.

I looked at her and tried to see what she wanted me to look at, but she was just staring out the window in front of the sink. Her hair was in a tight bun, which I assumed Meg did for her.

Crumpling the bag and shoving it into the recycle bin, I walked over to the window and stood next to Amy.

I looked out the window and into the window of Old Mr. Laurence's house. The boy Laurie was pacing in front of the window with a book in his hand.

"Do you think he's being held captive there?" Amy's eyes twinkled with the hope of something more interesting than a new neighbor.

I stared at him and watched as he set the book down, then took a seat at the grand piano directly in front of the window.

I had looked at this scene—the window, the piano—so many times while helping Beth wash and dry dishes, but it looked so different now that a boy was inside. Usually, I just stared at the red curtains and wondered if Old Mr. Laurence had ever thought about redecorating since the 1930s.

"He looks lonely," Meg added. She had moved behind me and was looking over my shoulder into the window at Laurie.

"Mom said he's from Europe. He was living there for years." Amy's voice was full of childish wonder.

"I wonder if he has a secret. A tragic European secret," I said, using a haughty but vague accent. When we were younger, my sisters and I would re-enact plays I wrote, and we would dress in our dad's oversized clothes and use fake accents to go along with the characters I created. My favorite was a man named Jack Smead, whose voice ranged from Australian to Jamaican and back.

I continued to stare at Laurie. The bridge of his nose had a bump like it had been broken before, and his hands grabbed the book again and he took a heavy breath. I could see his chest move up and down from our kitchen. He was fascinating.

"Mom said he didn't really have any upbringing. With his dad gone all the time and his mom an Italian artist or something," Amy continued her gossip.

I suddenly felt that everyone around me seemed more interesting than me.

In the room across the yard, Laurie began moving his mouth, the book in his hand. I strained to figure out what he was saying, but I couldn't read his lips. He stood up again, and the bottom of his white T-shirt caught on the corner of the piano, exposing the bottom of his stomach. There was a flash of black on him, but he shoved the fabric down so fast that I couldn't make out what it was.

"He has good eyebrows," Meg said.

I couldn't look at his eyebrows. I was still thinking about his stomach.

"If I were a guy, I would want to look like him," I said to my sisters. He looked like he knew the world, like maybe he owned part of it.

Amy went to say something to me, but she must have thought better of it because she closed her mouth and looked out the window again.

"Why do you think he's here?" Beth asked.

I didn't want to tell Beth and Amy what he'd told me the day of the Christmas party. For some reason I felt like that would be betraying him somehow, which was a ridiculous thought, since these were my sisters and he was a complete stranger.

"Imagine giving up Italy to come to the bottom of Louisiana," I said, staring at his hands as he turned the pages of the book. I tried to look at the cover to see what he was reading, but I couldn't make it out. "And with awful Old Mr. Laurence," I groaned, watching Laurie sit back down, put the book aside, and spread his hands over the keys of the piano in front of him.

"Jo, don't be mean. He's not awful," Beth told me.

He was awful, though; he always yelled at us for walking on his grass. Over the summer he'd told Meredith that I snuck out of the house and I got grounded for a month. On top of that, every time he saw us outside he was always yelling, "Those damned Spring Girls!" He acted as if I shattered the windshield of his car on purpose. I was just trying to learn a sport so my parents would feel like they had a normal child. My interest in softball only lasted a week.

"I would live in that big house with him whether he's awful or not," Meg said.

Beth joined us finally and leaned against the window, her other shoulder touching my own.

"They do have a beautiful piano," she said with longing dripping from every word.

Laurie's fingers moved so roughly over the keys that I swore I could almost hear the music from inside our kitchen.

"When I'm a successful writer, I'll buy you the best piano ever created," I promised my sister, and I meant it.

"Most writers can't even pay their bills, let alone buy a piano, Beth. So, let's say when I marry a rich man, you can come over and play mine," Amy said.

Ugh, she sounded like Meg, always talking about getting married, but at least we knew Meg was actually old enough to be married.

Amy danced around the kitchen and stuck her hand into the bowl of chips, pulling out a handful of cheesy dusted fried potatoes cut into triangles. They were her favorite. Her orange fingers always grossed me out.

"And what if the man you love is poor, but a good man? Like Dad?" Beth asked Amy. Beth stuck a pod of coffee into the Keurig for Meg and pulled the handle down.

Laurie's head began to bob along with the movement of his fingers. It was fascinating to watch. He was the opposite of Beth when she played, her calm fingers gliding over the keys, smooth as butter, and her eyes closed in the tranquil melody. Laurie's fingers were violent to his keys, combatively smashing over the ivories, and his eyes were wide-open as he played.

My heart was beating from inside my chest to the backs of my ears as I watched him. I could barely hear what my sisters were saying.

"Well," Amy said, "it's not like being stuck with a big nose or something. I have a choice of who I love."

"People aren't stuck with big noses anymore anyway. You can get that fixed easier than you can get a boyfriend," Meg replied.

My eyes were still on Laurie as he played. I had never seen anyone so oblivious of their surroundings as he was then. We were staring at him—well, at least I was—and he didn't notice at all. He was too involved in whatever he was playing.

"What about you, Jo? Would you marry a poor man if he was nice?" Amy asked, her little body moving around the kitchen still. She had a can of orange soda in one hand and orange chips in the other.

I didn't look away from the window. "I wouldn't marry anyone for money. I don't want anyone to have that type of control over me. And besides, I'm going to make enough money on my own."

Amy snorted. "Sure, Jo."

I couldn't even gather enough anger toward her; I was too fascinated by the boy framed in the window.

"And what about you, Amy?" I said coldly. "You think you're going to have a rich husband? I hate to break it to you, but—"

"Jo," Beth's voice broke off my sentence.

"Stop talking about boys anyway, Amy. You're too young," Meg said.

I didn't mention that by seventh grade Meg had already kissed a handful of boys.

Amy took a swig of her orange soda, and it left a line of orange above her lip like a mustache. She quickly licked it away. "We'll all grow up someday, Meg. We might as well know what we want."

Laurie wiped his forehead with the back of his hand, and his blond hair moved, touching the tips of his shoulders. I tried to image what my husband would be like, but as usual, I couldn't picture him.

I didn't even know if I wanted a husband. They seemed like a lot of work, and I'd never met a boy who I could even consider letting take me to dinner, let alone marry. I stared at Laurie, and his fingers stopped cold. I ducked down just as he looked toward our window, and Beth laughed when I popped my head back up.

He was still sitting there, but the book was back in his hands, and he had stopped playing music.

"What have you been working on lately, Jo?" Beth asked, to change the subject from matrimony and riches.

A lot of things, I wanted to say. I was only a few paragraphs short of finishing my longest piece, an essay on female sex trafficking in Cambodia. I'd spent more time on this piece than anything I had written before. I knew that Mr. Geckle would never allow me to publish it in the school newspaper, so I was planning on sending it to *Vice* myself. It was a long shot, and they would probably never even read it, let alone publish it, but sending it in was something I had to do for myself. Once I did that, I would be ready for anything. Mr. Geckle could only control my voice within the walls of White Rock High.

"Nothing special," I started, even though I was lying through my teeth. It *was* special; it was the most special thing I had ever written. I felt it deep in the whites of my bones.

"I read your paper about sex slavery. The one on your laptop," Amy began. I whirled around and grabbed her arm. The soda can dropped onto the floor, and fizzy orange liquid sprayed onto the tile.

"You *what*?" I shouted at her. She pulled back from me, but I held her arm.

"It was open on your laptop!" she yelled in her defense.

"I don't care!" I let go of her when I felt Beth's eyes burning on me.

It wasn't that I didn't want anyone to read it; I was mad because I thought my laptop was the one place where I had privacy from my three sisters, and Amy had just ripped that away from me.

Meredith came barreling into the kitchen and I stepped back, away from the orange puddle on the floor.

"What the hell is going on in here?" Meredith stepped around the mess and let out a deep breath before anyone answered her.

"Nothing, Meredith. Everything is fine," Beth said, and grabbed a towel hanging on the oven door. She laid it down, and both Amy and I stopped glaring at each other as Beth cleaned up our mess.

"Who was fighting? I heard yelling." Meredith's voice was steady, and she wasn't in the mood for our games.

"No one." Beth bent down. "We were just messing around. Don't worry, we're cooking and getting everything ready for tonight. I'm almost finished with my cheese ball."

Meredith looked at the four of us and shook her head. I figured that she didn't believe Beth but didn't feel like fighting on New Year's Eve. Meredith had a glass of clear liquid in her hand, and I thought she should have another. She had never before looked as tense and tired as she did lately.

She told us to be careful and not make any more messes and left us in the kitchen.

I gave Amy a look and turned back to the window. Laurie was gone.

I went to my room and closed the door and wrote to forget how mad I was at my sister.

7

meg

My makeup was done and I had just finished blow-drying my hair. While I was waiting for Jo to get out of the shower and curl my hair, I picked up the book she had slid under my pillow on Christmas. Honestly, I hadn't opened it since then, but I had a few minutes, so I lifted the black cover and turned to a random page. It began:

my favorite thing about you is your smell

I read the words in silent awe, and then read them again, and Shia's hands, dirt under his fingernails, came to my mind. He was always dirty, always planting something or helping some old woman or other move her furniture around or some such. He always smelled like the earth, like a garden.

I couldn't believe he was back—and *worse*, I couldn't believe that I was thinking about him right now. John would be home in a week to see me. I should be thinking about John's clean, strong hands, and the way he always smelled like fresh cologne and laundry detergent.

He wouldn't dare to wear ratty T-shirts or dirty sneakers the way Shia did.

"Jo!" I yelled.

It was eight thirty, and everyone was going to start arriving at our house around ten. By "everyone," I mean a few of the neighbors and their kids. I didn't invite any of my "friends," since half of them weren't talking to me over a rumor that wasn't even true. That's what happens when you're labeled the school "slut" in a small Army town. It follows you past graduation. I didn't mind so much and still don't, really. If they were truly my friends, they would know that I wouldn't do what they are accusing me of doing. The same thing happened to me at Fort Hood, and it was so much worse; the rumor mill here seemed like child's play.

That night we would have followed our tradition of celebrating at home, but Jo and I got a last-minute invite to the Kings' house for Bell Gardiner's engagement party, so we decided to stop by there for an hour, then make sure we were back home by eleven. I didn't want to go, especially because I was afraid to see Shia there, but I had assumed since the party was at the Kings' huge estate, many people would be there and lessen my chance of running into Shia.

"Josephine!" I shouted again.

While I waited for her, I flipped to another page in the book she'd gifted me.

The poem there was simple, and began:

how can our love die . . .

Stunned, I turned a few more pages.

he isn't coming back . . .

Underneath the poem was the word *wilted*, as if the poem was signed by Wilted. I thought of the bouquet of flowers on Mrs. King's nightstand. The card was signed by Shia, and the red petals were wilted. I touched the corner of one and it broke off, falling onto the wooden dresser. I thought about how he left so suddenly and how much time I'd wasted wishing that he would come back.

Trying to push those wilted flowers and his shining green eyes out of my head, I slammed the book shut and tossed it onto my bed just as Jo came strolling into our room.

"I'm here!" she said with a smile.

Her hands were full. In one hand she held the curling iron and her phone, and in the other she had a handful of Bugles. Her long hair was down, touching the top of her hips as she moved toward me and stood behind me at the vanity. Her face was freshly scrubbed pink, and her pale skin was glowing.

She would never listen to me when I told her how lucky she was to have such flawless skin. Beth and I suffered from acne the most, but mine had cleared up since I started working at Sephora, where I got to try all the new skin-care products from the best, most expensive brands, for free.

"Your makeup looks so good," Jo said.

She plugged in the curling iron, and I parted my hair, clipping up the top of it so she could curl the bottom.

I stared into the mirror and smiled at my sister. We had been getting closer lately, and I was starting to see a change in her. She was no longer my little Josephine who ran away from home when Old Mr. Laurence trapped a raccoon in a cage and wouldn't let it go. She was growing up so fast, and that meant I was, too. I was ready to be older; I hated being on the cusp of being a woman, because I felt like one but wasn't treated like one.

"Big curls, please."

Jo nodded and went to work.

"Do you think Amy will be able to stay up tonight?" I asked as she curled a chunk of my hair. The strands were hot when she let them out of the barrel and they fell onto my shoulder.

Just as she started to answer, Amy bounced into our bedroom.

"Jo. Meg. Whatever you do, you have to tell me how the party is."

"We will. Are you trying to stay up? Or will you be asleep when we get back?" I asked as Jo wrapped another piece of my hair around the metal barrel.

Amy shook her head and moved around us. She grabbed a tube of lipstick from my vanity and leaned down into the mirror as her small fingers pulled the top off, revealing a deep purple shade.

"I'll be up." Amy's fingers turned the tube around and around as if she was trying to figure out how to use it. "You guys will have all the fun. Did you hear that Bell Gardiner is engaged! I can't wait to see her ring! Ugh, you're going to have way more fun than me." Amy sighed heavily and licked her lips before she smeared the stick across her lips. When she was done, she pulled back and looked at herself in the mirror.

"It's going to be a blast. And of course we know, Amy. We were invited." Jo rolled her eyes.

Amy pouted. "Stop rubbing it in."

I didn't particularly care about Bell Gardiner's engagement,

or her at all. She was one year older than me and had supposedly been going to move to Florida for college, but she only
made it as far as the French Quarter. Rumor had it that she
worked at a bar downtown, right in the center of the Quarter,
somewhere between Bourbon and Royal. Of course she was a
bartender, like my aunt Hannah.

"How big do you think her ring is?" Amy asked, her little
sock-covered feet moving around my small bedroom.

Jo and I made eye contact in the mirror.

"Who is she even engaged to?" Jo asked.

I shrugged my shoulders and closed my eyes. Who knew?
Not me, nor did I care. I felt bad for the poor man who asked
her to marry him. I could have made up excuse after excuse on
why I didn't like her, but the main reason was Shia. They had
dated briefly during the end of my junior year, their senior, and
those two weeks felt like the longest of my life.

"Who knows. Probably some soldier," Jo said, looking at Amy
through the mirror.

Amy's eyes lit up. "Can you imagine? Everyone is lucky but
me." She sighed.

"Lucky? To be engaged at twenty?" I responded to Amy.

Even though I had a catty response, I had grown up wishing I would find the love of my life at a young age and have the
security of being someone's wife. I knew I was jealous of Bell
Gardiner, and though I would never say it to my sisters, I was
secretly hoping John would propose to me when he came home
for leave the following week.

Beth's voice came from over by the door, where she was
leaning against its frame. "I'm glad I don't have to go and be
with all those frightening people and try to think of things
to say."

She hated to be around crowds. I felt a slight guilt when I got the Facebook invite for only Jo and me, but Beth would much rather be home with Meredith and Amy than at a crowded party with me and Jo.

I gave Beth a sympathetic smile and looked back at Jo.

"Is that what you're wearing tonight?" I asked her.

She nodded and looked down at her all-black outfit. Black jeans, black shirt. A thin line of pale skin showed just above her hip. I couldn't remember the last time I'd seen Jo in a dress. Probably that one Easter where Meredith made all of us wear matching dresses and carry matching baskets to get family pictures done. Gah, they were horrendous. They were probably on some BuzzFeed list of corniest family photos.

"What's that smell?" Amy asked, and sniffed the air. It smelled like burnt . . .

"Oh my God, Jo!" I yanked my head away from her, and a chunk of my hair was smoking, still on the barrel of the iron.

Amy screamed louder than I did, and Jo dropped the hot curling iron onto the floor.

"Get it off the floor!" Beth yelled. "It's going to burn the carpet!"

I stared at my hair and ran my fingers over the hole in it.

Jo began, "I'm sorry! I—"

"I can't go anywhere like this!" My eyes welled up with tears, and as much as I didn't want to yell at Jo, I was always going to be that girl who cared about what her hair looked like.

"I ruin everything," Jo mumbled, barely loud enough for anyone to hear her.

Her words made such a sad sound that I wanted to comfort her. But I just kept staring at the chunk of my hair she'd burned off and I didn't know what to say.

Amy clucked around me and pulled the bow from her white hair. "Here, put this on, you'll barely notice."

I took the bow from her hands and put it in my hair. I never wore bows, I was too old for them, but there was something edgy, a little baby-doll-like, about the way the black bow wrapped through the front of my hair.

I looked at myself in the mirror and straightened my back. I couldn't let my burnt hair ruin my night. I still looked sexy. I liked the contrast between my dark makeup and my girlish bow.

"You're so pretty, Meg. I hope I'm as pretty as you when I get older," Amy said.

That made me smile. Leave it to little Amy to give me the extra confidence boost I needed. Bell Gardiner would look flawless. I knew she would. She always did, and her fiancé was probably some rich Southern gentleman, and she was going to spend her party showing off some beautiful diamond, and I was going to spend the party sulking and reminding myself that I had someone, too.

John would be home soon.

John would be home soon.

"John will be home soon," Jo said, stealing the words from inside my head.

I smiled at her effort and pushed my feet into my heels.

8

The driveway to the Kings' house was packed with black cars and people in their New Year's best. My feet were already killing me, and every time I looked down at Jo's sneaker-covered feet, I wished I didn't care so much about what people thought of my appearance. If I was like Jo, I would have worn flats and jeans. We passed an SUV and I looked at myself, using the window as a mirror. My sparkly dress was tight and my hair was already falling out of its curls.

I looked at myself again, trying to be more like Jo. I looked hot, I knew that I did; I just had to remind myself a few more times.

"God, it's so crowded," Jo said, waiting for me to catch up to her.

The Kings' estate was a massive, two-story, square, tan house with thick white pillars on the porch extending up to the second floor. The long shutters on the bottom-floor windows were painted black, and since I had last been here a week prior, someone had strung up strands of white twinkling lights on the black fence upstairs and down the front pillars. The house was always beautiful; it had been my dream home since before I even stepped inside, but that night it seemed even more magical. Flowers were everywhere. Purple bellflowers draped over iron trellises, and blue flowers that I didn't know the name of overflowed from hanging baskets.

The real estate in southern Louisiana was my favorite of what I had ever seen. I loved the old, square houses with shutters and pillars, and the eeriness of it all just made it even more appealing to me.

When we finally stepped onto the porch, my heart was beating so fast and my toes were aching in my heels. I spotted Mr. Blackly, the doorman for the estate, and he smiled, waving for me to cut the line at the door. I couldn't believe a line had formed at the door. It didn't surprise me too much, though, since the Kings' home was the biggest anywhere near the post. It was a large double-gallery house. I loved that style of home, especially when the houses were in the Quarter.

One day, I had asked Mrs. King why she didn't move closer to the French Quarter, and she had looked at me with a smirk in her eyes and said, "Because, darling Meg, I love my diamonds." She looked down at her wrist, and it sparkled under the lights in her bathroom. I nodded and swept blush over her dark cheeks.

I tugged Jo by the arm of her denim jacket and we pushed through the crowd of people waiting to get inside. I didn't recognize a single face in the sea of them.

Mr. Blackly told me to have fun and drink some champagne for him. I was even more surprised when we got into the living room. All of the furniture was placed the same as always, but there were little tables full of appetizers, and tucked in the corner was a full bar. The man behind it was shaking a metal cup in one hand and pouring liquor into a glass with his other, and I felt like I was at a Gatsby party.

"This is freaking insane," Jo said into my ear.

I agreed with her as we made our way into the parlor to look for someone I knew, anyone but Shia.

The first person I spotted was Bell Gardiner, standing over by the piano. She was wearing a long emerald-green dress, and I couldn't help but look down at her left hand. Her ring sparkled from ten feet away, and I could see that the color matched her dress. It was beautiful. My petty dislike for her grew instantly. She smiled at the man in front of her, and I wondered if he was her fiancé. Since he had a fairly large bald spot on the back of his head, I hoped he was. I was petty, but at least I could admit it.

"Has it been an hour yet?" Jo pulled her cell phone out of the back pocket of her jeans and checked the screen. "How has it only been five minutes?" she asked, and shoved the phone back into her jeans.

Jo grabbed a little cucumber sandwich, and we continued to explore. A few minutes later, I saw Reeder and the Laurie boy standing by the bar. When I told Jo I wanted to talk to them, she shook her head and told me to go for it but she was staying put.

I didn't want to leave my younger sister alone in such a crowded place, but I was bored out of my damn mind.

"Meg." Reeder smiled when I approached him. He wrapped his arm around me and I leaned into his expansive chest. He was monstrously big.

I had known him since I moved to Fort Cyprus. It didn't take long for the student body to hate me and he was always so nice to me. He used to drive me to school on the mornings that he had patrol, and he was one of the only guys I had ever known that I felt safe around.

One sloppy night my senior year when John had broken up with me, I went to a party and drank my weight in vanilla-flavored vodka. I was a stumbling mess and Reeder showed up with his friends. It was the first time I had seen him out of his uniform, and I hung all over him like a bee to pollen, and when he drove me home and walked me to my back door, I leaned up and tried to kiss him.

I had never been turned down by a boy, or man, before that night, and I haven't been since Reeder gently declined my advances. He said I had had too much to drink. He was right.

"There are so many people here," I said to the two of them. I wondered how Reeder, a military police officer, had become such fast friends with the greasy, leather jacket–wearing boy from Europe. I didn't trust a boy with hair like that.

"For sure. Happy New Year!" Reeder raised a glass of clear liquid, and I grabbed a flute of champagne from a passing server's tray.

Laurie looked at me and took a swig from a can of Coke. Gross. "Where's the other girl? Your sister, I assume?"

"You shouldn't assume."

The corner of his mouth pulled into a smile. "Well, where is your nonsister?"

I focused on him, looking right into his eyes. They were jet-black; it was unnerving.

"She's not interested in you," I told him.

Jo had never had a boyfriend, and no freaking way was this guy going to attempt to be anything close to it. Boys like him didn't want to date; they only wanted one thing, and Jo wasn't ready to give that to anyone.

"Hmm. You're a real peach." He ran his long pale fingers through his blond hair.

I turned away from him, not wanting to feed his ego or irritate him enough to want my sister even more. I knew how boys like him were wired. I searched for Jo by the table I'd left her at, but didn't see her there, or anywhere. I knew she was capable of handling herself, more so than me even, but I couldn't shake the uneasy feeling that had planted itself inside my stomach the moment we walked through the door of the party.

I told Reeder that I would see him later and didn't so much as look at Laurie before I walked away to find Jo. I pushed past big balloons with the numbers of the new year, grabbed another glass of champagne, and went to find my sister.

9

jo

*E*very inch of the Kings' house dripped with disparity and greed. It drove me up the crown-moulded wall to walk through a house so full of excess, when on the way over here we'd passed by a group of homeless men sharing the scraps of a meal they'd dug out from the trash of the creole restaurant just off base.

Of course I knew that the Kings couldn't feed the entire city. Well, maybe they could, but it's not their fault that there are people less fortunate than them—but it was hard to remember that as I walked past a table full of neatly placed lines of bottles of champagne.

I always hated the feeling that crept over me when someone was staring at me. I had an uncanny ability to feel their eyes on me the moment they hit me. I waited a few seconds to look up, and when I lifted my eyes, I saw a tall man with brown hair staring at me. He was dressed in his Class A's, making me wonder why he was wearing his military dress uniform to a New Year's Eve engagement party. When he saw me staring back at him, he smiled. I didn't like the way his face changed when he smiled. It wasn't friendly or welcoming; it was expecting and assuming.

Since I didn't know what else to do but smile back, I did just that. It was a tiny, awkward thing, though he must have taken it as an invitation to approach me because he set his beer bottle down on the closest table and made his way over. I looked around for Meg but couldn't find her, so in the brief moment the soldier flicked his eyes away from me, I dipped between two elderly women and turned around the corner.

I took another corner and another until I passed the kitchen, full of staff, busying themselves to feed the hundreds of people crammed into the mansion. The smell of corn bread and rosemary made my stomach grumble angrily. I should have eaten more than Bugles and a cucumber sandwich all day.

As a man carrying a tray walked through the archway, I grabbed a snack as he passed. Looking down at the food in my hand, I thanked my lucky stars that it was meatless. It looked like some sort of tomato salsa on bread. I recalled Beth making something like that before but couldn't remember the name of it. I took a bite and my stomach grumbled again.

I kept walking, looking behind me to be sure the man wasn't following me. Not seeing him, but wishing to take no chances, I took another corner and walked up the empty staircase near the back door. It was so quiet back there, and I wondered for a second if I should even be in this part of the house. Meg had told me a few times that Mrs. King was weird about certain rooms of the house, but I really wanted to get away from the party, if for only a few minutes.

I passed two closed doors and reached the end of the hall-way. There was something in the corner . . . It looked like a bench, but I couldn't see clearly because a curtain covered part of it. I walked closer to see if I could hide there for a little bit.

I pushed the curtain aside and immediately bumped into a statue sitting atop a marble podium. My hands shot out in front of me to steady it before it crashed to the floor, and once I finally settled it, I spun around to sit on the bench.

"Ow!" a male voice grumbled, and I jumped back up.

Laurie was sitting on the bench with a can of Coke in one hand and my arm in his other.

I jerked away and pulled back the curtain to escape. "Sorry! I didn't see you here."

Out of all the places in this mansion, he had to be sitting in the only quiet spot I could find.

Laurie put the soda can down on the floor in front of his feet and looked up at me. "It's okay. I was just hiding back here."

Even sitting down, I was reminded of how tall he was. His mouth was open, and I looked at it briefly, just enough to feel the heat in my cheeks, then looked away.

"I'll go." I turned away from him.

He touched my elbow. "No. Stay."

When he said those two simple words, I felt something like déjà vu, which wasn't possible since I had only spoken a few words to him. I thought maybe I was losing my mind, mixing dreams with reality, but I swore I had heard him say those two words to me before.

"I just don't know anyone and I'm not great at making con-versation with strangers, so I would rather hide back here until it's time to leave."

"If you don't know anyone, who tells you when it's time for you to leave?" I asked.

He tilted his head and stared at me a moment. His legs were so long that they sprawled out to the rug on the floor. I hoped it wasn't animal fur that he was pressing his black boots into.

"Good question." He smiled at me. "And, what about you? Who tells you when it's time to go? Your older sister?"

I shook my head.

He stared at me for what felt like minutes but was actually only about ten seconds. I counted five breaths while I waited for his lips to move. His lips were so full, like mine, and I wondered if he got called mean names in school the way that I did, or if his good looks saved him from the ridicule of his peers, the way they did Meg.

"So, what are you doing at the party if you don't know anyone?" I asked.

He patted the seat next to him and I sat down, keeping as much distance as possible from him. The bench was so small that it was only about two feet of space.

"People-watching."

"And how was that? Did you see any people you liked watching?"

What did that even mean? I silently asked myself.

He seemed to understand and smiled at me. "Your sister is nice to watch, that Meg Spring." His hair was pulled back into a bun, and I thought he should be a model.

"Oh. My sister, *of course*." I laughed. "*Everyone* likes to watch Meg."

"I can imagine that to be true."

He leaned against the back of the cushioned bench, and I stared past him down the long hallway. This house seemed even bigger from the inside than the outside. Old family portraits were on the wall, hung in perfectly symmetrical lines.

"It's a little creepy, right?" He spoke quietly and quickly, and his lips moved so fast. "To have immortalized the entire family and hung them on the walls up here where guests obviously aren't supposed to be?"

"Yes, very."

"So, what about you? Who are you watching out there?"

I shook my head. "No one."

It was true. I wasn't watching anyone the way he was watching Meg. Laurie's face was turned away from me, and he was fixing the cuffs of his dark jeans just above his boots.

When I could no longer stand the ensuing silence, I asked, "Is it true that you're from Italy?"

He looked at me. "Yes. My mother is Italian. A painter. I lived there when I was young, then we moved to the US, and last year I lived there for the school year, until I got sent back here."

His tiny accent made sense now. I pondered whether it would be rude to ask him to speak Italian for me, just so I could hear it.

"What's Italy like? I want to go to Europe so badly. When I work for *Vice*, I have this entire plan of places to go and stories to cover. I want to see so many more places than here; I've seen the same things over and over my entire life. The same people, the same mentality." I got so lost in my own words and dreams for my future that I had nearly forgotten where I was or who I was talking to.

"So, Jo Spring. You've got dreams, do you?"

I decided right then that even though I would most likely never have another conversation with him, I needed to hear about Europe. "Yes. Shouldn't we all?"

"Are you speaking generally, or about me specifically?"

I knew then that this was what Meg had warned me about. Boys who play games. Laurie Laurence was definitely a boy who wanted to play games. Word games were only the beginning.

I could play, too. It didn't matter that I had never had a boyfriend. I had three sisters. I was the queen of games.

Okay, so maybe Meg was the queen, but I was the princess. For sure.

"I really need to get going," I told him, instead of moving my piece onto the board. I knew that I could play games, but I didn't want to. I wanted to hear about Europe and the world outside my little one, but he didn't seem willing to share.

"What? Why?" He stood up with me, but I hurried away, closing the curtain behind me before he could speak.

Checkmate, Laurie, I thought as I rushed down the stairs.

10

meg

"Have you seen Jo?" I asked Reeder when I finally found him again.

I had searched the living room, the dining room, and the kitchen, and couldn't find my sister. I was beginning to panic, imagining Meredith's reaction when I came home without Josephine.

I pulled my phone out of my purse and checked again, to be sure she hadn't called or texted me back.

Where the hell did she go? I wondered. *She better not have left me here.*

It had been close to an hour, and I was ready to go home. I hadn't seen Mrs. King once since I got to the party. Even though I had spent nearly every day in that house lately, I felt out of place when it was full of strangers.

Reeder told me that, no, he hadn't seen Jo, and I made my

way to the backyard of the house. I grabbed my third glass of champagne and pushed through the back door. Crowds of huddled bodies covered the expansive lawn, and so many lights were strung on the trees. It was beautiful until I heard the shrill voice of Bell Gardiner herself.

"Meg Spring! What on earth are you doing here?"

When I turned to her, she smiled so brightly that for a moment I was convinced that we were friends. But a tiny, barely noticeable falter in her smile reminded me that we weren't. As much as I didn't have a reason to not like her, she had even less of a reason to be staring at me like I was intruding on the occasion somehow. At least two hundred people were crammed into the estate, and I could guarantee that most of them didn't have a clue who she was.

"I was invited." I managed a smile for her.

No way in hell was I going to let her know she had crawled under my skin so long ago and stayed there.

Her blue eyes sparkled under the canopy lights. Her dress was barely attached to her slim body; only one string on her left shoulder kept the green satin on her body. The entire back of the dress was cut out, showing her creamy skin underneath. She wasn't even wearing a bra. Bitch.

"Oh, were you?" She paused to look me up and down. "That's great."

I looked at the woman next to her and assumed it was her mother. She had the same dark hair and blue eyes as Bell.

"Congrats on your engagement," I told her.

She shot me a pitying look. "It must be hard for you."

I looked around at those surrounding us and realized everyone had fallen quiet. They were watching us like we were the series finale of *Gossip Girl*.

Bell looked down at her ring, and I fumbled for words. Why would it be hard on me? John was coming back next week from West Point. I couldn't imagine that her fiancé would have better stats than that.

I decided to behave like a mature adult and smile instead of spit in her face. The thing I hated most in life was to look foolish in front of people, and there was Bell Gardiner trying to make me look pathetic and less than her and her stupid green dress and big emerald engagement ring.

"I'm happy for you, really, Bell."

I turned to walk away and saw Shia approaching.

Oh no, no, no, I thought to myself. My fists balled at my sides and I didn't want to be stuck between those two. Not that night, not ever.

"Shia, honey!" Bell waved her hand in the air, and I stopped moving my feet so my brain could try to think of something witty to say if either of them sassed me.

Where was her fiancé anyway? If he loved her enough to buy her such a beautiful ring, why wasn't he standing at her side at their extravagant party?

I tried to dodge Shia's eyes as he neared us, but I couldn't. I hated the way he always pulled me back to him, even when I hadn't seen him in so long. He was wearing something I never imagined I'd see him in. His black dress pants and black button-up shirt perfectly matched the black blazer he wore. Before that night I had only seen him in jeans and T-shirts.

I tried to look away from his green eyes, but couldn't find it in me.

"Look who came to congratulate us." Bell Gardiner's words went right over my head until she reached for his hand and pulled him to her side. He kissed her hair.

My legs went numb. I couldn't begin to form a coherent thought as I watched her take his hand between her two.

Her ring shone, blinding me.

What the hell kind of joke was this?

Bell Gardiner and Shia King?

How?

Why?

He regarded me coolly. "Thanks for coming, Margaret."

Margaret? Since when was I Margaret to him?

A dark memory interjected that I had probably become Margaret when I left him waiting for me at the airport. That's when I became a full-name acquaintance.

"It's nothing," I said. The words were like glass shards in my throat.

I couldn't believe that I was living in a world where Bell Gardiner and Shia King were the happy, engaged couple that this party was for. I didn't even know the two of them were still in touch.

All the hours I spent with Mrs. King in this house, at the store, at her country club, and she never once mentioned anything about Shia and Bell. Or Bell and Shia. Or this party. Not once. Really, she barely mentioned Shia at all—she mostly talked about her two daughters, who she was so proud to talk about. Both of them had graduated law school, following in the footsteps of Mr. King, the most prominent, most wealthy lawyer in the entire state of Louisiana.

"Isn't this party great?" Bell asked.

I knew she was talking to me. I was afraid that I wouldn't have the strength to look up at her and meet her eyes, so I remembered what Meredith always told us: *"Never, ever, let any-*

one take your strength, girls. Don't let anyone make you feel less than whole, and if they try, show them who you are." She had told the four of us girls that so many times that by the time I was ten I had it memorized. I think she said she read it in a book when she was pregnant with me.

I lifted my eyes to Bell Gardiner and Shia. My smile stretched my cheeks, and I hoped my lipstick was still in place. "It's great, really. Thank you for inviting me. I lost Jo somewhere. I'm going to go find her, but you two have a good night."

I didn't give them enough time to so much as blink before I turned away, trying to confidently sway my hips as I disappeared into the crowd.

My eyes were stinging when I found Jo leaning against the wall and drinking a glass of champagne.

"You shouldn't be drinking. Meredith will kill me," I said.

Jo rolled her big brown eyes at me. "It's fine. I won't tell her. Are you ready to go?"

Her cheeks were red and I wanted to tell her about Shia and Bell, but I needed a minute or thirty. "Have you ever drank before?" I grabbed another glass of champagne from the table next to us, downed it, and reached for another.

"Yes. Once. Beth and I got into Dad's liquor stash when we were at Fort Hood." She smiled. "We were *so* sick the next day."

A vague memory of Beth holding Jo's long hair over the toilet popped into my mind. "I can't believe Beth, out of all people." I laughed a wry sound.

"Did you ever find out who Bell Gardiner's fiancé is? I haven't even heard anyone talking about it. I think everyone just came for the free booze and finger sandwiches. No one likes Bell Gardiner."

The champagne bubbled and burned in my mouth.

"I don't know," I lied. "But you're right about no one liking Bell Gardiner."

So many times I had wanted to share more with Jo, to let her grow up faster than my parents wanted to let her. Meredith was good at teaching us to be strong, to be capable, but she lacked in teaching us anything about the reality of being a teenager. She told me once that she had to grow up too fast and didn't want that for us. I understood that to a point, but Jo had probably never even kissed a boy, I thought with wonder. By her age, I had slept with three. I didn't apologize for it then, and I definitely wouldn't now.

"I have to pee. Then can we go?" I sucked down the last of the liquid. I'd lost count of how many I'd had. My chest had stopped aching, but I couldn't help but think about Shia and Bell. It made no sense to me. Their personalities couldn't be more different. With his extensive travel, how did they maintain a relationship at all, let alone keep it strong enough to be engaged? How long had they been together? I didn't have a clue. I had kept tabs on his life, or thought I had, but clearly I was slacking in the cyberstalking department. That, or he didn't care enough about her to even so much as mention her online.

11

I easily found my way to the upstairs bathroom, the one that was connected to Ineesha's room. She was the oldest daughter of Mrs. King. I wondered if Ineesha was here, too. I hadn't seen her, but it would be even stranger if Shia's sister hadn't bothered to come to town for his engagement party. I stood in front of the mirror for a few minutes before I struggled with my Spanx and relieved myself.

On my way out, I thought I heard male voices talking low, but in a fury. I paused by a heavy painting hanging on the wall. I knew the painting well. It was of the entire King family. I didn't have to look up at it to know that Mrs. King was wearing a vivid red dress and that a young Shia sat at his mom's feet, a teddy bear in his small arms. His cheeks were chubby from childhood, and his hair was long on top; clusters of curls sat on his head.

I saw the painting every day that I walked through the empty halls upstairs. Now, as I tried to listen to the conversation through the open door of the room closest to me, I looked around to make sure no one was coming. I hid behind the corner wall. The halls were empty; only faint voices and the echo of music downstairs could be heard. I was surprised that it wasn't louder up here, given the number of people in the house.

My stomach turned. The King estate always felt so empty. I could always hear my own footsteps clomping on the original hardwood floors—which Mrs. King loved to tell me were from the 1860s—to the high ceilings, which complemented the original crown mouldings that clung to the crème walls. Mrs. King was so proud of her home; she talked about the detail on the stained-glass windows in the attic with far more pride than on those rare moments when she spoke her only son and his "adventures" around the world.

I began to feel bored and wanted to go back and find Jo, even though she was grinding on my nerves with that Laurie boy.

Right as I took my first step away, I heard a voice I recognized.

"You don't know that!"

Shia was speaking loud and deep. I slowly slid my feet across the floor, quietly moving closer to the voices.

"I don't know that?" a booming voice howled toward the empty hall. Something fell and broke against the floor. It sounded like glass smashing.

"You know nothing, boy! You think just because you went on some child's mission and fed a village of people that you know about the world? Well—"

The voice cut off and I heard Mrs. King say something unintelligible next.

I had never met Mr. King in all my time at the King house. I had only heard his voice once, when he had called the house phone to speak to his wife. His voice was the deepest I had ever heard.

"Are you happy now? You made it clear that you don't want me to be a part of this family!" Shia yelled.

I wondered if Bell Gardiner was in the room. I couldn't help my constant craving for drama. It usually wasn't a coincidence when I found it, but that night I was actually minding my own business, just using the bathroom—trying to get away from the drama of Bell—so it had to have been fate that brought me to hear the argument they were having.

It was strange, though, because unlike in most cases, as I stood in the hallway listening to Mr. King yell at his son, I didn't feel the adrenaline rush from the drama of it. I felt the hairs on my arm tingling and my back straightening.

"You never deserved to be a part of this family!" Mr. King shouted. "You're my only son, the only one who can carry my family name, and look at you!"

I thought I heard the sob of a woman.

Bell Gardiner, maybe? I thought to myself, inching closer.

I drew a deep breath and took one last step toward the door. I had never been in that room before, but I knew it was Mr. King's office. I had passed it once when the door was open, but the only thing I remembered about it was the large desk in the center of the room. Now when I peered around the doorframe, I saw three people.

Shia stood closest to the door, his back turned to me. Across from him was Mr. King, a man almost the height of Reeder. His skin was a deeper brown than Shia's and his eyes were dark, but they looked so much alike that it surprised me.

Mr. King stepped toward his son, who turned in profile to meet him. Shia's shirt was untucked now, hanging low below his hips. His face was pulled into a tight grimace, eyes closed and mouth twisted at the corners.

"I thought by now you would be done wasting your time on these childish games," Mr. King said, his voice going right back to a shout.

Shia spun around and looked at his mom. "Childish games?" He pinched the bridge of his nose and walked in a jagged line across the carpet. "I'm doing what I'm passionate about! Do you have any idea how many people I've helped? Fed, taught to read—and here you are still telling me that I'm a child?"

The chime of a cell phone seemed to shriek throughout the room. It rang and rang until Mr. King finally snapped, "I have to take this."

The clattering of his shoes on the floor echoed back to me—almost through me—in the hallway.

"*Of course* you do," Shia said, but his father didn't respond.

My chest tightened, and I thought about the first time I met Shia King. We had just been stationed in southern Louisiana from the middle of Texas, and I was walking alone around the French Quarter. I remember leaving my sisters and Aunt Hannah at a frozen-yogurt shop, to explore for a few minutes alone. I had never been to the French Quarter before, and it was the one thing I was looking forward to when we got the news about our PCS—permanent change of station—to Louisiana.

I wanted to move from Texas after what happened during my freshman year. It felt like a godsend when my dad sat us down, nervous and ready for the worst reactions from us, and told us girls that we were moving that summer. I cheered, ready to get away from the torturous assholes at my high school. Jo threw a fit, Beth was smiling, and Amy didn't care at all.

That summer was the summer I reinvented myself. I dyed my hair dark, dark brown, and I cut my bangs. I learned how to do my makeup, and I felt like I could start over.

That particular day, the sun was beating down on my skin as I walked around the cobblestone streets. My shoulders were sunburned within twenty minutes. I was walking aimlessly, just wanting to explore the streets. The sweet smell of sugar led me down Decatur to a creole praline shop.

The building was beautiful; the outside looked so charming, so New Orleans. Blue metal that resembled lace ribbon draped over the windows. It was impossible to think anyone could pass this place without going in. My mouth was watering and my body was overheated and I wasn't the only soul who came out that day. I was about the twentieth person in line in the big room. The air-conditioning was on high, blowing loudly from the ceiling.

Little carts were full of souvenirs, with the logo of the store on everything from T-shirts to mugs. I grabbed a mug because I couldn't resist.

"You have to try the chocolate," a voice behind me said.

I turned around to see Shia standing there, his smile youthful and his eyes frosted green.

"I've never been here."

He smiled at me and glanced at my mug. "I figured."

I turned back around.

A few moments later, his fingers tapped my shoulder. "You didn't get the chocolate," he said as I took my first bite of the crunchy praline treat.

I almost got the chocolate, but chose not to just to spite him. Our relationship kept with that pattern. Him giving me advice and me doing the opposite, just to prove a point. It's why we would never work. We tried a few times, but neither of us had the patience to put up with the other.

"Meg? What are you doing up here?"

Mrs. King's voice pulled me from my walk down memory lane. Her square chin was raised, and I stood up straighter, trying to come up with something to say.

And yet her tone smoothed over her words, as if her husband and her son hadn't just been screaming at each other like the family tree was being chopped down.

"I'm, uhm"—I paused—"I'm looking for my sister."

I heard shuffling inside the big room and wanted to get moving before Shia came out and saw me.

"Your sister? The little blond one or the one with the long hair?"

I wanted to tell Mrs. King that I actually had three sisters, but I felt it wouldn't do any good; she didn't seem to remember their names even though I talked about them all the time. Well, I wouldn't say all the time, since I didn't actually speak much around Mrs. King, but when I did, I talked a lot about my younger sisters.

"That's the one, yes. I'm sorry to disturb you." I looked around me, trying to avoid her heavy gaze. She was so damned intimidating.

I looked at her outfit and wondered if I would ever dress like her when I was older. Her maroon blazer matched her pencil skirt perfectly, not even a fraction of a shade off. Around her neck was a thick rope of pearls, and her lips were dark fuchsia. She was a beautiful woman in her late forties. I couldn't imagine what she looked like when she woke up. Even when I came in the early afternoon to do her makeup, she already had her hair done and she was usually dressed to the nines. Perfectly paired jewelry and all.

I wanted to be like her when I grew up.

I don't think she wanted me to notice the way she glanced

back to the open door as we began to walk down the hallway. "It's fine, dear. Let's go downstairs," she said neutrally.

Mrs. King was at least five inches taller than me in her stilettos. The way she could walk in them made my already aching feet feel even more pathetic. I had a long way to go.

She made me feel both the oldest and the youngest I could ever be.

I looked up at my boss, and she turned to face me as we passed the upstairs bathroom. The door was closed and a thin line of light was cast on the floor. It was quiet, so when she spoke to me, her voice was as soft as a sprinkle of confectioners' sugar.

"Have you enjoyed the party? I'm sure you heard some things you shouldn't have. We can just forget about that private family moment, can't we?"

I nodded. *Yes, please.*

I hoped she didn't call me out for calling out sick for work and being here, dressed up and obviously not sick.

"Of course. And, yes, the party is stunning. I'm happy for your son, and for all of you."

Her smile slid up her dusted cheeks. Whoever did her makeup tonight did almost as good a job as I do.

"I wouldn't be *too* happy," she said so low that I almost thought I had imagined it.

Neither of us talked as we crossed the upstairs of the house. The music and voices from the party downstairs carried up to where we stood. It was weird how quiet it was upstairs. In my parents' house, I can hear every single noise from wall to wall. *I will have a house like this by the time I'm thirty.*

"Do you want to have a glass with me before we rejoin the party?"

I never thought I would see the day that Mrs. King would invite me for a drink. I didn't even know what the glass she was offering would be full of. But at that point, I would have gulped down a cup of molasses just for the sense of inclusion.

"Sure." I tried to keep my smile chill, not too excited. Mature girls keep their cool. All the time.

I followed her into a small butler's pantry. While we walked, I pulled my hair out from behind my ears and tugged down the hem of my dress. After she pulled down a black bottle with a diamond-shaped sticker on the front, she turned to me.

She pointed above my head. "Grab two glasses."

When I looked up, there were racks of glasses and goblets. Everything from champagne flutes to beer mugs. I grabbed two cups that I thought looked good for whatever it was that she was going to have me drink. When I handed them to her, she turned her wrist around, and her watch sparkled under the light. Everything about her dripped elegance and class. She gave me an approving smile, and my heart leaped. She then opened a small fridge built into the wall. She bent down, and I heard ice clinking into the glasses.

I read the label on the black bottle: HENDRICK'S GIN. I had had gin only once until that night, with my ex–best friend from Texas, Justina. That was an awful night. The beginning of the end of our friendship.

"Here we are." She slid my glass to me and set hers down. Her slender fingers wrapped around the glass bottleneck and she yanked the top off. Her crème-brûlée nails looked so posh and beautiful against her dark skin as she poured the clear gin over the ice cubes.

When she finished, I waited a moment, hoping that she would pull out a mixer of some sort. She didn't. She just took a drink of it straight and said, "I don't drink often, but when I do, it's the real deal."

I smiled and followed her lead, raising my glass to hers. I took a small sip and my tongue burned, but truly it wasn't so bad. It was a hell of a lot better than cheap beer or the wine coolers my friends in Texas always stole from their moms' stashes. To that day, I couldn't stand the smell of wine coolers—they reminded me of those fake bitches who ruined my life in Texas.

Mrs. King put her glass down on the counter in front of us. "So, Meg, are you seeing anyone?"

I couldn't help but wonder how her lipstick wasn't smudged even a bit.

I nodded and hoped that I wouldn't choke when I went to speak.

"Yes, Mrs. King. I'm dating a man named John Brooke. He's graduating from West Point next week." I wanted her to be impressed.

"I know him, I believe. Good for you, he'll take care of you. That's all we can hope for."

The way she said those words grated on me a little, but if she weren't anything close to right, why did I mention John's West Point graduation?

"Yeah" was all I said.

"Let me tell you something, Meg." It wasn't a request. She was going to speak regardless of my response.

I nodded anyway. I took another sip of gin, and it burned just a touch less than the first.

"My son thinks he knows everything about the world and the way it works. He has these illusions of himself being some type of savior." She waved her hand in the air like she was dismissing someone who wasn't there. "All we want for him is to be successful. We want him to make our family proud and carry on his father's legacy around here. Do you know how much pressure is on our family already? To be the wealthiest family around here *and* be black?"

My boss's eyes fell on me, and I wasn't sure how to respond. I didn't know how much pressure there was. I only knew the way people talked about the Kings, as if they were somewhere between a fairy tale and royalty.

"My son has a responsibility to carry on our name. Both of my daughters did what they were supposed to—hell, even *more* than they were supposed to. Ineesha graduated top of her class and is now the youngest partner in her firm's history. My youngest daughter's husband is running for Senate. And here's Shia, wasting his time in these countries, letting the delusion of liberty affect his future. He dropped out of college, for Christ's sake."

I didn't know what to say. I didn't feel qualified to give advice or even comment, but I wanted her to keep talking.

"What would you want him to do?" I asked.

She didn't hesitate. "Go to law school. Enjoy this engagement to Bell Gardiner. Listen to his father."

"Shia doesn't want to be a lawyer, though?" I wished I could clip my mouth shut.

Her eyes hardened a little, but she nodded. "You're right. He doesn't want to, but when he's an adult living in a house like this, he will thank us. Wouldn't you be happy living in a house like this, Meg? Even if you had to make a few sacrifices to get here?"

I looked around the butler's pantry, which was nicer than most rooms in my parents' house. "Yes, I would be."

When Jo and I talked about the future and our plans for it, I always felt reflexively guilty about wanting to be a mother and a wife. Jo has a different plan for herself, and the idea of being a wife and mother, without a career, would be hell for her. But for women like me and Mrs. King, there's no shame in it. Is it so bad that I would sacrifice a few things to be a wife and a mother? No, I didn't think it was. To Jo and Meredith, yes, but to me, no.

"I knew you had your head screwed on right. Why couldn't Shia have just done what we said and enrolled in law school? It's still not too late; his father has connections. He could get accepted now, even after wasting two years pedaling around the globe. He just won't listen to us, that impossible child."

It was weird to hear Mrs. King talk about Shia like this, like he was making all these mistakes, when sometimes I wished I could be like him. I wished that I didn't care what people thought about me, and I wished I could leave my family to travel the world. I wished I was brave enough to. At least for a little while.

"I'm sure he will come around. He's lucky to have parents like you," I reassured her, feeling slightly traitorous.

Mrs. King's smile would have made up for my guilt if Shia hadn't walked by the open door just then and given me a look that said he'd heard every word we'd said about him.

12

jo

Meg had been gone for twenty minutes by the time I got bored and wanted to leave. Well, to be completely honest, I was ready to go the moment we stepped through the wrought-iron gate separating the Kings from the rest of the world. It really did feel like some alternate universe where rich people stand around shoving tiny spoons of caviar into their mouths and wash it down with expensive booze. This was a world I never wanted to end up in.

Fortunately, the champagne *was* helping things.

"Isn't this party beautiful?" a tall woman asked me. I had to turn my neck up to see her, and even when I did, I couldn't see much of her face. She was wearing a big, feathery hat on her head. She was an elaborate, rich peacock. Perhaps just as useless.

"It's just delightful." I changed my voice to that of a Southern belle, and the woman clapped her hands.

Like, actually clapped her hands.

"It is! That Bell Gardiner is lucky to have the chance to marry into the Kings'. Can you imagine?"

Her delight and sense of wonder surrounding this family made my stomach turn. To me, the Kings were wasteful, boring, and about as narcissistic as they come. This party showed that. Almost as much as the creepy paintings of the five of them, strategically placed in every single room I'd been in so far. Maybe it was true that having your portrait painted stole your soul. Or was it having your photograph taken? I couldn't remember, but it would explain what had happened in this household. I didn't know much about them, but with Meg's hatred for Shia and her complaints about the coldness of Mrs. King, I needed to do little investigating of my own. This lavish party was enough.

"I can't imagine. I bet it's, like, so much fun to be stuck in this big old house with nothing to do but drink champagne and complain about your life. Like, *so* much fun, right?" I moved my hips when I talked, and a smile crept across my face when the woman frowned down at me.

"*What* is your problem?"

Her outrage was ridiculous. She acted like I was talking about her own sister or mother; maybe that was the case, but I didn't know.

"Nothing. I'm just saying. I heard that if you move into the house, you slowly start to turn into a robot. It's crazy. Bell Gardiner." I nodded in the direction of the long table the woman of the evening and her friends sat at. Her groom was the only one missing from the group. The empty seat next to her stuck out like a sore thumb.

"You are . . ." The woman huffed, and her beady eyes popped out from under her outrageous hat. I didn't want to stick around long enough for her to find the words, so I dipped between a server and a group of tall men.

I wanted to go back to the hidden bench, but I didn't want to take the chance of Laurie coming in and trying to play his games with me.

I pulled out my phone and texted Meg: Going home. Meet me there when you're done. Can't take it anymore.

Meg was fine by herself. She stayed out almost every weekend and didn't come home until hours after I fell asleep. I grabbed another tomato bread and smiled at the gigantic security guards at the front of the gate on my way out.

I pulled out my phone to order a ride from Safr, but when I looked around the street, the quiet darkness of it called to me. I could walk for a few minutes and get some fresh Louisiana air into my lungs and some silence into my head, then call a car to take me the rest of the way home. Well, to the gate of the post. Drivers couldn't get through the security gates without a sticker on their car. Sometimes I got lucky and got a driver with a sticker or a military ID to take me through, but not always.

From here the gate was only a ten-minute drive, and from the gate it took me about five minutes to reach my front door. I could be home before long and put my pajamas on and hang out with my sisters. We had traditions that we followed every year. Beth and Meredith would fill the kitchen with food, and when Aunt Hannah came over, it was even better. Well, the food was. Not the awkward silence that rang hollow through the room between my mom and her sister. Amy always ran around asking everyone what their favorite memories were and told hers first. Meredith and Amy always fell asleep before midnight, and Beth always woke Meredith just before. We would hug and dance at midnight, and Dad would always light sparklers and we would always yell *"Prost!"* when we clinked our glasses together. My dad had learned it in Germany, and we loved saying it.

I missed my dad. I was beginning to think about him every hour. When I was younger, it felt easier to distract myself from missing him. I was busy with school and with my writing and could pass the days faster. But now that I was paying attention to the world around me, it was not so easy.

My teachers talked about the war, and my Twitter feed is full of politics, most of which conflict with what I'm learning in school.

I felt so much younger just last year.

Meredith always told me that being sixteen was unlike any other age. When you're fifteen, you don't drive yet, you're most likely not dating yet. I had started my period later than all of my sisters, aside from Amy. I felt so young until somehow, without my noticing, last year I was thrust into early adulthood. Every day was something new, and I felt the world getting smaller with each sunrise. My sisters think I'm being dramatic, but times are different now, even since Meg was my age two years ago.

Only a month more and my dad would be home. He would be back and life would lighten up just a little bit. I would have someone to debate with, someone to bounce my ideas off of. I was proud of my dad, but couldn't help wishing he wouldn't have signed up to be an officer. Guilt bloomed in my chest and I took back my thoughts, mentally apologized to Dad and the universe, and thought again. I was lucky he was coming home. I knew that. But no matter how much I knew that, it didn't make it feel much better when he was gone.

I walked past an empty field and thought about the privacy

all this space afforded. I bet that the Kings owned this land, too, since there were no houses on it. Only cattle. Two eyes stared at me from the darkness, and I walked a little farther from the animal. I was fine with cats and birds, but large farm animals were not my thing. Just like on most days in southern Louisiana, the air got sticky at night. It was still cold, but tonight was warmer than the morning. I searched for more cows and tried to stay under the streetlights in case any cars drove past. Meg hadn't texted me back yet, so I hoped that Meredith wouldn't freak out if I came home without her.

I didn't think so, but I would see what happened. Maybe Meg would text me back or call me before I called a car. I texted her again: Meg, where are you?

I thought I heard a branch snap behind me, but I also knew how my imagination worked. Anytime there was ever too much silence, my mind would create something to keep it occupied. It was why I wrote—to dump out some of my wild imagination.

Another snap. Okay, so there is something behind me. A cow?

Let it be a cow . . .

I turned around, and Laurie was walking about ten feet back. He raised his arms in the air. "Don't shoot!"

He laughed and I glared at him. Was he following me?

"Why are you following me?" I shouted. He was only about five feet away now; his long strides carried him quickly to my side. His shirt was untucked and his blond hair was pulled back away from his face.

"I'm not. I just saw you walking and wanted to join you." He smiled and slid his tongue over his lips.

I looked up at his eyes. "That sounds a *lot* like following to me. What do you want?"

His wet lips were glistening under the streetlight. "I'm heading home, too. Why not go together?"

Hmm. "It's a long walk from here. In case you didn't know." He probably didn't know, since he'd just moved here, and I sort of loved that I knew more than he did about this.

He chuckled and shook his head for a second. "You are just so pleasant, Jo Spring."

I didn't smile. "Aren't I?" I pointed to the paper cup in his hand. "Is that coffee? Where the hell did you find coffee?"

I'd seen tables and tables of champagne and two full bars, but no coffee.

"It *is* coffee. Do you want it?" He held it up.

I nodded and grabbed it. It was still hot. "I'd take coffee over compliments right now."

I lifted the white plastic lid from the cup. I sniffed it to make sure it didn't smell like alcohol. The champagne I pretended to like was more than enough for me. After that night, I really didn't understand why people like to drink so much. Adults, maybe—they have more to worry about—but teenagers? I don't get their love of alcohol.

I snapped the lid back on. Was this safe? I hated that I had to question that.

"You take a drink," I told him, handing the cup back to him.

His eyes went from mine to the cup, and he grabbed it from me. Besides tilting his head to the side, he didn't do anything before he took a drink. He gargled it like mouthwash and smiled after he swallowed it, sticking his tongue out to prove it was all gone.

"The walk here is only ten minutes if we cut through the cemetery," Laurie said a few moments later.

"The cemetery?" We couldn't just cut through the cemetery. It was closed and gated.

And a little creepy. Honestly.

"Yeah." He kicked a rock with his boot. It slid across the dark street, and all we could hear was the chirping of crickets and the vibration of grasshoppers in the fields around us. Coming up was a cornfield that was always so dark that every time I walked past it, I couldn't help but picture Amy's pick for last Christmas's horror film: *Children of the Corn.*

"It's faster. Trust me. I cut through the cemetery all the time."

It irritated me that he knew this and I didn't. "It's also closed."

"So? I can help you over the fence if you're worried about it. Most girls can't climb it. I'll help you." He offered a smile.

I loved a challenge, and the way he said "most girls" annoyed me. "I'm sure I can handle it. I don't need your help." I smiled back at him and followed him down the road.

"It shouldn't be this hot outside. Summer is going to be brutal," Laurie said.

I looked over at him. "We're talking about the weather?"

He laughed through his response. "Guess not."

The cemetery was marked by a big red wooden gate.

"Ready?" Laurie asked with a smirk that was a challenge wrapped in a big red bow.

"Yep." I began the climb a second before him, and I didn't need his help over the steel fence. I made it over and down by myself and only ripped my pants in two places. The jeans were a worthy sacrifice to my cause of self-sufficiency.

We were silent as we walked among the graves. Laurie told me that if we disturbed the dead, they would disturb us, too.

I knew he was just talking shit to me, but I still shivered and walked a little closer to him, making sure my steps were as light as possible until we reached a paved road again. We were almost to the gate. I could see it in the distance, only a few minutes' walk ahead.

Laurie had only just moved here—how did he know more about my town than me?

"So, Jo. What are you passionate about?"

"What a random thing to ask." I laughed, trying to keep up with his long strides.

"Not really. I'm curious."

Laurie shoved his hands in his pockets and slowed to walk just a little behind me.

"I want to know yours, Laurie." I stretched my back as high as I could. "You tell me something about you. I'm not into games."

"Hmm, Jo. Somehow I don't believe that."

He smiled and the moon shone brighter.

13

"*I*'m not going to let you walk with me if you're going to be obnoxious," I replied.

I didn't want to spend the entire walk home playing guessing games and having him make cryptic and not-even-close-to-productive comments about everything I said.

"I won't be. I promise only my best behavior from here on out." He lifted his hand and drew a cross over his heart.

It was cute. I laughed.

"Let's talk," he said, and began firing question after question at me. By the time we reached the gate of the base, I had talked to him so much that the walk had flown by.

Where did I get my name?

Why did I like to be called Jo instead of Josephine?

Which of my sisters was the oldest? Which was the youngest?

I had learned little to nothing about him, besides that I thought I wanted to be his friend.

When we approached the gate, I wasn't sure which lane to go through. One of my nonmilitary friends once told me that the gate was like a toll gate. Laurie seemed to know which way to go, so I followed him to the far-left lane. The lights above us were so bright, and the military police guarding each lane were holding big guns strapped to their uniforms.

Meg's friend Coleman was the gate guard, whose job it was to check our identification and welcome us to the "great place" that was Fort Cyprus. He didn't give us a hard time at all before he let us through. He didn't even check our IDs. He probably wanted to sleep with my sister, like the rest of the soldiers we knew.

"Tell me why you always scowl, Jo."

When I informed Laurie that I did *not* always scowl, he asked me again and I glared at him. I wondered if all boys were interesting like him. My dad was, but some of the boys in my school, and even older ones that Meg dated, seemed less stimulating than plain yogurt.

"So, Jo, can I assume you have a temper to go with that glower?" Laurie asked when we passed the Shopette just beyond the gate.

The Shopette was always crowded and had the best hot food and tastiest less-than-a-dollar cappuccinos, which came pouring out of the machine within thirty seconds. Whenever we checked out, I would look at the receipt as a big reminder of all the money we'd saved by not paying taxes on our cappuccinos, Tornados, and Krispy Kreme donuts. My dad would say that we should always use the resources the Army provides for us. During the school year, my dad would fill up his big jug of coffee there every morning. I loved the days when he could drive us to school. It was usually only once a week, but he talked the whole way.

For a second, I forgot that I was standing with Laurie while my dad was seven thousand miles away. A line of cars pulled out of the parking lot, and we waited on the curb.

Laurie looked like the type of boy who stayed out late.

"My dad says I do have a temper. He says that my quick temper, sharp tongue, and restless spirit always get me in trouble."

Laurie laughed at that. "Your dad seems to know what he's talking about."

Laurie sniffled and pulled a tissue from his pocket. He wiped his nose and waved for me to walk in front of him. I stepped down off the curb and made a joke about not falling that time, but I don't think he got it.

"So, Laurie. You've asked me all the questions. My turn." I didn't look back at him, and I made sure to keep my pace a few steps ahead.

"What is there to do for fun around here?"

"Nothing. I'm always trying to figure that out, too. But there's nothing," I told him, distracted from my turn to interrogate him.

"You have to make your own adventures, Jo."

When I looked over at him, I felt like he could read my mind.

He creates his own adventures, I thought.

"Do you want me to come inside?" Laurie asked when we reached my driveway.

The curtains were open and I could see Meredith sitting in Dad's armchair and Aunt Hannah sitting on the couch. Amy was on the other end of the couch with her phone in her hand. I didn't see Beth, but I was sure she was in the kitchen. I checked my phone, and it was only ten forty-five. Meg still hadn't answered me.

"Sure. My family can be . . ." I looked inside and wondered if my mom and aunt would yell at each other before or after midnight. "But you can come on inside. We have a lot of food and stuff."

I looked over at Old Mr. Laurence's house, which was pitch-black. I gestured to the house. "Do you need to tell him or something?"

"No." Laurie laughed. "He's in bed. He won't even notice."

"Is he as awful as everyone says he is?" I blurted out.

Laurie stopped walking for a moment, and we stood in the middle of my driveway.

"Do you want to hear how our morning went today?"

I nodded and tucked my long hair behind my ears on both sides.

"This morning the driver took us down to the Quarter, to this little place where my grandpa likes to get his pies for the holidays. There was this little fish shop, and while we were waiting, a homeless woman came in begging the owner to let her scrub some fish in exchange for some scraps for her family to eat. She had a little boy with her who looked like he hadn't eaten in days."

My stomach turned.

"So, the owner of the fish shop says no and shooed them out of there. So my grandpa tells the guy off, buys a whole bag of fish, and takes them outside. He handed her a wad of money, the fish, and a bottle of water." Laurie looked down at me. "He even smiled at the toothless little kid, and that man hardly ever smiles. He's tough, but he's a good man. Don't listen to rumors that bored women make up about him."

I was stunned . . .

But I loved the plot twist. I loved the entire idea that people were never who we thought they were. It was silly to think that the first impression or even the tenth was enough to know an entire human being. I wasn't buying it; besides, it made it more fun when Old Mr. Laurence turned out to be a Care Bear, not a grizzly.

"Is that your mom?" Laurie pointed to the house.

I saw Aunt Hannah standing in the window.

"No, that's my aunt. That one is my mom." I pointed to Meredith, sitting on the chair. She had on an old cotton dress, and her hair was wrapped up in a floral cloth.

"Let's go." I tugged on Laurie's jacket and he followed me through the creaky door.

Amy sat up when we walked in, and I saw her little hands fly up to her hair to fluff the blond strands.

Meredith watched us quietly, but didn't move from the chair.

"Uh . . . Hi, everyone," Laurie greeted the awkward room, and waved his hand in the air.

"Laurie is going to spend New Year's with us, okay?" I told everyone.

I didn't wait for anyone to respond before I led him into the kitchen. The lights were on the dimmest setting, so I turned the knob up. Laurie squinted a little, but I kept them on high.

I pointed to the food. "Eat."

With a little smirk, Laurie grabbed a handful of chips from a bowl. Leaning over the counter to look inside the tops of the Crock-Pots, he lifted the lid on the barbecued sausages and scooped a ladleful onto a styrofoam plate. Those were my favorite before I stopped eating meat.

"Let's talk some more," Laurie suggested.

"I've talked a lot already, and ask Beth, I can talk all day. I never know when to stop!" I laughed. I felt much calmer when I was back in my house and away from the fancy party at the Kings'. It didn't surprise me that Meg got caught up in it. I suspected she wouldn't be home before midnight.

"Beth is the one who never comes outside, right? The one

with the rosy cheeks who always carries a laundry basket?" Laurie asked with interest, then he shoveled a spoonful of little sausages into his mouth.

A thin line of dark barbecue sauce dripped down his shirt, and he rubbed it in. If I had done that, Meg would have scolded me and told me to change my clothes. Boys seemed to get away with everything, and it ground on my nerves.

"Yes, that's her. She's my girl. She's the most decent of us all," I said with loyalty. It was true. Beth was better than all of us, even Meredith.

"I always hear you guys calling for each other when I'm sitting in the main room over there." His chin motioned to the house next door. "And when I look through the window, I always see you guys crowded around each other at the table or on the couch. It's nice."

I didn't know what to say. We had eavesdropped on him a few times, so it's not like I could be upset about it, and I wasn't anyway. I knew so many nosy people.

"How do we seem from the window, Laurie?" I asked out of curiosity.

"You seem like the great American dream I grew up hearing about."

My head turned a little to the side, and I dipped a cracker into the cheese ball Beth had made for me.

"I can assure you that's so far from reality. We're far from the American dream, but I will be close soon. I'm moving the moment I graduate high school and never looking back. I have it all planned."

"Where do you want to move away to? Won't you miss your sisters?"

The oven started beeping as he finished asking that, and

Beth came shuffling into the room. Her cheeks reddened all the way down to her neck when she saw Laurie.

"Beth, this is Laurie. He's spending New Year's with us."

Beth was dressed in light blue jeans with two big holes in the knees and an oversized T-shirt from our trip to Disney World last year. She was wearing Meredith's apron with wild-indigo strands printed all over it. Her hair was pulled back and barely held with a tie.

"Hi," she said, then busied herself with the oven.

She didn't talk much.

Amy came bouncing into the kitchen, and I noticed her newly shiny lips. She hadn't been wearing lip gloss or that dress a few minutes ago. I could only assume it was for Laurie's benefit.

"Hi, Laurie. Thank you for coming to our party," Amy said in a voice that I had never before heard from her.

He was the height of two of her. Her little cheeks were so red.

Beth laughed from her place by the oven, and I checked my phone again. I wasn't worried about Meg, but I was annoyed that she would just drop off the earth like that just because she was around a bunch of rich people.

14

I pulled my beanie over my hair.

It was nine in the morning on New Year's Day, and I couldn't sit in the house any longer and listen to Amy complain or Meg talk about Shia and Bell for another minute. I grabbed a broom and put on my strongest boots. I could sweep the driveway or something.

"What in the world are you going to do now, Jo?" Meg asked.

"Going to exercise." I smiled and batted my lashes.

"You already took a walk this morning, and it's cold outside. You are crazy for wanting to go out when we have a lit fireplace and Netflix." Meg looked to Beth for support.

Beth didn't seem interested in taking anyone's side.

I lifted my broom into the air. "I'm not like you, Meg. I can't just lay around all the time. I need more adventure than that."

Meg huffed and pressed buttons on the remote. I left her alone and made my way outside. The driveway was actually pretty clean, so I wasn't quite sure what to do with the broom I'd brought outside with me. I looked over to the Laurence house and counted the windows on its front. Six. The house was made from stately stone, and the yard in the front was better maintained than ours. Fort Cyprus would send someone out to cut your grass and maintain your landscaping while your head of household was deployed.

The Laurence house didn't look like an officer's house; it looked like a general's house. It was nice, all matching patio furniture and a black town car parked in the front. It looked lonely, sort of lifeless. No kids were playing outside or teenage girls yelling inside, no shoes on the porch. There were always shoes on the porch at our house.

As I stared at the details of the Laurence house, my imagination started to run wild. I imagined the house as an enchanted palace, full of useless splendid delights that no one actually enjoyed. I wondered about Old Mr. Laurence's family and why only his grandson was ever at his house. I knew it could be the simple military-family answer, that no one lives in the same state as their family because of PCSing. Laurie had already told me that his dad was in Korea.

I looked up to the second-story window, and by the time I realized Laurie was standing there, staring right at me, it was too late for me to move. I waved my broom in the air, and the window resisted as he yanked it up.

"How are you?" he asked.

I shrugged. His nose was red, and from down on the ground his eyes looked puffy. "How are you?"

"A little sick. I'll be fine."

"Are you going to stay locked in there all day?" I didn't know the level of comfort you're supposed to be at with a boy before you initiate hanging out, but I wasn't sure if I cared so much about what I was supposed to do.

"Are you offering your company, Jo?" He grinned at me from the window. When he smiled, he no longer looked sick.

"No." I grinned back at him.

"You *should* offer me your company," he said, sure of himself.

I think I liked how confident he was. I wasn't sure then if it was genuine, but I wanted him to stay around long enough to find out.

"Come on, Jo Spring!" he called from the window above me.

"I'm not sure I would be much fun if you're sick!" I yelled up. "I'm not that nice or that quiet!"

I heard Amy talking inside the kitchen, watching my exchange with Laurie.

"I wouldn't want you to be!"

I shook my head. I did want to get to know him better, and it was my turn to ask all the questions. But I did need to ask Meredith and make sure she was okay with it. I couldn't imagine that she wouldn't be, but I had never asked to go inside a boy's house before.

"I have to ask my mom if I can come in. Now, shut your window before you get even worse!" I turned from him and carried my broom inside. I went through the back door and found Amy, Beth, and Meredith all standing in the kitchen.

After ten seconds of silence I finally asked the three of them, "What?"

"Nothing," Meredith said, her lips turning up into a smile. She looked like she was up to something. Her heart-shaped face was staring out the window, up at Laurie's. I walked over to check what she was looking at, and I saw Laurie standing in front of the mirror, taking a hairbrush to his hair.

"It's not a big deal," I told them. "You guys shouldn't be so nosy!"

Amy started making kissing sounds with her little pink lips. Her blond curls bounced around her face. "He's so hot, though. You're so lucky," she whined, kissing the air one more time.

"Amy!" Meredith and I said at the same time.

"What?" Amy's hip jut out and she looked sixteen for a second. "He is."

Amy grabbed her phone from the counter and asked Beth to make her breakfast. Beth immediately began to move around the kitchen, opening a cabinet and pulling out a loaf of bread.

"So, Meredith, do you mind if I go next door to hang out with Laurie?"

She was mid-drink of her coffee, so she swallowed and shook her head. "No, I don't mind, Jo. Do you feel comfortable going?"

Amy looked up, raising her golden brows.

"Yes, I do."

"Then I trust you to go there. Text me in an hour to check in."

Beth shook a jug of orange juice, and if I wasn't in a hurry to get next door, I would have been useless like Amy and gotten her to pour me a glass.

When I walked down the hallway, I passed a mirror . . .

I looked like hell. I hadn't even thought about the way I looked when I saw Laurie, or that I was wearing black leggings, a Pac-Man sweatshirt, and dirty Vans. I thought I would be sweeping the driveway, not hanging out with Laurie inside his house.

I didn't feel like changing, though, and he'd already seen me in this outfit anyway. It felt like a lot of work to consider my clothes and get primped just for a boy. I never understood that concept, because what happens when you move in with someone? Do you have to set your alarm for an hour before they wake up just to get ready? No, thanks.

I went into the bathroom and brushed my teeth, raked Amy's hairbrush through my hair, and tucked my hair behind my ears. My hair always got so oily, so fast, and I didn't feel like breathing in the powdery fumes of Meg's dry shampoo, so I shoved my beanie back on my head.

Then I leaned into the mirror and studied my face. My lips were their usual puffy selves, and my thick eyebrows were unruly again. Meredith always told me to leave them be until she took me to get them waxed. She even pulled out pictures from ten years ago when the tiny-eyebrow trend was in. I was glad I came after that period in beauty history.

I still had sleep in my eyes, so I wet a warm rag and wiped them, plus my mouth. Before I could find something else to do with my appearance, I shut the light off and walked back to the kitchen.

"Here, take him some of the leftovers from last night." Meredith handed me a covered dish, then gently set a pie on top of it. The pie was from Christmas. It was Meredith's cherry pie recipe that no one except Dad ever ate. Since Aunt Hannah was here now, it seemed like she wanted to make up for missing Christmas by making as many pies as humanly possible.

"Okay, okay." I blocked Meredith from putting another pan, this time meatballs, on top of the stack. On the edge of the kitchen island was a little bowl of the barbecued sausages that Laurie seemed to like the night before, so I grabbed them and loaded them on top.

"Careful, you'll crush that pie," Meredith warned me. Beth grabbed the stack from my hands and dumped the sausages into the big dish on the bottom.

"I'll get the door," Beth said, moving past Meredith to help me. Beth's eyes looked a little tired, I thought.

I adjusted the pans in my arms and walked through the backyard.

"Jo! You're not wearing that?" Meg cried from inside the house. I continued across the yard and didn't look back at my sister.

When I got to the door of the Laurence house, I rang the doorbell twice before someone answered. I was just about to walk away when an elderly man pulled the door open. His hair was white and almost transparent, but was combed neatly and looked like even the wind couldn't move it. I recognized him immediately as Old Mr. Laurence.

"Send her up!" Laurie's voice carried down the stairs, and Old Mr. Laurence waved me in.

His eyes were suspicious and the oddest shade of river-green I had ever seen. Laurie's eyes were so dark, it surprised me that he looked so different from his grandpa. Old Mr. Laurence had a sharply squared jaw, and his thick shoulders reminded me of someone on TV, but I couldn't think of who.

Thanking the old man, I walked toward the staircase and saw Laurie making his way down. My arms were killing me. The interior of the house was so strange. The curtains were maroon and massive, draping over the hunter-green wallpaper. There were so many curtains, it was distracting. The random candlesticks and books everywhere reminded me of the set of *Downton Abbey* or something. It was messier than I had imagined, especially compared to the view from the windows I usually snooped through.

"Do you need help? What is all that?" Laurie's long legs carried him down the staircase quickly, and he reached for the food in my arms.

He led me back up to his bedroom and set the food on a

desk near the door. His room seemed bland at first glance, but as I looked closer, I saw touches of magic everywhere. From a distance, his wallpaper looked like black squiggles on a white sheet, but when I walked over to it, I realized it was sheet music.

Against the wall farthest from the doorway was his bed. The sheets and pillowcases were all white and burlap and reminded me of an IKEA ad. The Louisiana sun was beaming through his big, open windows. It was warmer in the room than outside, and the ceiling fan made a nice breeze. As Laurie pulled the Tupperware lid off the sausages, I explored his bedroom. He didn't seem to mind, because he sat down on the edge of the desk and started eating while I flipped through the pages of an old coffee-table book with *Barcelona* on the front cover. The pages were filled with bright, vivid pictures of beautiful beaches and tapas-style food.

"Have you been to Barcelona?"

His mouth was full of food. He nodded.

"Was it wonderful?"

He nodded again.

I couldn't imagine how it would be to be so young and have traveled so much. Being an Army brat, I have moved with my family a few times, from Connecticut to Texas, and now outside of New Orleans, but that was nothing compared to traveling Europe and having an Italian artist for a mother. I loved Meredith so much, but I didn't get my love for writing from her.

I put the Barcelona book down and grabbed a notebook full of scribbles.

"Not that." Laurie grabbed it from my hand before I could flip to any of the pages.

It made me want to see it even more. "What is that?"

"It's a book of drawings, but I'm not good at it."

I let him hide it away from me. One day, when we were friends, I would ask again if he would show me.

I moved to another part of his room, near his bed. He had stacks of graphic novels in languages that I didn't even recognize. Next to that were empty bottles of Coke and two glasses of what I assumed was water. On the nightstand, his wallet lay on top of a *GQ* magazine, and was stuffed with cards and receipts. I picked it up in my hands and started looking through the cards. Honestly, who hoarded so many cards? There was an Urban Outfitters gift card, a punch card for Panera Bread, a business card with a Realtor's name on it.

Before I could see any more of them, Laurie said my name and then, "Um, what are you doing going through my wallet?"

I felt myself getting a little anxious. "Just looking." I shrugged and turned around to him.

He was holding the pie plate in his hands. but he didn't seem upset. He half-smiled at me. "Is that something people around here do? Pick up someone's wallet and go through it?" Humor was in his voice. "Imagine if I picked up your purse and opened your wallet!" He sat down on the small sofa in his bedroom.

"I don't have a purse." I guess it could be considered invasive to go through someone's things like I just did. The wallet felt heavier in my hands and I dropped it back onto the nightstand.

"I have three sisters." I couldn't help but laugh at myself. "We don't have any privacy. Sorry." I took a few steps away from the nightstand and tried to find something else to look at.

"Did you know that the Russian language doesn't have an original word for privacy?" Laurie asked.

His couch was big enough for both of us to sit on, so I sat on the opposite end from him. An orange pillow with a fox's face on it was between us. I put it on my lap and touched the soft fur. For a second, I thought his comment was a random thing to know, but then I remembered that I knew that, too.

"I did know that, actually," I said rather proudly.

Laurie's chin turned to me. "Did you? How?"

I didn't think he believed me, and I found that funny. "I read it in a book once."

"What book?"

"*The Bronze Horseman*. It's a—"

Laurie shot up from the couch. "I know it! It was my mother's favorite book. Well, books. I read the trilogy last summer."

"No way."

Laurie was definitely the most interesting boy I had ever met.

"Yes, way. The Italian version cut some of the text—can you believe it?"

I liked how he got excited easily. I did that, too, but Meg always told me it was immature. If Laurie was immature, then so was I.

"What? Why would they?"

"Not sure. But they did."

"What were we talking about before?" My head was fuzzy when I tried to remember what was happening before I was on the couch with Laurie.

"Who cares? Let's talk about your aunt and your mom. Are they sisters?"

I told him about us girls' theories about Aunt Hannah and Meredith and the drama between them. I told him more than I should have, but I felt like that was okay. For a second I thought about Meg and how River had tortured her when they broke up. I had to remember that guys can be important to me, but I'm more important. I want a career and I want to be taken seriously. I couldn't imagine being someone's wife and liking it. I didn't think anyone was out there that I would like enough to share the remote with.

His phone rang twice while I was talking, and when I stopped for a moment, he said, "It's my mom," with the kind of shy smile that boys in magazines wear.

I wondered if he knew that he looked like a troubled musician or a struggling actor. He had the polish of a well-groomed politician's son, but the wit of a bartender's son. I stared at his mouth and the slow way it moved when he explained things in detail with memories from Rome and Boston and how he somehow loved the two equally. I wondered what the girls that he usually dated looked like. Not that pretty girls couldn't be smart, because I knew they could be. I knew many. The thing was, though, that pretty girls are sometimes taught that it's their job to be pretty and not to be smart.

I wondered if boys were taught the same. Once, Meg told me that girls who were prettier had easier lives. I didn't believe her then, and I didn't think I could ever agree with that. I wondered if the pretty girls Laurie could date were ever interesting. It wasn't fair to assume they weren't, but since I didn't have much social experience, I only had the basic stereotypes to base my ideas on.

After a few minutes, Laurie changed the subject. "What about high school?"

I groaned. "I hate it. I can't wait to be a journalist. Or a businesswoman. Or a writer, or all three."

Laurie's expression changed and I thought he wanted to say something, but he kept tapping his lips with his fingers and pulling at the corners of them. I used to do that when I was younger, and I constantly had the worst red rash around my mouth. Meg called it my "ring around the rosie," and Amy told me it was a disease. There were two types of people, I supposed. Well, three, including sweet Beth, who helped rub cream on my lips before bed.

I started telling him about high school and how I felt about my teachers. Mostly Mr. Geckle, and how he kicked me off the newspaper and demoted me to yearbook. Laurie laughed a lot and looked pissed a lot, especially about Mr. Geckle and his red cheeks and hairy fingers.

"You have such a funny way of explaining things and telling stories. It's so . . . so . . . true, but told in a way I wouldn't have thought of," Laurie said. "When I was younger, my dad had this girlfriend who talked like you. She lived in New England some-where, and she was like a Gypsy or something."

I laughed like it was a silly thing to say, but I loved the comparison.

"Do you want a tour of the house?" Laurie asked me the third time his phone rang.

But by the time we reached the big staircase, Meredith had texted me and told me that my dad would be calling in twenty minutes. I told Laurie I had to go, and he showed me to the door.

Old Mr. Laurence was watching me and opened his mouth like he wanted to say something before I left, but he turned away and disappeared behind another door.

15

meg

"Jo? Jo? Where are you?" I cried, standing at the bottom of our staircase.

I heard a small "Here!" from upstairs. It sounded like it was coming from our bedroom, and sure enough, when I got there, I found Jo reading *The Bell Jar* and covered shoulder to toes in our dad's plaid blanket that usually rests on the back of his armchair.

This was Jo's utopia: a bowl of Bugles on her lap and her fingers gripping the binding of a novel. It gave her some sort of refuge; we all knew that. Meredith reminded us of our strengths and our weaknesses. Jo was smart—education would come easy to her. And me, well, I was beautiful and charming. I may not be as book-smart, but I'm street-smart, and sometimes that gets you further in life. We would see.

Jo would be fine, and Amy would be, too. Beth was the only one I worried about.

"What can I help you with?" Jo's eyes regretfully pulled away from her book. She held the edges tightly in her hand, careful not to lose her place.

"Look." I held up the screen of my phone, showing the Facebook invite with Bell Gardiner's smug face on it.

Ugh, why would she even invite me? Just to rub it in my face that she's part of that family now?

"Miss Gardiner, soon to be Mrs. King, invited us to the King family's New Year's Day dinner. Isn't that nice?" I stomped in a line. I was trying to be calm, but I didn't have much patience at that moment.

Jo sighed and closed her book. Her eyes were full of maturity and wisdom when she spoke. She was changing and evolving every day, it felt like.

"Do you really want to go, Meg? Or is this some weird social sabotage that we shouldn't get ourselves involved in? It feels like a setup to me. I've read stories that started like this," Jo finished, full of skepticism and fire.

"Jo," I sighed. She just didn't get it. I didn't want to go per se, but I sort of had to. I had to pretend that I wasn't bothered by Bell Gardiner's new fiancé, new thoroughbred family that I longed for, dramatically. I didn't care about her advancement into a part of society that a woman who works at a bar has no business being in.

I could work my way up to that same level; I just needed time. Bell Gardiner was older than me and had a head start anyway. When John got back, I would make up for it. I would be with a man who adored me, and that was all I ever wanted in life. Well, that and beautiful, sweet, happy children, a nice house, and a good marriage. I knew that Jo didn't share the same values, but I hoped she would have my back on this.

"Yes, I want to go. What are we going to wear?" I asked her, changing the direction of the conversation. I only had two hours to get ready. It was obvious that whatever reason Bell had for inviting me in the first place came as a late thought, which annoyed me more than the randomness of the invite did.

Jo pulled the blue-and-gray-plaid blanket away from her body and looked down. "What I'm wearing is fine?" She revealed a gray T-shirt and dark blue jeans with rips up the legs.

"You have to wear a dress, Jo. You *have* to. Look at this invitation! There's going to be matching silverware and people serving us dinner—you can't wear jeans."

I usually loved Jo's chill Los Angeles style, but not for something like this. Mrs. King would be offended as hell if I brought my sister to her annual New Year's Day dinner wearing jeans.

"I don't own a dress." Jo shrugged like it wasn't a big deal at all. And fair enough, to her it wasn't; but for me, this was monumental. There had to be a reason that Bell Gardiner was inviting me. The invite hadn't come from Mrs. King, as I would have hoped. I didn't expect to be invited at all, but it would have been a totally different story if Mrs. King herself had invited me, especially since we had had some QT last night.

So I had to be on my best behavior with Mrs. King, and Jo's wearing jeans wouldn't cut it.

"Josephine. You have to wear or a dress or I can't go." I tried not to let my voice crack.

I hated that I was so worked up over this. I couldn't help it. When I thought of Bell Gardiner dazzling in that green dress the other night, it made me panic and imagine how dressed up everyone would be in such a formal setting. I couldn't stand to be the one person who looked like they didn't belong.

"Jo, please. Can't you wear one of Beth's or mine? Just find something to wear! But it has to be a dress." I was anxious.

Jo sat up and set her book on the desk at the end of her bed. "Then I won't go. I don't like these snotty, negative-energy social hurdles. They're pointless, and I don't care who likes me and who doesn't."

She was being ridiculous. I didn't know how two sisters could be so different. It didn't seem possible that this long-haired, long-legged firecracker was my blood. She couldn't care less about her reputation or what boys, or girls, in her grade thought of her. Honestly, I cared more what the women thought; they were the ones judging. Sometimes I thought I wanted to be more like Jo, but when I imagined the lonely realities, I quickly broke with the ludicrous idea.

"Come on, Jo."

She closed her eyes and held them shut, the way she always did, and I let my mind wander for a moment. I thought about Shia. What he would wear, how he would act around Mr. King after their fight yesterday. My stomach felt like I'd drank rotten milk. I hoped this feeling would let up before the dinner. When I would worry like this, my dad had a way of talking me down. My dad, Shia, Jo . . . they were all so different, yet somehow tied to me and my life.

"You can wear something of mine, Jo. Anything you want."

I was being *so* helpful.

The moment she nodded her reluctant assent, I ran off to shower and shave and pluck and plump.

Two hours later, we were standing by our front door, Jo wearing a denim dress of mine. One of the straps was hanging a little off her shoulder, and her long hair was toppled over to one side, the part in the middle nonexistent and messy. It fit her so well. Jo had that type of face and thick hair that could pull off the messy look. When I tried that, I looked more bedhead than beach waves.

She looked like she was in California, not Louisiana, but she looked completely striking. She always did. Women in Sephora would pay forty bucks a pop for the natural blush on her cheeks.

"We're doing this," I said to her, and she nodded her defiant head at me and I somehow knew she would be down for anything I asked her to do. It made me love her more, and I felt our bond grow. It had been happening a lot lately. Jo was finally at that age where we could relate again. At a few ages it always fades a little, like twelve and fourteen through sixteen. But now she was almost seventeen, and I finally felt like she was cool to hang out with again.

"We're doing this." She smiled back at me.

I always loved her, but sisterly love is different from friend, complete-comfort love. There were things I'd told my friends in Texas that I would be absolutely humiliated about if Jo or sweet Beth knew. Lately Jo had been blurring the line between sister and friend.

It made me feel good, having another person to trust. Of course I trusted my mom and all of my sisters, but trust and ease don't always go hand in hand. It was hard to find those people, and I tended to trust the wrong people again and again.

Just as I was going to call the Uber, Jo pushed my hand down, shaking her head. A random limousine pulled from the Laurence driveway into ours. When the door opened, I tried to tell the driver he had the wrong house, but Laurie popped out of the roof of the car. It was an older limo and looked sort of tacky, but Jo's face lit up like the Fourth of July when she saw him bow his head and raise his hand like an usher to guide her into the car. I didn't like the way he turned away after helping her in, like I wasn't even there. It wasn't the attention I was jealous of; it was that I didn't think he was good enough for Jo.

Jo needed an old soul with a steady hand and durable ego. Her suitor needed to be reliable enough to guide her and keep her emotional whims grounded. Laurie, the European-raised grandson who wore Chelsea boots and a man bun—Jo wasn't ready for that type of maddening teenage dream.

"Your chariot awaits, Spring Girls!" Laurie yelled to me as I struggled to get past a big box on the seat.

"I'm not Mr. Laurence, I'm Laurie," he was telling Jo as I sat in the seat directly across from them. A three-foot gap was between the two of them. His hands were twisting off the top of a glass Coke bottle in his shirt, and Jo smiled when he handed it to her.

"Laurie Laurence, what an odd name," Jo said, and lifted the bottle to her lips.

"No"—he laughed—"my first name is Theodore, but I don't like it. If you must know, when I was young the guys in my class would call me Dora, so I changed it to Laurie when I started high school. We moved to South Italy from North; it was easy to start over."

Jo's shoulders shifted in excitement, and she tapped her Coke bottle to his. They looked like they were going to prom, but Jo refused to go to prom or homecoming, or even football games. I was at every one, cheering in the student section. We couldn't have been more different. When they took another drink, a thin rope of soda spilled over Jo's lips, down her chin, and onto the light denim dress.

"Tell me about Italy, I need to hear everything," Jo said, wiping at the stain with her hand. She was giving me a migraine.

Laurie handed her a napkin and told her it wasn't that bad. She laughed and sat back against the leather seat. I noticed a sense of familiarity with him that I thought was off, but the most I could do was talk to my sister about it later. Maybe every girl, even Jo, needed a Laurie to waltz into her life and right back out, leaving her deflowered and ripened. Maybe that's what Jo needed, to fully develop. She was sort of stuck at that shy homebody-girl stage, and that was great for her, but it made it harder to make friends in school.

Then Laurie started speaking about his school in Vevey, where the guys all have the same haircuts and they try to sleep with their tutors. When they went on their spring breaks in Switzerland, they told the other boys about their attempts, and Laurie didn't say it, but Jo and I both knew it must have made them feel more like men.

I felt weird witnessing Jo's first ongoing flirtation with a boy. We had no brothers and very few male cousins, and those cousins we had we didn't even know, so boys were like a different species to us. I got past that in seventh grade when I got my period and my chest and hips grew. Boys started to notice me, and girls started to be mean to me.

I never wanted to run the school like Shelly Hunchberg, but I wanted to have friends. I settled for a group of semi-awful girls who mostly just obsessed over YouTube and matte lipsticks. They became more awful the older we got, and they took someone else's side over mine, and from then on we hadn't spoken to one another. I didn't want Jo to go through those social trials. No matter how teachers or parents wanted to deny it, the years between sixteen and twenty were hard. Jo was at the beginning of the trial.

I zoned out whatever Laurie was feeding to Jo and stared out the window. It wasn't a far drive. I was already walking into a wasps' nest; I needed to stop worrying so much about Jo, too. I wanted to keep my sister sheltered, but I didn't think it would help her in the long run. To feel anything, you have to know the highs and the lows, I thought. If I kept Jo away from making her own mistakes, she would never learn how to navigate. I saw it all the time with my friends. Their parents coddled them and they learned nothing about how the real world worked, and the moment they were fired from Forever 21, they hysterically called home, their iPhones clutched in their shaking hands, and begged to come back. I saw it time and time again.

I still lived with Meredith and planned to until John and I were engaged. I didn't know when it would happen, but I knew it would be somewhat soon. In the military, it was even better for your reputation if you were married. I was completely ready to be the perfect officer's wife. I still had some learning to do before I mastered the domestic parts of my role, but I had the social cues down. Even though Jo didn't see it, there was more to being a military wife than baking and chauffeuring a van full of kids around. It was about being strong, being capable of running an entire household, and supporting your husband and country in the best way you could.

We passed a row of big houses, so I knew we were close to the Kings' place. Jo and Laurie were still babbling about Europe.

John Brooke would give me the best of everything. He was stable and handsome. He was the whole package. I had lusted after security my entire life. That's something Shia would never have been willing to give me—despite his family's money, he was ready to throw everything away, adventure after adventure. John could give me stability. John Brooke was a nice guy who didn't talk much, but when he did, he always had the wisest things to say.

"Meg said my dress is too big. She made me wear it," I heard Jo tell Laurie when he helped her out of the car. "You can laugh, too," she said to him while looking at me with a smile on her face.

Laurie didn't laugh.

He only looked down for a second and whispered something to her that sounded like "You don't have to wear a dress," and she stuck her tongue out at me.

I couldn't help but laugh at the tiny fleck of innocence left in her. I knew it was going to evaporate soon; I had noticed her body beginning to bloom over the past summer.

Jo grabbed my hand when we got out of the car and squeezed it tightly as we walked through the gate of the King house again. Shia was standing in the doorway, and he saw me before I could dodge him.

I tightened my grip on Jo's fingers and leaned in for Shia to kiss my cheek. I didn't want to be formal with him, but I had a role to play. So did he, which is why he kept his lips pressed to my cheek only just as long as he needed to.

I pulled away and stepped back. My maroon dress was already clinging to me in the time between leaving the limo and walking to the front door. The estate looked entirely different from the night before. It had been less than twenty-four hours since I had been here, but it was completely transformed.

The first difference was that there was no crowd. The Kings were all lined up on the stairs, waving like true diplomats, and then there was Bell Gardiner, her hair slicked back into a tight bun. Little hairpins were sticking out of the sides, and I could smell the hair spray on her from feet away.

Without looking at me, Shia smiled at Jo. "Thank you for joining us. It'll be fun, I promise." He squeezed her shoulder, and I watched her relax. He was good at that.

I looked over to the side to find Laurie staring at me. Jo looked at him and then at me, and her shoulders slouched a little. Laurie waved at me, maybe it was mockingly, but I shooed him away and gave my jacket to a man at the front who looked an awful lot like Christopher Walken.

First, I headed toward the hallway bathroom. Unfortunately, Bell and her mother stood exactly in my path. Avoiding them, I crossed through the kitchen instead, and spotted Mrs. King. She was standing next to the marble island in the center of the open kitchen. Jagged gray swirls cut through white marble, and the paint on the archways and crown moulding was the exact same shade of gray. The room looked like an old parlor.

"Meg," she said when she noticed me.

Her elegant hand held up her wineglass, and she gave me an imperial smile and waved me over. Jo and Laurie followed, and I shamelessly hoped that Mrs. King wouldn't see the stain on my sister's dress.

Mrs. King set her glass down and hugged me. Laurie kissed both of her cheeks in that way that they could do correctly, because they both had traveled to Europe. I saw Jo studying the gesture of *faire la bise*, and I heard Laurie explaining it to her as we all walked toward the dining room, and I just knew she would soon start air-kissing everyone she saw.

Jo was definitely going to leave this town the moment she turned eighteen. She reminded us of that every day. A man with red hair stared at the top of Jo's dress, and I reached over and lifted the strap up her shoulder.

My feet were killing me; I had barely let the blisters from

yesterday heal before I put my feet through torture again. Twelve chairs were spread around the long oval table, and I walked around slowly to find the seat with my name written on the little place cards. When I found my name, my seat was directly across from Shia and Bell, and four seats down from Jo. I thought about asking them to move my seat, but I didn't want to be difficult.

Throughout the dinner, course after course of delectable food was served. The entire six-course meal was a lot like a typical creole *réveillon* dinner, which was a staple of a New Orleans–style Christmas, but the Kings were having it on New Year's Day. Somehow that seemed fitting. This family could change the date of Christmas itself, and many people would follow.

During the meal, Jo talked to Laurie and Shia King about the food, although I also watched her gag at the foie gras on the little plate in front of her. She picked around half of the courses, and Shia ate a bite of soufflé from Bell Gardiner's fork. The waitstaff were quick and efficient. When Jo spilled a spoonful of leek soup on the table, they quickly covered the spot with a new napkin, and they used little hand-sized brooms to sweep the crème tablecloths between every course.

I made it through dessert, the cocktails, and the coffees that came after, and even the awkward speech by Mrs. King. She thanked her husband for his warm heart and thanked her son for spending the holidays with them, and I looked at Jo, who was looking at Laurie. I dared to be rude and pulled my cell phone out of my bag. On the home screen was a notification of a text from Amy: How is it, lucky girl? You don't even know how lucky you are!

I didn't reply to her, but I texted Meredith to tell her we made it just fine, even though it was late, then I tucked my phone back into my purse and hung it on the back of my chair. I followed most of the conversation around the table. Everyone was talking about theater and galas and their own accomplishments. I nodded along to the pissing contest around me. Honestly, it made me feel a little bitter to sit there and not have anything to say besides that I was working for Mrs. King and used to work at Sephora. Even Bell had more to say than me, and she was a freaking bartender. Shia traveled the world, his family was loaded from Mr. King's success, and Mrs. King raised three functioning members of society. I couldn't even say I was an actual makeup artist; I was just good at it. The matriarch of the house did try to help keep me afloat in the conversation and complimented my talent for makeup, telling them how I managed to make her look ten years younger. As I went to reply, Bell and her mom took control of the conversation, so I just kept my head nodding and my lips closed while the servers cleaned around us.

I needed some fresh air; I was going to lose my mind if I didn't go outside for a minute. I noticed a few seats at the table were empty, so I grabbed my glass of water and stood up. I tried to get Jo's attention, but she was waving her hands around and looking back and forth between Laurie and an older man I'd never seen before.

I figured she was fine; her cheeks were flushed and her shoulders were relaxed. Since she looked like she was lecturing them, I left.

I took my time walking down the hallway and out to the back patio. I could only hear faint voices coming from the dining room when I got outside. The patio was empty, and I sat down on a black iron chair and leaned my elbows onto the matching table.

I looked around at the perfect landscaping, and it intimidated me. So many things went into keeping a property like this. I'd always dreamed of a big house and a gorgeous yard. Yet I didn't know if I was capable of remembering to have the bushes trimmed. The twinkling lights from last night were still up, and it was a beautiful Louisiana night, about seventy degrees with a slight breeze that picked up the loose bits of my hair and pushed them back down. I was oddly at peace before my bubble was popped.

Shia's voice was the thumbtack. "Find anything interesting out here?"

I shook my head, not ready to give up my peaceful serenity outside and definitely not ready to talk to Shia.

"No. You should go back inside. Nothing out here to see."

I tried to be funny, but it just didn't land, and Shia walked toward me and sat down across from me. The chair creaked when he sat down, and I tried to imagine how it felt growing up in a fairy-tale land where even old outdoor tables are enchanting. But I knew enough to know it wasn't fair to say his life was a fairy tale.

"So, despite your having been here last night and tonight, my mom says you've been sick. Are you feeling okay, Margaret?"

He was already so close to me and he leaned in farther. The crickets were even silent; I held my breath. I could smell the honey on his lips. He was so sly in that way. He made you crave him, but then he would vanish and leave you thinking you imagined the whole thing.

"I'm fine. Thanks for asking." I turned the other way and unpinned my hair. I wondered if my makeup was still in place. I hadn't thought about it since dinner.

Did I smell like shrimp gumbo? Shia King didn't smell like

gumbo, or even the garlic-soaked artichokes I'd watched him devour. He smelled like his earthy self, like rain and lumber with a hint of cologne. His outfit surprised me the more I stared at it. I hadn't allowed myself the liberty of taking him in fully, but now it was just us, and he was staring hard at the ground.

His shirt and his jacket were almost the same color olive, and his dressy undershirt was buttoned all the way to his neck. Little black designs were printed on it, and he was wearing dark gray boots. He looked like he stepped out of New York City or Milan. I suddenly worried if he could see the outline of my strapless bra. I couldn't wear clothes like Bell Gardiner could, but I knew I looked good in that maroon dress. I just had more to cover.

"I didn't realize you and my mom were so close." He eyed me and brought a glass to his lips. "Until I heard you talking about me last night. I always knew you were more like her than me, but I didn't realize just how similar the two of you are."

"She just wants the best for you, Shia. You're her only son. They want the best for you—"

"Oh my God, Meg! Do you hear yourself? You're sitting here . . ." He paused and his eyes focused in on me. He tapped his fingers on the center of the vinelike design on the table. "You're a clone of her. Last night when I looked in the pantry, it was eerie how alike you looked. You were holding your glasses the same way."

His shoulders shuddered and I recoiled.

Part of me couldn't hide that I was flattered that Shia thought his mother and I were similar, but maybe that was why he liked me sometimes and hated me others.

. . . and he had called me *Meg* again, finally.

"You're lucky your parents care so much," I said.

Shia rolled his eyes and dropped his head back, looking up at the starry sky. "I used to think you got it, Meg. But you just don't get it. It is what it is."

The way he shook his head made me feel like he was judging me immensely.

I jutted my arms out and stood from the table. "You don't know anything about who I am or what I get."

If I had had any water left in my drink, I might have sucked it down or thrown it at him, I wasn't sure. I wanted drama; it was how we were.

"I did at one point. And you know it." His eyes were unwavering as they stuck to mine.

I stepped around my chair and past him to storm across the yard. If my shoes had been less murderous, it would have been much easier to make a classy, sassy getaway. Instead, I ended up on the ground, struggling to yank my foot from a dirt hole. Shia was standing over me, a flat look on his face as he pulled my shoe out.

The heel snapped and he pointed to my ankle. "That looks bad."

I shifted my eyes to where he was looking.

My ankle was throbbing in an unnatural way. I hadn't noticed the burning pain until he mentioned it. Which was weird. Jo would have a theory about that; she had theories for everything. I wanted to ask her.

"Here, let me help you up." Shia reached for my hands.

I jerked away and shifted my weight, shaking my head. "Get Jo. I don't need your help."

He threw his hands up in the air, but didn't say a word as he walked inside to get my sister.

I was humiliated in the worst way, and I could feel the tears stinging the backs of my eyes. I needed to get the hell out of there as soon as possible. I couldn't believe I had gone there anyway—what the hell was I thinking? I didn't know. I sat on the soft grass and waited for someone to come back. I should have stayed in my seat at the table and I wouldn't have looked like such an idiot.

Jo ran out the back door, moving so quickly in her flat boots. I should have been smart like Jo.

My skin felt clammy. "I've sprained my ankle. It was those stupid shoes, I tell you." I moved my body a little and my foot throbbed. "I don't think I can stand up."

"I told you those shoes were awful for your feet. They weren't worth it, were they?" Jo rubbed my ankle.

"I need to get home. Call a car or something." I didn't know how I would get through or around the house, let alone into the car, but I would find a way.

"Laurie!" Jo called loudly.

I scowled at her and swiped my hand through the air. "No way. Don't have him take me. I'm sure he wants to stay. Jo, I don't—"

I stopped midsentence. Laurie came strolling out of the house, Shia behind him. I was completely mortified. I bit down on my cheek and tried to lift myself up, but the second that I put all my weight on my knee, I fell back over and yelped in pain.

"Meg. Stop moving," Shia told me.

I huffed and would have told him off if Mrs. King hadn't been swirling in behind him. She looked concerned but a touch bored. It was strange; I didn't want to be the center of attention in this crowd the way I usually did.

"It's fine. I just need to get to the car," I told the gathering crowd.

"I'll take her home. It's fine," Laurie said, pulling his phone from his pockets. He grumbled a few words, hung up the phone, and shoved it back into his jeans.

I liked the way he watched Jo everywhere she went. She disappeared and came back with a big brown stain on the stomach of the dress she was wearing. She was truly a mess. Mrs. King didn't even look at Jo. It was like she wasn't even there.

"It's so early, Laurie. You're sure it's okay?" I asked.

Jo looked at him.

Laurie shook his head. "I always go early. I do, really. Let's get you to the car, it'll be pulling up any second. I'll help Jo get you home."

Laurie lifted me up in his arms before I could protest, and I watched Shia's eyes burn into his back until we disappeared into the house.

16

beth

*L*aurie came barreling through the house, Meg stuck to one
of his sides. His T-shirt was bunched into her fist as she hob-
bled. Jo was holding her up from the other side, and I checked
for blood. I didn't know why, but I guess living in an Army town
will give you different instincts from your average person.

I didn't see any blood and Meg wasn't crying or screaming,
so I rushed over to help. Meg's face was gray and she was wearing a beautiful maroon dress that now had green grass tracks
down the side of it. I dropped to my knees and gently lifted the
bottom of her dress up to check her ankle before I moved it.

"It's broken, Beth. Isn't it?" Meg cried.

Laurie stood awkwardly over Meg with his hands stuffed in
his pockets, bending at his knees.

"No, Meg. It's just sprained. Let me get some ice. Don't
move," I told her, and climbed to my feet.

When I got to the doorway of the kitchen, I called back to Jo, "Don't let her move!"

Meredith walked into the kitchen, her hair in pins and her dress dragging on the floor. "What's going on?"

I pulled open the cabinet drawer closest to her and grabbed the plastic bags. "Meg sprained her ankle at the Kings'. Looks pretty bad."

My mom pulled the freezer door open and helped me fill a bag. "Is that the Laurence boy?"

I nodded. "He seems nice."

She closed the freezer door and leaned against the counter. "I think so, too."

Meredith followed me back into the living room and thanked Laurie for helping Meg. Jo said the same to him and disappeared upstairs. She never came back. Laurie kept looking up at the staircase over and over for the next hour before he finally gave up and left. I didn't think Jo knew how to handle boys, especially tall ones with long hair like Laurie. It probably never occurred to her to even say goodbye to him.

That was Jo; she was always in her own world. It was one of her best qualities, but she had to learn when to check back in.

～

The next morning, I woke up before everyone else and started the coffeepot, fed the fish, and watered the plants. It was only eight, but I figured I should make breakfast. I didn't know if we had everything I would need, so I searched the cupboards and the pantry for ingredients.

Eggs—check.

Milk—check

Toast . . . I moved a bag of tortillas and found a loaf of wheat bread behind it. I thought a pack of bacon was somewhere in the freezer so I investigated. Underneath a bag of frozen chicken breasts, I found a pound of bacon. I turned the hot water on and let it run over the meat to thaw it. I missed my dad and how he always woke up early with me and helped make breakfast. We would talk about music while we folded laundry, and it felt so deserved, that time with my dad. Looking back, I realize I thought those hours would never end. They seemed so infinite during the year he was here, even though they shouldn't have. I should have been used to him going; we all should have eventually gotten used to it. But it was the opposite.

As I waited for the oven to heat up, I flipped the bacon over. My dad used to tell me about the concerts he and my mom would go to. They were Bob Dylan fans in the nineties, and I remember one year I heard them stumble into the old house in Texas, and my mom was laughing so hard that I thought she was crying. I hid by the doorway and watched my dad lift her off her feet after he chased her around the kitchen. I remember how tightly he hugged her to his chest when he finally caught her. The parents in my memory are so different from the ones I know now, but that's life. I was lucky to even have both of my parents under one roof.

Amy strolled into the kitchen when the bacon had begun to smell up the whole house.

"Yum." She took a seat at the table. She pulled her phone out of her pocket and didn't say another word. Mentally, I kept coming back to the fact that Amy's pajamas were too small; the pant legs stopped at least two inches above her ankles.

After a while, Meg hopped into the room and poured herself

a cup of steaming coffee as I pulled the pan of bacon out of the oven. She hopped over to the table on one foot and sat down.

"I think I spilled some," she whined when her butt hit the chair.

I told her I would wipe it up, and she smiled at me and told me thanks, that her ankle was killing her.

Jo and Meredith were the last to join us, and by the time everyone was sitting down, Meg's face was turned into a grimace and Amy's finger was still scrolling.

"Man, isn't it weird how now we are supposed to just go on with our lives after the holidays? Everything will go back to normal when you guys all go back to school," Meg said through the eggs in her mouth.

"I wish it was Christmas and New Year's all the time. Everyone would be even more stressed and have even less money," Jo sniped.

"Jo. Stop it," Meredith said, but smiled when she turned away.

We all ate breakfast, and Amy talked about some food trading thing she was doing at school when they returned from break. I offered her whatever I could, and she blew me a lipgloss kiss from where she sat. Meredith said she had sent Dad an email last night and hoped he would be able to Skype today. I felt like the calls were coming less and less lately, and I had read the emails between him and my mom about his upcoming mission. I knew that his platoon was being sent on a mission because he said that he would be gone for over a week.

I liked it much more when he stayed on the FOB. I wasn't like Jo, who read every hashtag, or like Amy, who was blissfully unaware of most current events. I was in my own lane right between, and when you added taking care of my mom and sisters on top of that, I would say I had a toll road or two on the three of them. I was worried sick over Dad, and I hoped that he would call Mom soon.

"Meg, I need a ride to work tomorrow. I can't take any more days off this month. My manager will kill me," said Jo.

She was picking at her plate. Her veggie omelet had to be cold by now. I made it before I made the French toast. Jo was the only one in the house who didn't fight over my French toast, except when Dad was home. My dad's mom taught me how to make it, using wheat bread and a little extra nutmeg and a *dash of sass*—I heard the last part in her voice. She had a Midwestern accent, even though she said there was *no such thing*. There was that voice again.

Jo and my dad were the only people who could be trusted around a plate of warm chocolate-chip cookies. Yet the two of them would eat an entire bag of chips in one sitting. Jo and her Bugles were best friends forever. The omelet I made sure as hell wasn't. Something seemed to be wrong with her.

"I can barely walk, Jo. How can I drive you anywhere?" Meg pointed to her propped ankle.

It was definitely much less swollen than last night.

"I can't miss work again, and the bus takes so long to get anywhere."

Meredith left the room, and I was going to follow her soon. Jo and Meg needed to figure this out on their own, and my mom seemed to be a little spaced out, anyway. She was probably exhausted with worry.

"Meredith!" Jo said in a calm voice. "Are you busy Tuesday? I can get a ride there but not home."

Meredith popped back in and asked what time she got off and told her that she may have to wait an extra twenty minutes before she could get her.

"I have to pick up Aunt Hannah from work, too," she explained.

"Thank you." Jo smiled at Meredith.

When my mom left again, Amy turned to Jo and said, "It's not her fault that she can't drive you. She's hurt."

Jo seemed to consider what Amy was saying. She spun herself in the chair to face Meg. "I'm sorry. I know it's not your fault. I'm tired and finishing that piece. It's stressful."

Meg couldn't even try to hide the surprise on her face. She was always so collected, and I could tell that Jo's honest apology shook her a little. Me, too.

"Th-a-a-a-nks," Meg replied, drawing out the word, sounding confused. "It's fine. I know you have a lot going on."

Meg's shock transferred right on over to me, and something occurred to me. Meg and Jo had been spending a lot more time together than they ever had before. I had been hearing their voices at night lately, chatting away while everyone was in bed. I hadn't heard that sound since we were kids, when Meg used Jo as her cosmetic guinea pig after bedtime. Jo's pillow was always covered in makeup the next morning.

"And why don't you just have Laurie take you, since he's your boyfriend now?" Amy touched Jo's arm, and Jo slid her hand away. "Who would have thought Jo would have such a hot boyfriend. He's almost *too* hot." Amy touched the screen of her phone and looked back up to the three of us.

Jo's response was flat. "Shut the hell up."

"Just sayin'." Amy smiled and looked at Meg for approval. She worshipped everything about Meg.

A few seconds passed, and Jo stood from the table. "I'm out," she announced, and left the room. I was next. I needed to finish my History assignment on my mom's laptop before midnight. I knew I would regret working on a World War Two assignment right before bed. It was one hundred percent going to give me nightmares, but I was behind on my schoolwork because of lazy Holiday Fever.

When I walked into the living room, Meredith was sitting in Dad's recliner with her eyes closed. I bent down over her to grab the laptop from the side of the chair; she opened her eyes, scaring the hell out of me.

She started laughing when I gasped.

"Sorry, baby," she said with a smile.

She always looked so young when she smiled. My mom was beautiful, but sometimes it seemed like she had aged five years in one. I was worried about her and couldn't wait for my dad to be home.

"I have an assignment to work on. I'll bring it back before I go to bed," I told her. She smiled at me, looking a little sleepy.

"That's fine. You can do it down here if you want. I'll be quiet. I'm just going to watch *Criminal Minds*." She lifted the lever on the recliner, and the footrest sprung to life.

I laughed. "No way you'll be quiet if you're watching *Criminal Minds*."

She talked through every scene, constantly trying to guess who the killer was and shouting at the TV.

She laughed and shrugged. "I still think the FBI should have a watch on the writers of that show. It's some seriously twisted shit." She said that every single time we watched the show together. I was the only one who could stand to watch it. Amy was too squeamish, Meg was too big of a chicken, and Jo was too literal. She would pick apart the plot holes and legalities of everything.

I loved this time with my mom, when she was happy and distracted.

"Come on, Beth, stay down hereeee," she whined, and pressed her hands together like she was praying.

I tried to hold a straight face as I sat down on the couch and tossed her the remote. "Only talk during the commercials. Promise?"

She dragged her thumb and index finger along her lips like she was zipping them and pretended to toss me the key.

17

*I*n the few weeks that passed since Christmas, things had changed.

Jo and Laurie became inseparable.

Now that Shia was out of the country again, saving the world in his way, Meg was back to work at the King house. John Brooke would be home very soon, and it was all Meg would talk about. She was always so flustered while pretending not to be.

Meredith kept herself busy, with Aunt Hannah coming over more than usual.

Everyone was hunky-dory except Amy, who got suspended from school for continuing to trade food in class after the teacher told her multiple times not to.

Apparently, the principal was alerted when Amy was caught with a full-sized key lime pie inside her desk. A pie. In her desk. When she'd asked me to make it for her, I didn't bat an eye. I figured it was for some school celebration, so I made her one from scratch that was supposed to be a homemade replica of Petite Amelie's recipe.

So, Amy was home with me for a week and Meredith asked me to teach her while I was home. My online classes only took me around two hours a day to finish, so I had plenty of time during the next five days of her suspension. My sister was sitting across from me at the kitchen table; we had the house to ourselves that morning.

"I want to go to Laurie's house again," she complained through a spoonful of her cereal.

I dipped my spoon into the bowl and popped soggy rings of Cheerios into my mouth and, in the same mumbled manner she had spoken to me, asked, "Why?"

"Because!" Her sigh was heavy and dramatic. She was always the emotional one, more so than Meg even. Amy always seemed to be floating above the clouds. Meg was the most grounded of us, Amy the least.

"They have everything there. A big yard. They even have a golf cart parked in the backyard," she whined.

I thought of the scooters and the bikes my parents had spent months saving for and had to remind myself that Amy was only twelve. She didn't understand that she was being a spoiled little brat. "How do you know?"

Amy was always sneaking around. I heard Meredith telling Aunt Hannah that she should put a password on her laptop if she didn't want Amy to go through it.

"I just do." Amy had a glimmer in her eye as she went on. "We should just move in over there. There's a library for Jo, a piano for you, and Meg loves the greenhouse. I'm sure we can find something for Meredith."

It was true, Old Mr. Laurence had the most beautiful grand piano in his house. I had only seen it up close once, last week, when I went into the house for the first time.

I smiled at Amy. "We might run into a problem getting Old Mr. Laurence to give up that big house to us."

Amy nodded, her blond curls rubbing against her shoulders. "You could convince him. One of us could even marry the old man!"

"Ew. You wouldn't!" I gaped at my sister, mostly teasing, but I didn't like the way she was already talking—in only the seventh grade—about marrying an elderly man for money. Who knew where she got that—maybe Meg?

"I would! So should you," Amy said in a faux Southern accent. "I would do just about anything for a better life. If I was Old Mr. Laurence's wife, I could paint all day and drink tea and be a proper Southern woman." Raising her spoon up, Amy lifted her pinkie into the air.

I laughed a little at the change in her voice, but I didn't like how quickly this conversation had gone awry. I needed to talk to Meredith about Amy's comment, but honestly, I didn't know what to say. I didn't know anything about getting married, or even talking to the opposite sex.

Instead of giving her bad advice, I said, "If you put as much energy into math as you do planning your life as a trophy wife, you could at least have a diploma."

Amy smiled, and the dimples in her cheeks flashed at me. Her teeth were so straight, but just a little too small for her face, making her look younger than she was.

"Whatevs."

"That term is never going to be a thing, Amy."

Eye roll. "It already is, Beth."

"Be happy with what you have."

She shook her head. "I want more."

"Well, if you want more, then work for more. No one is going to hand you anything, and the sooner you realize that, the easier your life will be. Look at Dad: he does all of this for us, to make sure we have a good life." I reached across the table and touched her hand. "I know it's hard, but just try and be a little grateful."

Amy looked down at the table, and then back up at me. "I thought he did it because of his patriotic duty?"

I laughed a little. "That too. Now, let's go get your math booklet and let's do some work."

With a sigh, Amy took one last bite of her breakfast and followed me to the coffee table in the living room, where I spent two hours teaching her how to long divide. Her school textbook was so much more advanced than I thought it would be. She was already learning to subtract fractions. I don't think I was learning that until at least ninth grade. I helped her add and subtract negatives without using our fingers, and she giggled when I got a few of the answers wrong. I quizzed her and she got better each time.

Sitting across from Amy, I felt like a big sister for the first time in a while. It felt like I was living inside one of those pure, family-friendly, Americana-themed television series where siblings hold hands and never want to rip each other's heads off. Meg used to watch one of those shows, and we were all obsessed with it, but for the life of us we couldn't remember what it was called. We remembered that a curly-haired girl talked to the moon, and that her neighbor had a crush on her, but not the title. A few months back we'd spent an afternoon searching the internet for it, but failed to find it again.

I got along with all of my sisters, usually. Jo and Amy fought the most, and consequently they hardly spent any time together. Amy and I would hang out more since I was always at home.

I wondered if she liked hanging out with me the same way

she did Meg. I doubted it. Meg taught Amy how to straighten her curls with a flatiron and how to paint little flowers on her big-toe nail. When they were speaking, Jo taught Amy how to write short poems; they would read them out loud to each other, and I'd heard Jo telling Amy ghost stories about the French Quarter. Last Halloween—while Aunt Hannah watched Amy—me, Meg, Jo, and Meredith went on a ghost tour in the Quarter. The theme of the spooky tour was all about female murderers. It was awesome. Jo told Amy all about it when we got back and got cool points for that. Knowing Jo, she might have been trying to scare her sister, but instead it intrigued Amy.

I tried to think of what I brought to the sister table for Amy . . . But when nothing came to mind, I distracted myself by asking, "What do you want to be when you grow up?"

"Old Mr. Laurence's wife." She laughed.

"Seriously."

She shrugged and looked up at the ceiling. "I want to be like Meg."

"Meg? In what way?"

I didn't want to say that Meg hadn't accomplished much in her life yet, but I had a feeling that Amy meant that she wanted to look like Meg.

"You know"—Amy shrugged—"I want to wear lipstick and tight dresses and be popular and pretty."

Amy's shirt had a little stain on the collar, and I wondered who'd taught her to care so much about being pretty. "It's not your job to be pretty. It's your job to make the best for yourself, but it isn't your job to be pretty. You don't owe anyone that."

"Sure, Beth."

And honestly I was a little surprised she'd even been listening to what I'd said.

18

*L*ater that night, Jo was late for dinner and Meredith sent me next door to collect her. Meredith had strict rules about all of us being home for dinner during the week; it was one of her things. We could go out before and after if we wanted, though I never found myself wanting to. I enjoyed peace and quiet and conversations with my mom and helping her with the daily routine that my dad left behind when he was deployed.

Jo knew Meredith's rule and had never broken it until that week, when she was late three days in a row. Meg was the only other one to ever break the dinner rule, but since she'd turned eighteen, Meredith let her do as she pleased, for the most part.

Meredith could have gone to fetch Jo herself, but lately I'd gotten the feeling that with each day that passed it was a little harder for Meredith to leave the house. We all helped as much as we could. Jo had been working much more than before and started paying her own cell phone bill. Meg was the taxi driving us around, and Amy . . . well, Amy was young and didn't help much. When I was Amy's age, I was already helping with dishes and laundry, but Amy was a very young twelve, and sometimes it seemed like she didn't have a clue about responsibility.

As I slid my feet into my sandals, I reminded myself that I was helping Meredith by going to fetch Jo. I hadn't left the house since I got Jo from the Laurence house yesterday. Sometimes I would take long walks around the neighborhood alone, just to get some air and comfort Meredith. I knew she worried about my anxiety, but I was happier being inside and didn't mind my own company. I preferred it.

Meredith was trying to find the bay leaf in the pot roast and Amy was setting the table as I got ready to leave the house. It usually took me a few minutes to make sure I had everything. I sometimes wished I would never have to leave the house. I even had this whole invention idea to use those tubes like the bank does and send food and supplies through fast tubes so people would never have to leave their houses.

"Beth, are you almost ready? Dinner will be done in ten minutes."

"Yes, Meredith." I walked out the back door and crossed the yard.

I looked for any hint of life inside the bow window in the back of the Laurence house. The kitchen looked empty from where I stood. Laurie and Jo were inside somewhere, and maybe that would be it. I hoped. Old Mr. Laurence always intimidated me with his bushy eyebrows and scowling face. I had never seen a person who looked so annoyed at being alive. I wasn't exactly a ray of sunshine, but Old Mr. Laurence made me look like a rainbow.

Laurie didn't seem to have his grandfather's permanent scowl. I had seen him be soft with Jo last Saturday, when he stayed at our house so late that they fell asleep on the couch together. Jo's head was leaning on Laurie's arm, and his mouth was slightly open as he breathed in and out. His body was so long that I almost tripped over his legs when I tried to wake them up.

Their friendship made so much sense to me. Their insurgent personalities found each other at an Army post full of people who follow commands in almost every part of their life. I thought that I would make a good soldier. Jo, not so much. She loved to question authority in every bit of her life. Sometimes this got her in trouble, like when she busted Old Mr. Laurence's window, or when she wrote a full-page spread in her high school's newspaper about the effects of PTSD on soldiers returning from war, and her teacher, Mr. Geckle, basically told her she had no chance of that article getting into the White Rock High paper, so she slipped it in just before printing. Luckily, she only got one day of in-school suspension as a punishment. I always hoped she wouldn't get herself into too much trouble, but knew that slipping pages into the newspaper was child's play compared to what she was capable of.

When Jo was with Laurie, I felt a little less worried about her. And Josephine was the sister I worried about the most. She was the most inspired of us all, and she had passion that could burn a field of wildflowers, but I didn't know if she would be able to put it out when need be. She needed Dad. She needed someone who could help her turn her fiery passion into productive change. Jo was always a fighter, from refusing to have her Barbie date Ken, to walking out of class when asked to dissect a frog.

Dad was always good at bringing her back to earth. He explained to her that Barbie doesn't have to date Ken, but they *can* be friends, and he wrote a note excusing her from the rest of the dissection project.

I missed Dad, too. I missed how Meredith was when he was around. I knew as a military kid I was supposed to be used to this life, the yearlong deployments with only one year between. My life was supposed to just go on as normal when he was gone, but sometimes it was hard. I often found Meredith curled up in his recliner, with a wooden picture frame in her hand. Inside the five-by-seven square was a picture of my dad before he became an officer, Staff Sergeant Frank Spring, in full battle rattle. His heavy gun was in his hands, and his smile took up his whole face. He always looked younger in pictures, Meredith would say. She would tell me so many things about him when I would help get her to bed from the recliner. Some nights she would cry, and other nights she would smile and tell me a happy memory from when they were young. I knew Meredith missed being young, and that made me a little sad for her.

When I gently rapped on the Laurences' door, my heart was pounding. I hated to be in situations like this, when I wasn't sure what was going to happen. I liked when I knew where I was and who would be at the door. I wasn't great at handling the unexpected. I counted to ten on my fingers and looked through the big window again. The kitchen was gloomy, all old cherrywood and dark granite. A huge clock was hanging on the wall, set to 9 p.m., but when I pulled my phone from my pocket and hit the home button, it was only twenty minutes after five.

I knocked again, this time a little harder, then glanced past the kitchen into the living room. A row of picture frames adorned the mantel. I couldn't see the images inside them, but there were a lot. A shadow moving in the kitchen made me jump and edge away from the door. The shadow came closer and I saw a flash of white hair.

Dammit, Jo.

Old Mr. Laurence pulled the door open and waved me inside, then turned his back to me. He didn't make eye contact before he turned, he didn't say hi . . . nothing. He did lead me to the staircase and wave his hand in the air again. I nodded to thank him and walked up the stairs; when he disappeared, I ran the rest of the way up. It reminded me of when I was young and would run from the dark hallway bathroom and jump into my bed, clearing the chance of something under it grabbing me.

I didn't know which room was Laurie's because when I came yesterday, I met them in the library. Now, I passed a bathroom with a big claw-foot tub and a walk-in shower. The hallway was dark, even though the sun wasn't fully gone for the night.

When I got to the next-to-last door, I could see a sliver of light cast onto the hardwood floor in the room. Walking slowly by it, I realized this was Laurie's room. My sister was lying on his floor with a book in her hand, her usual relaxed face was wreathed in a smile, and she didn't notice me standing in the doorway. Laurie was on the bed, his eyes on his cell phone, and the speaker on his desk was playing soft electronic music. I knocked on the door and said my sister's name. Laurie called me inside.

"You're late for dinner, so Meredith sent me over here to get you."

Laurie didn't say anything, just lifted his head up, waved at me with his free hand, his phone in the other. I noticed that he had on loose-wearing bracelets made of strings and beads.

Jo checked her phone and nodded. "We were just talking about the library here. You should see it. There's a huge piano in there, it's so dope." Jo sounded like a teenager from a Karen McCullah movie.

"I'm the only one who plays it, and seriously, I barely touch it. My grandpa's had it for-fucking-ever," Laurie commented from the bed. "Come in, Beth, you can sit down."

I walked to the chair in the corner of the room. A stack of magazines was atop it, which Laurie indicated I should move so I could sit down. I sank into it, and the black leather was warm and smelled like cedar and tobacco. A long, body-length pillow was on the floor next to the wallpapered wall. The Laurence house had more of a New Orleans feel to it than ours, likely because it was much older than ours. We were only the second family to live in our house, even though Fort Cyprus was so very, very old. Meredith said there had been a fire in the original house, started by the youngest daughter of the last family to live there. The house burned to the ground and the father was severely burned, but everyone survived.

Our house was a newer build with gray siding and a deep porch. The Laurence house was in the Greek Revival style, on the corner of Nightshade and Iris, and it had more books and tchotchkes than I'd ever before seen in my fifteen years. There was an old feel in the air of the place. It tasted like cinnamon and clove. There were shadows in every corner, and I immediately saw what Jo saw in it. Jo craved danger, and here it was, in the safest way possible. The creepy house didn't have a personality like that of our house. In the Laurence house, darkness crept around the walls and lingered through the thick air.

Laurie's room was full of things. Everywhere I looked there were posters, records, books, barely a foot of uncovered space anywhere.

"Beth, what kind of music do you like? Your sister was just telling me you love Bastille."

Jo didn't say anything and I didn't look at her. Laurie was

nice, but I hated talking to people I didn't know. It made my skin itch.

With a burning breath in my lungs, I responded, "I do. I play the piano and keyboard. A little on guitar, but I'm awful at it."

"Shut the hell up—you are not!" Jo said from the floor. She clicked her feet together. Her black bootees were missing a buckle on one foot. I meant to fix it, but had forgotten. She broke it the same night Meg and Shia got into their last big fight a few months ago. Until this week, Jo had gone back to wearing sneakers and lace-up boots.

I felt my entire face burn. "I'm not that good."

"I'm sure you're great." Laurie smiled at me and set his phone down.

My cell phone started ringing from my bag, and Jo sat up. The ringtone was an Ed Sheeran song that my mom had listened to every single day since my dad left.

"She's calling." I stood up quickly. I gave Laurie a little wave and waited for Jo by the door.

She told me and Laurie that she had to run to the bathroom for a moment. Well, technically she said, "I'm gonna pee. I'll meet you downstairs."

So I walked downstairs alone. I passed the room that I could see from the window in our kitchen. Even before I went inside, I had known about the piano from seeing Jo watch Laurie play it through the window, and I saw it up close and personal when I came into the house the first time. I looked behind me, hoping no one would be around. It was clear. There were always house-keepers or someone coming to the house, or worse, I didn't want to run into Old Mr. Laurence again.

I walked over to the piano. The sleek Seiler was positioned just in front of a wide, oak-paned bay window. It was the window I'd often watch Laurie play through. I slid my pointer finger over a sharp black key, and a thin layer of dust coated the tip when I pulled it away. I blew it off and sat down on the bench. The typically quick beat of my heart slowed slightly as I rolled my shoulders and lifted my hands in the air, my thumbs hovering over middle C. I didn't know how loud the instrument was going to be, but I tapped my thumb on the key to gauge it. It was pretty low, and I cared slightly less if someone caught me now that I was sitting here, touching the keys. It had been so long since I had played on anything but a cheap keyboard, and since Meredith let me start homeschool, I had been using the old keyboard my parents got me for Christmas four years before.

After playing for a few seconds I realized I wasn't playing a song I knew; my fingers were playing the familiar keys of a song I was working on before I left school. I gave myself a few more seconds to play before I pulled my hands away and left the room.

Seeing a shadow in the hallway on my way out, I hoped it was Jo or Laurie.

19

meg

John was coming home today.

I couldn't believe he was finally coming home.

I had been counting down the days and the hours and now the minutes until he was back at Fort Cyprus. I was dressed in a long black shirt with a heart neckline and cutout shoulders. I wore a peekaboo shirt once before with John and he couldn't keep his hands off me. I hoped it would be the same this time. I had been playing over so many scenarios in my head regarding how it would go when John got back to me.

I sat down at my vanity and checked my email on my cell phone.

I had one, from John. My heart sped up and I clicked it immediately.

The message was from only a few minutes ago. The subject line read *Tell me*.

Hey Meg,

What's up? I've been thinking a lot about when I get home and I
don't think I can do this anymore. I'm confused.
    I'm sorry.

2nd Lieutenant Brooke

I read the message again and felt the blood drain from my face.
After the fourth read, I tossed my phone onto the vanity
like it was on fire. My makeup-brush canister went flying and
scattered brushes all over the floor. They rolled past my feet,
and a thick kabuki brush stopped at the cutout toes of my Steve
Maddens. I had gotten a bloodred pedicure because John liked
my toes painted. He told me that once.

I remembered every compliment he had ever given me.

John Brooke didn't say much. His words came less often, but
that made me appreciate them more.

I was trying to be rational, to think before I made any moves,
but it was hard. I didn't know if I should respond, delete it, or
forward it to someone for a second opinion.

Where was this coming from? John would be home that
night, in just two hours! What could have happened in the last
day and a half that would make him so confused? The last time
we talked, he teased me about my dislike of superhero movies,
and I promised to watch at least one with him. He talked about
his mother up in Maine and his sister who had just had her
third baby. There were no signs of anything being off.

I told him I couldn't wait to touch him again. I went into a
little detail on what I had planned for him. The line was silent
for a beat, then he sucked in a breath and told me I was killing

him. It made me melt from the inside out, and I couldn't wait to touch him. I thought we would be in a warm hotel bed by ten tonight. I thought he would be inside me, telling me how much he missed me as he made love to me. How much he needed me and felt lost without me. In the morning, we would have fancy hotel pancakes with things like purees and powdered sugar on the side. I was supposed to feed him fancy pancakes and tease him until he rolled me over onto my back and made love to me on high-thread-count sheets.

What would I tell people?

What was I supposed to tell *Mrs. King*? Oh, you know, John Brooke broke up with me instead of proposing, and now I'm single and Shia and Bell Gardiner are still engaged, and I'm single, working for you. Did I mention I'm single again?

How could John do this to me? And through fucking email? It shook me to the bone, all of my muscles aching at the same time. This feeling was insanity itself. The burning anxiety of the social failure alone was enough to put me in an early grave— add to that being single again and dealing with everyone hearing that he ended things through email.

I should have known it was all too good to be true. This was a typical move made by the ever-predictable men in my life. My ex-boyfriend River had done the same thing, only through text message, and after sending private pictures of me to half the school.

To walk into a computer lab and have my picture blinding me from every screen . . .

I still didn't know who did that, but it was probably one of my group of old "friends." From River, to them, to John. I shouldn't have even been surprised that this pattern continued in my life.

"What's going on?" Jo's voice came to my ears as if through a tunnel.

I didn't know what to say to Jo about what was happening in my world. I didn't know if she was old enough to handle it, or if my ego was durable enough to take a hit like this. Looking back, I cared way too much about what people thought of me, but at the end of the day, my reputation was more important than anything. I had worked hard to build it back up when we PCS'ed to Fort Cyprus. Though I could feel my image slipping between my fingers, I fought against it. I wasn't ready to let the veil slip away from my life. I straightened my back.

"Nothing." I swallowed. I could feel the sting of tears.

My eyes moved to Jo but she wasn't looking at me. She was looking at the mess I'd made on the floor. She picked up my phone from where it was lying on the vanity, facedown and covered in white powder.

She looked down at the screen, and I just let her. I changed my mind so quickly—wasn't that part of going crazy?

"Read the screen." I sighed in defeat.

If John was confused, I needed to try to clear his head. But if there was no chance, then I might as well start the breakup narrative before he could.

Jo's eyes widened as she read the email. "What the hell does this mean?"

"I don't know, Jo." My eyes burned hotter with the threatening tears.

"Isn't he supposed to be here in a few hours?" Jo stepped over the mess I'd made and sat down on the edge of my bed. "Did you write him back?"

"No!" I shook my head. "Should I?" I was reluctant to admit that I didn't know what the hell to do.

"I would. He's your boyfriend. You should be able to call him."

Like it was super-obvious that I should be able to call John and just talk it out simply because he was my boyfriend and that was that. Oh, Jo. She had so much to learn about boys and relationships and how to navigate the minefield.

"You don't get it," I told her.

"How don't I?"

"You've never had a boyfriend until Laurie—"

Her eyes went wide and a flush touched down her neck and up to her cheeks. "Laurie *isn't* my boyfriend."

"I can't just call him. It doesn't work like that. If I call him, he's going to do one of two things. He's going to *really* break up with me, or not answer. Both are horrible options. Right now he's just *confused*."

Now Jo was confused, and I thought it was fascinating and a little simple of her. "So . . . you just wait until . . ." She made it seem so black-and-white, but nothing about this was anything but gray.

My phone made a noise in Jo's hand and she almost dropped it to the floor.

"Email," she said, so gently, "it's an email. From John Brooke."

I turned back around and looked at her through the vanity mirror. She was holding the phone up so I could see the screen. I felt wild. And hunted. And scrambling for solid ground. With a deep breath I told her to read it to me.

Without hesitation, she started reading. "'Hey Meg, I'm sorry for what I said earlier. I didn't mean it. I'll see you tonight. I can't wait. Second Lieutenant Brooke.'"

I stared at Jo and waited for the blood to start pumping through my body. "See, he was just having a little cold feet.

Everything is fine. If I would have called him, it just would have ruined everyth—"

Another email alert.

"John again." Jo's eyes were on the screen.

My heart pounded. *What is going on?* "Read it!" I yelled at her.

"'Meg, I really can't do this. Don't call me or text me again. I'm sorry. Second Lieu—'"

John's words coming out of Jo's mouth were so heavy on my chest, I didn't want to hear any more. "I got it!" I yelled.

I wanted to grab my phone from her hands before it dinged again, but I couldn't move. My head was spinning and I was running my hands over my jeans. I hooked my fingers in the rips and tugged.

"I'm sorry, Meg." Jo was next to me. She raised her hand into the air like she was going to touch me, but she couldn't do it. My sister was never affectionate, and that was okay.

"It's fine."

I looked at myself in my mirror and tried to find what John Brooke no longer wanted about me. Immediately I thought about River and Texas and wondered if someone told John that he was dating the whore of Fort Hood. That had to be it. It couldn't have been my styled hair, the curve of my boobs. It had to be that he found out about my past there.

I stared at the thick eyelashes glued to my eyelids. The box said *Minx*, and the eyelashes had a sexy curve to them. Were they too much?

My cheekbones were shimmering and my lips were plumped and painted a deep red. I took so long getting ready that day, wanting to look perfect for our reunion. I felt like an idiot, all dolled up for a man who thinks email is an appropriate form of relationship communication.

It had been months since I had last seen John. Our reunion was supposed to be special and reaffirming. I had painted my nails, buffed my heels, and was wearing sexy red lace panties and a matching push-up bra. I made sure my skin smelled like coconut, and I used my last paycheck from Mrs. King to buy a new pair of Steve Maddens. I had managed to look French Quarter Ritz-Carlton appropriate.

I couldn't imagine what people inside that posh hotel wore. I remember hearing the Kings had their anniversary party in one of the ballrooms there. Shia had complained about the old-fashioned, Southern-money feel of the hotel, that they hadn't redecorated in one hundred years.

Now I would never see it. I wouldn't know.

I scraped my fingers through my hair, yanking out the bobby pins holding the unmanageable small fringe behind my ears. I grabbed my makeup wipes and pulled back the sticker so quickly that it ripped.

Jo was silent as I wiped the dark lipstick from my lips. I'm sure she could feel the shame rolling off me in sticky, sinful waves, crashing at my feet. I wore my best lipstick for him, and that meant something, especially since I couldn't even use my discount on it.

I tried to make myself laugh about caring about my smeared lipstick over my shredded life. I wished that I didn't care as much as I did, but that just wasn't real—and I wanted something, anything, in my life to feel real. Even if it was a horrible sensation.

My fake eyelashes were stuck to the glass on my vanity counter, and I searched for something between my smudged lipstick to the tips of my polished toes and saw Jo, bright eyed and natural and brilliant behind me.

"Why don't you want to get married, Jo?" I hoped she could bear the weight of my question.

"Shit like this," she said, with half a smile.

"Seriously."

She shrugged and sat down on the corner of her bed. "I don't know. It's not that I don't want to, I just don't think it's something that I need to be focusing on right now"—she paused—"or anytime soon. I want to be a journalist, a writer, more than a wife. I'm fucking sixteen, dude."

Her answer sounded so simple. So juvenile but so knowing all at once. Only Jo could do that.

"It's not that I just want to be someone's wife, Jo. I want to have a job and stuff, I just want someone to enjoy my life with. You were too young to remember when Mom and Dad actually acted like they loved each other; maybe that's why you don't care as much."

Jo sucked in air through her lips; the sound almost seemed like a laugh. "I don't think that has anything to do with it."

I wasn't sure if it did, but it made a little more sense than me just being desperate for male attention and affection. I wanted what I saw my parents had had at one point. I still remembered when my dad came home from Afghanistan two deployments ago and the look on his face when he saw my mom running to him. So many people were on that field during the welcome-home ceremony, but she found him before we did, and she let go of Amy's hand, shoved it into Beth's, and took off for him.

I didn't think I would ever be able to forget the way he held her and the tears in his eyes when he picked Amy up and held her to his chest. She was about eight at the time and we all wore

T-shirts with our last name on the back and whatever randomness we decided to paint on them with the sticky paint tubes.
Amy's said WELCOME HOME DAD with the stick figure version of
our family. My dad asked my mom to keep those shirts for him,
to make them into a quilt someday.

My dad was a good man, and John Brooke was, too. What
was so bad about wanting to spend my life with a good man?

"Do you know anyone who's in love beside your own parents?" I asked.

Jo shrugged. "In real life?"

"What other life is there?"

She looked at me, then at her hands. Her fingers ran over
her comforter. "Books, TV. So many lives."

I wanted to correct her, to make sure she didn't actually
think that words in a book from the inside of an author's mind
or actors on a screen in our living room were the same thing as
reality. I thought she had to know better; she was just being her
whimsical, artsy self.

"Oh, Jo, you have no idea what you're talking about." I
sighed. I loved her, so I would be gentle with her, but she was a
child. She was smart about some things for sure, but she knew
nothing about relationships. It worried me. Imagining Jo as a
mother to a newborn was like imagining Shia King wearing a
crisp black suit in a courtroom.

"I disagree, Meg." Jo picked at her nails, not looking at me.

I made a little noise of annoyance. "Okay." I laughed a little.
Sometimes she thought that she knew everything. "That doesn't
mean you're right. You haven't had any experience dating at all."

Jo sighed and her hands lifted from her lap and she ran her
open fingers over the front of her hair. When we were young, Jo
had the worst cowlick right in the front, just next to her middle

part. At sixteen it was still there, but slightly less noticeable, her hair was so thick.

"Do we have to keep talking about this?"

"What?" My insides felt like I was hollow. Hollow and anxious at the mention of John's name. I felt pathetic and confused. "My boyfriend who is supposed to here in a few hours just broke up with me via email!" My voice rose and my throat burned.

I stared at my phone by Jo's lap. It hadn't gone off in a while, but somehow I could still hear the email notification echoing in the silence in my room.

My chest rose and fell—and Jo wasn't even trying to comfort me. She was just sitting there with her eyes slowly moving around the room and her hands calmly folded on her lap. Oblivious and righteous.

"Just go, Jo." I sighed.

I didn't know what else to say to her, and I knew better than to think Jo would say any of the things I needed to hear.

Where was Beth?

20

I was done crying by the time I settled on the couch between Beth and Amy. Meredith made comfort food for us,
and I sat there with a blanket pulled up to my chin and a bowl
of mac and cheese on my lap. My feet were stretched out on
Amy's lap, and she was almost asleep. It wasn't even eight yet but
I was ready to go to bed, too. Jo was sitting on the floor with her
laptop on her legs, and I wasn't mad at her anymore. I couldn't
blame her for not caring about something she didn't understand.

Selfishly, I wished for someone to break her heart, but then
I took it right back. I wouldn't wish that on her. I changed the
name in my head and wished into the universe that Bell Gardiner would have her heart broken. I didn't take that back.

"There's a car in the driveway," Meredith said. She leaned
over and pulled back the thick curtain covering the front window.

I took another bite of noodles and cheese and waited for the
headlights to disappear in the window. Since we lived in a cul-
de-sac, people often used our driveway to turn around.

I heard a car door shut, and Meredith used her legs to push
in the footrest of Dad's recliner.

"It's a man," she said.

My first thought was that my dad was home early to surprise us, but that wasn't likely; he knew how much Meredith hated surprises.

"Who is it?" Beth asked.

"I can't tell . . . it looks like John—"

I shot up from the couch and ran to the window, bowl in my hand and all. I saw John Brooke walking up my yard, wearing his uniform and a serious expression across his familiar face.

"What is he doing here!" My voice came out as a screech, and Beth was by my side in an instant.

Amy's face twisted in horror. "Oh, no! Meg, he's here and you're wearing *that*."

I looked down. My flower-print shorts and pink tank top couldn't have been further from what I had planned on wearing when I saw him again. Why the hell was he here? Wasn't his string of emails enough?

Beth took the bowl of mac and cheese from me just as his knuckles started tapping on the front door.

"Don't let him in!" I shouted into the panic filling the room.

"That son of a—" Meredith started.

"Why not? Maybe he—" Jo started, too.

I couldn't think straight. Why did I take my makeup off? My eyes had to be swollen. Why was he here?

"Yes or no, Meg?" Meredith asked when she was on her feet.

I thought about it for a second. Should I say my piece to John Brooke? Should I let him have it for breaking up with me over email, then showing up to my house?

He knocked again.

"Let him in," I said, hating that I looked like shit.

Jo was a statue, sitting on the floor still, typing away.

My mouth tasted like truffle, and I knew I smelled like a mushroom and looked like hell. My fingers smoothed over my hair as Meredith opened the front door.

"Hey, Meredith, how are you?" John's voice was so deep.

Meredith turned to look at me, and John stepped into the light. He was wearing his West Point uniform, and his hair was cropped shorter than I'd ever seen it. His blue eyes found me, and I couldn't help the cry that ripped through my lungs and splattered all over the floor. John's face fell and he moved toward me, his hat in his hands.

I turned around and rushed down the hallway to my room and slammed the door behind me. Heavy footsteps pounded toward me, and a soft knock touched the door, but John opened it before I could respond.

"Hey," he said shakily.

I stared at him in all his West Point glory. His entire body seemed to have grown from the last time I'd laid eyes on him. The gold buttons on his gray uniform were so shiny. He looked so polished, and I . . . well, I looked like a damn mess.

"What do you want, John?" I hoped that I sounded intimidating and in control, not like a nineteen-year-old who'd just spent the last two hours crying over a boy.

Except John didn't look like a boy anymore. He looked like a man.

"What? Meg, what's going on?"

I ignored the voice in my head telling me to look in the mirror on my vanity. Seeing my mess of a self would only make things worse.

"What's going on?" I laughed. "You tell me, John. What the hell is going on? Why did you even come here?"

His reddish-blond brows pulled together over his light eyes, and he took a step backward, toward my door.

"Go ahead and leave if you want to!" I yelled at him, all sense of sanity going out the window closest to me.

"What the hell? You knew I was coming. We had plans, remember?"

"Yes! We did. But you're confused, remember? You must be so confused that you forgot to email me and say you're coming after all!"

I felt my legs getting weaker the louder my voice went. I sat down at the edge of my bed and put my head in my hands.

"Meg." John's voice was soft. "I don't understand what's going on. I don't know what you're talking about. I came to pick you up so we could go to the Quarter for the weekend. I just got in, picked up my car, and came here."

I looked up at him. *What?*

Was he lying? I looked at the clear confusion on his face and the tiny movement in his shaking hands. I didn't know what to make of this.

"Are you trying to tell me that you changed your mind?"

John walked toward me, and I flinched when he grabbed my hands. He dropped them. He knelt in front of me and I focused on the structure of his gray uniform, the brown stitching, the high collar reaching up under his neck. His face was red, it always was a little, but he really did look confused.

"Meg, please tell me, what's going on?" John's soft voice touched me in featherlight caresses, soothing my anger from his rejection.

"You emailed me." I grabbed my phone from under my pillow where it was charging and yanked it toward me.

"Emailed you?" His freckled hands grabbed mine and

wrapped around the phone and my trembling hands. I pulled away and he let me, and I opened the email chain.

Holding the phone in my hand, I lifted the screen to him. His fingers wrapped around the sides of my iPhone and his eyes strained to read the small font.

A few seconds later he started shaking his head. "I didn't send that. I didn't. I wouldn't do that, Meg."

I looked at him and let his claim sink in. Was he lying? I searched his eyes and I couldn't tell. Who would do this to me if he didn't?

Shia was the first person who popped into my head.

Was that possible?

"Meg, look at me." John's fingers lifted my chin so I looked into his eyes. "Meg, I've missed you so much. I came here expecting you to be happy to see me."

He half laughed and my mortification sank in. Of course John wouldn't do that to me.

I took my hands from my lap and brought them up to his head. "Oh, God, I'm sorry! I'm happy to see you." I ran my long nails over the sides of his short hair and down his smooth, freshly shaved face. "I missed you so much."

His eyes closed when my fingers ran over his mouth, and his lips parted under my touch, blooming into a smile. I didn't kiss John, even though I wanted to. He didn't kiss me either, but he was never the most affectionate anyway.

I heard a voice outside the door, and it didn't even bother me that my sisters were being nosy little shits. I didn't care. John was here, right in front of me, and freshly minted from West Point.

I sighed, remembering my ungodly appearance. "I looked very, very different earlier before the whole email thing."

"You look fine. Beautiful." John reached for my cheek and ran his knuckles across my skin. "I've never seen you like this."

Anxiety swirled in my chest. I hadn't planned on letting John see me without makeup anytime soon, if ever.

I asked him to give me a few minutes to pack my bag for the weekend and sent him out to socialize with my family. When he opened the door, Amy and Jo were busted eavesdropping, but he just laughed and gave Amy a salute. As they walked down the hallway, I heard John explaining his old-fashioned uniform to Amy, and my mind immediately had me wondering how he would fit into my family. He was so calm, even after my yelling at him in front of them.

If that had been Shia and I accused him of something he didn't do, he would fight me tooth and nail and make me grovel for his forgiveness. Shia was too emotional, too headstrong. John Brooke was strong, too, but in a gentle way.

John Brooke was good for me, he really was.

21

John thought of everything. He'd hired a town car for us to be chauffeured to the Quarter in, and we sat in the back of the car, all heart-eyed and naïve love. It felt like prom without the awkward blow job in the back of River's car. John had a bottle of grocery-store champagne that tasted like strawberries and bliss. During the dark drive, he held my hand between his on his lap, and I sipped the bubbly from a plastic flute.

"Tell me about your graduation. I'm sorry I couldn't make it."

"It's okay." His smile reminded me that he didn't exactly invite me in the first place, but I wasn't upset about it anymore.

I wasn't.

We were only boyfriend and girlfriend, so I understood why he wouldn't want me to come to New York and have a great weekend with him, getting to know his family and new friends.

Sometimes I hated that military girlfriends didn't get the attention or recognition that the wives did. And other times, I sort of believed what Jo said about the military culture forcing soldiers to get married young. At the same time, these men and women go through so much for their country, why should they do it alone? The saddest soldiers I knew were the ones who didn't have wives or kids waiting for them back home. Sure, most of them had parents, but it just wasn't the same.

Would John Brooke still want to marry me after my meltdown? He didn't send those emails. I knew he didn't. To reaffirm, I looked over at his face. Were there changes since I had seen him last? Our entire relationship had been long-distance. That should have been a sign, but it wasn't. Rather, it made us stronger; that's how it was with the military. He seemed the exact same, even less outspoken, if that was possible. His hands were still covered in light brown freckles, and his nose still had that little dip in the end of it.

I looked beyond him, to my own reflection. My bare face stared back at me, and even in the dark I could see the circles under my eyes. I never went anywhere without makeup, and there I was with John, on my way to the Ritz looking like a complete hag.

He continued to tell me about his graduation ceremony and how he could hear his mom's proud sobs as he crossed the stage. I imagined that any parent would be proud as hell of their child for graduating from West Point, though not having met her, I wondered what kind of woman she truly was. He squeezed my hand and lifted his lips into a smile when I looked at his smooth face. He looked so good in his uniform. It was special. He was special and his uniform helped show that.

"I would love for you to meet my mom someday," he told me when our town car pulled onto the main highway. The car glided smoothly in and out of the lanes; it all felt so different from my Prius or my parents' purple Cherokee, like we were floating over the pavement. "She would love you." His thumb brushed over my skin, a little pattern that felt like comfort and the affection that I was in need of.

She would? I wanted to ask, but I would have seemed insecure, and a woman should never, ever, let a man know she's insecure. Meredith taught me that, and there I was practicing what she preached, finally, after nineteen years. Her advice was coming in handy now, especially when the man in question just encountered me in my pajamas with mascara rings around my eyes. I needed confidence to erase that image from his mind.

I looked up at John, and he leaned down to kiss my cheek. He couldn't have sent the emails. I didn't have a clue who did, but I knew it wasn't him. It couldn't have been.

I tilted my chin toward him, and I liked the way the passing streetlights lit up his face as we sped past.

"I would love to meet her." I made sure my lips touched the corner of his, just enough to let him feel their warmth, but not enough to be satisfied.

When we arrived at the hotel, the car pulled into a covered driveway, and two valets rushed over. One of them looked like a guy I went to high school with, and I tried not to hold it against him. Our bags were scooped up, even my makeup case, and I tried not to cringe when the familiar-looking one roughly dropped it onto the cart.

John held my hand as we walked through the maze to get to the lobby and the elevators. Couples were everywhere, older white couples that smelled like hair spray and money; each man we passed had a thick watch around his wrist. I wasn't in Fort Cyprus anymore.

The woman behind the desk was friendly, with deep-rose lipstick and fake eyelashes. She asked if we wanted to upgrade to a Club room, and John said we did. She began to explain the benefits of the Club level, like we got our own open type of area. I think she called it a lounge, and the lounge was full of fridges of water and soda, and in the center of the lounge was a table full of food being served buffet-style.

I just focused on absorbing the energy of the place and trying to erase any tension still left in me from the email mishap. I looked at John the whole time she talked, and while the bellhop took our bags, and while we rode the elevator and walked the long hallway.

Our room was beautiful, just like I knew it would be. I decided that I was going to pretend that I didn't feel all mixed up inside, and I was going to talk myself out of the throbbing headache that was haunting me from earlier. John was there with me, right next to me, holding my hand and doing things to make me happy. I owed him more than puffy eyes and a sad look on my face.

The bellman finally left us alone after he explained nearly every inch of the room and its amenities. The bed was already turned down, and I laughed at a memory from a few summers ago.

"What?" John asked. He wasn't holding my hand, but he couldn't because he was unpacking our stuff.

"I was thinking about this time when my family was staying at a hotel in Houston, and they turned the room down while we were at dinner, and Jo was convinced there was a ghost in the room." I laughed again, remembering how wild she was over it. "She made my dad check the closets and under the bed, but it didn't really make sense, since you can't see ghosts."

I looked at John and he had a smile on his face. "Jo is something else," he said with a soft look on his face.

I shook my head. "Yes. Yes, she is."

"Are you hungry? Did you eat dinner?"

I didn't remember if I had eaten or not. I couldn't have even guessed what time it was.

"Are you hungry? You just got off a long flight. I bet you are."

He nodded. "A little. Do you want to go out? Or order in?"

Room service was a lavish novelty that I wanted every part of.

"Would you mind if we ordered in? I'm not ready or anything . . ."

He looked down at his own clothes, his perfectly tailored uniform, and back to me, in my leggings and sweater.

"The email thing really ruined my carefully orchestrated plan." I tried to swallow the burning in my throat.

I was still so confused and still angry about being fucked with in such a hurtful, pointless way. It had had such an effect on our night together—I wanted to try to forget that it happened. Until tomorrow at least.

"Room service, it is." John nodded and climbed into the bed. "What do you want to eat?" He began reading off the room-service menu.

22

jo

"How many times are you going to say that?" Amy whined, dragging her arms in front of her little body as she walked across the living room.

"As many times as it takes," Beth said. "You have to finish your work tomorrow before we go to the park."

I wasn't paying attention to their entire conversation because I was taking my version of an adventure across the room, sitting cross-legged on the floor. I put Amy's old step stool in front of me and rested my laptop and tea on top of it. It was the closest thing to a useful desk I had; the desk in my room blanks out my brain every time I sit behind it. I've never written more than one hundred words sitting at it, and Meg and I have had it in our bedroom since we moved to Texas. I didn't even know how many years ago that was. The desk was cursed.

I was reading a *Teen Vogue* article, a piece by an at-the-time freelancer named Haley Benson. She wrote about taking a trip alone and how it changed her life. She took herself to breakfast, lunch, and dinner and went on walks across the white sandy shore of an island somewhere far from Louisiana.

When I googled her, I found that she was born in Georgia and recently got a promotion at the magazine. Her brown hair was medium length, twisted into a loose braid in her Facebook profile picture. Imagining what I was doing in reverse, the idea of a random, somewhat nosy, but mostly admiring teenager looking me up online and hoping to have a little bite of what I had didn't seem possible.

I hated times like this, when I started wondering what in the world I was thinking when I had set my mind on moving to New York City someday.

I wasn't like the other girls in my school or online who binged on too many *Gossip Girl* episodes and thought they belonged in the Big Apple. I was more like the wishful, somewhat sad, but mostly hopeful want-to-be journalist with zero experience, but tons of knowledge, who stayed up late every night staring at a screen and consuming every bit of the world that I possibly could. In school they never tell you that most of the arts- or media-related jobs are on the two coasts. I wasn't into the California sun, so NYC it had to be.

Plus, living in a big city would afford me invisibility among the sea of floating souls. I couldn't wait.

I should have been working on my piece instead of fantasizing and worrying about my escape, but I was ready to move on. I hoped that people weren't lying when they said that high school will only make up a tiny part of your life. According to my teachers, my performance in high school would shape who I became as an adult, what kind of job I would have, how accepted I would be in the world. They preached about how important SAT scores were and brainwashed me to believe that I would actually use long division in my life after White Rock High.

Meredith confirmed that I wouldn't.

Then there's Roy Gentry, one of my favorite poets, who was severely bullied in high school and practically screams that high school doesn't fucking matter once you leave it. He says that half of his graduating class didn't even remember his name or why they made four years of his life hell; it's always the popular ones who fall the hardest in the real world. Reading his social-media posts made me happy that I didn't peak in high school, and I really, really hoped for Meg's sake that high school never mattered in the real world. Her experience was much worse than mine.

I started thinking about the vast numbers of people who move to big cities and have crappy, strange roommates and make minimum wage folding T-shirts while waiting to get hired at their dream company. This was on my mind because another thing the internet taught me was that a huge percentage of the articles making it online and into print were written by seasoned journalists, not by high school students who share a room with their older sister. I had to make my voice stand out from the veterans', and in my piece I needed people to know about what was happening in Cambodia.

I closed out Haley Benson's Facebook page and her piece and opened my browser. I was almost finished with my article, and afterward I would get sucked down the rabbit hole that were internet forums. I could spend hours reading the insanity in the forum comments and was mildly obsessed with seeing what the people in the deepest, darkest corners of the internet had to say. I opened a private tab and closed out whatever Amy had opened. I hoped Amy wasn't seeing things she shouldn't be seeing on my computer, and a quick look at the history seemed to indicate all was safe. I closed another tab, a Google page.

Last week Amy was on LiveJournal reading my old entries that I posted in junior high. They were full of drama and essays about school lunches, and they made me laugh now, but I still didn't want my little sister reading them and harassing me over them for the next month. It was my fault because I left the site open, but still.

It pissed me off that I never had any privacy. I hated that my parents wouldn't let me put a password on my computer. Even though I should have known better, I defied them once, and my dad randomly checked it, found the password-prompt screen, and took away my laptop for two weeks.

I guess I should be grateful that Amy uses her phone for most of her internet usage, and Meg only uses my laptop when she wants to watch makeup tutorials on YouTube. She says her screen is too small to see the contour, whatever the hell that means.

I opened my Word doc and scanned through the paragraph I stopped my last round of editing on. Just as I finished reading, the screen went black, and I panicked immediately. My throat tightened. I yelled for my mom—what else could I do? My finger repeatedly tapped against the power button, and I let out a little burst of breath when the low-battery warning flashed on the screen before it all went black again.

"Can you hand me the power cord?" I said to nobody in particular. I shared my parents' charger ever since Meg randomly brought a mutt puppy with skin tags hanging from his cheeks home last summer and it chewed through mine. I should use some of my next check to buy another one. I always meant to. Less than a year later, the dog ended up being part pit bull, and Fort Cyprus animal control took him from our yard and euthanized him within forty-eight hours because we couldn't find him a new home. My dad had to carry me out of the shelter office and cover my mouth when I wouldn't stop screaming at the asshole behind the desk.

My mom stepped in and, seeing the situation, replaced her alarm with the usual gentle look on her face, a velvet smile, and cloud-soft blue eyes. "Jo, you've been online for a while now. Why don't you go do something? Go to the movies, ask one of your friends if you can come over. *Something.*"

"What friends?" Amy said, and laughed until Meredith shushed her. "Take me to the movies!" Amy righteously demanded, reminding me just how great her company was.

Meredith shrugged and looked me flat in the eyes. "Or you can help me organize the garage."

I closed my laptop and stood up immediately. "Actually, I think I'll go for a walk."

I stretched my arms out with somewhat of a flourish and slid my feet into my dirty Vans. Meredith kept promising to take us to the outlet mall right after Christmas, but now we were at the end of January, and Christmas itself barely came last year. So, for now I hoped the small hole over my big toe didn't expand.

Right before I closed the door, I heard Amy ask Meredith if she could go with me. I hoped my mom would say no, but I held the door open a little just so I could know whether I needed to run.

"Amy, let's make something cool, like zebra-striped cake or

sugar cookies shaped like flowers," Beth began, her voice full-on sweetness, convincing and easy to cave in to.

Amy's excitement rang out and I closed the door. I was glad I dodged that one, honestly.

On my way down the driveway, I texted Meg to make sure everything was going okay with John. What happened tonight made no damn sense. From the breakup emails to her smearing makeup everywhere, to him pulling up like a white knight with a rental car instead of a horse, and, finally, to her riding—well, driving—off into the New Orleans sunset with him.

Honestly, I didn't know if he was lying, or if she was confused, or what the heck was going on with them. All I know is that I wouldn't be so quick to run off with him without an explanation of the emails—or any proof that he hadn't sent them.

I hoped that it was miscommunication. I didn't think Meg could handle rejection like that. Especially not after waiting months and months for him to finish at West Point.

The sound of a stick snapping jolted me back into my surroundings. Looking around, I didn't see anyone, but I crossed the street anyway. Likely it was an animal, hopefully not a skunk. I had been sprayed three times in my life already, and that just wasn't normal. Skunks obviously had it out for me, and I wasn't in the mood to scrub my body with cans of tomato juice again.

As I finished my loop around the block and walked past the Laurence house, I couldn't help but look at its giant illuminated window. I could see so much of the overcrowded living room, all of the furniture so aristocratic and overdone. I was starting to get used to the place, but I still felt a little weird going over there. I wondered if Laurie was around. It was somewhat early; I stopped walking, debating whether to knock on the door. I hadn't realized that I didn't have Laurie's phone number, and it seemed a little weird, but everything with Laurie felt that way. He lived in his own world, one I liked visiting.

The front door of the house opened and a woman walked out.

No, not a woman, I realized. A girl, a teenage girl.

No, not a teenage girl, it was a snake with long blond hair and a prickly voice . . .

I stared like a deer in the middle of the road that didn't move as a car barreled toward it.

Shelly Hunchberg crossed the lawn and clicked the key fob to her little green Volkswagen. I couldn't believe I didn't notice it earlier, that unmistakable little booger of a car.

Why was she at Laurie's house?

Then the silhouette of Laurie himself filled the doorway, and he stood watching her until she pulled out of the driveway. Gravel crunched under her tires, and I hated the noise.

Shelly Hunchberg, out of everyone? How did she even *know* Laurie? I knew the town was small, mostly Army families, but Laurie didn't even go to our school.

"Jo?" Laurie called out suddenly.

I thought about bolting, but that would have been even more awkward than my sort-of spying.

"Jo? Is that you over there?"

"Yep!" I squeaked out. My voice sounded weird.

The light around Laurie disappeared as he closed the door behind him and stepped off the porch. We met in the middle of the road. He was wearing a black long-sleeved T-shirt and dark jeans at least a size too big, and his hair was wet and hung just below his shoulders.

"Hey." He sounded a little out of breath.

"Hi," I said, even though what I wanted to say was *Why did*

*you have Shelly evil wench Hunchberg in your house? Don't you
know she's awful and the biggest bitch at my school and she'll suck
your soul . . . and probably other parts of you . . . dry?*

"What are you doing out here? Just roaming around?"

I shrugged. Why did everything feel so weird all of the sudden? "Pretty much. Meg is with John Brooke, Amy's being annoying, and my laptop died while I was editing. So the night air it is."

Laurie laughed and tucked his hair behind his left ear. "Why do you guys call him John Brooke? Like he's some superimportant agent or president or something?"

I told him I didn't know why, exactly, but I thought Meg started the trend.

"What's he like? Is he as enthralling as your sister thinks he is?"

"Not exactly." I laughed. "I mean, he's nice and everything, though."

"'Nice'?"

I didn't say anything else because I didn't want to be an asshole and laugh at John Brooke's expense. He was upright, maybe uptight, but he wasn't bad.

To change the subject, I asked Laurie how his day was. He told me that he went on post with his grandpa to get his ID card renewed and then went to dinner at a restaurant that served only crawfish. Crawfish pie, crawfish soup, crawfish everything.

Laurie changed his slight Italian accent to a Southern one. "'Panfried, deep-fried, stir-fried. There's pineapple shrimp, coconut shrimp, pepper shrimp, shrimp soup, shrimp stew, shrimp salad, shrimp and potatoes, shrimp burger, shrimp sandwich . . .'"

I was laughing at the end. "Did you seriously memorize *Forrest Gump*?"

He nodded. "Not the whole movie, but a lot of it. It's one of the best."

I agreed with him, though it was a strange talent to be able to recite so much of it.

Laurie glanced back at his house. "Do you want to come inside? Or go for a walk? I'm kinda hungry."

"Sure," I said, even though I wanted to say, *Didn't Shelly evil spawn Hunchberg just feed you the fruit of her loom or loins, or whatever the saying is?*

Instead, we walked across the street in silence until Laurie threw out another Bubba quote and I laughed despite myself.

23

meg

The food was delicious, particularly a decadent arrangement of strong cheeses that came with something called a Hurricane Po' Boy, which was topped with barbecue sauce and crispy shrimp. John overordered and we had so much food left, including a completely untouched crème brûlée.

I totally planned to pick at the burnt-sugar topping sometime before bed. Or maybe we could even have some fun with it.

But John looked like he was half-asleep on the chair, and I was so full that I could barely move. Still, being alone with him, at last, I either needed a bath or to run a marathon. Since I didn't want to hack up my lunch like a model from the nineties, I crawled out of the feather fluff bed and wandered past John and into the suite bathroom.

The bathroom area was largely covered in dark tiles, the sink and a sizable mirror separate from everything else. The shower was huge, as was the Jacuzzi; it was even bigger than it looked in pictures.

I ran the perfect bath, and soon bubbles were piling up a foot or so above the tub's edge. John undressed while I called my mom and managed to sneak into the water before I could even steal a glance of his body. We hadn't been together since he had had a two-week break back in October. I was more nervous than I had anticipated, and my bloated cheese-stuffed stomach was no reassurance.

When I got into the bathroom, John was neck deep in bubbles and his eyes both calmed and enticed me.

"Come in, I'm a little lonely in here." He smiled.

He was a man of few words, but he knew what words to use, and when. I pulled my sweater over my head and let it fall to the floor. His eyes were on me, taking me in, devouring me, which made me excited enough to almost forget about the food baby pushing on my stomach.

I took my pants off, and John's eyes ate my body up like Sunday brunch at a Southern country club. I pushed my arms against the sides of my chest and got a little wet when water splashed up over the sides as he shifted. I loved what a woman's body could do to a man. Not what it could do *for* them, but *to* them. The boys at my high school always called me a tease, and I was. I loved it. They wanted me—and couldn't have me—so they pretended they were too good for me and called me names and passed around pictures of my body, which they would never be able to touch themselves.

When my panties slid down my smooth, pampered legs, John's mouth went slack and his eyes barely blinked. I stood up, adrenaline flowing through me, licking at the tension I felt from him. I stepped out of my panties fully and eased into the tub. The water burned my skin as I submerged myself into the soft bubble bath. I sat opposite John in the big tub, a sea of bubbles floating between us. I felt like I had so much to say to him, but at the same time didn't know what to talk about.

Then it was quiet, the only noises in the room being the soft sounds of the bubbles popping between us. John's short hair was still dry on his head, looking lighter than his wet chest hair. I wanted to touch him, so I slid over to his naked body, and he parted his legs, letting me settle my back against his chest.

"I missed your body," he said, his hands exploring my neck, my chest. John Brooke's hands were never rough; they always carried in them some sort of timidity that made me feel like he was a little bit of a challenge.

I pushed my ass against his front and felt him hard against me. "I missed yours."

His hands grabbed mine and he turned me around. He moved my hands between his legs, making me take his length. I felt powerful as I manipulated his body with light strokes. I felt like a goddess when his head tipped back, and my hands felt like they were connected to the earth. Meredith always told us that a woman's body is the most divine, most powerful entity in the universe, that it creates life—and can end it, too. She taught me to never be ashamed of my body or my sexuality.

Though I would guess that she didn't exactly mean for me to take it as far as I invariably did.

There I was, a sexual predator, practically the graceful version of a porn star, using my hands and body to bring my prey to ecstasy. I watched my man's eyes and made sure he knew I was thinking dirty, dirty things about him and couldn't wait for him to be inside me. I even said as much and took pleasure in the spring girls   203

watching his face change. Blinking eyes, open mouth panting my name, and he was getting closer, so I pumped faster and asked him if he wanted me to fuck him, and he could barely nod because he was so captivated by my body and the way my hips moved as I straddled him and put him inside me. He stuttered a line of words and spilled out my name as he came so quickly. As flattered as I was that I had accomplished what I intended to even faster than I had planned, I knew from our history that once he came, he was down for the count for a while.

He kissed my neck and gently pushed me off him, cradling me at his side. I moved back in front of him and laid my head back on his chest. Then there was more silence.

We sat that way for what felt like hours, and when I heard John's light snoring behind my ear, I turned to find his eyes closed.

I was exhausted and I knew he had to be, but here I was completely naked in a bathtub with him and we had barely touched before he came. He was asleep. Eyes closed, breathing hard, mouth slack. Sleeping.

I was naked and soapy, and he was sleeping.

The Ritz in the Quarter was insane. I felt a world away from my parents' house and the stained tub and the dishes that Beth washes and dries and everyone lets lie on the counter for a day before Beth puts them away.

I wasn't going to sit in that fancy-ass room while he snoozed in the bathtub. I needed a night out, but I didn't want a night alone, either.

I moved away from John, making sure he didn't awaken. It blew my mind that the tub was big enough for me to sit on the other side and rest my chin against the lip of the tub, feet spread out, and still I wasn't touching John's body.

The emails from earlier scratched against my mind as the bubbles thinned over the cooling water. I thought I left the life-sabotaging bullshit from my peers back in Texas. I dealt with two full years of shit and made it out of Fort Hood and to New Orleans only a little stained. I couldn't think of anyone who would waste their time sending me fake emails, except maybe Bell Gardiner? That girl with her tiny waist and long black hair would totally be vindictive enough to do that. And petty enough. She hated me for no reason other than my relationship with Shia, if you could even call it that. I thought it was sad the way girls turned on each other over boys instead of allying together. Bell Gardiner was a little too old to be sending fake emails, but she still wore white eyeliner, so I couldn't put anything past her.

Bell Gardiner could have Shia King. From the day he left Louisiana for his first humanitarian trip, I had convinced myself that I didn't want anything to do with his green eyes or the beautiful tawny brown of his skin. I didn't care that he thought Bell Gardiner was better than me. John Brooke was certainly a better match for me than Shia. It shouldn't have been a competition.

But it was. Shia was probably fucking Bell Gardiner while I sat naked in lukewarm bathwater with a snoring boyfriend.

A snoring boyfriend who had just graduated from West Point, at least.

Shia was probably on top of Bell Gardiner, promising her the same shit he promised me.

"We're going to travel the world together, Meg."

"I can't wait for our future, Meg."

Once he even told me that he couldn't wait to tell his mom that we were together, and I even believed him.

I had visions of us holding hands, walking the streets of Mexico City, eating fresh fruit from street carts. He never believed that I would leave with him, and that's what corroded our relationship, his refusal to believe that I would leave my mom and sisters to travel the world with him.

As I looked over at John Brooke asleep in the bathtub, I still wasn't sure if Shia was right about me.

Shia King was pushing himself into my mind from wherever he was, and it was messing with my head. I was lucky to be here in a huge, expensive hotel suite with John Brooke, soaking in a tub in the center of the French Quarter. Poor John, he was so tired, and I was being the worst kind of bitch by thinking about Shia.

I moved back to John and reached between his legs. He was soft for a few seconds, but when John stirred awake, so did the rest of him. His eyes flew open and his body jerked a little before he remembered where he was, then he closed his eyes, rested his head on the lip of the massive tub, and let me play with him.

I started slow, with my hand tight around him, moving from top to bottom, and I felt his hands on my shoulders, turning me around. His mouth found mine immediately and he moaned through our lips.

"Touch me," I said into his mouth.

His hands were timid as they explored my breasts, and his fingers completely avoided my nipples, which drove me insane. I couldn't tell if he was doing it purposefully to wind me up, but I wanted to believe he was. I didn't know how many women John had slept with, but I definitely knew I wasn't the first.

His hands slid down my torso until he stopped between my legs. I was panting. He was groaning and so, so hard in my hand. I was losing myself in the rhythm of his kiss, his hand between my legs, pushing in and pulling out. Climbing onto his lap, I wrapped my arms around his neck and lowered my body onto his again.

John's eyes closed as he entered me and I sank down on his length. He was so thick, even though not that long, and I felt my mind drifting into the familiar state of desire.

24

jo

"Do you want a coffee?" Laurie waved for me to follow him into the kitchen. "Decaf or regular?" he asked, taking my getting up as an answer.

He opened a drawer and pulled out a box of coffee pods. As a barista, it made me roll my eyes, but the pods were nothing compared to the decaf offer.

"Decaf?"

He nodded.

"Decaf isn't even coffee."

He popped a Dunkin' Donuts pod into the machine.

I rubbed my temples in a dramatic way and walked closer to the instant-coffee machine. "Your blatant disrespect for the bean is killing me right now."

Laurie threw his head back and his hair was all over the place. "Hey, not all of us can be a barista extraordinaire."

"You don't have to be a barista extraordinaire to not want to drink coffee-flavored water," I teased.

He set two mugs out on the marble counter. One had a penguin on it, and the other had the saying NAMASTE IN BED inside the outline of a sun.

I pointed to the mug. "Nice."

He was the kind of boy who had quirky coffee mugs but drank decaf. He made no sense to me, but I liked the contradiction he was.

Once our "coffees" were ready, I followed him upstairs to his bedroom. I could smell his room before we even stepped through the doorway. His familiar homey smell coated my senses and immediately relaxed me. It was weird the way that worked.

"What cologne do you use?" I plopped down on the couch he had inside his room and put my feet up on his old oak coffee table. He'd told me it was from Spain and his mother had paid a fortune to ship it across the sea.

"I don't know actually." Laurie got up and walked over to his dresser and grabbed a little glass bottle.

Instead of asking me why I wanted to know, or giving me a weird look, he read the name of the cologne. I had never heard of it, and his accent made it sound even more exotic and expensive than I'm sure it was.

Over his decaf coffee, he continued telling me how he felt about his dad's sending him away to live with his grandpa, who didn't understand the way young men work. Laurie was a lonely yet social being. He confounded me.

"Do you miss your dad still?" Laurie asked me when he sat down. "Or are you used to this life now?"

"I miss him still. I don't want to ever be that used to this life that I don't miss my dad anymore."

Laurie chewed on his bottom lip and asked me if I thought it made him a bad person to not miss his dad. I told him no, that if he was a bad person, he would never have asked that question in the first place. He took that in and we sat in silence while we finished our drinks in a peaceable calm.

Hanging on Laurie's wall were old movie posters in no apparent pattern at all, held up with red tacks. The movies on the posters ranged from the original *Planet of the Apes* to *Almost Famous*. As with the other parts of Laurie, I kept trying to find the common thread among them, something that would solidify at last what kind of person he was.

Laurie stared at me while I looked at the posters. I could feel his eyes on me, though I wasn't uncomfortable, which itself was a little strange.

"You hungry?" he asked eventually.

"I'm always hungry."

He stood up and reached for my hand, and I hesitated for a second before I let him take it and lead me out.

On the way down the grand staircase, Laurie pointed to a row of family portraits on the walls. They were all in different frames of the same size. One of the frames was made of dark steel and had a picture of a row of men in uniforms. Not that everyone was dressed in Army green, though; some wore Navy white, some Air Force blue. At the end of the row stood a little boy, Laurie, the only one in the picture who wasn't dressed in a military uniform. Dressed in a black T-shirt and ripped blue jeans, he couldn't have been older than twelve. A thick mass of blond hair covered his forehead, and he wasn't smiling.

"A picture is worth a thousand words," he said in a taunting voice, and I examined the rest of the pictures while we finished the walk downstairs.

Near the bottom of the staircase were a few yearbook-style photos of more men in uniforms.

"How often do you see your mom?"

He shrugged. "It's been a while now, but since I moved to the States, I usually see her once every six months. Christmas and summer break."

I couldn't fathom living in a different country from my mom and dad, and living with my grandparents. Granted, I hadn't seen my dad's parents since my dad's commissioning ceremony almost two years ago. They stayed at a hotel right outside our post in Texas and came to the house once during the weekend they were there. My dad said my grandpa was sick, but that Sunday morning, the six of us, my parents and my sisters and me, went to Golden Corral for breakfast, and they were there, sitting at a table only two away from us. My grandpa was shoveling down sausage links and looked pretty healthy to me.

As for my mom's mom, well, she and Meredith were in one of their nonspeaking tiffs, and I stopped caring a while ago when I couldn't untangle their off-and-on moods. It never seemed worth the effort.

I would rather live in the janitor's closet of White Rock High than live with any of my grandparents.

"Do you miss Italy?"

"Italy or my mom?"

"Both?"

"Yes to both."

He didn't elaborate, and I didn't ask him to. I was collecting little pieces of Laurie every time we talked, and I could be patient while I put them all together.

When we got into the kitchen, Laurie pulled open the

industrial-sized fridge and tossed a little box at me. I struggled to catch it, but when I did, it was a Yoo-Hoo.

"Oh my God!" I held the carton up in front of me and couldn't help the blossoming smile spreading across my face. It was like a blast from the past looking at the blue logo written over yellow. I pulled the little straw off the back, pushed it through the directed spot, and took a long gulp.

"So good, right? Our housekeeper brought them home a few weeks ago, and I'm obsessed. It's like chocolate milk," he told me, like it wasn't a staple of millennials' upbringing.

"You didn't have these when you were a kid?" When he shook his head, I added, "The world is so big. You know? I swear most houses here had these bad boys at the ready."

Laurie's laugh was light like raindrops. "Better late than never." He took a drink and licked the chocolate off his lips. "The world is small, not big."

I looked at him and he turned away, to open the fridge again. He didn't seem to find what he was looking for and shut the door.

"How do you think it's small?" I asked his back as he raided the pantry.

"Maybe we should order something? Pizza? Chinese?"

As yummy as pizza sounded, I hadn't brought any cash with me and wasn't sure my card would clear because I'd bought a new laptop case and put the rest toward my move. I wasn't the best at budgeting, but I was sixteen. I didn't have to be.

"I didn't bring any cash," I warned him, but he was already holding the mailer with all the sales on it.

Laurie looked up at me through his thick blond eyebrows but didn't say anything. He pulled a cell phone from the pocket of his dark jeans and licked his lips again. They were a little

too big for his face, but I was sure that made him like honey
to girls his age . . . and probably my age, too. Meg always said
that boys would like my plump lips, but so far, outside of a few
obnoxiously gross remarks about them, the boys didn't seem to
care. They liked Meg's boobs more, which I thought was ironic
because lips could make boys feel better than boobs could.

"Yeah sure," he said into the phone.

Was it possible to order pizza without being on hold first? I
didn't think so.

"What do you like on your pizza?" Laurie asked.

"No meat, please."

He ordered a large cheese pizza and bread sticks and we
went back upstairs to wait. He never did explain to me how the
world was small to him, but I knew he would someday.

25

beth

Amy was sitting at the kitchen table apologizing for the fifth time in five minutes. The bitter smell of burnt dough was thick and cloudy in the room. I opened the back door to try and air everything out, but the air was stagnant, intent on making Amy cough up a storm. Her blue eyes were bloodshot on the whites and she was holding her chest.

"Amy, go upstairs until it clears up in here. This isn't good for you to be breathing in." I waved my hand through the white fluff in the air between us.

It was a dramatic cooking failure on my part. I should have watched Amy set the oven and made sure she turned the dial to 325 degrees, not 500, and I definitely should have double-checked before I slid the pan of sugar cookies inside and set the timer.

Amy kept her butt on the chair. "I'm fine. Look, it's clearing."

I couldn't believe my mom hadn't gotten up from the couch yet. The kitchen was blocked off by a wall with an archway to enter, but she had to have been able to smell the smoke. We smelled it from upstairs in our bedroom, with the window open and one of those wax burners mom used to sell.

I opened another window, the one just above the sink, and I looked over at the Laurence house. I knew just where the piano was positioned even though it was dark in the room. Just before I turned back to Amy, a light in the downstairs flicked on. Laurie, followed by my sister Jo, walked past the lit-up doorway of the piano room. I wondered if they were dating. It would surprise me because of Jo's fierceness when it came to herself, but maybe she was ready to have her first boyfriend.

Jo was the last one out of all of us to have a first kiss; even I had been kissed by two boys—who I never wanted to kiss again.

"What's happening?" Amy was beside me, standing on her toes to get a clear view through the window.

"Nothing, nosy rosy." I poked her side and she tried harder to find something interesting across the yard.

"Are they making out yet? Having sex with each other?"

"Hey! Shhh!" I bumped my shoulder into Amy's. I was smiling when I corrected her. "They aren't having sex," I whispered. I paused. "And, what do you even know about sex?"

Amy looked up at me. Her baby blues were perceptive and her smile reminded me just how in tune with the world she was. At twelve, I played with my older sisters' dolls and was part of my school's choir. At twelve, Amy had the world in her palm, and with the flick of her index finger she could see which one of her classmates was dating another, and with the tap of her fingers she could have a conversation with someone in Japan.

"You don't want to know." Amy laughed confidently.

"The internet?"

She nodded.

More than a few times, I had been concerned about what Amy was looking at on the internet. From videos of people fighting to those gross clips of people getting boils popped, she scrolled and scrolled through things that would have tortured me at twelve. Just last week, I was folding laundry and Amy told my mom and me about an eight-month-old baby whose own mom beat it to death. The way the words slid out of her mouth sounded like she had completely missed the horror of the whole story.

I began to warn her to be careful, but she finished my sentence in a voice that I assumed was meant to mimic mine.

"On the internet. You never know who's out there. It's not safe." She bounced a little on the tips of her toes when she said the words.

I touched her thin shoulder and turned her to face me. "I'm serious. With all the articles you read, you should know that sometimes people in the world are fucked-up."

I used the curse word because I needed her to take me seriously. I didn't want her to think about it as much as I did, because while realistically I knew that the chances of something happening to me were low, the statistics were still scary as hell.

"Amy," I prodded when she didn't answer me.

She jutted out her little square chin at me. "You're paranoid, Beth." She laughed. Sometimes she thought everything was a joke.

Her teeth were small and her canines were sharp, and sometimes she was too much for her own well-being, but I fiercely wanted to protect her. Jo and Meg, too. Even though I wasn't the oldest or the youngest, I still had more responsibilities than all of my sisters combined.

"I'm trying to help you. It will become more real to you as you grow up."

Her expression softened and she took a deep breath. "I'm not a kid anymore, Beth."

She looked at me with sympathy in her eyes and on her face, and I shook my head. Before I could say anything back, our mom came walking into the kitchen with a confused look on her face. The lids of her eyes were so swollen, I could barely see the blue of them, and her hair was a blond mess, her bangs covered in sweat.

"What's wrong? Are you girls okay?" She moved her head slowly to examine the room, but it was almost like she thought she was whipping her head around.

"Yeah, sorry. We burned cookies." I waved my hand through the air.

My mom's face did a complete three-sixty. Her eyes even opened a little. Just a little, though.

"Are you okay?" Amy asked, looking at Mom, then to me.

My mom nodded and combed her fingernails through her bangs and touched the top of her hair. The front of it always stood in a little poof. Meg had been trying for years to convince her to get rid of it, but she only downsized it. A little. Just a little.

"Yeah, I'm fine. Just tired. I've had a headache for two days." Her voice was all croaky, like a frog.

I walked over to the cabinet and grabbed a cup to get her some milk. Amy said she wanted to go to bed, and Meredith kissed her forehead before she wrapped her arms around Amy's waist and squeezed.

"Ten minutes on your phone, then put it down. I'm going to come up in thirty minutes. That gives you enough time to shower and wash your washables, brush all your brushables"—Amy was suddenly five again, smiling at the saying my mom used on all of us growing up—"put your pajamas on, play on your phone, and be in bed, blankets covering your coverables"—another smile from Amy, and me, too, this time—"and lights off. Okay?"

Amy nodded, and my mom told her she loved her.

After my sister left, my mom settled into drinking warm milk and waiting on an edible batch of cookies to finish in the oven. It was a little after nine, but it was a Saturday, so it was okay for Amy to be up and Jo and Meg to be gone. With my being homeschooled, every day sort of felt the same after a while. I stayed up later than everyone else in my house on most nights, and sometimes my mom would stay up late with me watching horror movies or talking over infomercials. Other nights she would make Jo and the rest go to bed and I would be lying on the couch listening to music and all she would do was kiss me on the forehead and tell me she loved me.

More than a few times Jo threw an absolute fit over me being "the favorite" child, but it was because I was the one who helped our mom run the house while Dad was gone.

"Have you heard from Dad?" I asked.

My drained mom stared at me for a few seconds. She even took a drink of her milk, swished it around in her mouth and all, before she responded. A slow shake of her head was enough for me to know she hadn't.

Something between an earthquake and a sigh came out of me, and I put my elbows up on the table and rested my head. "How many days has it been?" I asked, even though I knew good and well.

"Four."

"Fo-our," I repeated. Four days had felt like four hundred. "Did you ask the FRG?"

My mom nodded. "Two more days and I'm going to reach out to the Red Cross like I did when my dad"—she paused and corrected herself—"your grandpa died. They've helped me get ahold of your dad."

"What if Jo or Meg, or even Amy, asks?" But I wanted to know what was up, too.

Meredith's robe was falling off her shoulder, and I saw that she was wearing my dad's clothes. She did that a lot, but during blackouts it was worse. Since my dad was an artillery officer, he would go on missions for days at a time without being able to speak with us. Unfortunately, this felt the same as when someone was injured or killed, when the Army would block out all communication until the family was notified. Those days usually felt like holding your breath while someone repeatedly kicks you in the gut.

Jo and Meg hadn't asked about Dad, but I wasn't judging them over it. They had to handle things in their own way, and they both had busy lives. I was the one who spent 90 percent of her time inside the house. The other 10 percent was split up between the grocery store, sometimes to the PX, and random walks to the Shoppette down the street.

"I don't know, Beth. We'll just have to tell them. I don't want to hide anything from them. I just hoped we wouldn't need to mention it." Mom's lip quivered, but she sucked it right back in. "I hoped he would message me by now."

There was a knock at the door, and my mom's face curled into something that looked like a creature from the stories Jo used to write. My brain flew to exactly what Mom was thinking.

We both sat perfectly still.

"It's not possible." My mom's breath was ragged, and waves of tears were just on the brink of spilling over.

I moved toward the door and my mom grabbed my arm. Her fingers were tight and I saw only panic on her face.

"No, it's *not* possible," I told her, and gently unhooked her from me.

I looked at her again to tell her it would be fine. She usually believed me, but swirled up in that moment, I didn't know if I could be trusted.

My heart was violent inside my chest as I crossed from the kitchen tile to the soft carpet of the living room, and my throat was closing, my chest a tick away from heaving as I pulled back the blinds. A car was parked in the driveway, but our porch light was out and all of us kept forgetting to replace it, so I couldn't make out what type of car it was.

Another knock.

Just before my head started swimming along with my insides, I wrapped my hand around the door handle and yanked it open.

And instead of a destructive landslide, I found Shia King walking backward away from the porch, muttering something to himself.

He raised his hands in the air when I stepped onto the porch—if you could call our series of cement blocks a porch. "Sorry, Beth. Were you sleeping?"

I shook my head.

"Oh, okay, good. Is Meg here?"

His T-shirt had a lion's face on it and looked like it had been worn a lot.

I shook my head.

He nodded, and his tongue slowly skated across his lips. "Okay," he said, sounding defeated.

I always liked Shia, even though I didn't talk to him much.

By the time he'd started coming around, hanging out with Meg, I had begun distancing myself from people.

"Well, I'm going"—he drew out the words—"to go."

The street was so quiet and even more lights were on inside the Laurence house.

"Wait," I managed.

Shia whipped back around and waited for me to speak.

"She will be back Monday."

"Where is she?" I must have worn my apprehension on my face because before I could respond he said, "I'm sorry for asking. If you don't want to tell me, it's okay."

I wasn't as transparent as Jo, but I was close. "No, it's fine. She's with John Brooke." I felt a jab of guilt right below my ribs.

He nodded like he already knew, and I thought he was going to say something besides "How are you, Beth?"—but he didn't.

I told him I was good, and after ten more seconds passed, my mom came out onto the porch and barreled past me. She was crying and her sobs were slicing through the still Louisiana air as she rushed toward Shia with her robe flowing behind her.

He stepped back and nearly tripped. His face was twisted into something I could only describe as pure panic. He had to be confused by her rabid behavior. I was, and I knew that she assumed he was a messenger delivering earth-shattering news and she was so tired.

"Why are you here?" Her fists were crunched into balls kept still at her side.

"I came to talk to Meg."

My mom let out a little sound like something between a sigh and a scoff. I thought she was going to push Shia, and I guess Shia thought so, too, because he moved out of her way, backing slowly to his car.

"Why would you think Meg wants to talk to you?" my mom practically yelled, no longer crying. It went away that fast.

I shut the front door behind me and took a few steps toward where they were on the grass.

"I don't know. I'm not sure she does," he told my mom in a tone that made me wonder what Shia did to Meg.

I knew all about Meg and Shia's drama while it was going down. I held my sister's hair back while she threw up into our kitchen sink after one particular fight with him. She never could handle stress and, just like our mom, vomited easily. It was one of those Friday nights where she told my mom she was "going out," which meant she was parking the car in the back of the gym parking lot on post and waiting for Shia. Meg told me about their make-out sessions once, but I let the secret slip in front of Meredith, and Meg never forgave me. She called me "Ophelia" for months. I hated being called my ex–best friend's name as an insult, but I had betrayed her the way Ophelia had betrayed me.

The last time Meg cyberstalked my old best friend, she was dating River. It wasn't that I expected Ophelia to return even a speck of what I felt for her, but I never could have expected her to date someone as disgusting as River, even if she didn't know firsthand how slimy and slithery he was. But she did know, some of the story at least.

Ophelia helped us tear down the demeaning sheets of betrayal. Then she dated him. More than once. But when we first moved here and Meg met Shia, we spent a few nights a week at "my piano lessons."

"She's with John Brooke, Shia. *That's* where she is!" my mom exclaimed, sounding slightly deranged and more like my oldest sister than herself. "He took her down to the French Quarter for a couple of nights. John Brooke just graduated from *West Point*, Shia!"

Shia didn't say a word.

"John Brooke is a nice man who makes my daughter very happy."

Shia remained stone-faced.

Mom kept going. "He came tonight to get her after a little email mess. Would you happen to know anything about that?"

Shia's dark eyebrows pulled together. He shook his head. "What email mess?"

I didn't know Shia well enough to know when he was lying, but in general I was pretty good at telling stuff like that, and he seemed honestly confused. Jo said this trait would get me far in a journalism career, but in reality, it hadn't even helped me make it out the front door.

"Someone sent Meg an email that they shouldn't have sent, pretending to be someone they weren't, and caused her unnecessary pain. Since she doesn't have a big group of friends here, I'm sure it will be easy to narrow down the already small list of suspects and figure it out. Who else would want to hurt her for no apparent reason?"

"Not me." Shia lifted his hands to his chest and touched his fingers to his worn T-shirt. "What kind of emails?"

My mom shook her head. "I'm not going to share her business with you. What are you doing here? What did you come to talk about?"

Shia looked at me. I looked away. He seemed to be struggling with what to say to her. I didn't blame him.

"Well?" she pushed.

The normally outspoken Shia hesitated to take my mom's

bait; he seemed to know better than to be too vocal to my mom when she was like this.

"I just wanted to talk to her. I don't know if she would want me to—"

"She's my daughter and you've hurt her. You're either going to tell me what you wanted to talk to her about, and I'll tell you where she is, or you're going to get in your fancy little car over there and drive on back across town and try again next time."

Shia was a few inches taller than my mom, but right then he looked so much smaller.

He sighed and turned his body toward the Laurence house. I wondered if Jo and Laurie would hear the drama outside and come out. I didn't know if Shia would live to see his wedding if Jo came out and found Meredith like this and Shia backing away with that guilty look painted on his face; she would rip him from the ground. Meg never wanted anyone to know about her and Shia's meet-ups, and I was sworn to secrecy. I was really, really good at keeping secrets, except from Ophelia.

My mom stepped to one side and leaned against my dad's Jeep.

Shia dipped his chin and pulled his head back. "Mrs. Spring, you know I have always liked you"—his pink tongue darted over his lips—"and I would never disrespect you, but I have no flipping idea what you're talking about."

The front door opened behind me and a light danced across the grass. "Who's here?" Amy asked from behind my back. I felt her hands touch my back as she passed me.

"Hey, Amy. How's it going?" Shia said. He seemed so uncomfortable, but was trying to be polite.

"Go inside, Amy," Meredith warned.

"Mom . . ."

When Mom snapped her eyes back at Amy, my little sister wrapped her arm around mine.

"Let's go inside, Amy. Mom and Shia are talking," I nudged. I had a feeling she would put up a fight.

But my sister had, like, this flare in her eyes . . .

I didn't know what was coming, but as I turned to pull her inside she wouldn't budge.

Shia looked from my mom, to me, to Amy. "Look, Mrs. Spring, I was only trying to find Meg and talk to her—"

My mom got so close to him that I wasn't sure if she was going to kiss him or push him. "Talk about what? The emails you sent to her to try to ruin her relationship with John?"

Shia shook his head. "I would never do whatever you're talking about, Mrs. Spring. I wouldn't hurt Meg."

Amy sank back a little, and her face was flushed.

"You've already hurt her! You think you're soooo much better than us, don't you, Shia King?" Meredith taunted him. I wondered how much liquor my mom had snuck into her mug tonight.

"What?" He rubbed his shaved head. "No. I—"

"Just leave, Shia! Get the hell away from us and go back to your fancy mansion in—"

"Mom!" I finally stepped in to stop her rant. She liked Shia; she was just taking her anger out on him because he frightened her.

She glared at me, and I shook my head. Her eyes were murderous, and for a second I didn't recognize her.

Without a word to Shia, or to me or Amy, my mom stalked inside the house and slammed the front door.

"Sorry about that. She's—"

"It's fine. I get it." Shia's voice was sad.

"Let's go." I tugged at Amy to follow me into the house.

Just before we got inside, she turned back to Shia and yelled, "She's at the Ritz in the Quarter with John Brooke!"

~

When we got inside, and Shia's fancy foreign-styled headlights shone through the window before disappearing down the street, my mom asked, "Why did you do that, Beth?"

Her voice wasn't loud, but that was the worst part for me. She was mad, but she was never the type of mom to yell at us all the time. Ophelia's mom was like that. Ophelia would run down to my house when her dad came home with whiskey on his breath.

"You were yelling at him, Mom. He didn't do anything wrong that we know of," I said, explaining myself.

My mom sighed and rested her arms on the back of the recliner. "Well, at least he doesn't know where she is."

I looked at Amy and then at my mom.

Amy sauntered past both of us. "I told him. I'm sorry, but neither of you were going to help him."

"He didn't need to know where she was. Your sister is fine without him, and she's with John."

I didn't agree that Meg was fine without Shia, but I still had to scold Amy for her loud mouth. "It wasn't your place, Amy."

"I just think he loves her," my little sister said.

Mom laughed. It wasn't real. "What makes you think that?"

Mom sat down in Dad's recliner, and Amy sat down on the red beanbag chair, swishing as she sank into it.

"Because he's here," Amy said, like Mom knew less than Amy did at twelve.

I sat on the couch and put my feet up. The blankets on

the back of the couch always smelled like our house in Texas. My mom used even more scented wax-cube things then, and the smell would never leave the fabric. I grabbed Dad's eagle blanket, the one that smelled like cinnamon toast, and pulled it over my legs.

"And that means love, how?" Mom asked. She seemed to be less angry now. More of the mother I knew and loved, and less like Aunt Hannah when she drank too much and got angry over the smallest things.

"He lives far! And he's engaged to Bell Gardiner! But he still came all this way. Of course he loves Meg."

I laughed at Amy's seventh-grade explanation of love.

Mom did, too. "It doesn't work like that, darling. If boys like you, or love you, they will show it. You will know. If we have to debate it or question it, he doesn't love you—and even if he did, if he doesn't show it in any way beside showing up to your house at ten at night while engaged, he isn't worth your love anyway."

I wondered if the same rules applied with girls, too.

"Not anymore. Maybe when you were young."

Meredith scoffed and looked at Amy with a soft disbelief. "Shia King hurt your sister, and after everything that she's been through, she doesn't need any more of that. No emails, no rich kids who think they're too good for my daughter." Mom turned back to me. "You both should know better. I've told you what to put up with, and what not to. Meg doesn't need to be putting up with Shia's bullcrap, and, Amy"—Mom looked right at her—"you don't need to be helping Shia mess with your sister's life. She's happy with John Brooke."

"What did Shia even *do* to Meg? Why don't we like him again? Because I'm pretty sure he's the richest, hottest guy around here. His jawline—"

Amy was practically salivating when Mom interrupted her. "Amy, is that what you want to do in life? To be loved by cute rich boys?"

"Yes!" Amy squeaked. "Yes, of *course* it is!"

"And then what? What happens when you're in your thirties and your cute rich boy grows into a not-so-handsome, rich, spoiled man and, God forbid, something happens and you're left alone to raise children alone, with no job experience at all."

Amy sighed. "Mom, seriously. That isn't going to happen. I'll make sure my husband will always be hot." Amy giggled.

Mom's face was hard. "I'm serious, Amy. You need to make sure you have a job and your own skill set. And you can't go around judging boys only by the way they look. It's not fair when boys do that to girls, so we shouldn't do it either."

"I'm going to marry someone like Dad, and he'll stay around forever and help me raise my daughters." We knew this tactic of Amy's—to say something you couldn't disagree or argue with and thereby hopefully end your absurd argument with her.

It made Mom smile despite herself. "I hope you do. And I hope you have three or four daughters just like you. You know what they say?"

I did, because Mom had said the same thing to Meg so many times. Meg talked about having kids more than any sane nineteen-year-old. I was sure she would be a good mom someday, but I thought she could listen to Jo and wait until she was older to worry about such things.

"No. I don't want to know what they say." Amy rolled her head back, and my mom tapped the tip of Amy's nose. Amy laughed. "Don't tell meeee."

"They say whatever you put your mom through comes back

to you twice as bad when you have a daughter. So keep pushin' it and I'll get my revenge when you have an Amy Junior."

Mom tickle-attacked Amy's sides, and my sister's laughter bounced off the walls. It was a good sound, helping to diffuse all the tension of what had just happened.

Once Amy got away from my mom, she sat next to me on the couch. Meredith turned on a movie, the original *Halloween*.

Right before it began, Amy asked Mom if she was really going to tell Meg that Amy sold her out to Shia.

Mom turned to look at Amy with a funny look, said, "I sure as hell am," and went back to the movie.

26

jo

*L*aurie's room was a mindfuck. It was layered with contra-dictions. Like a record player from Urban Outfitters with a Halsey record spinning, to an autographed box set of old WWE wrestling tapes. He was so fascinating but so ironically normal it made him a character to me.

I could have written forty thousand books about Laurie. Maybe someday I would.

I kept my trip around Laurie's world going and walked over to the desk. He kept encouraging me to snoop through his things, like it was a game.

"Tell me if you find anything that surprises you," he said with a pen in his mouth.

"Oh, I will."

I opened a drawer, and he changed the song on the record player through his phone.

My fingers felt something soft like fur and then something cold and metal. "What the hell?" I jerked my hand back and wiped it across my jeans.

Laurie was on his feet, moving toward me. I wondered if his grandpa was home.

"What?" Laurie shoved his hand in the mystery fur drawer and I closed my eyes.

It could have been a dead hamster or a wild rat. Gross.

When he pulled his hand back out, a black-and-red fuzzy key chain was dangling from the tip of his index finger. "It's just a rabbit's foot." He swayed it closer to me and I jumped back.

I hadn't seen a rabbit's-foot key chain in forever, but I remembered when Meg used to have a bunch of them from her job at the skating rink near my middle school in Texas. She had a purple one hanging from the rearview mirror of her first car, an old Buick Riviera with a tan paint job and brown wood interior. The dangling foot creeped me out.

"Ew."

"It's not ew. It's good luck."

I shook my head. Meg used to say the same thing. "An animal's foot is not good luck. Nature wouldn't allow such a cruel thing."

Laurie stood next to me, rubbing the thing. "That is such a human thing, isn't it? To claim that the severed foot of an animal is ours for good luck. How fucked-up?"

"Yep."

"Is that why you don't eat meat?"

"No. Well, in a way, yes. I guess so. Not rabbit's feet directly. Can you put that thing away?" I pointed, with my face bunched up in disgust. He tossed it back inside the drawer and snapped it shut. I was done sleuthing for now.

"I think it's cool. I mean, I don't plan on changing my diet." He tapped on his stomach to drill in the words. "But it's cool that you do what you want and believe in something."

"I believe in a lot of somethings."

"Oh, I know you do."

We sat down on opposite ends of the couch. I was closest to a circular side table that was painted gold and had our Yoo-Hoo cartons on them. I couldn't remember which one was mine, and it would have been super-awkward to just assume and grab one and start chugging.

"So, do your sisters have boyfriends? I know Meg has John whatever-his-name-is, but what about Beth and Amy?"

I leaned up and pushed against his leg. "Amy is twelve."

He shrugged, and his face was the definition of *And . . . ?* "I had my first girlfriend well before twelve. Her name was Lucia, and she had the prettiest curly hair."

"And why did you and Lucia break up?"

Laurie ran his hand over his hair. It was so wavy now that it had air-dried. "Well, I thought we were exclusive, and she was dating all the boys in my class. It broke my ten-year-old heart. I've really never recovered."

I rolled my eyes. "Sure. But seriously, no, Amy doesn't have a boyfriend. Beth doesn't either."

I didn't want to tell him that I thought Beth would never have a *boyfriend*. It wasn't my truth to tell.

"Do you?"

His question didn't feel as crass as those words would typically sound coming from a guy like Laurie. I don't know why my brain kept thinking that—*a guy like Laurie*—because I couldn't decipher what that meant.

"No. Do you?"

"Have a boyfriend? No." He smiled at me, showing his teeth. He had what Meredith called rich-kid teeth.

"A girlfriend," I clarified. Shelly Hunchberg sashaying out of his house was sitting on the tip of my mind and tongue.

"Not really."

I looked up at the ceiling, wondering if Laurie had ever broken a girl's heart before. I suspected that, yes he had. Of course he had. Boys like him were made just for that. I hoped some of the girls who would fall in love with him would make it out to the other side stronger, not less whole than before him.

"None here," he told me.

Hm. "None here as in Fort Cyprus or the United States of America?"

Laurie laughed and jerked his leg, making it bump into mine. I moved away and his smile grew even more.

"Fort Cyprus."

"What about Shelly? Is she one of your girlfriends?"

More laughter from him. "No. What do you know about her, by the way?"

"Nothing you want to hear, I'm sure. How do you guys even know each other?"

"Her mom sent her over to bring us a packet for that fund-raiser thing they're doing."

"What fund-raiser thing?"

"I don't really know, but I guess my grandpa told her I would go."

I wondered what the fund-raiser was. I bet it was some cookout-type thing. The sun had been coming out to play for the last few days and Shelly's mom, Denise, used any reason she could find to throw a "fund-raiser" where she'd be the center of attention.

If Meredith didn't know about it, I didn't want her to.

"She seems okay," he said. "Cute. A little bossy."

I didn't think I liked the way his words pressed into the sides of my body. I suddenly didn't want to know anything else about his opinion of Shelly. Or anyone who Laurie would find cute but a little bossy. I didn't want to draw the faces of the girls in Laurie's past. It struck me as odd that I had never thought of these girls or wanted to know who they were before.

I wasn't jealous, was I? I wasn't sure, but it confused me.

The tops of Laurie's cheeks were red. "Have you had any boyfriends here?" His voice came out higher than it usually did. I didn't look at him. "In the United States of America?" He used his Italian accent to play on the way the words sounded.

"No. Not really." Not at all.

He made a noise in his throat. "How many boyfriends have you had?"

"What? Like ever?" The answer was zero unless a weeklong internet relationship with someone I met in the re-blogs of a Tumblr thread counted? I didn't think so.

I'm not sure how invested Eurosnlife17 was in our short-lived rendezvous, but since he asked for nudes a week later, I figured he had a few other online lovers in whatever the internet version of a little black book is.

"Not really," I finally answered Laurie. I could hear the hesitation in my voice, but wasn't sure that I cared. "I didn't really talk to that many guys, I guess."

I watched the curve of his neck as he swallowed. "Hm, why not?"

I didn't feel like I had a specific reason per se; I just simply didn't.

I started talking, mostly to give myself an answer. "I don't know, I just didn't. It's not that I tried not to date, it just never happened. I have plenty of time," I told him and myself.

That was okay, too, I thought. I didn't date like Meg and was still a virgin. I didn't know how it felt to have a boy's hard body under me, and I didn't know what to do with my hands while kissing. I hadn't learned those things yet, but I was only sixteen. Yes, I would have liked to find someone in my school fascinating enough to date, but I wasn't given many options.

No way in hell was I going to settle for a guy like River, who broke up with Meg through a text message a week after she had sex with him and ruined her life for almost two years. I didn't want to be humiliated by a boy like Josh Karvac, who refused to wear any shirt that wasn't a jersey and only dated Meg because River said she gave good blow jobs.

Sometimes, and very, very selfishly, I thought about how lucky I was to have a sister who had so much experience so I knew better. I didn't want to be known for giving good blow jobs, I wanted to be known for my words and my voice. The problem was that boys didn't seem to care as much about a girl's voice as they did about silencing it by shoving their dicks down her throat.

"No one at your school ever tried?" Laurie asked.

I looked at him, but focused on the reflection of the ceiling lights in the pupils of his eyes. "Define *try*."

He grinned.

"Not really. There was zero effort."

"That's hard to believe."

"I saw this same conversation in a movie."

He smiled. "I'm sure. It's the age-old tale of the edgy, sarcastic teenage girl who has no idea how beautiful she is and has never had a boyfriend. It happens all the time." His hand moved in a circle in front of his face, and humor creased his cheeks.

"Don't call me edgy," I said, pouting.

"Don't wear a choker." He laughed, and I felt his stare touch my neck.

My hand flew up and I touched the velvet strap around my neck. "I like chokers, asshole."

His eyes lingered on me. "So do I."

I gulped and felt anxious all of the sudden, like something awful was about to happen but it was out of my power to stop it.

I wanted the prickly touches of anxiety to go back where they came from. The few inches between us felt nonexistent, and I could smell the cigarettes and drawings on him.

I stared at Laurie and he stared at me until he broke away and finally spoke. He was staring at the wall when he said, "I'm sure you'll find a boyfriend in New York."

"I hope so." I stared at the wall, too, and wondered why I was lying. I didn't care about having a boyfriend in New York. I cared about having a job and maybe a cat.

"Me, too," Laurie said, and I thought he was lying, too.

"Do you have any questions about the dating game?" he asked a few seconds later.

"The dating game? Why is it a game?"

He looked at me. "Because that's what people do. They take everything that's supposed to be good for them and over-complicate it. We were put on earth to procreate and get married and keep the earth going, that's it. That's our purpose and everyone makes it so much more complicated."

I couldn't have disagreed more with him. "I hope my only purpose to the universe isn't to procreate and keep the earth populated. That sounds like some shitty dystopian novel. I want to have more purpose than that. Maybe I don't want to get married and pop out babies. Maybe I want a career and I want to live alone and travel and sleep in and hop on a plane any second I want. What's so bad about that?"

"Nothing is bad about it." Laurie moved a little closer to me, but I don't think he noticed. "I just don't agree. For sure I want to play a vital role in the universe and all that, but I also want to get married and have a family and spend my time with my wife and kids."

"You do?" My mouth was dry. It was weird to hear a boy Laurie's age be so animated about having a family.

"Yeah. I don't want to be like my dad." Laurie's voice was low and he looked around the room like someone could be listening. "Or my grandpa. He has this big house, this legacy military career, but that's it. When he dies, all he's leaving behind is a single shitty father of a son and a whiny spoiled grandkid."

Laurie told his truths so openly, it was fascinating. "What do you want to leave behind?" I asked.

"I haven't figured it out yet, but I know it's going to be something more important than stripes on a uniform." He felt really close to me. "What do you want to leave behind?"

"I don't know yet, but I want it to be epic."

"Epic," he repeated, intensity in his gaze. "I can see your gravestone now, Jo Spring, daughter of Meredith, leaver of epicness."

"Laurie Laurence, son of an Army general, father of a thousand babies."

His hand wrapped around my knee and he playfully squeezed. "A thousand? That's a little much, and my name isn't *Laurie Laurence*," he whined, and I giggled like he just slipped a love note into my locker.

When I looked at Laurie, he was moving toward me, an inch a second, he couldn't have been moving slower. His hair had fallen down over his forehead, and I couldn't stop staring at the small scar cut into his bottom lip.

I felt his mouth touch mine before I was able to form a single coherent thought. I didn't know how we got here, from laughing and teasing to kissing. Maybe that's how it always was, I wouldn't know. All I knew was that my mouth opened and this kiss was softer than I expected. His lips were wet and soft like Aunt Hannah's pudding. Our teeth didn't crush together like Meg's first kiss. He didn't taste like syrupy caffeine like I always thought my first kiss would. Right then, in that room, Laurie's mouth tasted like danger and faint cigarettes.

I suddenly understood why people craved the taste of tobacco. Laurie's tongue was sweet and earthy, and my eyes closed on their own when he kissed stars into me. I felt his hands on my hips as the control slipped from my body. He was putting all of his strength into his hands, it seemed, as they gripped my hips. My sweater was so thick, bunched into his large hands; he grasped tighter.

"Damn you, Jo." He burned the words into me and pulled me onto his lap. Blood pounded in my ears, and I pushed my fingers through his thick hair.

His kiss was just the seed. His fingers turned to branches, rooting themselves into my body. My hands became no longer my own, and I thought that this was why Meg put herself through all the pain that boys bring along. For that feeling. It was worth it, I thought, as Laurie flipped my world upside down. How quickly my mind changed from smart, thought-out conclusions to sappy syrup dripping from the trunk of a tree.

When his hand touched my stomach, I shifted my hips to be closer to him. His eyes echoed my own right back to me. I felt another feminine milestone inside me, budding and blooming and exploding into rich petals of womanhood. Isn't that what it's supposed to feel like? An explosion inside my body? I didn't think my body was strong enough to handle much more, but when the doorbell rang and interrupted us, I was thrown right back into reality and hoped that Laurie and I didn't just ruin everything we had.

27

meg

*E*ach morning at home I waited for the sun to wake me up. I could feel its warmth through the jersey-knit curtains stained with cigarette smoke. The extra layer of tar clinging to the fabric didn't do much to keep out the sunlight. The curtains in my room had been Meredith's—hence the sunflower print on them. My mom had been obsessed with sunflowers her entire life. She had bowls and sundresses, key chains and a steering-wheel cover, all with big blooming sunflowers on them. It made gift shopping for her beyond easy.

When I woke up that morning, I wasn't tucked into the bed that I had had since I could remember; I was in a king-sized bed made out of the finest clouds old Southern money could buy. The hotel bed was lush under my heavy body and deliciously cool against my skin. I got up in the middle of the night and turned the digital thermostat down to sixty-five and slept like a freaking baby after that. This thermostat was accurate, unlike the dated one in my parents' house, so when it said it was sixty-five, it actually was. The Ritz in the Quarter was a sensible and luxurious mixture of modern and classic. I wondered what it would be like to wake up in such a place every morning.

I could wake up next to John in a house that my parents weren't in control of. I wondered what a house without so many people would be like. Meredith always said that I would be bored without the noise of my younger sisters, but apparently John is noisy enough himself. To my surprise, John Brooke wasn't much of a cuddler, and he was loud in his sleep. I could have sworn that in the past he slept with his arms wrapped around me. I remembered when we stayed at the Red Roof right outside the post gate and I woke up sweating, with his body around mine. He didn't snore then either, not that I could remember—and those whale noises wouldn't be easy to forget.

It had only been three months. Why did it feel so long?

He's a back sleeper and he snores. And by snores, I mean he grunts out noises that sound like grizzly-bear mating calls and coughs like he's choking on his own breath. I hoped his snoring was temporary. Maybe he was going to need some time to adjust now that he was away from West Point's early mornings. I was crossing my fingers and toes. Good thing those nose strips existed. We would need to grab a box of those before tonight.

My dad snored like John—only worse, if you can imagine it. Dad's midnight calls into the wind were one of the reasons Meredith slept in the recliner so many nights when he was home. Here I was already thinking about every night for the rest of my life. To say that John and I had an exciting, comfortable night would be like saying it made sense that Dan Humphrey was Gossip Girl.

Our lavish room on the Club floor was pitch-black. Thick curtains kept out every ounce of sunlight from the outside world. The longer I stared at the ceiling, the more of my sight returned, but I still hated not being able to see in the room.

Jo always loved to linger in the dark like a freaking bat, but not me. I sat up a little, rubbed my hands together to warm them, and moved across the king-sized bed to check the time on the alarm clock on the nightstand. The room was cold, and I was topless. My nipples were hard, and John didn't so much as move when I touched his back with my cold, peaked chest.

The screen on the alarm clock flashed two ones and two zeros. I couldn't believe I had slept that late, but sleeping on clouds will do that to a lady. Maybe John's snoring wouldn't bother me as long as we had the kind of luxurious down comforter of the Ritz.

I felt rich here; even in the dark of the room I felt like royalty in a space fit for a queen. In the Quarter, I felt so far away from Fort Cyprus. The bed and room seemed like they were nestled somewhere in the rolling hills of Tuscany, all the way across the ocean. The idea of Tuscany made me think of Shia, who had posted pictures of himself in beautiful small towns in Italy, drinking wine and eating whole baskets of fresh bread with fresh handmade mozzarella. He posted pictures from the rocky coast of Naples to the beautiful structure of the Milan Cathedral. He said he went to Italy as often as he could.

I would travel someday. Mrs. King had told me that there were military bases in Italy, England, and Germany. Living in Europe, Jo says you can take a train to any country to visit for the day. She says that's why families in the U.S. who save up their entire lives to go to other states hardly ever leave the country. It's too expensive to travel outside of the country. Even Disney World costs thousands. A bottle of water there costs more than a case from the grocery store. It's one of the many things Jo is aware of that I had never thought about. Social media has changed the world.

Camera phones ruined my high school years. I can't imagine what Twitter and Instagram will do as they grow.

Still, I learned a lesson. I spent most of my time online scrolling through pictures of the people who graduated before me and seeing their babies popping out left and right. When I was in high school, most of my friends were older than me, so now most of them were twenty-two and on their second kid.

Back then I had this rule: I wouldn't take the school bus after the first week of school, so I molded myself into the cool freshman with big boobs and a naïve attitude. I always had a ride. It annoyed me how much I cared my entire high school life about what boys thought of my body. What a waste of my time and energy. I never knew how in control of my body I actually was.

"John," I whispered, but he didn't budge.

I imagined I could make out the blondish red of his hair and his tightened jaw in the blackness. Amy once said he looked like he was constantly pressing his top and bottom teeth together. He had the face of a soldier, the face of a prom king. I cast my vote for him by pressing my lips to the back of his neck.

"Ugh." The groan echoed through the darkness. I kissed him again and nipped at his skin just slightly. "Meg, please. I'm dead tired."

His words stung me right in the face, but I had to consider that he had been on someone else's schedule for almost four years. He had to wake up at the crack of dawn for PT, and West Point had much more strict qualifications than for the regular enlisted soldiers. John Brooke was in the elite. One of the best of the best. He deserved to sleep.

I wasn't going to sit and pout about his not wanting to wake up with me, even though we'd been apart for months. I needed to consider how he felt, how tired he must be. So, after ten more minutes of staring at the ceiling, I dragged my body out of the comfy bed and made my way to the bathroom.

When I flipped on the switch, the lights were bright, too bright for my eyes. I swiped across the switch again and turned on the dim lights on the ceiling. I set them as low as they would go. My cheeks were red in my reflection, as usual, even under the muted light. I hated that no matter how much green primer I slathered across my rosy skin, it was constantly red. I got my mother's skin, as did Amy.

I turned on the cold water in the marble sink and sprayed the dark roots of my hair with dry shampoo, raking my fingers through the white powder. I brushed my teeth, secretly hoping that John would wake up before I was dressed. But he didn't, and twenty minutes later I found myself with a napkin shoved into the front of my cotton sundress, digging my teeth into an authentic Café Du Monde beignet, alone. The powdered sugar blew all over my lap, latching its way into my navy dress, but I didn't even care. They were that good.

I took a swig of coffee to make it feel more like breakfast and finished the plate in less than five minutes. The coffee at Café Du Monde was good, and that they only served it two ways made it feel like a luxurious thing. It wasn't like Starbucks, where I ordered a Grande Iced Caffè Latte, extra shot, extra ice, please. At Café Du Monde, you get two choices: coffee black, or mixed with milk. I got it *au lait*—half coffee, half hot milk.

As the minutes ticked on, I got worse and worse at pretending I didn't care that John didn't wake up for me. Should I have tried to wake him up again? I didn't know, so I washed the thoughts away with another gulp of coffee. I was surrounded by people, a tourist group from China, all dressed in crisp, clean clothing, sharing a couple plates of beignets. A little Chinese girl with a bright smile pointed at a pigeon eating from a plate a few feet away. An African-American family wearing matching MERRIWEATHER FAMILY REUNION shirts were getting up to leave, and I watched as a girl with beautiful natural hair, about my age, tapped the shoulder of the waitress and handed her a large tip. A group of teenagers, all mixed races, were laughing and shouting at a table near the back. An old white man ate with a little girl who couldn't be over five and a woman who looked like an older version of the little blond girl.

New Orleans was a soup pot of different kinds of people, and I loved it. Military bases were like that, too, but they were never as beautifully crafted as a city like this. Government buildings were mostly brown and tan, whereas New Orleans was a complex mix of creole- and American-style houses with lots of color and detail. In the air, I could smell coffee, sugar, cigarette smoke, and the sun all at once. I could see every skin shade, every walk of life, while sitting at the little iron table outside Café Du Monde. It was still early in the afternoon, so there were more empty tables than I had ever seen, but it was still pretty packed.

"You finished, honey?"

I looked up and smiled back at the older waiter with a missing tooth. He had something sweet about him. Maybe it was the silver hair and weathered wrinkly face. He looked like he'd had a rough night for at least the last four hundred nights.

"Yeah." I slid my plate over to him.

He made a *tsk* sound. "You're gonna waste all that sugar?" His voice was as high-pitched as his hair was gray. He had a paper cap on his head and a white uniform, the traditional uniform of Café Du Monde. Since the place never closed, I wondered if his shift had just started or was about to end.

My eyes moved to the plate he was taking away and the pile of white powder on the paper. It looked like cocaine, only a little better for you. He folded the wax-sheet liner like a taco and grouped the powdered sugar together. It was the same color as his hair.

"I'll tell you a little secret," he whispered to me in a conspiring voice. It made me think about when Jo used to wake me up in the middle of the night to go on an adventure. We would sneak out the back door of our house in Texas and pass through the broken gate to get to the community center at the end of our street.

I nodded, waiting for the man to share his secrets with me.

"A little local secret"—his voice went lower again—"is to pour some of this"—he gently shook the sugar around—"into that." He pointed to my coffee.

A smile broke apart my face, and I told him I would love to try it. After I mixed the leftovers in, I downed the rest of my sweet *au lait* coffee with the extra powdered sugar, feeling like I belonged in the Quarter now that I knew the delicious secret of the insiders. After I slid him a ten, I walked next door to torture myself. I did that often. I was the kind of person who was extremely self-deprecating as well as self-aware. The mix was a circus.

When I walked next door, the smell of candied pralines was so strong that I was instantly hungry again. I checked my phone for a text or call from John, but it only showed a voicemail from the concierge at the Ritz. What even? Nothing from John. I would bring him back some pralines. I had already eaten an entire order of beignets; if I ate any more, I would have to change my powdered-sugar-dusted dress. There was already a line for Aunt Sally's, of course, so I stepped into the end of it. The woman in front of me had a little dog in a purse, and I made a face at it. It growled and I jumped back a little, laughing at myself. The woman turned around and gave me an annoyed look. She rolled her sweet little beady eyes at me. She dripped sticky-honey-dipped Southern woman, the kind who would insult you and then follow with "Bless your heart." Basically my mom's mom.

I knew her type. Her eyes lingered on the white powder on my dress, and I wondered if my pouty lips and expensive eyelashes would let her know I wasn't some worn-down girl in the line for pure sugar on a wax sheet. "If you don't want attention, why carry around a dog in a bag?" I said under my breath.

She heard me and huffed, then turned back around. I smelled her Chanel No. 5 and checked for her huge rock—which was indeed decorating her manicured finger. Her ass looked great in the jeans she was wearing, and it made me want to roll my eyes, for no reason beside my own pettiness. I spent so many wasted thoughts bringing down other women. I hated to think about how often I had done that when I was younger. Jo and her documentaries had changed my perspective. I'm still not as angry at the world as Jo, but maybe I should have been?

The line inside Aunt Sally's was moving pretty quick, and when I made it to the counter to order, I fumbled with my choice between original and chocolate. I wanted both.

"Two chocolate please. And a box of mixed," I finally said after a two-second pause.

I handed the smiling woman my debit card and waited to sign the receipt. I wondered when Shia was going to leave New Orleans, and I wondered if John had plans to meet up with him. This store was full of Shia and the memory of our first meeting, pretty much right where I was standing. There should have been caution tape wrapped around the area, or at least around the man himself. I tried to think about John, my lovely John, who would probably be waking up right about now. The night before wasn't exactly the romantic, passionate night I had anticipated, but today was a new day, and I had pralines to bring to the table.

When I walked outside, I thought my mind was playing a trick on me.

But nope. It was actually happening.

Shia King was walking toward me, live and in the flesh, his eyes already on me. I couldn't run or hide. Well, I could, but he would for sure catch me if I did. And I didn't feel like running. This street was big enough for the both of us. But he was the worst possible person for me to bump into at that moment. The literal worst.

Even though I knew there was no way in hell he was going to let me walk by without at least a snarky remark, just to make a game out of it I turned the other way and took a bite of my praline. Before my teeth finished sinking into the caramel, his hand wrapped around my arm. I gently pulled away from his touch, but turned to him.

"Do I know you?" I asked with my mouth full. Shia made me lose my manners like no one else. His mother would be horrified by my classless chewing with caramel stuck to my teeth.

He started laughing, but there was no noise. His body shook lightly and he shook his head, his white smile so big and his teeth sinking into his bottom lip. I always lost my breath when he did that.

"Really?" He tucked his chin down a little and raised a brow at me.

I held my breath now, though, because he was engaged to Bell Gardiner. Bell Gardiner out of all people.

"Hmph. Not sure." I took another bite and started to walk away. I knew he would follow me. "You look like my friend's fiancé."

He popped up next to my shoulder. "Is that chocolate?"

I jerked away the praline before his fingers could grab it. "Maybe. What can I help you with, Shia?"

"So you do know my name after all?"

"Like I said, I believe you're engaged to my friend."

People were all around us. A couple pushing a set of twins in a stroller. The twins were wearing matching boat hats on their little potato heads; one of them made eye contact with me and smiled, and I smiled back at him.

His smile made me a little sad, but he was so charming.

"Hmm, don't think I am," Shia said.

The baby I thought I was having a moment with started crying hysterically. I continued walking.

Shia laughed next to me, then said, "Anyway, this is a coincidence. What are you doing in the Quarter?"

He was walking next to me, but backward. The sun was so bright that I had to squint a little when I looked at him. He was wearing an earthy-green T-shirt, and Jo's poetry book came to my mind again. The one that says *a little more human than the rest of us.* Shia's facial hair had grown out a little more than I was used to, and it made him look older than he was. I had never seen him in person with the beginnings of a beard—only on Facebook. When he was home, he always kept it shaved.

"Minding my business. You?"

He laughed without noise again. "I can't say the same."

I tried not to laugh. "What do you want, Shia? Where's Bell Gardiner?"

His smile didn't falter, not even a smidge. "Working. Where's John Brooke?"

Touché, asshole.

I didn't look at Shia. "Sleeping. Say, I didn't know bars were open so early on a Sunday. Or maybe you have a connection?"

I hoped my words annoyed him as much as I wanted them to. He was lucky I was even speaking to him. At least, that's what I was trying to convince myself.

"Ha-ha, Meg. Don't be jealous. It's not a good look on you."

I almost bumped into a man carrying an ice-cream cone, and he cursed at me under his breath when he had to basically jump out of my way. How was it that Shia was walking backward and he didn't run into anyone? He was too casual. Even the staple look he wore, and wore well: a T-shirt that said MANILA on the front with a colorful bus under the word, black gym shorts with a Nike check, of course. He must have had those shorts in every color. Shia was being so . . . *Shia*.

"I'm not jealous," I denied. I focused my eyes on a passing taxi van full of rowdy men, and they shouted something gross to a group of women all dressed in the same shirts. Only one was different: it said BRIDE on white instead of BRIDE'S BITCHES on black. The women shouted back and I looked at Shia.

"Gross," he remarked. His eyes followed the taxi until it disappeared and we couldn't hear the men shouting anymore.

"Very." I hoped those women were going to be careful in a

city full of taxi vans full of men full of frozen liquor slushies. I hated that part of the Quarter. I loved the rich culture and the food and the music. New Orleans held so much beauty outside of Bourbon Street. I dreamed of living in a town house in the heart of the Quarter. I would have to wait until my husband and I retired, as I figured I would spend most of my life on a military base.

"Wait, why are you here? Aren't you supposed to be gone by now?" I asked Shia.

We reached the corner of Canal and Decatur and had to stop at the crosswalk to wait for the light to turn. At least half a dozen people were on the sidewalk with us, but it didn't feel that way. They were all minding their own business.

"I'm staying home a little bit longer."

I looked at his face, into his eyes. "Why? Is Bell knocked up or something?"

His smile faded. "Really, Meg? You're going to be that immature?"

I was determined not to say anything—

"I'm *not* being immature," I snapped, a little loudly.

My eyes bounced from the ground to the people around us, to the traffic on Canal Street.

He cracked a smile.

"Go away," I said, not really meaning it.

"Nope," he responded, knowing I didn't. "I thought you and Bell were friends? Plus you kept saying I looked like your friend's fiancé."

I gaped at him. "Friends? You're joking, right?"

Bell and I were never friends. She was awful in that way where she was a wolf in sheep's clothing. Little passive-aggressive insults like "Meg, I know the best dermatologist if you need one" when I ran into her at the PX with one tiny little pimple on my chin. The only times she had been "nice" were questionable. She slid me a drink here and there at her work, but even that stopped once my aunt Hannah got a job behind the bar with her. Reeder, Breyer, John, and I went out in the Quarter each time John came back from New York for leave, but it went from my favorite to least favorite place overnight.

Shia smiled. "Okay, so maybe not friends exactly."

We had resumed walking, I forward and he backward even on the busy cross street. We were in the center of the Quarter and there was no shortage of people bustling through the warm Sunday morning.

"But you don't have any reason not to like her. *I* like John just fine."

My hotel was coming up. It was almost a perfect square of a walk back from Aunt Sally's to the Ritz. What was I supposed to do about Shia walking with me?

"You and John were friends. That's not the same thing." I pulled my phone out of my pocket and checked for something from John. Nothing.

"We weren't that great of friends, and why do you care who I'm engaged to anyway?" Shia shrugged. The green of his T-shirt went so well with his dark skin. He always looked so effortlessly put together, but he was more than his pretty face. As was I.

Shia had told me that exact same thing about John once before, that they weren't that great of friends. When I had asked Shia why, he'd only said, "Why do you think?" and opened the door to the black town car that would drive him to the airport that September.

There was a time in my life, only months ago, when I felt

like I was always saying goodbye to Shia. We were friends, and he was John's friend, too, but it wasn't like John felt a little empty when Shia would leave. Then again, John himself had been in West Point for the last three years. My friendship with Shia barely existed compared to my relationship with John, and I saw them each about the same amount of times. Often, I didn't think anything of the small amounts of time I spent with John; I only thought about how he loved me and was much more mature than Shia. Shia and I had barely been speaking lately. I wanted to pretend that I didn't know why.

"We've barely talked the last few months," I finally said. I couldn't let him make me crawl inside my head the way he loved to. He wasn't the kind of guy you just talked to casually, spitting out beige words just like everyone else. He didn't ask about the weather, he asked about your favorite type of storm. His conversations were rainbow colored, every shade. When Shia King talked to you, he climbed into your mind and took pieces out with him. He didn't ask everyday things like *How are you?*

"Would you have had anything to say to me, Meg?"

Last summer, right in front of Jackson Square, he asked me, *"What's the last thing that made you cry?"*

"I don't know. But I would have liked the choice."

We kept walking and I could see my hotel from where we were. The temperature was rising as the afternoon took over from the morning. He was being silent as he stirred my words, probably searching for an essay of an answer to make my head spin with thoughts I wasn't ready to have.

That night in front of that park, famous for artists selling their paintings, something started to grow in the gap between us. I didn't know much about art. I wasn't like Jo or Shia King.

However, I could name every shade of Tarte lipstick and the best type of haircut for your face shape. We all had our talents.

"How's your dad?"

"Hasn't called in a while," I told him.

That sticky August night was supposed to have been a normal night of me playing Taxi, driving Beth to her friend's house to "study" (back when she wanted to leave the house) and then dropping Jo off at work. Her last job was at a little coffee-and-crepe place right across from Jackson Square. I planned to walk around a little and maybe go to the mall, but I saw Shia standing outside the entrance and I had recognized him from Reeder's barracks room.

I spent Jo's entire shift telling him about a Facebook post from River. It was a meme about crazy ex-girlfriends because *I* was the crazy one. Riiight. He had not only spread pictures of my body that I trusted him with to half of the school, but he wouldn't stop posting stupid quotes about exes.

By the time I had spilled half of my guts to Shia, Jo texted me to pick her up from her shift. I couldn't believe how fast the last four hours had gone, and I couldn't believe I had gone that much into detail about the bullshit that happened in Texas. I didn't want that part of my life to follow me here to a new state, new life, but there I was pouring it out on the concrete.

Prior to that night, Shia and I had hung out maybe six times. Sometimes with John, sometimes with Reeder, but never at Shia's house. Always in the barracks rooms. I didn't even know he was a part of the Fort Cyprus royal family until Reeder let it slip one night in the field behind the Shoppette, but Shia talked his way out of further conversation about it before we even realized that's what he was doing.

After I spilled my guts to him like cheap red wine on a white sheet, Shia and I became friends, I guess you could call it. Then we got in a fight that night I was wearing a tiara on my head. He called me princess and kissed my mouth with cherry lips and a silver tongue. Neither of us wanted that night to haunt us, and then John asked me to take our relationship to the next level. Even during that, I kept hanging out with Shia, and he would try to convince me to leave town with him. He always laughed enough at the end where I didn't know if he was serious or not.

His silence now got the best of me and I turned quickly to him, annoyance spreading through me, and said, "John's in the hotel room waiting for me."

Shia's eyes stayed on the busy sidewalk ahead of us, and the light turned for us to walk.

"Liar!" a voice yelled from the middle of the street.

When I looked, a homeless man was standing there, his hands in the air and liquid draining from his full beard. Shia gently tapped my arm for me to keep walking.

My frustration bubbled over. "If you're going to ignore me, then get the hell away from me."

Shia laughed and I groaned. "I'm not ignoring you. I'm thinking before I speak. You should try it."

I rolled my eyes in the most dramatic way.

"I want to see John anyway. I'll come with you?" Shia offered, waited for me to nod, and followed me to the hotel.

28

beth

"Aunt Hannah called," I told my mom as soon as she walked through the door.

The wooden door shut and barely made a sound. It wasn't like our thick mahogany door in Texas that Jo used to throw sharp-pointed ninja stars into. That thing slammed shut every time the wind blew and shook the house with it. The door in this house looked like it was made from birch and could blow away with the wind anytime.

Mom set her purse down on the floor and walked over to the fridge. I saw the lines of tension sprout across her forehead, but she kept a straight face. "What did she say?"

My aunt had called three times before I finally answered, and she sounded like she was covering the receiver. I would have told my mom this if her under-eyes weren't the color of my jeans.

"That she needs you to call her back. She sounded stressed-out." I paused long enough for my mom to dip her head into the fridge to avoid me. "Is everything okay?"

Mom stood up and closed the fridge, a carton of eggs in her hands. "Yeah, yeah. Everything is fine. Did you get all your class work done? Are you still behind a week?"

Classic Meredith Spring, changing the subject even better than Amy. I knew my mom twice as well as my sisters did, so that meant I knew her every move. She didn't have many, but lately she had been cashing them all in. She was trying to distract me by asking for my homework and getting me to talk about myself.

"I caught up after Christmas break, remember?" I specifically recalled talking to her about it in the living room.

"Oh yeah."

My mom opened the cupboard and grabbed a mixing bowl. She hadn't been in the mood to cook lately, but I wasn't going to bring that up. I didn't mind cooking most of the meals around here, but I was happy taking the morning off. It was almost noon. Jo was upstairs writing in her room, and Meg was with John downtown. Amy was at the house of some girl down the street, so we were alone for the most part. I owed it to my dad to take any time I could to check in on my mom. He hadn't called in *days*, and her eyes were bloodshot this morning.

My mom's blond hair was pulled back in a claw clip. Her hair was thinning in the front, where she curled the pieces into one big curl around her hairline. Meg always begged her to let her give her a new style, but so far our mom had refused.

"How much longer do you have? I should know this." She pulled a smile out of the pocket of her favorite T-shirt. She slept in the T-shirt, printed with my dad's old company name over the image of a tank. It was so worn that the black fabric had turned gray and the tank had started to peel off. The decal now looked like a house or something, not a tank.

"Until May, technically, but I might be able to finish early."

My mom popped open the carton of eggs and inspected them. "Your dad has always wondered about next year. And the school sent an email . . ." Her voice fell a little.

My dad wanted me to go to "regular" school, I knew he did, but he would never just flat out say it. "What kind of email?"

She took a few eggs in her hands and walked over to the bowl on the counter. "Just an enrollment email for you, Amy, and Jo. Are you ready to go back to school?"

She stopped talking, and I figured that she was trying to collect her thoughts before she handed them out. She chose the weirdest stuff to treat me like a kitten about.

"Does Dad think I should go back to school?"

"That's not what I said. I said he's asked over the past few months if you were ready to go back."

"Why, though? Is something wrong with what I'm doing now? I'm ahead of schedule now, and I only fell behind one time and that was over holiday. Jo bombed that math test last week."

"It's not about the grades."

Mom began to crack the eggs against the side of the bowl. The eggs broke hard enough that I'm sure a few tiny shells went inside the bowl, but didn't want to point them out. I usually did it at the end, pulling out little shards of eggshell. My mom wasn't great at not getting shells inside, but at least she wasn't like Jo, who refused to look at the eggs. She ate scrambled meat that wasn't real meat and tortilla shells almost every day for breakfast. Or the occasional bagel stuffed to the brim with cream cheese.

I waited for my mom to explain why I was failing as a teenager.

"It's that you'll be in tenth grade. Freshman year is always tough, for sure, but you've had a break. Do you think it's time to try it again? Now that Jo could get you into Yearbook with her? You're so smart, Beth."

This wasn't the first time Mom had brought it up, but this time was much more direct than ever before.

"You don't get it. It's not about being smart, Meredith," I said accidentally. It threw her off, I could tell. My sisters had picked up Jo's habit of calling her by her name, but I liked to call her Mom. Sometimes I would call her Meredith out of my sister's habit, but I tried not to. "It's not about me being smart, it's about the majority of the school day having nothing to do with actual school."

"What does that mean?"

I sighed. I felt like I had explained this enough times in the last year.

"Is this about bullying? Because—"

"It's not about bullying, Mom. It's about no one getting that I don't want to be around people the way that Meg and Jo and Amy and you and Dad do. I can't learn with a room full of people. I'm sorry if it's not normal—"

"Beth . . ." Mom paused. Her tone was unreadable and her eyes were full of guilt. I didn't ever want her to feel guilty, I just wanted her to see that this wasn't about her. "I wasn't saying you have to go back to school. I was only bringing it up because of the email. You know what's best for you, okay? I trust you to know what's best for you, and if you want to be homeschooled until college, that's okay."

I knew I was lucky to have the option of staying home. Most

parents would have been the opposite of mine and forced me to "work through my anxiety," which my parents did try until I couldn't handle it anymore and started skipping.

"Thank you." I sighed, leaning against the counter.

I would have brought up that my college would be in home, too, but I just wanted the conversation to end.

My mom continued to make breakfast until Jo came down with her arms full of newspapers and said Laurie was going to come over later. He had been spending a lot of time with Jo, but I thought it was a good thing. She wasn't good at making friends like Meg and Amy. She wasn't as bad at it as I was, but still.

"What in the world?" Mom asked, gaping at Jo and her baggage.

"I'm looking for something," Jo said, as if that explained what in the world she was doing. The smell of bacon smothered the kitchen until I added onions to my mom's famous farmer's breakfast. It was a mash-up of potatoes, oil, butter, salt and pepper, bacon, sausage, eggs, and cheese. Jo got her own skillet with no meat, and I ate from both.

When we had devoured our plates, Jo said, "That was *so* good—thanks, guys," and went back to her stack of papers while I started washing the pans.

The phone started ringing again and I hit silence. Seconds later someone knocked on the door. Jo set down the newspaper she had in front of her face, and my mom stalled a moment before asking me to get it.

I hoped it wasn't Aunt Hannah, but when I saw the two officers standing in the doorway, I immediately took back my wish.

meg

I called John twice before Shia and I came back to the Ritz. He didn't answer, and I couldn't just barge into the room with Shia and wake John up. So while we waited for John to come back to life, Shia and I hung out in the hotel's Club Room, and I somehow found a way to eat more food. The room was actually three rooms, one with an extravagant lunch display set out across a huge banquet table. Meats, cheeses, little finger sandwiches made from cheeses I had never heard of. They had fruit cut into shapes and grapes on sticks.

The other two rooms were for sitting. I couldn't count how many couches and recliners filled the space. Inside these rooms, time hadn't moved forward in a while. I didn't know what year the decor was supposed to be representing, but it was definitely sometime when people loved floral-print everything. Shia and I found ourselves a nice four-person table in the corner, next to a flatscreen TV that had to be at least fifty inches.

Shia moved a cracker around his plate and scooped some hummus onto it. I didn't know anyone else who loved hummus. I smiled thinking about how Amy once called it "rich people food," and Jo told her to shut up and google something for once in her life.

"How long are you staying here in this hotel? It's nice, right?" Shia popped the entire cracker into his mouth. He chewed quietly; all that fancy Southern table training came in handy. I took an etiquette course on post when I was twelve, but Shia was groomed since birth to be a gentleman.

"One more night," I said, the bottom of my throat on fire. I reached for my water and finished answering his question. "And, yeah, I would say so. Look at this space." My eyes bounced around the room and Shia's followed.

"You do love shiny things."

I snapped my gaze back to him. "And what is that supposed to mean?" My annoyance barely held behind the corners of my smiling mouth.

He shrugged.

I looked around the room and focused on the hotel employee who was relining the table he had just cleaned with a fresh, crisp white tablecloth.

"Just saying. Do you not?" Shia challenged me. I saw his eyes flicker from the powder scattered across the chest of my dress.

"Not all of us want to throw away our trust funds and *not* go to college." Shia's eyes bulged and his knee hit the table before I registered that I had really said that.

Were we fighting?

I had just started a fight, I knew it, but sometimes that was the only way we communicated. What I had just said felt much more personal and a splash too harsh for our usual banter. Such banter didn't entail fighting normally; it was mostly calling each other out on our crap, but it never felt malicious, no matter how many times I told my sisters I hated him.

"Throw away? You literally have no idea what you're talking about. But you just stay up there on that pedestal, Meg. I had a call this morning with my friend in Cambodia, and she told me she removed two girls in one month from a whorehouse with the money we raised for her. One of the girls was twelve—the same age as Amy—and had been a sex slave for three years."

My stomach twisted.

He continued, "What have you done? Beside paint my mom's face on and take her dogs for walks?"

I sat there taking in every single word he said and stirred it and stirred it until my phone rang on the table between us.

I somehow found my voice. "I better get that," I said, biting my tongue.

John's name flashed across the screen and I swiped to answer. He told me he had just woken up, and when I mentioned Shia, John said he was going to work out in the gym, take a shower, then meet us.

When I hung up, Shia laughed, but it wasn't snarky. "Work out? He just doesn't stop."

"He's been in a routine." I thought he would have at least asked me to come back to the room while he showered, or to tag along with him to the gym.

"Yeah."

Shia looked up at the TV and rolled his eyes at the screen. "Our country is—"

"Don't start the political talk. I need more coffee." I groaned. He was like Jo: when you got them going, they didn't stop. I admired it most of the time, even though I wasn't as involved as they were, but not today. My mind went to the twelve-year-old girl in Cambodia. I tried to remember if Jo's essay was about the same place . . .

"Fine. How's everything going with you? Did you enroll in that makeup course yet?"

I instantly wanted to press rewind. I shook my head and took another drink of water. "No. Not yet."

"Why? It's coming up, in what—May?"

That he remembered that blew my mind.

Of course he did, the honest part of my brain countered.

"Yeah. I'm sure it's full now. The summer will be busy for me anyway."

I didn't know why I'd put off signing up for the course. I'd met an artist when he came into Sephora for the launch of a brand. He told me about a course he was going to in Los Angeles in the summer. The person teaching it was a celebrity makeup artist, and she was supposedly the master of the newest techniques. I wasn't technically trained as an artist and the course would give me a little more credibility, but it was all the way across the country, and expensive.

"Are those reasons or excuses?" That was one of Shia's favorite things to ask about anything, from the reason I didn't return his calls to life choices.

"Both."

"What's going on, Meg?"

I fidgeted in my chair and looked around the room. It was much less crowded than when we first arrived. Only four or five people were in the room, and one was an old man who had fallen asleep sitting quite rigidly on the couch with his glasses resting on the tip of his nose.

"With what? It's just a makeup course." I shrugged and drank the last little bit of my water.

Shia had stopped eating, and a server came by to clear our plates. I held on to the crostini on my plate, but Shia had them take his away. He tipped her, too, and I wondered how many people I was supposed to tip but didn't since we arrived. The bellman? The valet? The concierge when they drop off John's clean uniform in the morning?

"In life. You're not taking the course you talked about for weeks. And you're working for my mom, of all people?" Shia dragged out the sentence like he needed me to really listen to what he was saying.

"She pays me well. More than my other job."

He had a different relationship with Mrs. King than I did, and no matter how intimidating she was to me, I could only hope to be like her one day. She was everything I wanted to be.

"And you're doing what for her? Long term? Where is that going to get you?"

I didn't respond, so he kept going. He did soften his voice so it didn't escalate the way it could have. "My mom said you're trying to marry John. Is that true?"

"She said that?" The burning in my throat spread up to my ears and cheeks.

"Not literally. But she hinted. She was saying how we could throw you a big engagement party."

He paused, but I didn't think he was done talking. I interrupted him anyway. "Like your engagement party?"

He sighed and lifted the bottom of his T-shirt up to wipe his face. A line of his skin peeked out and I looked at my plate.

I wanted to look at him, but didn't want to give him the satisfaction.

"A little like mine. But more romantic, more real, I think."

"Mm-hmm." I sat back against the cushioned back of my
chair. I didn't know how romantic my engagement party would
be or why Shia was hinting that his wasn't real, but I didn't want
to play this game. A different woman came by with a pitcher of
water and filled my drink.

I swished an ice cube around in my mouth, and he sat
forward.

"So that's it? We're just going to pretend like we have nothing to talk about?"

"You mean your engagement?"

He shook his head. "No. I meant *you*. What happened to you
having to get the hell out of here?"

"I'm still planning on leaving."

He licked his lips. "When?"

"Soon. I don't know. My dad's gone, and Jo hasn't even graduated yet. I can't just leave them. I'm working and saving my
money."

The sleeping old man from the couch was now up and moving, searching through a basket of potato-chip bags on the
counter under the TV closest to us.

"Soon, huh?" Shia asked.

I was so annoyed that I felt like my anger was going to stain
the upholstered chair under me with blotchy black streaks.
"What's your problem? Why are you starting shit with me?"

"I'm not. I'm just wondering why you've changed your whole
plan around, and now what? You're looking at whatever base
John's gonna be stationed at?"

His response reminded me of his speech right before I was

supposed to meet him last fall. Winter had come since and now we were on the verge of spring.

"Seriously, Meg. You're nineteen. You have so much time to do your own thing before you become a—"

"Stop." I held my hand up. "Don't try to lecture me. You're engaged, Shia."

"Why do you keep repeating that? Does that have something to do with you, Meg? I thought I was delusional and made us all up in my head? So if that's true, why do you keep bringing my engagement up?"

He had me there. I didn't want to talk about the day we blew up whatever scraps of a relationship we had and now had this awkward, barely speaking faux-ship going on that scratched at my skin. I didn't want things to be so muddled between us. Arguing with Shia usually made me bloom with laughter and feel a little spark on the tip of my tongue, but as I sat here in the fancy Club Room in the luxurious Ritz-Carlton in the famous French Quarter in New Orleans, it felt like wading through a thick vat of maple syrup.

"Oh, don't hold your tongue now," he said after we stared at each other for a minute.

The old man walked away with three bags of salt-and-pepper chips and a bottle of Coke tucked under his arm.

I told a little seed of truth: "I didn't say you were delusional."

He laughed without a sound. "Yes, you did. You told Reeder a really, really not-true story about us. You've been telling yourself that same story?" he asked, but he wasn't asking.

"What was I supposed to say? I don't want any drama in our group. You shouldn't either. So I said what I needed to say to clear myself."

"It's always about you, isn't it—and who's 'our group'? No one talks to me while I'm gone. No one talks to John either, except me, and even that's not often. There doesn't have to be drama. I'm not River."

My pulse shot through the roof of the Club Room.

Shia kept going. "I wouldn't have been pissed at you for not coming with me. That's your choice and your life. But it would have been nice if you could have just told me you weren't coming to the airport. I would have understood if you would have just *told* me. Been honest with me." He cupped his hands together and moved them slowly.

"I thought I was being honest. I thought I could be like Jo for once and just jump on a plane and leave without a plan."

In a flat voice he said, "We had a plan. It was literally a planned trip with my dad's foundation."

"You know what I mean." His sarcastic semantics weren't going to get us anywhere. "I'm sorry I didn't tell you"—I remembered just how hard I left him hanging—"until you landed."

"I'm not ma—"

"Well, well, well, look who it is!" John suddenly exclaimed by our side, patting Shia on the back. His hair was wet, so he must have showered, but he couldn't have worked out so fast.

And just like that, they were bros and hugging and their smiles were so big and so fake, I could spot the insincerity a mile away.

30

jo

When Beth walked back into the kitchen, the color was drained from her face. On her heels were two men in Army uniform.

Meredith dropped to her knees before they spoke.

Beth rushed toward her.

I felt like my socks were rooted into the ground. I couldn't move as chaos erupted in the room.

My mom was screaming, but the voices of the men broke through it.

"Meredith, Meredith! It's just an injury. I only came because Frank is my friend. I'm sorry to have frightened you!" the taller man yelled.

My dad's supposed friend looked like he wanted to get the hell out of Dodge. His cheeks were so red and the newspapers from the counter were all over the floor.

"Where is he? Where's my husband?" Meredith demanded.

The other man took a step forward, and his boot covered a picture of a homecoming ceremony for the Scout platoon who came home last week.

"Germany. He's at a hospital there while he gains his strength to come home."

"Germany?" Beth asked.

I told her that most injured soldiers end up in Germany before coming home to the U.S.

Beth wrapped something around my mom's shoulders, and I felt like we were on an episode of *True Life* or something. It all felt like it wasn't really happening to us. It felt like an article on the internet. I read once that by watching too many documentaries and Facebook videos, you can become desensitized to violence in front of you in real time because your brain and memory are not able to tell the difference from watching it happen virtually.

The room spun a little until my mom calmed down. Beth got my mom to sit in Dad's recliner with a cup of something that smelled a little stronger than coffee.

Beth called Aunt Hannah and our grandparents.

Twenty minutes beforehand, I was rummaging through old newspapers in my room upstairs. I was listening to music and searching through page after page of homecoming ceremony coverage. I wasn't even sure what I was doing with them yet, but I knew Laurie had a plan when he gave me a list of names to search for. It suddenly seemed incredibly unimportant as my mom's shoulders were shaking under the blanket wrapped around her.

Aunt Hannah showed up thirty minutes later, and Amy came home from her friend's house and wouldn't stop asking

Meredith what was wrong until she got yelled at. Beth stared at the wall, and I stared at my computer. Aunt Hannah was just sitting on the couch, staring blankly at the TV on the wall. The mess of cords hanging from the wall and wrapped around the extension cord screamed *house fire*, but there were just so many things to plug in.

"Have you talked to Meg yet?" Meredith asked when Aunt Hannah brought her another drink. I didn't even have a mental comment on her drinking, I had no right to question her in that moment. I even craved a drink and I hated the taste of alcohol.

The only thing we knew was that my dad's tank ran over an IED on the side of the road and caught fire. Out of four men, my dad was one of two survivors. One of the men killed had just had a baby halfway through the deployment. It didn't seem fair, but I couldn't speak the word *fair* since my dad was alive. The men who came bearing the news told my mom that she could go to Germany and stay with my dad until he healed, and she said she would have to see if she could.

Beth and I stood in the kitchen with Aunt Hannah and went over our options if Meredith decided to go.

"I can drive Amy to her stuff and myself to work," I offered. "I just need to go get my license. I can go Monday."

Aunt Hannah peeked into the living room and came back to stand by the oven, which she turned off. It was on from when Beth and my mom were making breakfast, which seemed like another lifetime.

"I can stay most nights, but I work five days a week," Aunt Hannah told me. Beth nodded and wiped a chunk of brown hair from her forehead. "I can help out as much as I can."

"Amy's the only one who can't take care of herself," I said, just as Amy came walking into the kitchen.

"I can take care of myself just fine, Jo." Her tone was harsh, but I didn't blame her. We had all had a long day, and no one had heard from Meg yet. I considered calling Shia or emailing John, but I didn't know how much of a mess that could make.

"Anyway . . ." Beth opened the fridge and poured Amy a glass of milk. Beth grabbed a pack of Oreos and slid them across the table. For once in her life, Amy shook her head at the cookies.

"So, Jo, you'll need to take that test this week. How many shifts do you work this week?" Beth asked.

I didn't know off the top of my head, and I told my sisters and my aunt that I would tell them when I knew. I leaned my elbows against the cold counter and felt the room shifting and our lives changing with every passing breath.

31

meg

John sat down next to me with a twenty-ounce Coke in his hand and a plate of salad and little sausages smothered in sauce that looked like dark gravy.

"What have you two been up to all day?" he asked Shia and me, swiping a forked crouton through a puddle of ranch.

Shia looked at me a moment, like he was waiting on me to reply to John first. I wanted him to do the same.

"I was walking around the Quarter a bit. Couldn't sleep," I said.

I wound my hair around my hand and stared at my water glass. Water had collected in little pearl-like beads all over the side of it, and I ran my finger over the moisture, drawing little lines with my nail. Even the water glasses at the Ritz weren't just plain glasses; they were more like crystal goblets carved with unique patterns.

I quickly ran through my morning and ended with "And I got these," lifting the bag of pralines from the floor. "They are so good. I got a few of them." I smiled, and John chewed his food. I sat the bag back down on the floor by my feet.

John half covered his mouth and said, "Cool, the things with the nuts? The shop is cool, though; it's like Mexican or something?"

Shia coughed. Or choked. I wasn't sure.

How John gathered that assumption, I would never know, but I thought it was pretty basic knowledge that the French Quarter wasn't historically tied to Mexico. The Spanish yes; Mexico, no. Then again, I couldn't tell you where Spain was on a map. I knew it was part of Europe, sure.

"They're creole. Do you want one?" I asked Shia without looking at him, but felt his eyes hot on my face. Shia thanked me and asked for a chocolate praline, which I knew was meant to goad me.

"What?" he asked with a grin, knowing I couldn't say a word in front of John.

It felt a little too Nicholas Sparks for us to have met up at the same praline shop where we met for the first time. If I was the extreme hopeless romantic that Jo always said I was, I would have believed that running into him in Aunt Sally's would have been some magical fate marker that meant we were destined to run off into the sunset together.

But I wasn't that much of a sap. Only like half as much as Jo made me out to be, at most.

John shook his head when I handed Shia the wrapped praline, chewing his food with his mouth not quite closed. "You two are into the sweet stuff. Gross."

"Hmph" was the noise that came from my mouth.

Shia looked like he wanted to say something, thought it out, his eyes looking up at the ceiling and all, but didn't say whatever made him pause. He sat back against his chair.

A few seconds passed and he casually asked, "So, what's on the plan today? How's it feel to be back into the real world?"

John ran his hand over his smooth chin. He laughed. "It's weird, for sure. Mostly because I get to wear normal clothes"—his fingers plucked at his polo shirt—"for the day. I don't know. Meg planned the day, I think? Right, Meg?" John looked to me.

Say what?

I was under the impression that he was planning the whole weekend. In fact, I specifically remember John Brooke's sleepy voice cooing over the phone, "Don't worry about anything, baby. It's my treat to you. Just walk out to the car. That's all you need to do."

"Right?" he asked again, and while I was watching him gnaw on a ranch-smothered crouton, something shiny fell from his shoulders and disappeared into the stuffy air, leaving him a touch less colorful than he was in my memory.

"I didn't plan anything, actually," I said slowly, and I felt so awkward and didn't know why, exactly. "But I figure there's plenty of stuff we can find last-minute. Even if we just walk around or whatever. There's always something to do. We could do a ghost tour like we did with Reeder and them. Remember?" I looked at John, and Shia looked at me, and I looked at the table. "We're staying smack in the middle of the Quarter; there's plenty to do."

"Oh yeah. That's cool with me, babe." John lifted his hip to pull his cell phone out of his back pocket. "Whatever you want to do is cool with me."

I nodded at him, smiling. He smiled back, but only a little, and then he looked down at his phone in his hand. He had a brand-new iPhone and it took pictures like a professional camera. It was like a little computer in his hand. I wanted one so bad, but they were so freaking expensive, and Amy was already racking up the data bill on our plan so much that Meredith threatened to take her phone away every month. I couldn't add an expense and listen to my three younger sisters bitch about it. Amy didn't understand that I actually *worked* for most everything outside of the basics.

"Cool," I lamely responded. It confused me to no end why sitting at the table with Shia and John felt worse than when I was seventeen and had to get my wisdom teeth cut out.

"Hmph." Shia made the quiet noise from his throat, breaking up the silence for a second.

I wondered what he was thinking about, but wasn't about to ask him. That whole situation was pretty awkward.

It bothered me that I looked like an idiot in front of not only Shia King, but to John Brooke. I must have looked like I didn't put any thought into our time together. If I had known I was supposed to plan a romantic freaking getaway, I would have scheduled couple's massages at the spa inside the Ritz. I would have preordered breakfast in bed with strawberries and champagne. John was twenty-one—they would have let us. I would have planned the most perfect couples retreat weekend, just like I helped Mrs. King plan for a trip to Atlanta with Mr. King. They got $400 massages at the top-rated spa in Buckhead, and Mrs. King got a sugar scrub. When I booked it, I added the complimentary hour in the couples room. I didn't even have the chance to be that thoughtful for us because I thought John was in charge of everything.

I had been looking forward to this weekend for so long, but

now it felt messy and completely done on a whim. Where it had once all seemed so planned and organized, it now felt like no actual thought beyond booking a bed for us to sleep in had been done. John's time mattered to me, and I wanted him to feel that. Wasn't that the point of dating someone? To show them how good of a wife I would be? That was my point anyway. I wasn't sure John had a point.

If I were honest, I'd admit also that I wanted Shia to recognize my devotion to John. I wanted him to see it in his face like I saw Bell Gardiner's emerald flashing on her dainty finger. I could have used a hit of revenge; the sticky-sweet high of having control over the situation is like nothing else. No orgasm, not a slice of devil's food cake still warm from the oven, not even the poreless satin skin I had after using foundation primer for the first time could ever compare to the feeling of having the upper hand. With River, I never felt in control of our dynamic. From the first sloppy kiss (during a game of Seven Minutes in Heaven that I didn't even want to play) to the first time we had sex (awkwardly in the back of his car), he was always in charge, and it felt like something was constantly floating over my head when I was with him. I didn't know if it was the pressure of staying relevant to him and his group of friends, but something was always over my head, keeping me eager to be the wild girl, the girl who would lift her shirt at a party or blow River in one of his friends' rooms during a rager.

River told me how beautiful I was until he took my virginity in the backseat of his 1991 Lumina and asked for pictures of my tits. Then I became an object, and the comments about my beautiful big eyes changed into comments about my big breasts and ass, and I never heard the word *beautiful* again. I didn't miss it at the time, though, honestly, I lived for the sexual power I had over him. It's that feeling that I loved so much.

River didn't care about me, not really. Not as much as he cared about being the cool guy with the naked pictures of Meg Spring. There was even a rumor that he was making guys in our school pay him ten bucks for them. The girls got them for free, to pick me apart, to call me names and criticize every part of my body from my "pepperoni nipples" to the stretch marks on the tops of my thighs. The girls at my old school were worse even than the guys. At least the guys' comments weren't negative.

River was careless and thoughtless, and John was supposed to be the opposite of that. I was in control, holding the better cards, and if Shia knew I was happy with John Brooke, maybe it would make me feel better about him and Bell. Such was my illogical logic at nineteen.

With every week out of high school, I felt like I was getting to know myself more and more. I found out things about myself every day. Like new foods, different ways I could appreciate my life. Jo said I always took power too far, and that power can be silent, but I liked to shout and scream. I had been quiet my entire life, and after being tormented for being quiet, I wasn't going to shut up. Jo always told me that with my confidence, I could be a CEO of a big company in Chicago or New York, but I didn't feed off the crowd or thrive under bright lights like she did. I wanted to hear the sounds of children laughing and playing, and I wanted a yard.

I didn't have New York City–sized dreams like Jo, but mine seemed like much more fun. Jo wanted to be a little fish in an ocean, and I wanted to be an expensive, exotic fish in a beautiful clean tank. She didn't care about being admired the way I did. Not everyone could be like Jo, or Shia even—and I didn't want to be.

The second that my thoughts went back to Shia, he asked a woman passing by us what time it was. I knew there were big clocks on the wall and a phone in his pocket, but I assumed he was trying to make things less awkward by speaking to someone, anyone. I wondered which one of us would leave first. I started to think I was being paranoid about how awkward it actually was, since neither of them were making a move to leave or strike up a conversation. John was still eating, and Shia was playing with a yarn bracelet on his wrist.

I grew more uncomfortable with each second that ticked on. It was weird that they weren't talking when they were supposed to be "friends." The awkwardness ate at me until I started to think that maybe they were both conspiring against me? What would Jo make of this? She would definitely have a theory on the strange behavior of these two young men. John wasn't acting like we had just been reunited the night before.

When it came down to it, I just wanted to spend uninterrupted time with John. The more I thought about it, the more I realized that even though we were "dating," we hadn't spent much time together. Was Jo right about us when she said that we had no foundation?

But what does Jo know about dating? I thought. Well . . . at that point Jo had spent more time with Laurie than I had John, and she had only been friends with him since around Christmastime.

Hell, I'd spent more time with Mrs. King than anyone else in my life lately, aside from my family. I didn't have much of a social life between working and driving my sisters around. Shia was my friend, at least when I first moved to Fort Cyprus. Thinking about it, I couldn't remember when we became more than friends, or less, but I knew that if Shia wanted me, he would have said it. He never told me he wanted me, not the way John did. He asked me to leave the country with him, sure, but he used the word "friend" more times than I could count. Kissing friends, that's what we were.

Meg Spring was for kissing; Bell Gardiner was for marriage. It made me nauseous to think about.

So much gossip surrounded me everywhere I went, how did I not hear about Shia and Bell? I spent at least fifteen hours a week at his family's house, and I had no idea he was dating her. I knew nothing about their whirlwind relationship. I looked at Shia across from me and remembered the mysterious emails from "John" that weren't actually from John.

Still, I didn't think Shia would do that. He would just text me or come to my house and tell me to break up with John if he had a problem with us. I couldn't think of a single reason why he would care, but I was still nursing the Bell Gardiner engagement wound, so I wanted him to care just a little. But Shia was better than that; even if he cared, he wouldn't take his time to make a fake email address and send me fake emails from John to purposely fuck with me.

Who had time for that? Nobody. Nobody with anything real in their life.

Shia sat across from us with his eyes dancing the line between bored and focused on the TV above our table. A basketball game was playing, and knowing Shia had less than zero interest in sports, I knew he was avoiding conversation, or maybe didn't have anything to say. On a bookshelf behind John's back was a collection of encyclopedias, so I pulled a Shia and looked them over. They seemed so ancient sitting there. There must have been some wasteland full of encyclopedias and dictionaries whose existence was devalued when the internet took over the world.

Staring at the encyclopedias only granted me a minute or two, and the silence ticked on. Shia leaned his elbow on the table and began to look around the room. John was still looking down at his phone in his lap, and my water cup was already empty again.

What in the world could be so interesting? More interesting than me?

Shia stood up slowly from his chair. His fingers pulled at the bottom of his T-shirt. "Want some more water, Meg?" He looked straight into my eyes, and I knew he wanted to say something, but I couldn't tell what.

I shook my head no, even though I wanted more. My throat was still burning a little. Now it felt tight, like I was being pulled with such force that when I snapped, the tearing sound would, like a shriek, rip the awkward silence among the three of us. Shia grabbed my glass, and I had a feeling that John was in his own little world, not aware of anything.

And, boy, was he not. The tension and hyperawareness of our secret was boiling between Shia and me. And there sat John, too distracted by his phone to even notice that the stove was on.

I knew I was being slightly petty, and John probably had so many friends and family members to catch up with now that he was graduated from West Point, but I wanted more attention than the stupid device in his hand. John didn't say much of anything before Shia came back with a cup of water and a bottled water. I didn't think that John would have noticed that my cup was empty in the first place, let alone know to fill it up even if

I said no. But should he have? Should John Brooke have to play these games I couldn't seem to help but play?

"Well, I'm gonna go. I have to run by my dad's office, pick up Bell from Spirits, and then go home. It was good to see you, man," Shia said.

John squeezed my hand and stood up to hug Shia. Shia was taller than John, who stood about five foot eight and had a stocky build. My mind flipped through a picture book from the first time I saw him to the last, here today.

His and John's exchange was a few seconds long, and they promised to call each other. I didn't think they would, but I couldn't decide which of them would be the *least* likely to call. John seemed withdrawn, and Shia seemed like he didn't know what to say or do—which was a first. I didn't know if I should have been standing up and I waited too long, so Shia stuck out his hand and shook my hand. Like we had just done a business deal or met for the first time.

Not like he waited for me at the airport to leave the country with him and I didn't show.

When he was done shaking my hand, he walked out of the room so fast that for a second I thought I'd made him up being there at all. John grabbed ahold of the arm of my chair and yanked it closer to him. I yelped and he laughed, and all felt right in the world. Well, at least my tiny bubble of a world inside the Club Room of the Ritz in the French Quarter. I felt a little like Carrie Bradshaw in Paris with her artist, Alexander. Then again, Alexander ends up being a complete dick and the trip goes down the drain and ends with Big coming to take her home from Paris. Hmm. Worst analogy ever. Okay, so I couldn't come up with anything else, but I'm sure there was a

Chris Klein character from a few years back that would serve better.

John felt like the type of man who knew exactly what he wanted, and in that moment he wanted my mouth. His mouth was rough and I licked his lips to wet them before my tongue met his. He tasted like Pepsi and salt, but his face was so smooth. I remember thinking that he must have shaved after his workout and shower. I lifted my hand to rub his skin, and I almost wanted to open my eyes to make sure Shia wasn't in the Club Room anymore. John's hands went to my hips, and my dress felt so thin when his hands rubbed the cotton into my sensitive skin. I leaned into him and put my hands on his thighs.

His pants were stiff and ironed to purposely have a crease down the front of his leg. I kissed him for the way I acted when I got those stupid emails, I sucked a little at his tongue for not planning anything for us this weekend, and my hands traveled seductively up his thighs for bringing Shia back, though John didn't seem to care at all.

Someone on the other side of the room coughed, and I never found out if it was on purpose, but I broke away from our kiss and John smiled at me. His hair was cut so short that the redness of his forehead shined through, and his lips were blushed from our kissing.

"I missed you this morning." He kissed my hair. "I was so worked up after my workout, God, I missed you."

"I missed you, too."

I hugged around his neck and had turned his cheek to kiss him again when Shia came bursting back into the room. He rushed toward us and I broke away from John, pushing at his shoulders in my surprise.

"Meg. Call your mom," Shia said urgently.

Before I could ask him why, he shoved his phone toward my face. My skin tingled all over like hundreds of little thorns were poking me all over my body. I took his phone and called my mom's number, hoping the sinking feeling inside me was only hollowing me out because of the look on Shia's face.

"What's going on?" John asked Shia.

Shia didn't respond. I knew something had happened the moment my mom picked up the phone.

"Meg, Meg, please come home. It's your dad, please get here." She wasn't hysterical or sobbing; she wasn't herself, but was still calm and clear.

"Is he—"

"No, he's alive. But in Germany"—there was a long pause—"at Landstuhl."

I could feel my face heating up with each thought that ran through my head. *What happened? How bad is he? How are my sisters? How is Meredith? Is my dad going to die?* "How bad is it?"

John's brows were drawn together and he stared at me. Shia's hand touched my shoulder, and my throat burned until I gave in and let the sob break through my lips.

"He's going to be okay . . . that's all we know right now. But I have to leave and Aunt Hannah is going to need you to help around the house. I'm flying out in two hours, so I have to leave the house now."

"I won't make it for at least an hour." I had to pack my suitcase, my makeup from the bathroom sink. There was no way I would make it home in anything less than an hour.

"I know, we've been trying to get ahold of you. I'm sorry, Meg. But I have to go now."

"No, it's okay. I know, I know."

We hung up the phone as I looked from Shia to John Brooke. Their faces looked different to me, so I looked around the room. Nothing in the Club Room looked familiar anymore. More people were filling the space, it seemed. A space that was losing its luster by the second.

My dad.

His face flashed through my mind. Him walking in the house in his ACU, taking his combat boots off at the door.

"My dad," I managed to say.

Shia squeezed my shoulder a little harder, and I tried to control my tears when his thumb rubbed in comforting circles.

"What happened?" John asked.

"My dad was injured. We need to go. Now. Oh my God." My heart pounded so hard in my chest that it hurt. I pushed my palm against it, hoping to stop the pain. "Oh my God."

"John, call the car up and go upstairs and pack the bags," Shia said, lifting his hand from my shoulder. I immediately began to shake.

"Uh, okay. Meg, I need help with your stuff."

I tried to nod.

"Help? Just pack the bags!" Shia's tone was impatient and demanding.

John looked at Shia and stood up. His green eyes were on me, and the inside of my brain felt like a hamster wheel.

I grabbed my phone from my purse, and the screen was full of texts and missed calls from every one of my sisters, Jo more than the rest, but Amy's and Beth's names were there, too, along with Meredith's and Aunt Hannah's. They had been calling for almost an hour. Why hadn't I checked my phone? And how did Jo know to call Shia?

"I need to go." I stood up. "I have to get home. Now."

I don't know how the minutes passed from the lobby of the hotel to the thirty-minute car ride back to Fort Cyprus. The entire chain of events was all a blur, except for Shia sitting in the back, humming every song on the radio and softly rubbing my shoulder where my skin was touching the cold glass of the window.

32

jo

Once Meredith stepped out of the house and Aunt Hannah stepped in, my sisters began to lose their minds. Amy wouldn't stop sobbing in my dad's chair. Beth was just staring at the wall as if it were alive and fascinating. It wasn't. It had been over two hours since we learned that my dad had been blown up.

Blown up.

How morbid did that sound? In reality, that's exactly what happened. Two hours since things started shuffling and shifting inside our government-owned home. It started to click instantly that our house wasn't ours. Just like the Fort Hood house, even though I'd spent most of my life in that house. I had a scrapbook of memories in my brain. From Meg's first kiss to when my mom lost a baby and Meg read *Oh, the Places You'll Go!* to me every single night for the few weeks that Meredith spent crying at night. Amy learned to walk in that house, and I learned to read. I wrote my first essay in that house. Meredith still had it; I planned to hang it on the fridge in my first apartment in Manhattan.

When Frank got orders to Fort Cyprus, we packed up our memories in a big government-issued moving truck and followed it from the heart of Texas to the bottom leg of Louisiana. It only took us a day, including our stop in the middle of nowhere outside of Houston, where we stayed in an Americas Best Value Inn that Meg swore was haunted. We slept maybe two hours that night because of Meg's tossing and turning and Amy's complaining that she was afraid of whatever ghost Meg thought was fucking with us. Frank ended up doing a "ghost check," which included his special light—aka a little flashlight key chain he carried hooked to his keys around a belt loop. He searched under the beds and in the closets. All of the rest of us would have stayed fast asleep on one of the queen beds in the double room. Two hours felt so short then, and as I stood against the wall in our Fort Cyprus living room now trying to process what was happening, two hours felt so long.

Two hours later and Meg still wasn't here, Meredith was at the airport getting ready to board a flight to Germany, and Aunt Hannah had already found Frank's bottle of Captain Morgan under the sink in the kitchen, right behind the trash bags and next to the Windex.

Beth was sitting on the couch, closest to the wall covered in square frames with pictures of our family. I was on my dad's shoulders in one. I was wearing a ball cap and overalls, and we were standing in front of a bronze Walt Disney and Mickey Mouse statue. My dad's eyes were tightly squinting, making his face crinkle up like it does when he laughs hard. Beth was wearing acid-wash jean shorts, like she still does at fifteen. Her dark hair was almost always pulled back then in a loose ponytail just above her neckline. Meg was wearing cutoff shorts and a Tweety Bird T-shirt tied just above her belly button. We all looked so young in that picture.

The Frank that took us to Disney World and kept me up-to-date on news and jokes and music, and even corny dance moves, most likely wasn't going to be the Frank that came home to us. I didn't know how to process that. I knew what PTSD was, and I feared it for my dad's sake. But I didn't know what it would feel like to be around. I just wanted Dad to be okay.

"When will Meg be here?" Amy asked, sniffling with red-ringed eyes and pouty, chapped lips.

Beth responded in a low voice. "Soon, Amy. She's on her way."

Amy let out a sob and curled her knees to her chest. I wondered if it was that my dad was injured that made her cry, or the shock of it all: Meredith's leaving; Beth's silence; Meg's not being here at all.

I was starting to get angrier and angrier at Meg in her absence. I didn't think far enough to consider it unfair for me to be pissed at her. We needed her. Well, I didn't, but Amy wouldn't stop asking for her. My phone kept vibrating in my pocket, and Laurie's name kept flashing. I tossed my phone onto the couch and sulked into the kitchen. I didn't like that Amy's little mind was probably in shock. I'd read an article online that said the brain of a young adult can literally lose a small percentage of function during the shock of losing a loved one. I knew this wasn't as bad as losing a loved one, but I also wasn't naïve enough to think that part of our dad wouldn't be gone.

I stood at the counter and stared out the kitchen window. I

could see light in the big room, the one with the grand piano. I'd spent so many mornings watching Laurie's fingers assault the ivory keys. All of those mornings, even the one the week before, felt like ages ago. Was I still sixteen? Or had I been standing in the kitchen for days, weeks? My toes were numb. They felt so cold and I couldn't have told you why. Or if they even did. It's possible that my body made it up so I could transfer the pain from my heart to another part of my body.

Someone knocked on the door, and I didn't even jump. I thought it would be Meg, but it was Laurie. He was standing tall enough that I could see his shoulders and the tips of his blond hair through the window in the door.

What was he doing here? I didn't answer the door, but I figured he would just come back. I didn't understand why I didn't want to see him. I just knew it made everything feel much more real than it would if he wasn't around. I had been spending more and more time with him, and I knew him better than any other boy, ever, but I didn't want him around for this. This was about to get messy. Everything that held the Spring house up was about to crumble. I could feel the floor humming beneath me; it was only a matter of time before it started to rumble. Then the cracking, then the crumbling—and somewhere down the line of Laurie's lineage there was already too much crumbling and collapsing.

Laurie didn't need to get involved. We were already too many, and with Aunt Hannah slurping away on Frank's liquor, and Meg not even here . . .

"Who's there?" my aunt said behind me, heading toward the door.

"Don't!" I shouted, but it was too late.

Her hand swung open the door so fast that I realized she

must have been expecting more bad news to be delivered. Laurie came walking in, a big smile on his face. He was holding a bag of Bugles in one hand and in the other a bottle of that fizzy apple drink he tried three summers ago in Munich and has been obsessed with ever since.

"Hey!" He walked around Aunt Hannah to me. His chin turned upward and he scanned my face with laser eyes. "What's up? What's wrong?" he asked, like he could easily read me in a second's time.

I shook my head and untucked my stringy hair from behind my ears. He cleared his hands, dropping his stuff onto the counter. He didn't stop walking toward me, even when the glass bottle rolled off the counter and dropped to the floor. Luckily it didn't shatter, but I don't believe he would have turned back around if it had.

"Jo, what's going on?" Laurie turned to my aunt. "Hannah?"

She was immediately frazzled by Laurie. "Uh . . ." She looked at me for a second, then to Laurie. "It's Frank." She cleared her throat. "He—"

"Shut up!" I snapped at her just as Amy came into the room.

Her frail shoulders were shaking and she was wearing pajama pants that were too short for her blossoming legs. Her bottom lip looked like it had split open.

"Amy." I moved to her, wrapping my arms around her shoulders. She pushed at me, ducking under my arms. She never liked hugs from anyone except Dad and Meg. Meg used to give pretty good hugs, though.

"Where's Meg?" Amy hiccuped, and the oven starting screaming beeps into the room.

"Beth!" I snapped.

"Can you call her again?" Amy asked, tugging on the bottom

of my T-shirt. She felt so small in that room, like she was eight again and had sliced her toe open on her pink Razor scooter. She'd cried and cried for Meg, until Meg came home from River's house, albeit smelling like Smirnoff. Meg was lucky I never snitched on her, but I was starting to wish that I had every time Amy asked for her.

"I'll call her again." I patted Amy's back, which was wet from sweat. "Laurie, can you call Meg please."

The oven beeped again.

"Beth!" I shouted, and Amy cried harder. "I'm sorry," I told her, rubbing. "You're burning up." I shook out the back of her shirt.

Laurie had my phone to his ear in no time and disappeared down the hallway.

"How long until we'll hear from your mom?" Aunt Hannah asked us.

Wasn't she supposed to know that? Or at least not be selfish enough to ask us that? We were kids, even me. Meg was the only one of us who was an adult. She had a car and paid her own cell phone bill and car insurance.

And she wasn't here.

33

meg

When we pulled up to the gate, I was relieved to see Reeder on duty. It had me assuming that we would breeze right through and pull into my driveway in less than two minutes, but instead, we sat under the awning and John and Reeder exchanged *Hey, bro*'s and John went on a few sentences about his time in town and I held my breath on and off, waiting for the conversation to end.

"John. Let's *go*," Shia said, his head appearing between the front seats. "Meg needs to get home."

John whispered something to Reeder, something about my dad, and that got Reeder moving to open the gate. We drove through and I stared out the window. When we pulled up to the driveway, I ran up to the door.

Jo came barreling up, her arms flying in front of her body. "What the fuck, Meg?" she shouted into the air. She pushed hard at my shoulders, and I tumbled to the ground, my body hitting it fast. I thought she was going to hug me, not push me off my feet.

I scrambled to my feet, and Shia was standing in front of Jo, seeming to hold her back as she yelled at both of us.

"Amy's been crying for you! And you weren't fucking here! *Where the hell were you?* It doesn't take that long to *fucking drive back!*" Jo looked at the three of us, her anger rising. "You probably stopped on the way back to blow John Brooke! Or both of them!"

I had never seen Jo so angry before. She kept coming for me, and Shia kept her at bay. I got to my feet and headed for the house.

Amy ran to me and sobbed in my arms. "Is he going to die, Meg? Is he?" Her voice was so high-pitched.

"No, babe. No, no." I petted her hair. "Come on, let's sit down." I told her, not looking back at Jo, who had called me every name I had been called in the hallways of my high school in Texas. In the house, I went to Amy's room to get her quilted blanket with the little patches of color and carried it out to her on Dad's recliner.

My brain kept going back and forth between Jo's being pissed at me—Jo, who always seemed so in control and didn't need anybody or anything—and how my family was going to handle what was happening. I wanted to slap Jo for being such a selfish little bitch, but I knew it would just cause more and more drama in our family. I was so tired of drama. We had more important things to worry about now, like how our dad was holding up in the hospital and how we would make it weeks without my mom around.

34

jo

Amy was asleep on the couch, her cheeks still red two hours later. Shia covered her with a blanket while Meg slipped out from under her head. I sat on the floor staring at the three of them, with no words in my throat.

"Are you hungry?" Shia asked Meg.

The way she looked at him made me sad for her, for John Brooke, and, mostly, for Shia, who never stood a chance with my oldest sister. When Meg nodded, Shia immediately led her into the kitchen. Laurie was so quiet next to me that I had nearly forgotten he was there.

"You can leave, you know," I told him, staring at Amy asleep on the couch. Sometimes she looked so young.

"I'm fine."

I looked over at Laurie, and I couldn't figure out why he lingered. It had been hours since he popped into our chaos, and yet he was still sitting on the living room floor, long legs stretched out, as always. He looked the same as before my life changed in an instant, only his eyes were glossy and his hair was wavier at the ends.

"You can go, seriously. I'm fine," I told him.

He bent one of his legs at the knee and scooted closer to me. "Why do you want me to go so bad? I'm just sitting here."

"*Exactly*," I snapped. I didn't mean to be so harsh, but I didn't have the energy to apologize.

Laurie didn't say anything; he just leaned against the wall and shook his head a little. It pissed me off. Who did he think he was?

I was getting angrier and angrier with each passing minute. Laurie started clicking his tongue, and it pushed me over the edge. I shot up and went outside. It was cold, but the air was still sticky somehow. The porch was ice under my bare feet. The screen door slammed shut, and I kept walking into the yard. The door opened, and I groaned, spinning around on my heels.

"Jo—" Laurie called, and I watched him look for me in the darkness. I even thought about ignoring him and running as fast and as far as I could, but he spotted me.

"What's wrong?" he asked, as if my dad hadn't been fucking blown up and my mom wasn't on her way to Germany and my house was falling apart.

"What's wrong?" I yelled at him, not giving a shit that none of this was his fault. "What's wrong is that—" I stopped to dig for what exactly was wrong, besides the obvious. "Why are you still here? I told you to go hours ago."

"I can't just leave you like this. Your—"

"I can take care of myself, Laurie."

He sighed and stepped closer to me. The streetlight was shining directly on him now, and I wondered at what point we had moved to the edge of the yard. "I never said you couldn't, Jo. I'm just trying—"

"Trying what? To swoop in and try to make me feel better. Guess what? That's not going to work here, Laurie, because you see, my fucking dad is lying in some hospital bed fighting for his goddamn life right now!"

I knew I was wrong for yelling at him, but honestly, it just felt so good in that moment.

"I'm only trying to—" He tried to explain, but I cut him off again.

"Well, stop. *Stop* trying."

"Stop interrupting me!" he half shouted, and turned away from me. His fingers tugged at the hair closest to his scalp, and he looked at me again. "I'm trying to be here for you, Jo. Just fucking let me, for God's sake."

"God doesn't have anything to do with this."

"Jo, I know you're upset and—"

I couldn't let him finish a sentence, not tonight. "You don't know anything. My dad actually loves—"

I stopped myself. Where was this coming from? Even this version of me couldn't finish my hurtful sentence. But when I looked at Laurie, I realized that the damage had already been done. His face had fallen like a shooting star onto the grass, and I was struggling to find the voice I was spouting with only seconds before.

"You know what, Jo? Fine. I'll go. Have a good fucking night." His accent was so strong that I barely understood the last part as he dashed across the street and I stood there frozen inside and out, waiting for him to turn back around.

I never wanted to be the kind of person who lashes out at their family . . .

Laurie wasn't my family.

He was a random neighbor boy who I had spent the last few months getting to know inside and out, and he had done nothing wrong but try to be there for me. He wasn't my punching bag, and I needed to find it in myself to walk my ass over and apologize. I could smell bacon cooking from the kitchen, and my stomach growled despite the fact that I hadn't eaten bacon in years.

I thought about Shia and his comforting words to Meg and Amy as Meg played with Amy's hair until she fell asleep on her lap. John Brooke had left almost as soon as he arrived, yet Shia was still here. Swallowing my anger and pride, I crossed the street and knocked on Laurie's door.

He opened it after a long pause, and I stood there, silent until he waved me in. Neither of us talked until we got upstairs to his room. He had already changed into his pajamas, a white T-shirt and blue plaid cotton pants. His bed was a mess, like he had been trying to sleep but rolled around instead.

He sat down on the edge of the bed for a moment before lying down. His long body was almost too long for the bed, and I sat down on the edge of it. I lay down next to him, just as I had many, many times, and he clicked the lamp off above his head.

"I'm sorry," I told him in the darkness.

"I know," he whispered back.

35

jo

*O*ur house became something between a clinic and a
funeral parlor after my dad came home from his hospital stay in Germany. The mood had changed significantly,
and it was hard to remember what life was like before there
were ten doctors' appointments a week and people in and out of
our house like someone died. Even Denise Hunchberg brought
some sort of casserole over pretty much every day since the moment John Brooke helped Meg wheel Dad through the door. We
had everything from bar food from Aunt Hannah's late shifts
at Spirits, to Denise's Cheez-It casserole, to vibrant bouquets of
flowers sent by Mrs. King herself.

Meg must have been getting better at sucking up to the
woman, I thought.

The house became overcrowded and started to smell like an
office-party potluck. I had finally gotten my license, so I could

help take my dad to his appointments and take myself to work when I could. I thought I might have to quit my job at Pages if my dad's doctors kept adding specialists for him to see. Unlike Meg, I liked driving on the post with my dad; we had started our own secret get-out-of-the-house club.

My dad stared up at the clock on the wall in the waiting room. "They always make me wait so long,"

"Yeah, they do. I bet this will still be faster than Dr. Alaban," I said.

The pages of the *People* magazine I was scrolling through were stuck together, and I wiggled them apart. Apparently Jennifer Aniston was pregnant with twins! For the tenth time in the last year. And it was determined that they would most likely have her genetically superior locks of brown hair.

I would never understand people's obsession with her becoming a mother. So what if she didn't want to have children?

"No way. Dr. Alaban is just thorough, Jo."

I looked up from the faux news story on the page. "Thorough? Dad, he takes an hour to even get to the room and has to listen to your heart like ten times before he gets it."

My dad rolled his eyes. "Your generation is so impatient."

I rolled my eyes right back at him and leaned forward, tucking my leg under my body in the typical cushioned waiting-room chair. "We just don't like to waste time. Unlike yours."

He laughed at that. "Oh, you're not wasting time on the internet?"

"Learning, yes."

"Learning what? How to bully people or create hashtags for catastrophic events?"

"Touché."

The woman behind the desk smiled at me when I looked at

her. She was on the phone and seemed to be happy at her job. She remembered my dad's name each time we came to the neurologist. She was pretty, probably in her twenties. She looked like Angela from *Boy Meets World*.

"But your generation raised my generation to not like to sit around and wait for stuff."

"You also don't know what hard work is. You expect stuff to come to you. Not *you*." He waved his hand at me and smiled a little. I was getting used to the chip in the corner of his front tooth. Meg bothered him about fixing it, but he didn't want to.

"We expect things like free health care and some Social Security," I teased. It was true, but it wasn't either of our faults.

"Touché." He raised his fist and playfully tapped mine in a fist-bump. He drew it back and made a weird little *whishhh* sound, and I tried not to laugh.

"Dad." I bit down on my lip and shook my head. "No. Just no."

He shrugged. He told me I was no fun, and the office phone rang again. My dad ran his fingers over the healing skin on his neck. I felt like every day it got easier to look at his wounds. The first time Meredith gave him a bath, we heard her vomiting down the hall afterward. To drown out the noise, Beth started playing the piano Laurie's grandpa had given her, but Amy had already heard. I saw it in her cotton-flower-blue eyes when she stared down the hallway, then picked up her phone and went back to her cyberland. Sometimes I wanted to check her search history, but I couldn't go against my essential beliefs of privacy. No matter how badly I wanted to.

Amy was acting out; we knew it had to do with my dad's being home and everything changing so fast. Amy had to start helping Beth around the house, which, of course, Amy didn't want to do. But Meredith was busy, and so were Meg and I.

Within the six weeks since our dad had come back, Amy's teacher had already emailed Meredith about Amy's behavior. Dad said she was seeking attention, and I thought maybe she was, but of course she was. She was twelve and her dad not only looked different now, but he was a little different inside, too.

But of course he was; four deployments and rolling a Humvee over a roadside bomb on a residential street and barely surviving will do that to a person.

I could still see more of my original dad than my sisters could, but they barely spent time with him.

His jawline was so sharp, like Beth's and like Meg's. I thought I looked more like him than my sisters since I got his height. Our hair was the same dried-mud, milk-chocolate brown color.

His leg was still plastered, and the skin on his cheek had started to heal into a waxy coat. The skin they used to replace the skin he lost was so red. The week before, I showed my family a video about a group of doctors in Brazil who were testing tilapia skin on humans with burn damage. Basically a skin graft. Only my dad thought it was interesting and amusing. Meredith left the table.

I got my phone out of my pocket and had a text from Laurie. He asked what time I would be done and said he wanted me to come over when I got back from running around with my dad.

"Who you talking to that has you smiling that way?" my dad asked.

"Smiling? No one." I tucked my hair behind my ear and licked my lips. I wasn't smiling.

"Uh-huh."

My phone pinged and Laurie's name popped up on the screen.

"It's just Laurie," I told my dad when his eyes questioned me.

He jutted his chin out. "Just Laurie. Hmph. So, this Laurie kid is your boyfriend?"

I laughed. "No, Dad. He's not."

The clock on the wall loudly ticked the seconds by. It was louder than a second ago.

"I don't think he knows that. He sure *seems* like your boyfriend. You wouldn't hide that from me, would you?" My dad's mouth was a little crooked, and he said it would be like that from then on, that even two surgeries couldn't get his jaw quite back where it was before the blast.

I shook my head. "Dad."

It wasn't even that I was weirded out talking about boys with my dad; it was that I didn't have much to say about Laurie and me.

"Josephine. It's not like I'm going to lock you in the house or keep you from seeing him. I just want to know what's going on in your life."

I sighed. "Just because we hang out a lot doesn't mean he's my boyfriend."

"That boy is sprawled out on the floor of my living room every day. When he's not, you're over at his house. Seems like you're dating to me. When I was dating your mom, she kept trying to tell me we were just friends. Friends don't do the stuff—"

"Dad! Seriously!" I yelped in horror.

Not actual horror, of course; I knew that my parents were . . . romantic together, but I would be fine to never ever hear it come from my dad's mouth.

"What?" He smiled.

I rolled my eyes and started laughing. His chin tilted upward, and I could see the jagged crimson scar from the curve of his chin down to his collarbone. I was already getting used to seeing the new additions to my dad's body. Sometimes I noticed Meredith or my sisters staring at them mindlessly, like my dad couldn't see them doing it. I knew they didn't mean to, so I let them grieve and get used to the way it would be in this new version of our lives, after he came home.

I thought when he returned, it would be like before. We would go to Disneyland in Los Angeles for our vacation this fall. Meredith kept saying it wasn't nearly as magical as the one in Florida and was a third of the size, but Meg and Amy were dying to see the Hollywood sign and have a possible run-in with Robert Pattinson at the famous Chateau Marmont on Sunset Boulevard. Family vacations weren't exactly my favorite thing, but Meredith always told me that one day I would be glad that we had taken them.

"What's up with Meg and Brooke?" my dad asked.

I looked at him for one second and then at the scuff on my Keds. Meredith had told me not to get white shoes, but I didn't listen.

"Are you writing a gossip blog about your daughters' dating lives? What's with all the questions?"

"No, I just want to know what's happening. Hunchberg said Meg's trying to get married to Brooke. I laughed it off, but I actually don't know if that's true. And you know more than she would ever tell me."

"I mean, they're dating still. I think." I thought about how Brooke was coming over less, and Meg was spending more time at Mrs. King's and that Shia was in town.

"Not getting married, though? They're too young."

"John's what . . . twentysomething? And Meg is twenty."

"Yes, exactly."

"You and mom got married right after high school."

"Times were different then."

That was an understatement. Times were better now, for the most part. We were in another war, but weren't we always? I felt like people still got married young, around Army bases at least. The restaurants surrounding the post were filled with young wives of soldiers working as servers and bartenders. A few girls from Meg's graduating class were already married to soldiers stationed at Fort Cyprus. Women are more accepted into colleges and work places than when my parents got married, but the tough life of the Army made it hard for both.

"How was it so different?" I asked.

"Well, girls your guys' age don't have the same role as when your mom was marrying me. Especially in the military. It's a rough job, being gone and fighting for your life every other year. And then you add children in there, there was no time for the woman to work. In some cases yeah, but mostly this was the way it was. But with the way the economy is, it's nearly impossible to feed a family of four on the average soldier's salary."

I scoffed at the truth of that. "Which is complete bullshit."

"Jo!" My dad raised his voice a little and narrowed his eyes.

"Sorry. Anyway, it's crazy how soldiers can barely feed their families most of the time, but the politicians are spending billions on jets and dinners and whatever they put on their expense accounts. It's so fuc—" I stopped myself from cussing in front of my dad again.

The door clicked open and a nurse in Hello Kitty scrubs came out into the waiting room.

"Lieutenant Spring," she said, clipboard in hand.

"Do you want me to go back with you?" I asked my dad. Sometimes he did, and sometimes he didn't.

"Uh, yeah. Come on with me."

I pushed my dad's wheelchair down the hall and almost ran into the wall. I would need to get better at steering, I knew, especially since no one could tell us if or when my dad would walk on his own again. The nurse had such a sweet face that my dad didn't even complain to her about waiting so long. She told us her name was Sirine, and the tag on her ACU said ORLEN. She had her hair drawn back in tight strings, pulling at her scalp, and gelled or sprayed down. Not a single frizzy hair. I wondered if hair frizzies were against Army regulations.

The room was stark white and smelled like latex and some kind of cleaning product. I sat in a chair next to the desk, and my dad's chair was in front of me, next to the exam table. It was covered in thick white paper that always crunched when you sat on it.

"Are you in any pain right now?" Sirine asked my dad.

He widened his eyes at her. "You're joking, right?"

She smiled and faced the computer in front of her. "On a scale from one to ten, what level of pain are you feeling?" She pulled her military ID card out and pushed it into a slot in the keyboard of the computer. Her unpainted nails tapped away at the keys.

"I would say a good . . . two thousand."

"Two thousand, got it." She laughed. "So, Dr. Jenner will be in shortly. Let me just get your vitals the best I can."

When I checked my phone, I had a text from Hayton, the espresso-infused coworker who I worked the most shifts with, asking if I would cover her shift. No matter how long the doctor was going to take to come to the room, I wouldn't be back in time to take her shift.

My dad spent an hour getting lectured on different types of impact trauma and how he would continue to be monitored. My dad kept telling me that there was nothing to worry about, but as the doctor kept going and going, she made my bad feeling worse.

I wasn't sure if I trusted my dad the same way after that appointment.

36

beth

Spring came so fast that year. We were walking around the Quarter and the sun was beating down; it smelled like spices and spring flowers in the air. It was the second week in April, and we were strolling along the streets of the French Quarter Festival. I hadn't realized there would be so many people there, but Meg had begged me to come with her since she was riding with Laurie and Jo and didn't want to be the third wheel. So, we rode in Laurie's driver's black car, which smelled like new leather and Laurie. I still didn't know how rich his family had to have been to afford a driver at an Army base. Jo and Laurie talked about taking a trip to Cambodia after she graduated. Meg said she would hate to be trapped on a flight that was so long, but wanted Jo to post a bunch of pictures on Facebook.

I stared out the window mostly, and Meg was on her phone. The drive to the Quarter was easy—just a straight shot down

Highway 90 and we were there. The drive was so quiet compared to the streets of the festival; we were dropped off as close as we could get to Jackson Square. People were scattered on the patches of grass that dotted the square. Mostly everyone was eating. A couple were eating what looked like a crawfish platter out of an aluminum catering pan. My senses were on overload, from the different smells to the loud voices. I loved the aromas because I loved food, but not so much the ninety conversations that were going on around me.

"How fucking awesome is this?" Jo shouted. She radiated excitement, and Laurie tried to keep up with her as she bounced around us. "God, I love this city!" She twirled around in circles, and the bottom of her swing dress bloomed around her thighs like a dew-dripping flower with its stem squeezed between someone's fingers, twisting around and around.

Laurie watched her like he was spellbound. I didn't blame him. Jo had a confidence that most people would never have, and she had no fear. It didn't bother her that some people were watching her in her excitement. Laurie's cheeks were blushed, and his long blond hair was waving a little at the ends.

"What should we do first?" Jo asked us. She couldn't keep her eyes on one thing, but I couldn't blame her.

There were stalls and stalls of different types of traditional New Orleans cuisine, and booths selling everything from handmade soaps with local hibiscus to cone-shaped bags of kettle corn using, of course, sugarcane grown in the New Orleans area. I could hear a marching band close by.

"I'm starving. Let's get food," Laurie offered.

I didn't care what we did.

Meg had walked over to a booth selling what the little handpainted sign said was ALL NATURAL COSMETICS. Jo followed her

and Laurie trailed along. We waited for Meg to try on a deep
purple shade of eye shadow before we moved along to find food.
Laurie was like a kid in a candy store, naming all the options:

"Blackened-catfish po' boy! Crawfish étouffée!" Laurie's Italian accent was stronger when he spoke words that were closer
to other languages.

He was reading all the signs to us as we stopped at every
booth to gawk over handmade rings with big colorful stones and
hand-sewn purses made from dyed cotton. I grabbed a pink–
and-yellow one for Amy, who was at home with our parents for
the afternoon. Our dad had become increasingly irritable since
being home, and he still wasn't able to move his legs. We only had
a few more months, maybe a year, to find a place to live, since
he was going to be medically retired, and that in itself made the
house unsteady like a farmhouse table with a broken leg. Aunt
Hannah's friend owned a couple of houses somewhere that he
needed tenants for, but Amy was pissed off that she would have
to change schools. We could stay at Fort Cyprus; Meredith tried
to convince my dad that we should, but he wanted to move away
from the post, even though all of his doctors would be there.

Jo became an adult overnight. She was always going: driving
Amy somewhere, working, or taking my dad to appointments.
Her free time was spent watching the news and bickering with
our dad about who was the better night-show host, and Laurie
was still a steady shadow behind her. She took my dad for walks,
and they picked flowers for my mom to put in her hair like she
used to every spring and summer in Texas. I didn't know which
one had that idea. I guessed my dad. Jo was also spending so
much time sitting on the living-room floor with Laurie, her laptop resting on a stack of pillows.

She had been writing so much more than before. Sometimes Laurie would write, too; otherwise he would listen to music or watch whatever Meredith had on the TV, or he would be sleeping.

Jo was better served out in the wild. I was not. All of the conversations around me sounded like a ringing in my ears, and everywhere we walked seemed more crowded than the block before. The best way to describe it would be to say that I felt like I was standing on a stage, spinning in circles, while twenty people tried to hold a conversation. No one was actually looking at me, I knew that, but the logical reality didn't change the way my body and mind reacted to the noise.

I followed my sisters and Laurie to the back of the line for Antoine's Restaurant so Laurie could try their famous Baked Alaska with chocolate sauce. He smiled when Jo asked if it was actually chocolate, and she nudged his shoulder with hers. Jo was tall, but Laurie's legs seemed to take up half of his body, so even Jo looked short next to him. While we waited for his food, Jo pointed to a jazz band playing as they walked down the street. A small crowd was following them, and the music became louder and louder the closer they got to us.

Jo seemed happiest when she was with Laurie—well, outside of when she was tapping away on the laptop. She said things around him that surprised me and helped even me get to know her better. She scrunched her nose at the fish in his hands, and he asked her if she wanted to smell it. She scowled. They were playful, and it was a nice thing to see in Jo. Her mood had been so up and down since Dad had come home. All of us were handling the adjustment differently, and Jo was trying so hard to keep it together.

"Too many choices," Jo said by the third street we walked down.

Laurie was eating as we walked and somehow managed not to leave so much as a spot on his white shirt.

I couldn't decide either, and there were just so many people everywhere. Since I had left school, besides taking a trip to the grocery store, I was never around huge crowds like this. We got to a stall selling mood rings, and one of them caught my eye. The stone was yellow, sitting on a dark band that looked and felt like metal.

"How much is this one?" I asked the girl behind the table.

She looked to be about my age, maybe a little older, and had straight black-as-ink hair with steely-gray ends. It was cut to sit about an inch above her shoulders. Her dark eyes had glitter under them—like fairy dust sprinkled on her cheeks—and she was dripping in jewelry. When she stood up, I looked at her chest; it was covered in shimmering gold glitter. It looked like paint almost, and she was wearing layers of necklaces, all different, but somehow they all flowed together.

"Hmm, that one is twelve. It's a mood ring." Her voice sounded familiar, but I was sure I had never seen her before. I would have remembered. She looked like a Gypsy from a movie. Her nails were black and sparkly, and she was wearing a long printed dress with no bra underneath. The sides of the dress were slits, so I could see her rib cage covered in what looked like henna tattoos. I couldn't read the words on her left side and didn't want to be all gawky and socially awkward.

"I'll take it," I said, touching the ring. I looked back down at the rows and rows of mood jewelry. There were bracelets and other styles of rings, earrings, bangles.

"Everything is 'buy two, get one free,'" the girl offered. "Did you see these?"

I looked to Meg at my side, assuming the jewelry girl was

going to be looking at Meg. Usually that's what happens when, like now, Meg wore a sundress with a plunging neckline.

"These are glass." The girl's fingers waved over one of the rows of rings set in black-lined cases. "And these are quartz." She pointed to a smaller display box with maybe a dozen rings.

They were all pretty, and most of them were a deep blue while resting in the case. The one in her hand was yellow, and a dark green one was in the back row of the quartz box. The forest-green stone was set in a thin line of metal that looked like a vine. A little leaf was even set right at the bottom curve of the oval stone.

"I'll take the green one, too. Did you make these?" I asked.

A jazz band full of elderly men danced and played on the street behind me. My sisters and Laurie were waiting a few feet away. Meg was licking at the pink-and-blue spun cotton-candy cone in her hand. She pulled off a big piece and popped it on her tongue.

"I did. I'm Nat." Her long nails pointed at the sign on the table. It said NAT'S LAIR in deep purple paint against a piece of black chalkboard.

"I'm Beth. Nice to meet you." I pushed my hand out between us and she looked down at it, her lips turning into a smile.

"Nice to meet you, Beth."

"You can also call me Bethany," I told her for no reason at all.

She made eye contact with me. "You can call me Natsuki if you want to, but only my parents call me that."

"Natsuki," I repeated, and it felt a little funny on my tongue.

"It's Japanese. It means 'moon.'" Her name fit her well.

"It's cool. I don't know what Bethany means, and no one actually calls me that." I thought I saw something sparkle a little besides the glitter shining in her eyes.

Nat seemed like a character from a book or a sweet creature from another world when she laughed. Her body moved with her laughter, and she cupped her mouth. Her fingers were covered in rings, all different metals and shapes and stones. Her entire ensemble was like a costume, and she was far prettier than any other girl I'd seen since we moved from Texas, at least. The bangles on her wrists sounded like a wind chime when she grabbed a calculator from the table and started punching in numbers.

"You get to pick your free one now."

"Anything?" My eyes rested on a black-and-purple necklace. The gems were matte and not shiny at all, but it was beautiful.

"Not that." She laughed. "Something of equal or lesser price." She paused and nodded. "See, my parents always say I'm a horrible business owner, but obviously, they're wrong."

"Obviously." I laughed with her and noticed the way she kept looking at my mouth.

I knew better than to think she was staring at my mouth for any reason other than my having something stuck in my teeth, or maybe if I was like Meg and wore lipstick. But I hadn't even eaten anything yet that could have been stuck, and I wasn't wearing lipstick. When I looked at her long eyelashes and shimmering cheeks, I wished I had listened to Meg and let her put more on my face than BB cream and mascara.

"Take your time. I mean, there's a huuuge line behind you," she said with an eye roll, and I actually looked behind my shoulder.

No one else was there.

She was funny, and suddenly I felt incredibly plain standing outside this magical stall full of interesting jewelry and a

Gypsy-like girl who made it by hand. I was wearing a green T-shirt that said NEW YORK on it, even though I had never been there, and jeans that were ripped at the knees when my mom brought them home from American Eagle. Looking at Nat's sandals and the toe rings decorating her toes, I tucked my feet under the tablecloth so she couldn't see my unpainted toenails.

I decided to get my mom a midnight-blue ring with a black band. When I handed it to Nat, she smiled and picked up the calculator again.

"Homeschooling didn't help me with my math skills," she said after two attempts at figuring out the tax. "Wait, do I even need to add tax?"

"I have no idea." I shrugged. She was homeschooled, too. It made her even cooler to me.

"You know what?" She grabbed a little green bag from below the table and opened it. "You're my first paying customer of the day, so no tax for you."

I thanked her as she tucked my pieces into the bottom of the bag and filled the empty space with white tissue paper.

"I hope you like the jewelry, and if you don't, just pretend you do?" Nat lifted the calculator to show me the price, $25.

"I thought it was twenty-four? You were right about the homeschooling not helping your math."

I hoped that she would know I was joking, but I couldn't remember the last time I'd made a joke to someone who wasn't part of my family, or Laurie.

Fortunately, she caught on just fine and smiled. I wondered how old she was. How did she already have a business and I didn't even think I was going to know what I wanted to do with my life when I turned eighteen? Jo knew what she wanted to do right after graduation; so did Meg. Amy probably even knew at twelve. Nat knew and was out selling her jewelry at the festival.

I glanced over at my sisters again to make sure they were still nearby and saw a group of girls my age approaching the booth.

"Thanks again." I handed Nat two twenties from my pocket and she pulled a five and a one out of a brown leather bag and waved bye to me.

When I walked up to Meg, Jo, and Laurie, Jo was leaning against Laurie's back, and he was taking a picture of the top of their heads? I didn't ask why. They started doing that a few weeks ago. They even started taking pictures of all the food I made at home, and people on social media would comment that they wanted it or about how good it looked. Amy kept telling me that I should post videos of myself making food on some website she watches, but I didn't see where the time or courage would come from. Between my dad being home and my aunt Hannah coming over every other day to eat, to ask for gas money, or to sit on the porch with my mom while she had a drink or two, it was a lot. I also had schoolwork to do; I was so close to finishing my credits for ninth grade. I couldn't wait to be in eleventh, and I definitely couldn't wait to turn sixteen.

Jo said sixteen was transformative, and I saw something change in her when she turned sixteen. Meg, too. Just as I was thinking that eighteen and nineteen changed Meg so much, too, she wrapped her arm through mine.

"What did you get, babe?" She looked down at the bag in my hand.

As we walked, Meg tried on the jewelry. She held her hand

up and spread her fingers. I remember the sun shining through each one.

"These are fucking cool, Beth. How many did she have?" Meg reached past Laurie to Jo, who was just behind him.

"Oooh!" Jo said admiringly.

"We should go back there before we leave tonight," Meg offered.

I nodded, sort of wanting to go back to the jewelry stand, too. I should have gotten Aunt Hannah a necklace, maybe a black and amethyst layered one to wear to Spirits. The bar practically glowed moody dark colors that I associated with the Crescent City. My aunt Hannah seemed to almost never work anymore, but I thought maybe it just felt that way because she was coming over to the house so much more.

"Okay, so what's the plan? Do we want more music or more food, or what? We can grab a spot on the grass in front of Jackson Square where we came in and eat there. There's going to be fireworks over the river tonight." Laurie pointed behind me toward the Mississippi River, where rainbow colors would burst and bloom over our heads.

"What time is it now?" Jo asked, and instead of waiting for anyone to answer, she raised Laurie's wrist and checked his watch. "It's seven now, so we have about an hour of sunlight left."

We agreed to find a place on the grass and took turns getting food. A band was going to be playing at eight anyway, then the fireworks were scheduled for nine. I hoped that the grass wouldn't be too crowded by the time the show started, and when I looked around the festival, it seemed to have changed a little since we arrived. In just over an hour there were fewer kids, and more plastic cups full of alcohol in the hands of people swaying just a little more than before. The voices of said people were louder, too, and I suspected that the higher the moon rose, the rowdier the people would get.

The moon made me think of the jewelry girl, and I wondered if the moon made her bloom, too.

37

meg

My ass hurt from sitting on the ground, even on top of the two blankets Laurie bought from a vendor. The ground was hard and the spot we chose to sit down on was more dirt than grass, but I was having a good time. Jo and Laurie had obviously agreed to date each other, and he was everywhere she was. When she was eating truffle fries with a fork, his eyes followed up and down, and when she dropped one, he caught it with a napkin.

I thought maybe his obsession was with the fries, because, girl, were they good. But then he stuck the flake-covered fry between her lips, and she gave him a sheepish grin, and that grin widened as he moved a little closer to her. His legs were so long that they stuck out past hers, and his foot almost touched Beth's flip-flops. She was lying on her back, staring at the sky. I didn't want to bother her; I knew the crowd size had to be intimidating to her. She, unlike me, hadn't been through the madness that was Sephora on a Black Friday near an Army post. I figured that she needed the break.

"Is that Bell Gardiner?" Jo asked, her mouth full of potato chunks.

She grabbed a napkin and wiped her chin and lips. I looked across the grass, scanning the crowd for Bell, and found her after only a few seconds. She was wearing cutoff shorts with rips in them, flip-flops, and a dark orange tank top with a shawl over her shoulders. A shawl, really.

"Go say hi," Beth teased from the grass. I leaned over her and she closed her eyes, smiling.

"Should I?" I turned to Jo.

"Hell, no. No way. She was a total dick the last time she saw you and never even apologized. Don't even give her the satisfaction, Meg."

Beth added that I should only talk to Bell if she approached us. I wiped off my dress and straightened the ribbon choker around my neck. I tugged on one of the satin strings to even the two ends out. I ran my hands over the top of my hair. This heat hated my hair. The humidity in the New Orleans area was a good conversation starter for every week from April to August. When I first started working for Mrs. King, I complained about the frizz-causing humidity and she laughed and said, over a glass of pinot noir, *"Oh, wait until August. This is nothing."*

And, boy, was she right. But the weekend of the French Quarter Festival was only April, and my hair was already curling at the scalp. I had spent almost an hour pulling a flatiron through sections of my dark hair. Jo always hated the smell of heated hair, but I would burn candles of it.

I pulled a little bit of my hair over both of my shoulders and unsnapped my bag to get out a gloss for my lips. Beth was back to staring at the sky, and Jo was looking at Laurie's phone screen with him. I had the late realization that Amy would have been better to drag along to this type of festival than Beth was. Not only because Beth hated crowds, but also because Amy would have gone along with anything I wanted to do. I could have convinced her to do a lap around with me, and she would have gone up to Bell and her friends right beside me. Granted, it would have been lame as hell to have my twelve-year-old sister on my back, but Beth would find a way to avoid the confrontation altogether. I would go ahead and say that Beth was the smartest, most thoughtful of us Spring Girls.

The sun was starting to set and the grass area in the front of Jackson Square was getting more and more crowded as the light disappeared. Out of all the, I don't know, thousand people on the grass, we got mushed up against a group who looked to be my age at first glance. I scanned over them but didn't recognize anyone except one guy with white hair grown just a little past his ears. I couldn't remember where I knew him from and wasn't about to ask, so I just turned to Jo and made conversation.

"What are you two talking about?" I asked Jo and Laurie.

She laughed and shoved his cell phone to me. "Amy."

I read the messages on the screen and looked up at Jo and Laurie. Laurie looked a little uncomfortable, and Jo was smiling at me.

"Bad timing," she joked.

"It's not really funny, Jo." I took the phone and erased the messages. I looked up at Laurie when Jo acted like she didn't understand why it wasn't comical to show Laurie what Amy had sent her.

"What?" Jo's heart-shaped face tilted sideways and her lips pouted out.

Jo looked like a girl who would have been a model in the nineties, with full natural lips and thick eyebrows. Her legs were long and she walked like a pigeon on them, but had charm coming out of her ears. Understated beauty, a model for Calvin Klein or Guess.

"Laurie, cover your ears," I said.

He looked at Jo and didn't cover his ears.

"He can listen. It's *just* her period. It's not that big of a deal." Jo leaned forward and crossed her legs under her body. She stuck her flip-flops under the balls of her ankle bones so they wouldn't touch the ground.

"Just a period? Jo." I lowered my voice when Beth turned her head to listen to us.

"Meg. Seriously? You're censoring Laurie from hearing about menstruation? Half of the world are women, and they have periods. Including his mom. Plus, the boys in Europe aren't as sensitive to such a natural thing. Right, Laurie?" Jo looked over at him.

He didn't seem like this was a conversation that he minded having, but that wasn't the point.

"It's fine," Laurie assured me.

"What's fine?" Beth sat up and dusted the dry grass strands off her back.

I filled Beth in on what was happening and saw Jo roll her eyes. "Amy started her period while out with Dad and she's mortified."

"She didn't say she was mortified," Jo added.

I held the phone up and tried to read the deleted messages again. I bitterly wondered why Amy would text Jo about starting her period over me or Beth. Jo and Amy could barely stand each other, and I was the one who taught Amy how to curl her hair and put on eyeliner. I gave Amy her first bra when Meredith thought she was too young for one. But Jo was the sister Amy shared that moment with.

"She said"—I read off the screen—"'I'm so embarrassed Jo. I bled through my pants had to tie dad's shirt around my waist. Kill me please.'" I popped my eyes out at Jo.

"It's just a period, Meg," Jo said.

I groaned. I was all for Jo's liberal, free-spirited mantras and everything, but sometimes she passed things off as too unimportant when they deserved more attention. I knew that Jo was writing off Amy getting her monthlies because Jo had that mind-set where if you ignore something or are careful not to overreact, society will join in your belief. But Jo was only sixteen, almost seventeen, and she had no idea how boys who weren't like Laurie acted over a little blood. Not only the boys; the bitchy girls in school were much worse than the boys most of the time. Jo always sort of floated under the radar at school, whereas I was the beacon who couldn't stay under the radar if I fucking tried. I always ended up in the middle of drama, always. Like in eighth grade, when I bled through my gray gym shorts and a group of girls in my class drew angry red scribbles on a pack of oversized pads and stuck them to my desk.

"It's not just a period, Jo," I told her again, and hoped she would be able to go through her life always thinking periods weren't a big deal.

"Anyway, enough about periods." Jo laughed, and Laurie still looked unfazed by our conversation.

Beth lay back down on the grass despite the crowd surrounding us, and Jo started talking about her writing and that she'd almost finished a piece she was sending to *Vice*. I listened to her and Laurie bouncing back and forth in conversation, and I pulled out my phone and checked my notifications. I had stopped looking for John's name on the screen a day or two ago. He was in the field, which meant I wouldn't hear from him for days. I swiped up and cleared out a text from Meredith and one from Reeder, along with a text from Mrs. King. She needed me to come to her house early to do her hair before some kind of meeting being held there.

Mrs. King lived in a world from a television show where she held meetings and events for things I had never heard of. Either way, I needed the hours and always wanted to be a part of her kind of life. I sent her my reply and pulled up Facebook. I scrolled through pictures of my cousins on my dad's side's newest kids and pictures of my old neighbor's dog and her newly born puppies, while Jo talked to Laurie. I heard bits of it between my scrolling and got the gist of how much it pissed her off that the majority of people associated the French Quarter with booze, beads, and boobs, when the unique culture of the city was so much more than that. Laurie made a joke that I didn't hear, and Jo's chin turned up and she smiled at him so brightly that I almost said something to her. Instead, I turned back to my phone.

How was I struggling to keep a relationship and Jo had a boyfriend? Even though Jo would never let me categorize Laurie as her boyfriend, that's basically what he was. He was always sitting on the couch, and I always tripped over his long legs, stretched out all the way to the entertainment center. My dad started to get annoyed when he would try to roll his chair by. It was already a struggle to move the wheels over the rug, let alone with Laurie stretched out and asleep on the couch. The Laurence driver even took Jo to school most days.

I wondered how the next year of Jo's life would go. The animated look in her eyes when she talked to him with her hands, and the way Laurie stared at her lips—maybe reading them, maybe thinking about fucking them—when she spoke to him made the romantic in me weep but the realist in me prepare for heartbreak. I didn't have the best dating résumé, but it was extensive, so I did have experience.

I wondered if Jo would end up staying at Fort Cyprus if she and Laurie made it through the summer and her senior year. Long distance was hard; I knew that for sure. John and I jumped into a long-distance relationship, and look how that was ending up. It had only been a few months since I saw him last, but it felt much longer than that. I knew he was adjusting to his new duty station in North Carolina, but I had hoped my invitation to join him would have come by now. He was contacting me less and less, and I knew what was happening—I just wasn't ready to admit it.

Seriously, with every disappointment I felt from the guys around me, from River to even John, I felt my bones wear a little more, I felt a little more seasoned by the world. I knew plenty of women in my life who bounced from one disappointing man to the next, finding their identity in them and wasting away while catering to their husbands. It was especially common in military communities. Mrs. King wasn't like that; she married a law student when she was too young to know what marriage was and stayed with him, supporting him, helping Mr. King become the mogul that he became.

At nineteen, I would have been fine with that. I wanted that more than I wanted to become a makeup artist. I loved makeup, but I really wanted someone to go through life with me. Was that so bad? I knew Jo felt like I was abandoning my woman- hood by dreaming of a family and a life full of family vacations, teaching little versions of me and my husband to be decent hu- mans, and spending my holidays in a warm house that would smell like cinnamon and honey and be packed wall to wall with laughter and conversation. I'd spent my life having awkward family events. Meredith and Aunt Hannah always fought, no matter if it was someone's birthday party at a skating rink or Christmas dinner in my nana's dining room.

Once, after Amy pushed Jo into a pool at our aunt Han- nah's apartment building in Texas, Meredith told me that she and Aunt Hannah never got along until they were both in their twenties. But even then, Meredith was always having to bail Aunt Hannah out of the trouble she got herself into, and lately there was this weird tension between them.

So, my sisters and I were different. Each of us was a com- pletely different creature, and I couldn't wait until the day my family would go visit Jo in New York City, and she could show me her big, fancy office with marble desks and the latest Ap- ple computer. I was genuinely excited to see Jo grow up and try to conquer the world, and I would do the same, but my world would just be different from hers. I knew she would understand that someday and end her misjudgment of roles of women.

"Meg?" Jo's voice broke through my thoughts.

I blinked at her as I came out of the little fog inside my head. "Huh?"

"Do you want a water? We're going to get one."

I lifted my hand to shade my eyes from the falling sun. "Yeah, please. Beth? Do you want a water?" I turned to my sis- ter, who was possibly asleep on the dry grass.

Jo answered instead. "I already asked her. Man, you were out of it." Jo laughed softly. "What were you dreaming about?"

I shook my head. *Just about you and I being completely different people, you know?* "Nothing." I looked at Laurie. He was sitting behind her, running his fingers over the feathery tips of her long hair.

"Mhmm," Jo joked, and stood, brushing off her butt and legs. "We'll be right back. Don't move, please."

Laurie followed behind her and they disappeared into the crowd.

I stared into the crowd and heard one of the festival organizers telling people to sit down before the concert began. The group that had been close to us a few minutes ago was even closer now, and Beth was still lying there decompressing with her eyes closed, so I looked at my phone again.

I was scrolling for a few seconds before I realized that I was on Shia's Facebook page. I brushed it off as an impulse due to the months I racked up cyberwatching him. I would just have to break that habit. It would be hard, but I was only torturing myself, and now that we were Facebook friends, it felt even more intrusive for some reason. I could see even more of his life once I approved the friend request he sent me right after my dad came back from Germany. Now I could see his status and other posts he shared. I could also see pictures he was tagged in by Bell Gardiner, and I tried my best not to let them make me throw up the strawberry yogurt I had for breakfast basically every morning.

"Shia's there," I thought I heard a voice say.

Damn, I was getting to be a little on the paranoid side. I thought maybe I should have deleted him from my Facebook, but I told myself that would make things awkward since we were supposed to be keeping things civil. We wanted to be in each other's life, though at a distance.

"No way. Let me see," a girl's voice said right next to my ear.

"Swear!" another girl replied. I looked over, and they both were staring at a cell phone. I couldn't see what they were looking at, so I turned back to my phone. My skin was a little prickly as I continued to listen. It was like I had a sixth sense.

"Damn, whose tits are those?" a man asked. I looked up at him and he wasn't a man; he was a boy with scruffy brown hair so overgrown it almost covered his eyes, wearing khaki shorts rolled up just above his knee. His boat shoes made me think he was rich, probably from Lakeshore or Lake Vista. He smelled of privilege and Armani cologne.

"Some chick from—"

"Did we miss anything?" Jo's voice drowned out the response, and I turned to her. Paranoia took hold of me. I felt like everyone knew something that I didn't know. It made me itchy, and my heart was starting to pick up its beat.

"Not really. The music is about to start." I debated whether to mention something to Jo, but when I thought about it, I didn't have anything to say. I would seem insane. Completely.

Jo handed me a bottle of water, and it soaked my hand. Beth got hers, too, and I settled in my spot on the blanket and stretched my legs out in front of me. My hair was so frizzy, I could feel it when I touched it. The humidity was worse than in the morning, and my skin felt sticky and warm. I rubbed the beads of water from the outside of the sweating bottle over my legs spread out in front of me, and the group next to me was still talking about whatever was on that phone.

"How desperate do you have to be?" a girl whose voice I thought I recognized said. I could barely see her because I was sitting down and most of her group were still standing—despite a festival worker's request to sit the hell down.

"Well, she is a Spring Girl, and that whole family is nuts."

The words hit me straight in the throat and ached all the way down to the pit that was eating away in my stomach. I felt like I was being picked away at with a chisel as the group got more and more rowdy and the comments kept flooding.

"The one is like being held captive or something."

"Meg is a whore, and the little one is growing up to be just like her."

My body quickly turned to them, but not one of them even noticed. I was torn between knocking one to the ground and hoping for a domino effect, or leaving. A masochistic part of me wanted to sit there and just listen to the hateful shit they were saying about me and my sisters so I could obsess over it enough to start to think it was true.

"My mom said they're getting kicked out of their house because their dad's getting kicked out of the Army."

Whose voice is that? I knew it for sure . . .

It only took me a few seconds to find Shelly Hunchberg sitting on the grass a few bodies down from me. I felt the flame of rage flickering inside me.

"Jo," I said just as the crowd started to cheer over me with the first band coming onstage. Great timing.

"Jo," I said louder. Neither she nor Laurie heard me.

"Josephine!" I half shouted. and Laurie and Jo both snapped their heads toward me.

"What?"

I scooted closer to her and explained what was happening. The best I could.

Jo's eyes went wild. "So, they were looking at those pictures?

I'll go over there right now—" She was half yelling, but the sound of trumpets was so loud that she might as well have been whispering.

I hadn't even thought about the cell phone and what they were looking at on the screen. I think a part of me knew before Jo stood up and it was why I was feeling paranoid, but the rest of my mind didn't want to go there.

"Don't." I reached for Jo's arm and pulled her back down by her wrist. Laurie sat up more and was immediately alerted.

"Why not? If they're showing those pictures . . ." Jo's cheeks were red and she was talking through her teeth.

If they were, who was the source? How did those damn pictures travel from Texas to Louisiana?

The internet, that was how. It had to be.

My chest felt like it had caved in and smashed my heart as I tried to think clearly.

Was it actually happening? Yes, it had to be. They said names. I stood up, not knowing what else to do. I should have just left, but of course I didn't. Jo, Beth, and Laurie were on their feet, too. Before I could decide what to do, I heard an unmistakable voice from the group.

"And even John Brooke can't stand her. He's trying to break up with her, but she's so desperate." She laughed. "I heard Shia's mom talking about Meredith Spring being a drunk now."

Bell Gardiner. Her voice dripped honey and stung like a wasp.

I thought about the time I was at the pool in sixth grade and saw a wasp cut a honeybee's body in half and fly away with the lower half of its body, leaving its head just sitting there.

I thought about how Bell Gardiner was a cruel insect of a woman.

"What the fuck?" I said when I stepped into the little circle of bodies they had formed.

Jo was at my side, with Laurie and Beth behind her.

Bell's eyes didn't go wide; they turned into little slits like a serpent's eyes, and she came floating toward me like a ghost. She moved so slowly, like even if she was surprised to see me there, she wasn't about to show it. I could see a little hint of anxiety over me being there, but it wasn't as obvious as I would have been if caught red-handed talking shit about someone.

"Meg." She smiled a slithery grin at me, her eyes going from me to Jo to Beth to Laurie and back to me. "Hey."

Bell nudged the girl next to her and someone shushed us.

"What the fuck, Bell?" Jo's voice barked next to me.

"What? I didn't start it. It's not like everyone hasn't seen your sister already."

The voices around us got quieter, but the band onstage seemed to be getting louder by the second.

I didn't exactly want Jo to start a fight with Bell, but the realization that a group of strangers were passing around a phone with my naked body on the screen and talking about it less than five feet away from me was sinking in fast. I started sweating, and the air felt a little too thick. Everyone was starting to home in on me and realize what was happening.

Between the whispers of the crowd and Bell's faux-innocent face, I wanted to scream.

"What's your problem, Bell? Who the fuck do you think you are digging that shit up and passing it around!" Jo waved her hands at the group of Bell's friends.

Bell didn't seem to know what to say to that.

"Oh my God," I heard someone say from somewhere behind

Bell, and then Shia was there. I felt immediate betrayal. Of course he was in on it—how else would Bell even know there were pictures of me in the first place? "What's going on?"

Jo responded, "Your fucking girlfriend is passing this around." Jo snatched the phone out of Shelly Hunchberg's hands and shoved it into Shia's face. He barely looked at the phone before he backed away from Bell.

"The rest of you can go away now!" Jo shouted, waving her hand like she was swatting flies.

Beth looped her arm through mine, and Laurie stood behind Jo with a pissed-off look on his face. I hoped he would punch Shia right in the damn throat.

Sadly, he didn't.

"What are you doing?" Shia asked Bell.

She fidgeted a little, pulling the thin strap of her tank top up her shoulder. She looked a little less put together and a lot more worried, and I was trying to fight the burn of tears in the back of my throat. I couldn't cry in front of these assholes, especially not Shia and his bride-to-be.

"We were just joking around." Bell's voice was soft.

"It's not a fucking joke!" Jo shouted. I knew I looked pathetic letting my little sister fight my battles, but I was frozen in place and stunned into silence.

"Whose phone is this?" Shia held it in the air.

Shelly Hunchberg raised her hand and stepped forward.

"Really, Shelly?" Beth snapped. "Let's go, Meg." She pulled at my arm.

When I thought about it, there wasn't much I could do. I could either stand there and be humiliated as Bell acted like it wasn't a big deal that an entire group of people were mocking me and looking at my body, or I could leave.

I grabbed Beth's jewelry bag from the ground and turned to leave. I didn't even look at Shia. A woman with a baby strapped to her chest bumped into me, and her baby started to scream. It felt like a sign from the universe. A big, shiny *Fuck you* from the universe.

I heard Jo still yelling, and I heard Shia's voice calling my name as Beth dragged me through the crowd. All of the faces around me looked like River, like Bell, like Jessica Fox, who was supposed to be my best friend in Texas but taped a printed version of one of the pictures to my front door so that Amy found it when she came home on the bus. I remembered the look on my dad's face when he got back from "talking" to River's parents. My dad wanted to press charges for distributing child pornography, since I wasn't eighteen and River was, but I didn't want to deal with the humiliation and consequences at school.

Everyone loved River, and I was just a whore who gave boys blow jobs in the backseats of their cars to make them like me more. I was the girl with the big tits and the horny mouth. I got it. I sent pictures to my boyfriend and was going to be shamed to the end of the halls of Killeen High School for it. Well, apparently, I was going to be shamed on the streets of New Orleans, too.

When we neared the street, I remembered the fury that had radiated through Meredith when she stormed through the halls of my high school, demanding that every computer be wiped clean. I remembered the day I walked into the computer lab and Jessica Fox had set my boobs as the wallpaper on half of the monitors.

The air in my lungs was burning and I was out of breath. I stopped for a second.

Beth looked at my face and said, "Let's stop for a minute."

"Hey!" a girl's voice called to us from behind a booth.

"Shia's coming," Beth told me, and waved to the girl behind the booth.

"Get me out of here," I begged Beth. I didn't want to see Shia, and I only had about thirty seconds before the tears were going to be unstoppable. I was so mad, so fucking pissed at myself and the world for being so stupid. I should never have told Shia about those stupid pictures.

"Are you okay?" the girl in the booth asked. Looking over, I saw she was like some manga Gypsy princess, rivaling Vanessa Hudgens for Coachella queen. Her body was dripping with jewelry, and I realized the booth was full of the rings that Beth had bought.

Beth was talking to the girl, and I couldn't hear what they were saying, but Beth told me to come behind the booth and sit down. The moment my butt hit the chair, I let myself cry.

Shia walked on by without seeing us.

～

When we got home, Amy and my dad were sitting on the couch. Meredith was in the kitchen heating up a covered dish. We would never have to cook again, it seemed.

"How was it?" Amy asked. "It looks so cool online, how was it?"

I looked at Beth. "It was fine," she lied for me.

I loved her for it.

She pulled open her bag from the jewelry booth and distracted Amy with shiny mood rings.

"I'm going to take a shower," I announced to a roomful of

people who all said "Okay" to me like they didn't know why I was telling them in the first place.

I made it up to my room and collapsed onto my bed. I felt like a bucket of pig's blood had been dumped on my prom dress. I felt so dirty.

38

beth

The morning after the festival, I woke to Jo's and Meg's loud voices down the hall. Ever since Jo was a kid, whenever she got angry, her tone went a few octaves deeper. Meg was the opposite; her usually soft voice became a screechy kind of noise, a lot like the sound of Mrs. King's little dogs.

"You could have told me!" Meg yelled at her. "Weeks have gone by—and nothing!"

I threw my leg over the bed to get up. To go mediate whatever the hell was going on with my sisters. I was always the mediator. I was so tired, though; the festival noises, smells, chaos—it was exhausting. My entire body, mind included, throbbed when I lay in bed last night. Still, no matter how tired I was that morning, it wasn't that important. Not as important as whatever was happening down the hall.

"Don't blame me! You're *always* the victim!" Jo yelled back.

I closed my eyes for a second and stared at the ceiling. Nothing would change in the next few seconds. The day before had started so differently than it had ended. When it started, I was anxious, sure, but it was nothing compared to the end of the night, walking Meg through a crowd, hiding her in the mood-ring girl's booth . . .

I couldn't hear what Jo and Meg were yelling about anymore. I lifted my hand into the air, studying the stone on my finger, which had turned a light blue. The lighter shades of blue were supposed to indicate that I was relaxed. I wasn't sure that I believed mood rings really worked.

A door slammed, and Meg continued to yell. I got out of bed and followed the noise. In the kitchen, Meg was crying, leaning her shoulders against the fridge. Jo was gone, and the back screen door was swinging open.

My dad wheeled himself into the kitchen. "What's going on?" he asked Meg, who didn't answer. She only cried out, covered her face, and ran off to her room.

My dad and I both stared at the now-empty hallway for a few seconds before he said, "What is happening around here?"

I didn't know what to say because I didn't know, either, and I didn't know how much of last night my dad was even aware of. He had so much going on already himself, it was selfish to add another rock to his shoulders.

"I don't know," I said. "I'm sure they'll work it out, whatever it is." I looked at him. "Want some breakfast?"

My dad looked at me, at the door, and then down the hallway, slowly. He sighed, his thin shoulders visibly dredging up and right back down. He was wearing a gray T-shirt with a small hole in the collar. His outfits never varied much, just different-colored T-shirts and sweatshirts. Sometimes he would wear a button-up

shirt, when we went to restaurants or my sisters' school func-
tions. And even more rarely, he would dress in his Class A's when
there was a military ball or ceremony of whatever sort.

I always loved when there was a military ball for my parents
to go to. Meg had done Mom's hair and makeup for the last few
years, and she would always take us to the mall and let us help
her choose a dress to wear. That was one of the few times a year
we got to shop at the mall. It was pretty fun helping my mom try
on dresses; somehow, the JCPenney's dressing room would become the set of *Say Yes to the Dress*. Meg would have Mom twirl
and turn and bend down and stretch up, showing off every inch
of the dresses. We would always go to Friday's for lunch, and
sometimes even to Starbucks beforehand. My dad would get my
mom a corsage, and Amy would make kissing noises when he
slid it onto her wrist. Mom almost always poked his chest with
the boutonniere pin due to his habit of making her laugh at the
worst times. The memories I have of them are mostly fond, but
sometimes it's hard to square up the dad in my memories with
the man sitting in the wheelchair before me.

I checked the cabinets and fridge to see what I could make
for him. His appetite had changed since coming home. He says
the cocktail of medications the Army put him on made him too
nauseous to eat.

"What was all that noise?" my mom croaked, walking into
the room. She slid behind my dad's chair and sat down at the
kitchen table. The table was the oldest thing in our house, given
to us by my nana, before she and my mom stopped talking. I
wondered if Aunt Hannah talked to her still . . . I couldn't be
sure, no matter how much intel I had on the adult stuff around
us. The table was scratched, beat-up, and broken during our
PCS from Fort Hood to Fort Cyprus, and my mom's elbow was

resting right in the deep splinter of the glossy dark wood. She looked like she hadn't slept in days, even though she just woke up. She had been watching *The Twilight Zone* on the couch, a cup in her hand, when I got up to pee in the middle of the night.

"Meg and Jo were fighting over something," my dad answered.

When Mom asked for specifics, I shrugged and popped open a can of biscuits and started making everyone's meal.

Several minutes later, Meg came back into the kitchen right as I handed my mom her plate. Meg was calmer now, if a bit disheveled.

"Want some?" I asked.

She nodded, and her puffy red eyes focused on my mom, who was swallowing the pile of biscuits and gravy on her plate and washing them down with milk. A faint white milk stain colored her bottom lip as she chewed. I wasn't sure what she was looking at, but something on the wall behind me seemed to be entertaining to her.

"Did anyone call for me?" Meg's voice sounded like she had been chewing on sandpaper in her room.

"Call what?" my dad said.

I hadn't heard Meg—or anyone—ask that question in . . . years. Wouldn't someone have just called her cell phone?

Meg blinked and mumbled, "Never mind."

"What are you girls up to today?" my dad asked between bites. Clearly neither he nor my mom were eager to get into whatever all the yelling had been about.

When Meg remained silent, I guessed she wasn't going to answer, so I did. "I'm doing nothing. Some school stuff, laundry. That's it, really." I shrugged.

"That sounds like a blast, Beth."

It was a comfort that my dad still had his sarcasm. His tone wasn't as malicious or as callous as the comment would have sounded coming from say, Amy, and it came with a smile and knowing about his high school experience. He was a lot like me.

"Don't you have any friends around here?" he asked.

"You gave me so many sisters, I don't need friends."

We both laughed. His laughter was a little lighter than usual, but it still sounded so good in that yellow-wallpapered kitchen.

"Touché."

"Jo didn't come back yet?" Meg asked. She hadn't eaten much of the food in front of her. I thought about soaking the dishes before I made myself a plate, so the slimy gravy wouldn't stick to the pan, but I was so hungry and the gravy looked so, so good.

My dad answered, "No. She's still next door."

As far as I knew, no one knew for sure that Jo was at Laurie's, but then again, we all knew. That's where she always was. Laurie's, a shift at Pages, school, then back to Laurie's.

"None of you were going to tell me that Shia came here that night?" Meg pointed to my mom.

My mom snapped her head up, but my sister kept going. "He told me you all knew. He showed up there, and I didn't even know he was looking for me."

"Well, Meg, what difference would it have made?" Mom said, then went back to eating. She didn't seem to notice the stain of gravy oiling up her shirt.

Meg's eyes bulged. She wiped her mouth with a napkin before she spoke. "He came looking for me and I didn't even know!" It felt like her anger was going to make the house rattle. "I've been waiting for so long for him to do that, and you guys didn't even tell me. He's getting married—"

"Would that have changed? And John Brooke?" Mom pointed out.

Part of me wanted to step in, but another part of me didn't know what kind of tornado I'd be walking into.

I would never find out what Meg was going to say because Amy came rushing through the back door with puffy, wet eyes.

"What's wrong?" My dad asked, and I watched him struggle to get up like his legs forgot they couldn't quite move yet. He sank back down in the chair.

"My life! Everything sucks!" She stormed past us and twirled around when no one tried to stop her. "Fuck everything!"

Her cussing had my mom on her feet. "Amy, watch your mouth."

Amy huffed at our mom's warning and started to cry again. "Jacob Weber told Casey Miller that I tried to kiss him—and now everyone hates me!"

She paced around the room in a fury. I didn't know who either of those kids were, but I knew how rumors could eat at someone and ruin lives. I'd watched it happen with Meg in Texas.

"Why did he do that?" Meg asked Amy. My two sisters' heart-shaped faces had never looked as similar as they did in that kitchen, all puffy-eyed and pink-lipped.

"Because he's a dickhead!" Amy's voice turned into a cry like a puppy's when you step on its tail.

Mom didn't correct her language this time.

"He was the one who tried to kiss me!"

Our dad didn't say anything; he just looked at the women in the room as they started fluttering around Amy.

"Are you saying you didn't want him to?" Mom asked, on her feet and sharp-eyed in seconds. It was like she'd just shed a thick, groggy layer of skin.

"Where were you?" Meg petted Amy's hair like she forgot that she was midfight with Jo.

Amy leaned into her. "Ew! Of *course* I didn't want him to. He's kissed, like, every girl in my class." Amy's little nose turned up at the tip and always gave the illusion that she was younger than a preteen.

"Tell us what happened." My mom slid her hand behind Amy's back, but Amy pulled away.

"Meg," Amy whined.

My sisters shared a look, and Meg told us that they were going to talk alone for a minute.

My mom, my dad, and I all had our heads tilted a little, and I guessed that my parents were wondering when Meg and Amy had gotten so close. But I often caught them whispering and knew how often Amy crawled in bed with Meg, so I wasn't surprised by that. My head was tilted because Meg only cared about Amy right then, not herself.

39

jo

*L*aurie's room was a mess. It always had some type of chaos sprinkled around—a T-shirt hanging over the side of the headboard, or a day-old decaf coffee sitting in a chipped mug on his desk. But today, it was an absolute mess. An old-food odor and a musty smell that I'd rather not think about describing dominated the space.

"What the hell happened in here?" I asked him, kicking my way through a pile of clothes.

He was pacing around the bedroom like a madman. His long hair was hanging down, curling at the ends the way I liked. He looked like someone out of a novel. The stereotypical New York writer, born in Boston, or somewhere big. Not quite as big as the juicy, red Big Apple, but bigger than this little bubble of a town. Laurie, with his long golden hair, dressed in an oversize sweatshirt with patches on the elbows. He looked so smart, like he would write essays about climate or gun control, but still take your virginity after driving for hours to bring you to a field of flowers you Tumblred a picture of once.

His forehead was creased with a deep crinkle that made him look a little like Old Mr. Laurence, and like his dad from the array of pictures hanging in this big house.

"Hey," he said, not explaining the mess. "How's it going?" He lifted up a stack of magazines and put them back down on the desk.

"Shitty, actually."

He continued rummaging through his messy bedroom and moved toward the window, through which the sun poured, paling the walls and his skin. When I took off my cardigan and draped it over the back of his chair, he looked up at me.

"So, Meg is pissed off because I never told her that Shia came looking for her back when she was in New Orleans with John Brooke, months ago, the day my dad was hurt."

Laurie was listening, I could tell, but he was still moving around the room. It was making me restless, so I kept talking.

"It's just that when those assholes were talking about her yesterday, she's blaming me because she won't say shit to Shia or Bell." I sat down on the bed.

Laurie sat down next to me. "And this is your fault, how?" He always took my side in everything. I liked that. He would debate me after if he didn't agree, but his initial reaction was always to take my side.

"*Exactly*. She's always the victim. I get that she's pissed about what happened at the festival. I'm pissed, too!" I *was* mad—I didn't want my sister to be harassed by a bunch of dicks who peaked in high school, but she was acting like it was my fault when I wasn't the character assassin here.

I picked at the hole in the knee of my jeans. "It's like she thinks Shia coming to the house would have changed things."

"It would have, I think." Laurie paused when I gave him a look. He lifted his hands up, covered by the long sleeves of his sweatshirt. "Hear me out. He came to the house, then went to the Quarter, right?"

I nodded.

"If Meg likes Shia the way Shia likes her, then it was probably pretty important for her to hear what he had to say."

"But they *did* talk, eventually." I shook my head at Laurie. "Besides, he's engaged."

"You always see everything in black and white, Jo. Sometimes there's some gray in there."

I sighed. "Engaged isn't really a gray area. Either you're going to marry someone soon, or not."

"Either you're dating someone or you're not." Laurie looked directly into my eyes.

My chest tightened and I pulled at the strings of ripped denim. "Yes . . . and no. Sometimes it's more complicated than that."

"Like with us."

I looked away from his eyes, down to where his hands stretched his sweatshirt, down his fitted sweatpants and clean white socks, to the floor of the dirty bedroom.

"This isn't about us," I said.

"When will it be? You know my mom wants me to come back home."

I felt his words wrap around my throat and squeeze a little. Home wasn't across town or across the United States. Home was across the ocean. "No. I didn't know that."

"She does." His eyes were trying to keep hold of mine, but

I avoided them. "Why can't we just talk about it? I thought we would by now. You'll be applying to colleges soon. What then?"

Why was he choosing this exact moment to bring this up? Wasn't there supposed to be some tiptoeing around the subject, a couple more makeouts? Meg never explained this to me. By the time she and I were starting to grow closer, my dad came back and she stopped talking to me about things. We weren't close anymore; it was almost like we never were.

"Jo," Laurie urged me. I looked up at him and he moved a little closer to me. The big room felt so small, and Laurie's fingers were pulling at his sleeves. "If you don't want to, fine. Just tell me. I'm not going to force you. I just want to know what you're thinking. I never know what you're thinking."

"Yes, you do."

"Not about me. About everything else, yes. But never about me."

"You talk. I don't know what you want to say, or want me to say. You talk." It was true, I didn't know where to begin or end this conversation.

"Fine." Laurie rolled his eyes. He tucked his hair behind his ears and licked his lips. "Do you want to date me?"

"Is that how this goes?"

"Stop being sarcastic. I'm serious." His voice sounded small.

I took a second to think before I spoke. Something I knew I needed to do more often. "Sorry. I don't know how to be serious during this. I've never done this before, remember?"

He jerked his shoulders back. "Ouch."

I quickly raised my hands. "No, not what I meant. I wasn't insinuating that you have. I just meant that I literally haven't." I paused for a second. "Like, ever."

"If it's that uncomfortable for you—"

"No, it's not." I moved toward him when he backed farther onto the bed. "Just talk. Say stuff and then I'll say stuff." I was losing my breath. "Just go first." I bit into my lip a little too hard, and I caught Laurie's black eyes on my mouth just before he looked away.

"Okay." He dragged a long sigh through his lips. "My mom's been asking if I want to come back home. My dad got orders to stay in Korea longer, and she misses me now that my sister has friends."

I kept my mouth quiet while my head spun.

"The only reason I would stay here is if you're going to be around . . . I'm not saying that we have to agree to get married or move in or anything anytime soon, just that you'll be around . . ."

"I would be around." My voice was practically a whisper.

"What about New York?"

"Well, yeah. I would be in New York . . ."

Laurie's whole upper body sighed. "Yeah, so I would be here in Louisiana, and you would be in New York City?"

I nodded. "We would talk every day and come visit each other." People did it all the time. Right?

"So a long-distance relationship, then?"

He didn't sound particularly excited about this idea. I honestly wasn't expecting him to want a commitment type of thing with me. I thought we would stay friends, close . . . *best* friends, and maybe date someday when I was out of school, and his dad was home, and my dad was better, and I had time to worry about boys and matching bras and panties.

"I guess so. People do it all the time." I shrugged. "We would visit on the weekends."

"It's a three-hour flight, not to mention the cost of flights, and the drive is twenty hours nonstop." He had done his research.

"So, what do we do?" I asked.

Laurie shook his head, and I thought about the first time I met him, and the time when I slid down the driveway and flipped him off. The time outside the community center with Meg and Reeder. Laurie seemed so mysterious then, the classic heartbreaker.

He was so much different in my eyes now. He was my best friend. I liked him more than that—I knew I did—but it also scared me. I didn't want to be like Meg when River fucked her over. I wanted to go into my first relationship with my eyes open.

"Do you one hundred percent want to go New York? *Vice* has offices all over. One in Venice Beach, basically LA, one in Toronto . . . all over."

"I want to go to New York, I think." I'd never thought about Los Angeles. Toronto, yeah, but realistically it was hard to go outside the country for school. "You could come to New York."

"Could I?"

"Yeah? Right? I mean, why not? What are you doing here that you couldn't do there?"

He leaned back against his palms on the bed. "I don't know, but I don't want to live in New York. I hated staying there for longer than a few days. You haven't been, it's not as great as you think."

"*Yet*. I will be going soon," I told him, even though my parents still hadn't given me a clear answer if we could take a tour of a few campuses there. My grades were good, but I wasn't guaranteed to get into any of the colleges I wanted. Even after getting in, I still had to worry about paying for it, and my dad's

G.I. Bill money could only go to one of us. It had never been discussed *which* one of us, though.

"I think the long-distance thing would be fine," I told Laurie. "If I go to New York and hate it, we can figure it out then."

"So, what if I go back to Italy? I've got a friend in Milan I could crash with for a while. I would be closer to my mom, but still only a flight from you."

He really did his research. Almost too much . . .

"So you've been planning this?"

"Not planning, really." He scratched at something on his forehead. "Just thinking about it. Haven't you thought about it?"

"Yeah, I mean, a little. I didn't really think about it too much, but I kind of just thought you would stay here and I would go to New York and come home for holidays and stuff?"

"I don't know . . . What about boys in college? And the distance would probably eat at us. It usually does." Laurie sounded like he was digging for reasons for this to fail.

What I wanted to say was that statistically the person you're dating when young isn't who you end up with when you're older. Out of all the married couples I knew, grown-ups included, most of them were on their second marriage. Laurie was a part of me, and I knew it would rip out chunks of me when this stopped working—it wasn't an easy pill to swallow, but it was reality.

"I'm not concerned about boys in college," I said.

He smiled at me and reached for my hands. His skin was always so warm. He lifted my palm in front of his face and spread my fingers out, pressing them gently to his mouth, and I shivered all over. It was something, the way he made me feel. The way he made the blood roar behind my ears and popcorn pop in my stomach.

I leaned into him and he pulled me onto his lap. Each time we were alone, we crossed another line, made another move toward the dream of what we could be.

"We are so good as neighbors, nearby each other," he said inches from my face. My thighs were on either side of his lean waist; his thick sweatshirt was all droopy between us.

God, he made my head fuzzy. It pissed me off.

"Are you sure you want this? You won't be able to have Shelly Hunchberg come over and talk about fund-raisers when I'm in another state."

"Oh, shut up." He smiled. His warm hands were on my back. I could feel the heat of them through my thin tank top. "You will be the one falling in love with coffee boys and professors."

"No. I don't have time for them."

"You barely have time for me," he said, almost kissing me.

I didn't want to lie. "I know."

"You're important to me, Jo."

I looked at Laurie's face and counted the little batch of freckles just below his eye. His thick eyebrows were dark blond, relaxed, and his lips, they were carnation pink.

"'Kiss me, and you will see how important I am,'" I said as some cool girl who quotes poetry possessed my body.

"I read those journals. The Sylvia Plath—"

I kissed him to shut him up and decided maybe Laurie was right: there was so much gray.

40

There had been a line out the door of Pages for the last hour and a half. Hyper Hayton was excessively downing little cups of espresso to add to her own mania. Sam, this kid who I had only worked with twice, was having a hard time remembering orders. On top of that, he rang up the wrong freaking order four times in a row, which meant I had to remake four drinks in a row, and his shift wasn't over for another hour. I still had two hours to go, which meant cleaning up his damn mess. My feet were aching and my apron was stained with big brown splotches of coffee. My jeans were dusted with ground beans and the remnants of a glob of whipped cream, and I had somehow managed to get a nasty paper cut on my elbow from changing the receipt-paper roll.

I wasn't ever a graceful barista, but I wasn't usually this clumsy. I guess I can't say shit about Sam messing up orders. It was just that I couldn't stop thinking about this morning. The memory was so vivid, scorching hot in my head. Laurie had kissed me, like *kissssed* me. Like he kissed me harder than he ever had before. If Meg and I weren't fighting, I would have had her search the skin on my back for little moons left by his nails. I could feel them throbbing now, and my stomach flipped, right at the pit, and my mouth tingled. I missed him, I wished he would come into Pages and push me against the—

"Iced mocha for here!" Sam yelled to Hayton. Or me? I wasn't sure, but it about made my bones jump out of my skin.

"Oh, fuck. Fuck us. There's a line over there!" Hayton whisper-yelled at me, jabbing her little finger into the air to point at the bookstore area. She was right. Fuck us.

Pretty much the only shitty thing about working at Pages was when both sides were swamped with customers. Since I was one of only two switch employees, I could ring out customers on the bookstore side of the store, then pop over to tell a customer why they should devour my favorite poetry books, to make drinks, or to pop a bagel in the toaster oven when needed. Today was one of those days. I had been going back and forth since noon. I knew that after this line died down, I would be going over to sell books and have to remember authors' names and genres, the order their books go in a series, and maybe, just maybe, if I was lucky enough, my head would explode into book-page-themed confetti.

"Sorry," I heard Sam say.

"It's fine!" Hayton shot him her perkiest smile, looking a little like she was planning to skin him alive in front of the crowd. The image was vomit-worthy to say the least, and I momentarily cursed Meredith and her love of horror for its impact on my mind.

Pages kept getting busier and busier each week that I worked there. I hated the long drive to the Quarter, but I could totally see why people—both hipsters and non—flocked in to take pictures for their social-media posts. The funky blue floral wallpaper clashed with the rows and rows of books. In the back of the store there was a buy-here, resell-here section that was always busy, and where most of the actual bookworms bought their stock. But the aesthetic collectors wanted the shiny hardback that matched with their designer coffee cup and the pattern on their nails.

Pages was everything you wanted in a local hangout (tourist trap) of a bookstore. When word kept traveling about this place, and blogs kept posting pictures of it, and some chick with a million Instagram followers posted a fancy latte with a penguin drawn with foam here, it got busier and busier. Almost every person took a picture of their coffee, and I could always tell when they were going straight to Instagram. It's just *so chic* to drink a $6 white-chocolate coconut mocha! And what says designer coffee like a little design drawn on top?

But seriously, it is. And I not-so-secretly loved those pictures. Laurie's Instagram was full of pictures of us.

Laurie. My stomach flipped again.

The boom in business at Pages would have been cool before, but since my dad came home, I just didn't have time to work my ass off at school, then work, then home. I had become so busy driving back and forth to doctors, and Amy's Girl Scouts, and work, that by the time I tied the apron around my waist, I barely had enough energy to make an iced coffee, let alone keep a line going with pep in my voice and a smile on my face.

I was sweaty and had lost count of how many bagels I had toasted or how many vanilla lattes I had made. My tan T-shirt was clinging to the sweat beading on my back.

When I was thinking that nothing else could be added to my list, my phone vibrated in my pocket. I pulled it out to see my dad's name flashing on the screen. I ignored the call and shouted to Hayton that I would be back in a second. I didn't wait for her to answer before I dipped into the break room to call my dad back.

He answered on the first ring. "Jo, hey. Can you pick me up from Howard?"

He must have been at one of his appointments at the hospital on post. It felt like they were piling up. I didn't even know about this one.

"I'm at work. I can't. I get off at four, so like an hour. You had an appointment on a Sunday?"

I heard the blender turn on and prayed to God that it wasn't Sam making a blended drink.

"No, I went to the woodshop on post to see if I knew anyone, but it was full of new privates. Your sister dropped me off on the way to something." He paused. "I forget, but Meg dropped me off. Can you get me?"

"I get off in an hour."

"That's fine. I can sit and wait here."

A metal cup fell to the floor, and I cringed. The blender, the metal cup, Sam . . . bad collection there. I had like ten seconds, tops, before I had to go back out there and pull my weight, or I'd be here all day. I wanted to go back to Laurie's house . . . or just see Laurie . . . and I wanted to find out if Meg was still pissed at me over the Shia ordeal. My back was so tense, it felt like a hundred little needles were stabbing into the meat between my neck and my shoulder.

"No fucking—" I stopped and corrected myself. "No way.

Let me see if Laurie can come get you. I'll text you as soon as I know."

"Thanks, Jo. Love you."

"Love you, Dad."

I hung up and rolled my shoulders back, trying to relieve the throbbing. I wanted to lean against the wall, but I didn't want to get too comfortable. My body was exhausted all the way down to the tips of my toes. I glanced at the huge schedule board tacked to the wall in the break room. My name was on there four times for the week. That was about three too many. Was life supposed to be so heavy at this age? I should have been prepared for this. TV, film, and media in general prepared me for this. *Gossip Girl*, *Boy Meets World*, the imperfectly perfect dictation of what teenage life was like in my era.

Laurie answered the phone after the second ring.

"Hey, I have a favor to ask," I greeted him.

There was a noise in the background like a soft buzzing or swishing. "Hi. Okay?"

"Can you pick my dad up from the woodshop across from Magnolia hospital?"

"Now?"

"Yeah. If you can? Don't you have a driver sitting around waiting for you to call him?"

Laurie laughed into the phone. "Ha-ha. I do, but I'll go get your dad. I can actually drive. Can you believe that?" Playful sarcasm dripped from his accented voice. His "ha-ha" was almost missing the *h* completely.

"Gasp," I teased.

He was an awful driver. I limited his driving when we went

out together. Since meeting Laurie, I found myself loving being chauffeured around. I would still ride a public bus or metro any day, but sitting on black leather seats that were always the perfect degree of cold for the Louisiana spring while being driven by a driver who stays in his own lane, unlike Laurie, was pretty freaking nice.

"I'll leave now. I just need to finish my shower."

So that's what the swishing sound was . . .

"Thanks, Laurie," I breathed into the phone.

"No problem, Jo."

He hung up first, and I tried to think of anything besides him in the shower. Whatever he puts in his kisses should be bottled and sold to virginal girls around the freaking globe.

The bell on the wall rang right next to my ear, letting me know the lobby door had opened and scaring the crap out of me. I wiped my hands across my dirty apron and went back out to the storm in the store. Only there wasn't a storm at all. It was like the little bit of sunshine after a bad storm. The line was completely clear on the café side, and Sam was clearing the dirty tables. Hayton was putting her busy body to work by sweeping the floor behind the bar. Even the bookstore side was mostly cleared out: only two people were at the register. A blond girl and tattooed guy were checking out with a pretty big stack of used books. The noise had also died down, so that I could actually hear the music. The door opened again and Vanessa, our newest coworker, walked in. It couldn't get any better. I loved working with Vanessa. She carried her own weight, and she was funny, witty, and so good at her job that it made the shift sooo much better.

The chaos had cleared out. Laurie seemed to bring peace in the wake of him.

~

When I dragged my body through the front door of my house after work, Laurie was on the couch with his long legs across the worn-out rug from Mosul. He was wearing light jeans with rips in the knees, and the bottom of his white socks were dirty. Amy was perched next to him. The laptop was in her lap.

"And then she yelled at Jo, and Jo stormed off to your house. Meredith and my dad were pissed because of this creep at my school named Jacob Weber, who kissed me." Amy made a sour face.

I leaned against the wall to take my shoes off. I needed a shower. Immediately. "Amy, seriously?"

All I got was an eye roll from Amy before she turned back to Laurie. "Anyway, so yeah. It's so messed up."

I walked over to the couch and sat at Laurie's knees. If Amy weren't here, I would have sat between his legs like I could when we binged Netflix shows at his house.

"And none of my friends are in any of my classes this year." Amy sighed like she wasn't lucky to even *have* friends to begin with. Speaking of, Beth walked into the living room and handed Amy a plate of food. Little butter-cracker sandwiches with ham and cheese layered between them.

"Thank *youuu*." Amy air-kissed Beth, kicking her sock-covered feet against the couch. She had makeup on—little pink lips and cheeks.

"Damn." Laurie shook his head. His hair was tucked behind his ears, but he retucked both sides and kept talking to my twelve-year-old sister about her junior high crisis. "That's pretty brutal. Guys can be di—" He cleared his throat. "Guys can behave really poorly sometimes. Especially to girls. I wish I could say we get better when we get older, but I don't know if that's true."

"Some of you do," I told him.

I leaned back against his leg, and his hand began to rub my shoulder, the one farthest from Amy. His touch was harsh against the muscle, but the pressure felt so good. I was immediately relaxed. I reached up and pulled my hair down to help hide the affection from my sister.

"Yes." Laurie laughed. "Some."

Amy took a bite of her crumbly snack, and Beth stood over me. Her eyes were on Laurie's hand on my shoulder, rubbing the strain away. I wasn't embarrassed, which was kind of weird because I was around Amy. Not with Beth, though.

"I'm going to take Mom to the PX," she told us.

"I'm coming!" Amy announced, spitting little flakes of crackers on her white shirt.

Beth shook her head. "You should stay with Jo and Laurie. We are just grabbing a couple things and picking up Aunt Hannah's birthday cake."

"I don't want to stay with Jo and Laurie," Amy protested.

Since she had started curling her hair and wearing little diamonds in her earlobes, she looked older than Beth. It was strange. I swore that since she'd started her period, she aged two years. She seemed too immature for her body, with a thin black choker around her neck, and her jeans squeezing her little blossoming hips. She was going to have Meredith and Meg's type of body. I knew it. She already had bigger boobs than me and she was twelve. I wondered how she would handle it and if she would need me to remind her that she held the power of her body and to never let another person use it as a weapon against her.

"Look," Beth started whispering. "You can't get anything at the store, okay?"

"Okay. Fine?"

"I'm serious, Amy. You can't wait till we get there and beg for stuff because Mom and Dad have a lot of bills and that fundraiser is coming up."

I knew Amy always pulled that. She once had a midlevel meltdown in the middle of the PX over some body spray she wanted. My parents didn't spank us often, but that day, Meredith swatted her four or five times on the way to the car.

"Fine. Oh my God." Amy rolled her eyes.

Laurie squeezed my shoulder a little tighter and I turned around to Amy.

"Amy, chill," I told her.

"Mind your business, Jo," she sassed. She was giving me such a grown-up look that it was slightly terrifying, but mostly pissed me off. I hated when girls showed off in front of boys, and that was exactly what Amy was doing.

"Amy," I warned her again.

Laurie slowly moved his hand away from me.

"I'll just go ask Mom." Amy jerked her body off the couch so fast that the laptop fell on the ground. I freaked.

"Be careful!" I yelled, reaching for the laptop.

Laurie moved his legs out of the way.

"Guys," Beth cooed, trying to break the tension.

"Amy, seriously! Go, go to the kitchen or something. Get out of here," I seethed. The screen was frozen when I tried to log on to the home screen. "It's frozen! It's broken now because you—"

"Girls!" Meredith came into the room. "Cut it out."

"She broke the laptop!" I yelled. I didn't look at Laurie.

"Josephine! Stop it. Now!" Meredith was awash with anger. It was the most emotion I had seen on my mom's face in a while. It looked good on her.

Amy told my mom that she wanted to go to the PX, and when Meredith told her she couldn't, she grabbed the computer from my hands.

My sister was glaring at me, standing like a little lioness, with her lip curled up like she was ready to pounce, claws out.

"Drop it! Give it to me!" I screamed.

She lifted the laptop higher.

"Amy!" I yelled, trying to process what she was doing. Would she really trash our only computer knowing that if our parents couldn't afford to get her a glittery skirt or new pair of sandals, they sure as heck couldn't afford a new laptop?

I was full of rage and all I could think about was shoving her onto the floor, climbing on top of her, and shaking some sense into her. I could barely see straight when I started yelling back at her. Meredith moved toward her, but wasn't fast enough.

Amy started yelling, too, saying that I was a liar and she hated me. What did I lie about? Who knew? I didn't, but I told her I hated her, too. When Beth moved toward Amy, I pushed at her shoulders and she slammed the laptop to the floor. She screamed and dug her sharp little nails into my skin. Laurie reached down and grabbed the computer, carrying it away from further harm.

"Stop it!" Beth yelled, yanking Amy right off me.

Meredith wasn't even close to happy with us.

My dad sped into the room. "What the hell is going on?" his voice boomed.

Laurie looked away, just a little terrified of my dad's Army voice.

"The girls are fighting," Meredith explained.

"About what now?"

"I want to go to the PX," Amy said at the same time that I said, "She broke the laptop!"

"You broke the laptop? You're not going to the PX. Get to your room." My dad pointed his finger toward the hallway.

Amy sulked, glaring at everyone, Laurie included, and stomped back to her room.

"Let's go, Beth." Meredith sounded so exhausted. "They close early on Sundays."

Laurie waited for my dad to leave the room before he sat back down on the couch.

"Tell me the worst," I said when I sat down next to him.

The laptop was open on his lap, but I couldn't see the screen. He licked his lips and played around with the keyboard and the mouse some. "Okay, so it's unfrozen. I think it has some damage, though, and is loading slow. But . . ." He stopped and looked past me to the hallway.

The house was quiet except for the news on the TV and the ticking of the clock on the wall. Amy and my dad hadn't come out of her room yet, and I knew she was probably crying tears of guilt during the lecture Dad was surely giving her.

"But what?" I asked Laurie, moving closer.

He hesitated. "I don't know . . . I think I found something kind of . . . weird." He turned the screen toward me.

"Show me." I leaned in.

On the screen was an email inbox with Meg's name on it. Laurie clicked on the outbox, and I stared blankly at the screen while my brain processed what I was seeing. Only a few emails were in the sent box, and they were all to one person. Meg Spring.

"Open it," I told Laurie.

I read the email as soon as it covered the screen.

I couldn't believe what I was seeing.

41

beth

The PX tended not to be too crowded on Sunday evenings. The rest of the weekend was the worst time to go because all the soldiers were off work, but Sundays were sort of a family day around military bases. Mom and I came to the PX to get batteries and a few pair of jeans for my dad right after Amy broke the laptop in front of everyone, including Laurie.

Meredith was quiet most of the drive, and driving much slower than usual. I figured maybe she was tired. We all had so much going on, I didn't blame her. It used to take me over an hour to fall asleep every night. Not anymore; I fall asleep ten minutes after my head hits the pillow.

"Do they have thirty-six, thirty-six of the dark ones?" my mom asked me.

We were searching through stacks of folded jeans for my

dad's size. She had just told me the latest drama. Denise Hunchberg was being accused of taking some of the money from the fund-raiser. No one seemed to have proof, but Mateo Hender's mom claimed she did and posted on the FRG Facebook page that she was going to expose her. Since the women's children were dating, that would surely cause drama at Jo's school.

"Got them." I grabbed a pair of dark wash jeans and dropped them into the cart.

We were almost done with our small list, and I was getting so hungry. I had a Language Arts assignment that I had to finish by the time I went to bed, and I was pretty sure nobody else was doing anything about dinner. I would need to make something, and quick. It wasn't going to be hard, just time-consuming, and I had been hoping I could get some quiet time when I got home before Amy came into the room for bed.

"What's for dinner?" I asked.

My mom picked up a dark gray shirt and held it up in the air. A Nike check was on the little pocket. "They want forty dollars for this?" She gawked at the price tag in her hand and slid the hanger back onto the metal rack and grabbed a similar T-shirt from another rack. "I thought we could get Little Caesars when we stop by Kmart. I'm going to get the batteries there. I have a coupon." She pushed the cart toward the checkout line.

When Meg was in high school, she worked at Kmart for like two weeks before she quit. In that short time we became obsessed with the pizza at the Little Caesars inside the store. I smiled at my mom and my stomach ached. The checkout line took a few minutes longer than usual, even though not many people were shopping. I zoned out while my mom was making conversation with the thickly mustached clerk who scanned our stuff.

I started thinking about how fast this weekend had gone downhill. Between the festival, with Meg and Bell Gardiner, and Meg and Jo, and Jo and Amy at each other's—

"Uhm, it didn't go through. Try to swipe it again," the cashier told my mom.

My mom was startled, instantly panicking. "Okay." She swiped the card again.

A few seconds later there was an awful beeping noise and he shook his head. "Do you have another card?"

My mom lifted her purse onto the counter and dug for her wallet. She looked mortified, but I could tell she was trying hard not to. "I think I have my Star card."

She found it and it worked, so she bought a few Visa gift cards with it in case the other card continued not to work until payday, she said.

Wait . . . I realized. *It was just payday.*

The Star card, even though it could only be used on post, was a lifesaver back when my dad was enlisted and Meg and Jo didn't have jobs.

Neither of us talked until we got to the car. My mom started the engine, turned down the radio, and sat behind the wheel for a few seconds. She looked so much like Amy and Meg with their heart-shaped faces and the set of their mouths.

Over the soft purring of the car coming alive, my mom calmly asked, "Can I ask you a favor that I really shouldn't be asking of you?"

I nodded but she didn't turn her head. "Yeah," I spoke.

"Please don't mention this to your dad. I'm figuring it out."

She sighed, dragging her hand over her mouth like she was wiping off the truth.

"Mom, you know I will try to help you any way that I—"

She held her hand up, "This isn't something you should be worrying about, and I'm sorry for putting you in the middle of it. Sometimes I forget you're a child."

I wouldn't say I was a child. I helped manage the household, but it wasn't the time to bring that up. "If you asked Meg and Jo for help, they would."

"Beth . . ." She smiled. "That's not their job. I'm the parent. I know it doesn't seem like it lately." She looked down at the steering column.

"It's fine, there's so much going on. I get it."

She grabbed my hand on my lap. "Your generosity scares me sometimes, if I'm honest."

"Why?"

She shifted her legs and turned the headlights off. Not many cars were in the lot, and the store was about to close. The gas station next door looked like a ghost town.

"Because the world is just *so* big, Bug." My mom would sometimes call us bugs when we were young, but hadn't in years. "I worry about what will happen to you when your sisters all move out."

I half laughed, unsure how to take what she was saying. "What?"

"What do you plan to do after graduation? Or even for graduation—are you going to stay home until then?"

I nodded. "Yeah. If you guys will let me." I was honest, even though it made me feel like what I imagined a hangover would feel like.

She puffed out her cheeks and blew a mouthful of air into

the car. "Of course, we will let you. I would never force you to go to school if you hate it so much. I just need to make sure you're okay. Even staying home, are you okay? Am I doing what I should be doing as your mom for you?"

My mom's guilt was evident. And honestly, the Spring household wasn't perfect. But I believed that she was doing everything she could. Her nerves seemed to be getting the best of her lately. I'd seen her this sad before so it didn't shock me, but it was a different feeling to be the center of it. Part of me felt guilty that she was so upset over me, but a small part of me was desperate for the attention.

"I'm fine. I just learn differently than my sisters. Everyone's different, you know?"

She laughed. "Oh, I know. I'm serious, Bethany. If you need to talk to someone or maybe feel like seeing a doctor or something, that's okay. There's nothing, nothing, nothing, wrong with it. I will do what I can to get you whatever you—"

"Mom"—I squeezed her hand—"I'm okay. Thank you."

I looked at her. She looked more like the Meredith Spring I knew before this spring. The one with the sharp tongue and dark humor. The warrior with a whole world already on her shoulders who would still dance in the living room to old Luther Vandross songs.

"I love you and I'm fine. I just really need you and Dad to be okay with me not being at school."

"And you know if you like someone, whether they're purple, black, white, tan, or blue, or we call them a she, a he, or a who . . ."

"I know. I know." I smiled. She had been singing that little jingle since I was a kid. She always came up with little songs for random stuff. "I'm not dating anyone, I barely leave the—"

"My point exactly." She tilted her head down, giving me *the* look.

"Seriously, I'm fine for now, and if that changes, I'll tell you." She linked her pinkie into mine. "Pinkie promise?"

"Deal." I nodded and she smiled at me.

"Deal."

42

meg

Mrs. King was almost done with her monthly dinner for the board of her cancer foundation. She had me come over at noon to do her hair and makeup, direct the caterers, walk her dogs, prepare labels for her mail for the week. I didn't mind the personal-assistant duties, but would much rather only be handling her glam.

The meeting should be over any minute. The dessert was served fifteen minutes ago. I took the few minutes of downtime to touch up my makeup in the hallway mirror. My eyes were still a little puffy from the night before, and the redness in my skin had started peeking through my foundation. That festival wrecked me. It was like a time machine, and I was right back in Texas with a target on my back. I hated feeling like the two worlds were mixing. I had been thinking the past would never catch up with me. What a fucking idiot I was. I glossed my lips and fluffed my hair and tried to cover up the drama in my life one mascara stroke at a time. I caught my reflection in the mirror on the wall and put the wand back into the mascara tube.

Shia was standing there, his shirt covered in big patches of sweat. He wasn't moving. He just stared at me in the mirror. I looked away and quickly gathered my makeup into my bag and zipped it shut.

"Wait," he called after me, but I kept moving. "Meg!"

I turned the corner and walked down the hallway. Mr. King's study was right in the middle of this hallway, and even though he wasn't home, I knew better than to snoop around this part of the house.

I turned around to face Shia. "No! Get away."

"Meg, come on. Hear me out."

I shook my head. "No. No, Shia. You and Bell Gardiner can go fuck yourselves."

Shia laughed a little.

"This isn't funny. You told her, didn't you?" I lowered my voice. "I can't believe you. I know she's your fiancée and till death do you part and all, but I thought we were friends."

He popped his eyes out. "Friends, huh?"

"Shia."

"Margaret."

I looked up and down the hallway. The last thing I needed was for Mrs. King to walk out into the hallway with a group of board members dressed in their Sunday-dinner best.

"I didn't tell anyone anything about you. You know damn well I wouldn't. Bell said Shelly sent them to her, and she didn't know who sent them to Shelly. She knows she was wrong being a part of that shit, but it was Shelly at the center, for real, Meg."

I shook my head in disbelief. "You think I care who's in the middle of it? I'm mortified. I was humiliated in front of all of your friends and my sisters." I turned away from him when the tears pricked at the backs of my eyes.

"I know. I know you were." His voice echoed in the quiet hallway. Of course, this was one of the only areas of the house that didn't have a clock hanging on the wall or perfectly accenting a buffet table.

"I'm not talking about this with you. There's nothing to say. Now, I need to get back to work."

"Stop being stubborn. Aren't we past that?"

I turned around and raised my voice. "You and your fiancée went too far, and I have every right to be angry and hurt." I made sure he was looking straight in my eyes. "I hate you, both of you."

"She's not my fiancée," I thought I heard him say.

"Huh?" I looked down the hall again, checking to make sure it was only the two of us.

He licked his lips. "We aren't engaged anymore. I ended it on the way home from the festival. I'm sorry she was a part of that."

"Why?" My throat felt like I'd swallowed dirt and it needed to be watered.

He sighed, stepping closer to me. "So many reasons. I'm too young. She's too young. We don't know each other well enough. We don't have anything in common. She starts drama; she was shitty to you. The usual reasons." He smiled.

I caught my own smile just before it broke on my lips. "Are you being serious?" I couldn't tell for sure, but I thought maybe he was. "Why were you with her in the first place?"

He shrugged. "She's cool." He paused. "Well, sometimes she is. And she's funny and I haven't had a girlfriend in a long time, and I knew it would get my parents off my back about leaving. It would give my mom something else to obsess over."

"She worries about you."

"Yeah." He rubbed the back of his neck. The sleeves of his shirt were cut off, and like me, he looked tired.

"So now what?" I asked. Our conversation was moving so fast.

"I'm leaving Tuesday."

Whoa. "This Tuesday?"

He nodded.

"Okay." I swallowed my words and my shock. I knew he was leaving, and more than that, his absence from New Orleans wasn't going to change my life in any way. I had gotten used to his being gone in the short time I've known him.

"'Okay'? That's it?"

"What else do you expect from me?" I leaned my shoulder against the beige wall. The massive family painting on the wall hung at my eye level, and I looked at Shia's young face and that dang teddy bear in his hands, all captured in front of me.

"I don't know. Something more than *okay*."

"Why don't you say something to me? You're the one who obviously has something to say."

His eyes closed for a second and he came closer to me, backing me against the wall. "I'm sorry about Bell. I am. I didn't have anything to do with it, but I'm sorry still." He placed his hand at the base of my neck, just over the thin fabric of my T-shirt.

I was dressed too casually, a white pocketed T tucked into ripped black jeans that were tucked into black bootees. If I'd have known I'd be going up against Shia, I would have worn more comfortable shoes and a sexier shirt.

"What else can I say to you, Meg? That you drive me up a

freaking wall half the time? Or that I think you're a brat, or that I wish I could be what you want?" He inched closer.

Huh? He was going to kiss me. *Oh my God.*

This had to be a horrible idea. Jo would think this was a horrible idea.

"Don't even think about it," I said through a smile, turning my head when he moved his lips toward mine. "What is it that I want exactly?" I asked breathlessly. His palm was still at the base of my neck.

He grinned. "You want the officer's-wife life. You want to be like that, or like my mom."

"What's so bad about that?"

His body was only a few inches away from mine, nearly pinning me to the wall.

Shia gripped the torso of my T-shirt and pulled me to him. The moment our lips touched, heels clicked against the floor down the hall. I jerked away from him, and he gently wrapped his hand around my wrist. His mom was coming toward us, and I was trying not to panic.

"Don't run," he begged. "We need to talk."

"Meg?" Mrs. King was looking for me.

"Shit. Shit. Your mom's going to kill me," I groaned, stepping out into the light. "Coming!" I said as she laid eyes on me.

Her tan dress fit her body perfectly, and her laced-up heels went past her ankle. Her hair was sleek, a black river down her shoulders. "We're finished. If you want to come into the dining room while I clean up, we can go over next week and you can go."

She didn't seem to suspect anything, but then Shia stepped out of the corner and stood behind me. Mrs. King didn't even blink when she saw him. "You're back," she said to her son as he walked toward her. She was almost his height in her four-inch heels.

"Yeah, I only went to work out. I told you that."

"Your sister said your flight out is Tuesday."

I shouldn't have been there while they were talking about family things, but the only way out was past the two of them. I remembered the fight I'd witnessed from the hallway and prayed that history didn't repeat itself.

"Mom, I always come back." He reached out to hug her, and she pointed at his sweaty clothes. "Come on." He laughed, tilting his head, charming her instantly.

"You're going to put me in an early grave coming and going like this. Your sister is settling down, when are you going to?" She hugged him with one arm. The question was from a concerned mother, not the Mrs. King who cut my checks. She was always nice to me, but she was so, so soft with her son.

"I'm coming back at the end of summer."

The three of us began to walk toward the staircase.

"September is so long from now."

Shia was leaving in two days until the end of summer. That *did* seem so long from now.

"You'll be fine. Maybe you'll get lucky and one of the girls will get pregnant." Shia jokingly pulled away from his mom. My heart was finally slowing from our "talk" upstairs.

She rolled her eyes at him. "Very funny. They may as well, since you won't give me grandchildren. Okay, now go bother someone else in this house so we can get some work done." She shooed him away.

I bit back a smile, relieved the conversation had been light.

Shia kissed his mom on the cheek, waved to me without making eye contact, and disappeared from the entryway. I followed Mrs. King into the dining room, where the dinner had been held. She always reminded me I could sit in on the dinners, but I don't have the attention span for them. Two housekeepers were working around us to clean up, and Mrs. King grabbed a trash bag and started clearing off the table herself.

"It went extremely well. We're giving another scholarship, and we have some ideas for a new website. We need a designer. Do you know one?" She tossed plate after plate of mostly eaten food into the bag.

I started collecting the cups. "I think my sister's boyfriend is one?" Laurie seemed like the type. "I'll find out and tell you."

"Thanks, Meg. How was your evening? You ate, right? I hope you did."

I nodded and we moved from seat to seat. Mrs. King always made sure I ate whatever I wanted while she had her meetings, and I always picked places I loved to cater the dinners because of this. Most of the time I brought leftovers to my sisters.

"How was your time?" she asked again.

Oh my God, she's grilling me.

My throat was so dry.

"Good. I was just walking around and ran into Shia." I squeezed a tiny smile out like the last bit of toothpaste.

"I saw. How's John Brooke?"

My stomach dropped. I croaked, "Good. I mean . . ." She was cleaning so fast, I could barely keep up. Again, I wished I had worn more comfortable shoes. "He's visiting his family for a few days before he has to report to his first duty station."

"How many years does he owe the Army again?"

"Five."

"That's a long time," she told me, like I didn't know that already. The table was cleared off, and I was so, so ready to go home and get away from anyone with the last name King.

Maybe not Shia . . .

Hell, I was so confused.

"Yeah," I managed.

Mrs. King stood next to me, towering over me. "Let's go to the kitchen?"

She walked past me so I followed behind her and checked the time on my phone. I had been in this house all day. No one had texted me. Jo was probably still mad at me, and I could barely remember what we even fought over. Mrs. King walked to the sleek commercial fridge and pulled out a half gallon of milk.

"Can you grab two cups? And the green plate." She pointed to the plate of cookies in front of me.

I met her at the island and she handed me a glass of milk and a spoon. I slid the cookies between us, hoping that she already knew my schedule for the next week.

I took a bite of a chocolate-chip cookie right as Mrs. King asked, "Should I be worried about the way my son feels about you?"

I nearly choked. "Uhm, what?" my big mouth said.

Mrs. King was so calm and so well-spoken when she asked again, "Should I be worried about you and my son?"

I was careful with my response. "In which way?"

"In the romantic way."

"Why would you be worried?" I took a drink of the milk.

Mrs. King leaned on her elbows on the marble island. "The things that would worry me are cheating, patience, and the way our family name is carried on."

My chest tightened. "I'm not cheating on anyone. John and

I barely . . ." I didn't want to give her an excuse. "I would end things with John before I made a commitment to your son."

I didn't even know if I wanted to do that. I knew he was telling the truth about not telling Bell, but that didn't mean our relationship would ever make sense or last longer than one of his trips.

"And patience?" She dipped her cookie into the glass of milk.

"In what way?" I hated that I had to ask her to clarify, but if this was a test, I wanted to pass.

"He goes on these trips and he will be in villages with zero internet, and he will come home with no money in the bank because he gave it all away. He's a good man, and I'm proud of him, but there are limits to everything, and Shia needs to be with a woman with a lot of patience."

"Did you ask Bell Gardiner these things?" I just had to know.

Mrs. King shook her head. "Didn't need to."

"Because you already knew the answers?" I *still* just had to know.

"No. I knew it wasn't going to last long enough for the answers to matter."

Her response surprised me, but I didn't have time to think before my mouth took over again. "I think I'm patient."

I wasn't as patient as say . . . Beth, but I could wait for things that were worth my time.

"And the family-legacy stuff?" I asked.

I wasn't sure if I wanted to hear it. The Kings were so out of my league.

"Do you know what I care about more than the color of your skin or your last name?" she began.

"No." I sure didn't.

"I care about whether you're a warrior. Are you going to be able to handle the pressure of being in a family like this? Shia and his dad may not talk for months, but our family is number one in *my* life."

I nodded.

"And I don't care about what college you went to, or even if you went to college. I know it's not for everyone, and you millennials are so self-made nowadays, I get it. Are you going to be able to raise my grandkids to be strong and take on the world despite the color of their skin?"

I nodded again.

"I know this seems like a lot"—she smiled, lightening up the unexpected conversation—"and I sound like I'm hovering over him, but that's not the case. If this doesn't work out, it changes a lot of things. Your job could be compromised, the friendship you two have, the friendship we have. I don't want to waste my time or my son's time or your time, Meg, if you're not ready for this."

It still seemed a little intense, but honestly, I had been planning my wedding and naming my stuffed animals since I could talk. I wasn't like Jo. Being a mother was so important to me, and I had always known that no matter what race my children were, I would be their biggest advocate. I looked forward to my future as a wife and mother someday.

I was so far from that. Shia too. "I understand. Shia and I are just so far from that."

"Well, I want you to be able to think about the big picture. I would really hate to lose the working relationship we have now if you guys end up calling it off."

We had to call it *on* first, but I didn't tell her that.

"Mrs. King, I promise that if we . . . if we go there, I'll be ready for those things," I assured her, and myself. "All of them."

Shia and I couldn't just start dating. We would have to start as friends again, and that couldn't happen because he was leaving until after summer and it was still spring.

"That's all I'm asking. And don't tell him that I said any of this. That's the last thing." Her smile was warm enough to melt most of the awkwardness away. "Oh, and I need you to pass these cookies down to my grandchildren."

"Deal." I raised a new cookie in the air.

"Deal," she echoed, cheersing me with her half-eaten cookie.

For the next twenty minutes, we went over her schedule for the next week, including everything from dog-grooming appointments tomorrow morning to jury duty on Thursday. In between my adding things to her cell-phone calendar, I kept looking through the doorway, sort of hoping to see Shia again before I left. He only had two more days here, and I knew those days would come and go, and then, poof, he'd be on the other side of the world again.

But he never came through the door. Right as I was leaving with a pan full of leftovers, Mrs. King's phone went off on the counter where I'd placed it.

She lifted it up and read it as she walked me to the door. "Have a good night, Meg. And let me know if you want to take Tuesday off."

I nodded, thanking her, and got to my car as fast as I could. *What just happened?*

43

beth

*L*ittle Caesars pizza was empty save for us and the pregnant
girl behind the counter. Only two slices of pizza sat under
the warmer. I had known they were about to close and felt like
a jerk for coming in last minute, but it was worse now that I
was making a pregnant girl help us. Her name tag said Tawny,
and she had big brown eyes and really curly hair. She looked
so young.

"Hi." My mom smiled at her. Mom was always a polite customer and taught us to be the same. She was a little less perky
than she had been a few years ago, but everyone in the Spring
house was just a little more tired now.

"Hi, how can I help you?"

My mom asked pregnant Tawny to *please, please* make fresh
pizzas, promising her a tip worth her while, and apologized pro-
fusely. I didn't know what was going to happen that night after

the greasy pizza filled our happy stomachs, and the movie we choose to watch ended, and my mom and dad went to their room and we girls went to ours. I didn't know which of my sisters would be around tonight, and I hoped at least one of them would be there for me to talk to when my parents closed their bedroom door and my mom had to tell my dad that, once again, we had no money.

"Only jalapeño and onion on that side," my mom said, ordering Jo's favorite pizza. I hoped Jo had cooled down enough to be under the same roof as Amy. I hoped the next day my mom could tell my dad that I'm not going to public school ever again and that he would take it well and I could focus on my assignments.

"At least we aren't the only ones in here right before closing," a girl's voice said. It sounded familiar, and when I glanced behind me, I saw why.

Wearing fitted sweatpants and an olive-green T-shirt, leaning against the railing, was Nat, the girl who made the mood jewelry from the festival. Ugh, that festival. If we could just erase it from Spring family history, that would be great. Being at her stall was the only good part of that whole thing. She was so nice and even helped us hide Meg. Nat looked so chill in her street clothes. Her ears were showing beneath her ponytail, and I could see they were decorated. She was standing next to a man I assumed was her dad and pointing at the menu on the wall above us.

For a girl who I had only known for a weekend, I had sure run into her a lot. Well, the festival, she was working, so that was an easy explanation, but this? The chances of her and her dad being here . . . well, it was just weird. My cheeks were hot and I tried not to look in the mirrored wall behind the counter. Tried—and failed. I looked like I hadn't slept in a week.

"What did your mother want again?" Nat's presumed dad asked her.

With my fingers I tried to flatten the strays escaping from my ponytail, but it wasn't working well.

"Cheese and ham," she told him. He asked about her homework, and I was watching her when she looked over at me, catching my eyes.

She blinked three times quick and smiled. "Hey! I know you!"

"Hey." I waved back just as my mom turned around.

"Hi! Who's this?" She waved at Nat and her dad and introduced herself.

"Hi, I'm Nat." She smiled at my mom and thumb-pointed at her dad. "This is my dad."

"Shin. Nice to meet you." He reached out his hand to shake my mom's.

Nat turned to me. "How are you? How random we're the only people in town eating Little Caesars." She laughed a little and tucked her dark hair behind her ear. Her ponytail was so soft looking, the true Tumblr definition of a messy bun. Mine never looked effortlessly cute-messy. Ever.

"Good," I told her. I felt overly anxious for some reason. There was no line behind us or voices chattering over one another. Only pop music from a decade ago and the buzzing of the cooler in front of us. It was only the four of us . . . well, six including Tawny and her baby, but my heart was racing like I was standing in the middle of a Black Friday (now starting on Thanksgiving) sale at Walmart.

Nat was looking at me like I forgot to answer her, which I halfway did. "Right. We thought we were the only ones who still liked it."

Nat's face broke into a smile and she laughed a little. "Same."

Our parents were talking about school districts or something. I didn't know or care.

"What are you guys doing out? Fort Cyprus is so quiet tonight," Nat said, looking around the empty Kmart. I knew then that she was an Army brat because she called the entire town here Fort Cyprus. The few people around posts who weren't Army related called their town by its actual name.

"Running errands. We went to the PX." The memory made my throat dry. "And now pizza for dinner, then nothing, just watching a scary movie. You?"

"I love scary movies!" Her voice rose a little. She was so animated when she talked, it reminded me of Jo. She came closer to me, and Tawny came out to take Nat's order. She ordered for her family, and her dad stepped up to pay for it. "We went to the craft store and to get a tire-pump thing for some floaty thing."

"For your sister or brother or something?" I asked.

"No, my mom. It's for the yard for spring. It's kind of weird how much she decorates." Nat laughed. If only she saw my mom's house on Halloween or my grandma's house on Christmas. "I'm an only child."

I almost choked. "An only child?"

She started laughing. "Your eyes are like . . ." She popped her eyes out, laughing harder.

"I have three sisters," I told the pretty alien girl in front of me. *An only child? What would that even be like?*

"Three?" It was her turn to gape. "Wow. That's a lot."

"Yeah, it is." I grinned.

"My mom's birthday is tomorrow, so we were blowing all these yard decorations up for her and getting her pizza." Nat licked her lips and looked back to check on her dad. She looked so much younger without makeup and glitter and henna etched all over her creamy skin. I couldn't tell if she was my age or older.

"Cool. My aunt's birthday is tomorrow at our house," I said, for what reason I couldn't tell you.

Nat kept her smile. "Fun," she said, like she meant it. "I was trying to give my parents some alone time, but then my dad volunteered to come with me." She slapped her hand gently against her forehead. She made me laugh—it was refreshing. "That sounds so weird that I wanted to give my parents alone time."

My mom looked over at us, and I looked to Nat again, trying not to laugh. "A little. But I get it." My parents never had alone time.

"You could come to my house?" I said, but the moment I offered, I wondered if it was too much. Would my mom even be okay with that? Would my mom wait to bring up the money stuff to my dad until we were all in bed? I stammered a little. "I'll have to ask. I mean, if you even want to? I don't know—"

"Yeah. Sure. If your mom doesn't care. I mean it's only, like, seven. I could go home at, like, nine thirty? It's not like I have school tomorrow."

She turned to her dad and asked him.

My mom said yes, looking at Nat, her dad, then me. "How do you know her?" she whispered to me.

"She made the jewelry I brought home. The dark ring I bought for you." My mom hadn't worn it yet, but promised that she would when she went somewhere special.

"Really? Wow. She's only seventeen. Her dad said she wants to go to LSU next fall. But, yeah, she can come over, and you guys can stay in the living room and watch a movie."

"Mom . . ."

"The same rules apply to you that were on your sisters, not until you're sixteen." Nat couldn't hear her, thank goodness, but I wanted the conversation to end.

"Okay. Okay," I agreed, and Nat's dad nodded.

"I have this conversation with all my daughters. Meg and Jo, and now you." My mom was still whispering.

We'd never had to have this conversation because I'd never had any friends over, boy or girl.

"Okay," I said again.

My mom nodded and turned to Nat. "What kind of pizza did you get? We . . ."

It felt like everything around me was changing so fast since my dad got home, since Jo met Laurie, since Shia King came back, since Amy started her period, since me making my first friend in a really, really long time. I hoped that time would slow down in the coming summer—or was this what being a teenager was like? Everything came flying at you fast, and you just had to try to grab ahold of the good parts when you could?

44

jo

"I can't believe this," I said for the tenth time in the last five minutes.

Laurie was sitting on his bed, his fingers typing and clicking away on my laptop. I was so pissed at Amy. How could she be such a coldhearted little bitch?

"I'm telling Meg. I have to." I sat down at the end of the bed and pulled my phone out of my pocket. What a long-ass day. I was so fucking over today.

"That's not my business. You know what's best for your family. Look." He sat up toward me, angling the screen so I could see it. "Your essay was backed up, so it's here. I emailed it to my email just in case something goes wrong. You should really always send yourself your documents."

"That's it? You're done?" I raised a brow at him. He nodded. "Thank you, seriously. What a mess this is, Laurie. What a fucking mess of a family I have. Amy, man. I can't *believe* she would send those emails to Meg—Meg is her favorite one of us. Imagine what she has planned for me!"

I didn't want to imagine that, actually.

"Everyone's family has their own shit. You know that. Look at mine."

I agreed with a sigh. "Yeah, but at least yours is distant. It helps a little, doesn't it?"

He reached for the thin strap of my tank top and gently pulled me toward him. My fight with Amy seemed too distant in my memory to be only an hour ago; it was like this fight had started years and years ago and was only now coming to a head. Who knows what would have happened if Laurie hadn't have been there and I didn't have his house right next door to cool down at. When I leave the state, I won't have a sanctuary.

"It only helps a little. If any."

"I wish I could just go far away from here. But I wonder if I'd feel guilty leaving my family behind."

Laurie had his arm around my shoulder, but he pulled it down and cupped his long fingers over mine. He had become my closest friend. Closest family, closest everything, in the last few weeks. I'd started saying things to Laurie that I normally wouldn't say out loud—that's how I knew.

"A lot of people move away for college, you know? I've met Americans from all over the States walking the streets of Napoli, Paris, Berlin. You name it. People move away, it happens. It's a part of growing up, no?"

I nodded and leaned my head on his shoulder. He smelled like soap and rust. "Yeah. But Meg is working two jobs, and if she marries John Brooke, she'll move away, leaving Amy with me and Beth. One less driver, one less car. If I leave, one less driver. You get it?"

He moved the laptop off his lap and turned his body to me. He tugged at the unmade comforter rising up between us. "Yeah. I do, but that's not your responsibility. I know it sounds harsh, but you're responsible for yourself, and helping when you can, but that's it. If you stayed around here, you would be miserable. Your family would want you to get out if you want to. No?"

"I guess so. My dad was the first one who said I'd have to move because of my major." I shook my head. "You don't get it because your family isn't as close as mine. I literally share a room with my sister and live with both of my parents."

Laurie's face dropped.

"I didn't mean it like that. I'm sorry," I said quickly. "Sometimes I worry that if I leave, everything will fall apart. It's not even like I'm doing a lot to stop it."

"Talk to Meg about it. See what she says."

I nodded, agreeing with him. He reached up to cup my face. "We're all just tiny blips on your map, Jo. You don't belong here and you know it. I'm just hoping I'm good enough to drag along for the ride."

My heart sank. "You are," I whispered to him. "We're going to make this work long distance, right? That's if we make it through this year."

He rolled his eyes. "Really, Jo?"

I laughed. "Just saying. Let's get through this year."

"I have to go to my mom before that."

"I know. We will figure it out. It's going to be good practice for when I'm in college if we are still together."

Laurie didn't laugh that time or crack a smile. He looked at me. "Is that really what you think? It was funny at first, but you just say it over and over. What's the point in even trying this if you're not really going to try?"

I pulled back from him. "I'm trying. I'm joking. I'll back off . . . I just need to know for sure this is what I want and what you want."

"I thought we agreed that it was."

Laurie looked so exhausted.

We all did.

"We did." I rubbed at my neck. "I'm just being realistic and honest."

"Great."

We sat in silence for a few moments before Laurie finally broke it. "Jo, I need to know what this is. I'm not asking for a freaking lifelong commitment, but can we at least agree that we're dating, or not? I'm going to be going back home to Italy, and some people will be asking if I'm single . . ."

What? "What does that mean? Who would ask?" I stood up from the bed. It usually felt like the perfect size for us, but it felt so tiny now.

Laurie hesitated. "I just mean my friends, female friends, too. I'm not saying what you think I'm saying, but, yes, girls will ask me, Jo."

Of course they would. Look at him.

This irritated me beyond belief. Was dating Laurie always going to be like this? Girls ready to pounce on him the moment he didn't have someone?

"I don't understand why it's such a big deal to you to say we're together. If you are so unsure about it, what are we doing?"

I got defensive. "If you have so many options lined up back home, what are we doing?"

He shook his head. "You're being such a hypocrite. You know that, right?" His hands were in the air in front of him.

"Yeah. I do know. And you're a fucking player. I get it."

Laurie's mouth fell open and he moved off the bed and walked toward the door. He opened it, and I expected him to kick me out, but instead he just left. I waited less than a minute before I grabbed my phone and key chain and took off. His stairs creaked when you walked on them, and I usually loved the bit of personality it gave the house, but each squeak made me want to scream as I rushed down. The air was sticky and smelled like it might rain. I thought about taking a walk, but I really wanted to go home and lie in my bed.

When I got home, the house was quiet. The living-room light was off. but the big-screen TV was on, lighting up the room pretty well. My dad was sitting in his wheelchair next to his recliner, and Amy was lying on the couch, staring at the TV. Meg's Prius was in the driveway when I came inside, so I knew she was here somewhere.

"Meredith's not back yet?" I asked whoever was going to answer me.

"Not yet. They should be back any minute," my dad responded. Meg came walking out of the hallway and looked around the room.

"Oh, it's you," Meg sighed when she saw me in the television glow.

I told her I needed to talk to her. Now. I wasn't going to fight with her; that seemed like old drama. I needed to tell her about Amy sending the emails.

"Come with me upstairs for a minute," I said quietly.

My dad didn't respond, just kept his eyes on the show he was watching.

Meg agreed, and, of course, Amy whined that she wanted to come upstairs with us. I tried to remember back when I was twelve; was I as obnoxious as she is now?

"No," I snapped. No way was she coming.

Meg looked at me and I shook my head no.

"I'll come back and lay with you on the couch and brush your hair when I'm done talking to Jo. Deal?" Meg cooed.

Cooed to the twelve-year-old who tried to sabotage her relationship with John Brooke through sending false emails. If only Meg knew.

Amy agreed like the spoiled little lizard she was, and I followed Meg back upstairs.

"This better be good," Meg threatened me. She was wearing pajamas and a face full of makeup. Of course she was. "I just got home from an entire day at Mrs. King's house, fuck off," she said against my judging eyes.

She walked into our bedroom, and I followed, closing the door.

"I need to tell you something about someone close to us."

Meg looked beyond skeptical. I was so annoyed about my fight with Laurie and my family imploding. I was over it all and wanted to tell Meg to cut off the dumb-pretty-girl act.

"Cut the drama, what are you talking about?"

"I'm being serious. It's about those emails from John Brooke. The ones when—"

She cut me off with a wave of her hand through the air. "Like I don't know what emails you're talking about! Move *on*," she snapped.

"When Amy trashed the computer earlier, Laurie was checking it out and found an email address that Amy was logged in to . . ."

"What?" Meg looked at the door behind me and back to me.

I lowered my voice. "Yes. Amy was signed into the email address that sent you the emails from a fake-John email. I don't know why she would do that. But we have to tell Mom and Dad and say something to her, like now. How fucked-up is that?"

I expected a response, but Meg just stood there processing it all, so I paced around the room because someone had to be doing *something*.

"Amy? You're sure?" Her eyes were getting all red. I should've yelled for Amy to come up here and just put it all on the table.

"Yeah. I can say something to her if you want."

"No." Meg shook her head. Her brown waves touched her shoulders as she moved. Her hair was styled and her eyelashes were so long. She always looked ready for a camera or something. Even now. "I don't want to say anything to her."

What?

"Yes, you do."

"No." She just kept shaking her head. "No, I don't, Jo. What good will that do? She obviously did it for a reason."

"Because she's an evil little—"

"No, Jo. Because she's twelve and her dad got injured in Iraq, her two oldest sisters have boyfriends and are never around, her mom is drinking and barely notices when she's around. She's calling for attention."

"She's *seeking* attention."

"Even so. Think about why she would be? And why I can't just give her that attention and hope she never does it again? We have to think about how she's feeling, too. She's twelve and going through a lot. Think about how hard Dad coming home like this would have been for *you* at that age."

"Why are you so . . . so . . . I don't know. You're right about some of it, but why let her get away with it?"

"It's not really about getting away with it. She's my baby sister," Meg calmly explained.

She had too much patience. I was more of a revenge kind of girl.

"Let me handle it, Josephine." Meg plopped down on her bed. She picked up the little book I got her for Christmas and scrolled through the pages.

"Fine, *Margaret*."

It was quiet for a minute while I sat on my bed and Meg sat on hers. I remembered when we were little, she would talk to me sometimes and have me tell her my stories about Jack Smead. She would laugh and laugh until Meredith would come in and *shhh* us, threatening to take our internet away if we weren't quiet. Those days were so simple. Before boys and sex and money.

"I'm sorry about earlier," Meg finally said. "I was pissed at Shia and myself and took it out on you."

I looked at her and she half smiled; she was so pretty. She was a little wilted tonight, like a flower that needed a kiss from the sun, but she was still so pretty. Like Amy would be when she was older.

"I'm sorry, too. I really didn't think it would have made a difference. I didn't think about it, and I'm sorry."

She smiled. "Thank you. See, that's not so hard?"

"Ha, ha." I groaned at her. "What's going on with Shia?" I didn't think she would want to talk about it, especially not to me, but I asked anyway. It kept my mind off Laurie.

"I don't know." She touched her fingers to her lips. "He's leaving Tuesday."

"*This* Tuesday?"

She nodded.

So soon. "Oh, wow."

"I know." She looked away. "I'm breaking up with John Brooke. He's going to be stationed so far away and he's barely texted me the last few days and—"

"And you want Shia."

She nodded. "I think I do?" She looked terrified.

"So, what's the problem?"

"I'm so tired of the long-distance relationships."

Yikes. Another strike against Laurie's and my epic saga.

"So, go with him," I suggested. Meg could use some time out of this town. "How long will he be gone?"

"September." She paused. "I couldn't go. No way. I can't leave you guys here."

So she had the same worries as I did. "We would be fine. We'd figure it out. You should go." The idea of Meg leaving town was abstract. It didn't seem like something that would actually happen, but I hoped for it still. It would be thrilling. A change in the Spring house. A shake-up.

"I couldn't." She chewed at her bottom lip. "Could I?"

I nodded. "You can. Ask him."

"It seems so irresponsible. I'm not like you, Jo. I don't like surprises, and I don't like life on the road."

I shrugged. "How do you even know that? You've never tried it. You say you aren't like me, but that to me means you're scared."

Her face twisted. "I don't care if you think I'm scared, Jo. You don't know anything about life. You think you do because you sit around and watch documentaries all day? You've had a pretty cushioned life."

I was baffled. She couldn't be serious. "Me? So have you, Princess Meg. Sorry that I care about the world and you only care about fucking guys into marrying you to feed your crazy obsession. Good for you—go be a housewife, Meg, but don't give me shit because I don't want to be!"

She stood up, and I knew she was losing her temper, and that was fine because mine was already lost. "*Me?* You're the one who's judging *me*, Jo! I don't want to be alone, okay? And that's fine. You're so obsessed with being a know-it-all that you forget the most important part of being a strong woman!"

I was nearly shaking with rage. How was she pissed at me? I wasn't judging her . . . maybe I was, but so was she. She wasn't the only victim here.

"And what exactly is that? Enlighten me!" I shouted back, pushing myself off the bed.

"The choice, Jo! It's all about my choice as a woman. If I want to spend my time being a hands-on parent and at fund-raisers and family outings—I fucking *can*! I can do whatever I want! If you want to move to some big city, break up with Laurie and focus on yourself, go ahead! I'm not the one judging you! But at least I know what I want!"

I couldn't believe her. "You don't know what you're talking about! You can't even choose between Shia and freaking John! John Brooke, who's as boring as a snail, or Shia—who actually makes you act like a decent human being!"

The bedroom door opened, and Amy burst into the room. I couldn't stand to be around either of them, but when I tried to leave, Meg blocked me.

"Me? Look in the fucking mirror, Jo! You're a high school kid trying to tell me about life? You have Laurie right in front of you, waiting on you hand and foot, and just because you don't label it, that makes it better than me? If you don't commit to him, I hope he finds a nice girl in Italy who will."

Ouch. "Fuck you, Meg."

I pushed past her and ran down the stairs. Mom was pulling into the driveway when I walked past the front window, so I went out the back door. I stormed across the yard and couldn't believe the nerve of my sister. I knew exactly what I had with Laurie, and Laurie knew me better than she ever had.

I knew there was some truth in her words, and I wanted to prove her wrong about me. I knew what I wanted.

Laurie and New York. I could have both, unlike Meg. I frantically knocked on the Laurences' door, but no one answered. I knocked again, impatiently hopping from one foot to the other until I finally turned the knob to see if the door was locked. It wasn't, so I walked in toward the stairs. I didn't hear the TV blaring, so I assumed Old Mr. Laurence wasn't home.

My heart was racing. I hoped Laurie was home. I hoped he even wanted to see me.

I should have thought about that before knocking on his bedroom door, but I wasn't thinking about anything except seeing him. And there I was. Not in the sexiest outfit, not with freshly brushed teeth. What if he had a girl here? He wouldn't do that. I knew he wouldn't.

Just before I changed my mind and turned around, Laurie opened his door, looking confused and pissed off and so beautiful. He was so soft, so tender, compared to what I thought boys were going to be like. He listened to me, helped me, taught me. He had been there for me through all this shit with my family, and he was standing in front of me, waiting for me to speak.

"Hi," I said, out of breath now that he was in front of me.

"Hi."

I grabbed on to his shirt, pulling him to kiss me. Every part of me was bursting open, unsure if he would push me off or pull me in, and I moaned in relief when he wrapped his arms around my waist, crushing my body to his.

"What are you—"

"I'm sure. I'm positively sure. We can make it work. You can go anywhere, Italy . . ."

His tongue burned my skin as it traced around my pulse. When he pulled away, I missed the taste of him so badly that it hurt. It was that quick. It was like a switch had been turned on inside my body and the pressure in my stomach, throbbing in expectation, was going to rip me in half, I was sure of it.

"Yeah?" He licked at the most tender skin of my neck.

"I want . . ." I didn't know how to say it, but wanted to stay in control. "You."

I pushed at his shoulders, then found his mouth and kissed him, and led him to his bed. He fell back first and I climbed on top of his lean body. His T-shirt rode up past his belly button; the freckles dotted his tan skin like sprinkled seeds. His eyes were huge, blown-out black ink spots writing words that only I could read. I could feel his body reacting to me, and I thought about it. I knew this would change everything. I would always remember who I gave my virginity to. Always.

"I love you. I think."

His body froze and his hands touched either side of my face, bringing my eyes to his. "You love me?"

I nodded. "I think so."

He smiled and it touched his dark eyes, and his mouth touched my lips and he whispered, "I do, too."

I loved him. I was in love for the first time. My life was complicated, and my future was totally up in the air, but I knew that

I was in love with Laurie and there was absolutely nowhere I'd rather be than where I was, and that was what it was supposed to be, what this confusing mess of life was about.

I reached for the bottom of my shirt and lifted it over my head. Laurie searched my face, and I nodded, reaching for his hands and putting them on my breasts.

"I want you," I said again.

"You're sure, or you think?" He smiled.

I rolled my eyes at him playfully.

"It's going to hurt," he told me. It wasn't romantic or sugary at all. But it didn't need to be. That wasn't how life, or my relationship with Laurie, was.

"I know. I'm going to bleed and probably cry." I scrunched up my nose.

He laughed, biting at my neck.

"Okay, okay. I know the precautions. Let's just kiss a while and see—"

I kissed his lips and he rolled us over. I wasn't afraid of what was coming. I'd always wondered if I would be. Meg's first time was complete shit. I knew for sure mine would be better than that. Laurie told me how much he loved every part of me as he made his way down my body . . . I was breathing just fine, everything was calm, Laurie's mouth was so sweet between my thighs, and my head was clear and I wanted every second of this.

It did hurt, just as bad as I thought it would, but Laurie was so gentle, and we were both a little clumsy, and I loved him even more as I lay next to him and he told me about how many times he'd thought about this happening, but never actually thought it would. I loved how honest he was with me.

Afterward, when we'd been silent and cuddled there, I said, "I don't feel any different."

"Are you supposed to?" He rolled over and kissed my forehead.

I shrugged. "Yeah. I think so."

"So I failed?" he teased, and kissed me when I nodded.

My phone rang a few times, and I watched my sister's name flash up and then finally disappear.

"I need to go. I have to apologize to her."

"Did you come here, like just for that?" He looked at my naked body wrapped around his.

I shook my head. "Sort of?"

Laurie made me laugh, and I almost thought about repeating what we just did, but I had to get home.

When I walked home, each step my shoe made on the grass, I felt more and more powerful. I was blissful, not horrified.

I was loved, not used.

Meg opened the door just as I reached the porch. She stepped out and closed the door behind her.

"I'm sorry," I said at the same time she did.

"Me, too, Jo."

"You were right, you know. About Laurie." I looked in Meg's eyes, and she took in my face and opened her mouth into a big *O*.

"You!" she said loudly, then whispered, "Oh my God. You did it. Oh my God."

"Meg. Seriously." I laughed, covering my mouth.

"Jo, oh my God. Beth has a girl in there, you had sex with Laurie, and I'm leaving the country Tuesday. I just told Mom and Dad."

I thought about hugging Meg, but I didn't know if I should, so I followed her inside and passed Amy sleeping on the couch. I still thought Meg should say something to her about the emails, but I would let Meg decide what to do about that.

"Mom and Dad are in their room," Beth said from the couch.

She was sitting next to a pretty Japanese girl who looked familiar, but I couldn't put my finger on where I knew her from. They were watching the end of one of the *Halloween* movies, the third one, I thought.

Beth had never had a friend over before, and it made me happy. I was so exhausted—my body was aching from Laurie, from work, from not enough sleep. Things were changing so much, so fast.

My sisters and I were getting better at figuring out this thing called life, and I felt more ready to take on this big, small world with them and the rest of my sisters around the world.

acknowledgments

This book is so different from anything I've ever written, and I questioned myself nearly every page, until my favorite humans reminded me why I was writing this story. I often question myself—every second of every page. As a writer, I'm not supposed to say that, but I totally do.

I love this story, these Spring sisters, and in these acknowledgments, I want to thank my "sisters"—a.k.a. the women around me who encourage me to be my best self and live my best life: Rebecca, Jen, Ruth, Erika, Nina, Erin—you guys are my tribe, and I love you for your friendship, kindness, encouragement, and constant support for finishing this book, and for life in general.

Adam Wilson, another book down! We make a good team, even if I'm responsible for lots of future gray hairs because I can't make a deadline if my life depended on it. I appreciate you more than I can ever say, and I can't wait to meet the little one.

All of the production, sales, and marketing departments at Gallery—you guys are rock stars, and none of my books would ever see the light of day without you! Thanks for all the hard work! My copyeditor deserves a zillion virtual fruit (or cookie) baskets!

Chels, Bri, Trev, Lauren, and Diana, you guys are my OG's, and I love love love you.

Last but not least, my readers and publishers around the world—you guys have made my dreams come true. I was just a girl with a busted laptop and no idea what I was doing with my life, and you completely changed my life, and I will never be able to explain just how much that means to me.

To Ash and Jord, you two <3

the
spring
girls

anna todd

This reading group guide for The Spring Girls *includes an introduction, discussion questions, and ideas for enhancing your book club. The suggested questions are intended to help your reading group find new and interesting angles and topics for your discussion. We hope that these ideas will enrich your conversation and increase your enjoyment of the book.*

introduction

Four sisters desperately seeking the blueprints to life—the modern-day retelling of Louisa May Alcott's *Little Women* like only Anna Todd (*After, Imagines*) could do.

The Spring Girls—Meg, Jo, Beth, and Amy—are a force of nature on the New Orleans military base where they live. As different as they are, with their father on tour in Iraq and their mother hiding something, their fears are very much the same. As they struggle to build lives they can be proud of and that will lift them out of their humble station in life, one year will determine all that their futures can become.

The oldest, Meg, will be an officer's wife and enter military society like so many of the women she admires. If her passion—and her reputation—don't derail her.

Beth, the workhorse of the family, is afraid to leave the house—and afraid she'll never figure out who she really *is*.

Jo just wants out. Wishing she could skip to graduation, she dreams of a life in New York City and a career in journalism through which she can impact the world. Nothing can stop her—not even love.

And Amy, the youngest, is watching all her sisters, learning from how they handle themselves. For better or worse.

With plenty of sass, romance, and drama, *The Spring Girls* revisits Louisa May Alcott's classic *Little Women*, and brings its themes of love, war, class, adolescence, and family into the language of the twenty-first century.

topics & questions
for discussion

1. How does Meredith depict each of her daughters in the opening chapter? What does she reveal about their relationships with her and with each other?

2. "Meg divulged things here and there, but I was ready for more. I was trying to land in the sweet space between little sister who she trusts and mature sister who she can share her relationship secrets with. It was a thrilling yet dangerous shift, and I felt it inside me as it was happening" (page 56). Why is it suddenly so important to Jo that she gain Meg's trust? What about this moment made Jo crave a stronger relationship with her sister?

3. Jo is immediately drawn to Laurie, making Meg immediately distrust him. Why does Meg disapprove of Laurie for her young sister? She believes Jo is being naïve, but how does Meg's past color both girls' initial perception of Laurie?

4. Beth is the peacemaker and caregiver of the family. What kind of pressure does this place on Beth? Does her family disregard her needs in allowing her to take on such a role? Why has she assumed so much responsibility?

5. "I was completely ready to be the perfect officer's wife" (page 139). Meg is determined to become a military wife and settle down. She dreams of a life like the Kings'. How has her idea of the perfect life played into her relationships with John Brooke and Shia?

6. Meredith is a strong and capable mother, but her husband's time serving abroad has clearly worn her down. How has her withdrawal from their lives affected Beth and Amy in particular? Has her behavior had any impact on Meg and Jo?

7. As Meredith becomes less involved in the day-to-day, how does each Spring Girl step up to fill in for her? How do their new responsibilities affect their sisterhood?

8. Discuss Shia, John Brooke, and Meg's interaction at the hotel. Why does Shia go out of his way to find Meg? What does this exchange show Meg about her relationships with both men?

9. Meg, Jo, Beth, and Amy all respond differently to the news of their father's injuries. Describe each girl's reaction and why it does or does not fit with their personality. Meg and Jo have been growing closer, so why does Jo lash out so harshly at Meg?

10. "I wasn't sure if I trusted my dad the same way after that appointment" (page 305). What inspires this thought from Jo at the end of her father's doctor appointment? Until then, their relationship has appeared unchanged by his ac-

cident. What about their unique bond has helped Jo adapt the quickest to his injuries?

11. How will the girls adapt to having Mr. Spring home full-time and living outside of the military base? Will Meredith regain some of her former spirit now that her husband has returned home?

12. Are Amy's emails to Meg as John Brooke intentionally malicious? What was her goal in sending them? Does Meg do the right thing by not confronting her?

13. How do Meg, Jo, Beth, and Amy differ now from the way their mother described them in the opening chapter? How has each girl changed? Have their individual developments altered their relationships with one another?

14. By the end of the novel, each of the girls has begun to forge her own path beyond the limits of Fort Cyprus and their family responsibilities. What do you think of their choices, and what's in store for their futures?

enhance your book club

1. Meg, Jo, Beth, and Amy's atypical upbringing on a military base has shaped the women they will become. As you read, consider the differences and similarities between their childhood and your own. Imagine you were a military brat: How would that have shaped you differently? Which of the Spring Girls do you relate to the most?

2. Family is a central theme of the novel. Discuss the Springs' family dynamic. Is it what you would expect from a family with four daughters? How might your family react to the challenges these women face throughout the novel?

3. As you read, keep in mind the original *Little Women* by Louisa May Alcott. Aside from the contemporary setting, how does Anna Todd's adaptation differ? In conclusion, discuss if and how Anna answered any remaining questions from *Little Women* and what new questions her adaptation raises.

Connect with
Anna Todd on Wattpad

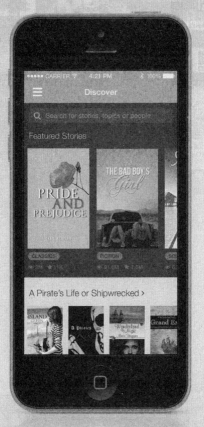

The author of this book, Anna Todd,
started her career as a reader, just like
you. She joined Wattpad to read stories
like this one and to connect with the
people who wrote them.

**Download Wattpad today to
connect with Anna:**

📖 imaginator1D